Everywhere House

A Mystery by Jane Meyerding

photo by Kathy Blanchard

Jane Meyerding was born in Chicago in 1950 and lived the first ten years of her life (mostly) in the midwest. After spending her second decade in the eastern United States, she moved to Seattle, where she seems to have settled quite comfortably. She works as a secretary and writes essays on political subjects—primarily nonviolent activism, feminism and anarchism. This is her first novel.

Everywhere House

A Mystery by Jane Meyerding

New Victoria Publishers Inc.

Published by New Victoria Publishers
PO Box 27 Norwich, Vermont 05055

Cover Design Ginger Brown
Printed on recycled paper
ISBN 0-934678-42-1

All of the characters in this novel are fictional and are not based on real individuals. Any resemblance is a matter of coincidence. The city of Seattle, the Lesbian Resource Center and the University of Washington are real, but the author has taken the liberty of rearranging many details to suit her own taste and convenience.

Library of Congress Cataloging-in-Publication Data

Meyerding, Jane.
    Everywhere house / by Jane Meyerding.
        p.   cm.
    ISBN 0-934678-42-1 : $9.95
    1. Women college students--Washington (State)--Seattle--Fiction.
2. Lesbians--Washington (State)--Seattle--Fiction. 3. Murder-
-Washington (State)--Seattle--Fiction. 4. Seattle (Wash.)--Fiction.
I. Title.
PS3563.E886E94   1994
813'.54--dc20
                                                    93-41740
                                                       CIP

THANKS

to those who read and critiqued—Carey, Kathy, Kerry, two Loises, Rebecca, Ruth, Sue, Xenia, and (just when I needed her most) Jane Hope; and to Esther Meyerding, who put up with the selfishness and bad moods required by the writing. Thanks also to Vicki P. McConnell who tried to edit out all the weird or unnecessary stuff; it's not her fault I was stubborn about some of it.

1. *March 1977*

Letitia and I were sitting on the floor of my room, upstairs in Everywhere House. Weirdly enough, even before the front door slammed and the yelling started I'd been sitting there thinking, Something's going on here, Terry. Something under the surface, I meant, because nothing much was going on at all, just to look at. Except in the sky outside the two big windows of my room.

We'd had rain showers off and on for most of the day, but by four o'clock we'd finally gotten some of that "partial afternoon clearing" so popular with the TV weather-guessers in Seattle. From where I was sitting I could see a band of clear sky stretching like a wide, solid-blue rainbow from north to south above the city. To the east, the grey haze of twilight was coming on, and to the west loomed a bank of angry purple clouds.

If I'd been sitting there with one of my housemates, I'd probably have said, "Wow, look at that sky! Waddya say we run up to Phinney Ridge for the sunset?" And I'd have been off, alone or with company. The view from Phinney Ridge—only about a mile west of Everywhere House—can be pretty spectacular on a late afternoon in early March. There'd probably be masses and masses of pink and white clouds, all shot through with gold as the sun slipped down behind the mountains over on the peninsula. And still that loom of greying purple over head and, behind it, the one clear slice of sky going bluer and bluer and bluer, all the way to black. Makes you wish you had some more cosmic way to applaud, it really does.

But it was Letitia I was with that particular Sunday afternoon, and I didn't know her well enough yet to act natural with her. We'd been discussing Virginia Woolf's *To the Lighthouse* for an hour, which was why she'd come over. Her suggestion.

A slightly delayed college student, I was twenty years old and in the second quarter of my first year at the University of Washington. Letitia was in the third quarter of her junior year. We'd met in a class on women novelists, co-sponsored by English and Women's Studies. Back then, Women's Studies tended to be called "eclectic" or "catch-all," depending on whether the speaker was for it or against it—one of those not-quite-to-be-taken-seriously departments that brought people together across the lines of academic class-standing and declared major. Even mating it with the English department didn't quite iron out all the wrinkles of unorthodoxy that clung to the very idea of Women's Studies in 1977.

1

The class felt like a cross between a regular academic course and a conscious-ness-raising group, just because of the Women's Studies connection, and I liked that a lot.

I liked Letitia, too, and I was even beginning to wonder if someday I might not like her a lot. If I could ever get her figured out.

She had a slightly olive, oval-shaped face with masses of dark brown hair sort of hovering around it, floating down like a soft brown cloud from a center part. Some people would've called her brown eyes protruding, I guess, but when she half-closed her eyelids and those long, smoky lashes swept down...I found no fault. Her eyebrows were firm and black, set high over her eyes, and her nose was short and unremarkable. But it was her mouth I was trying not to look at. It was wide and generous, with deep pink lips that looked as soft as a rose petal caught just at the hour before brown stains appear at the outer edges and the flower is plucked from the bouquet. "This one's wilting already," we say regretfully, and caress the petal between thumb and forefinger before throwing the bloom away. Our touch leaves a bruise, the flesh has become so soft, so tender.

What really floored me about Letitia, though, was that she almost always seemed to be coming at me and holding back at the same time. From the very first time she came up and talked to me after class, I felt she was looking for something in me, waiting for something to emerge from my inner depths so she could reach out and connect herself to a special part of me that only she suspected I carried hidden inside. But at the same time, she sort of held me off, as if she didn't want to get too close and then find out she'd been mistaken in thinking I was the one. It's like she was trying to get me to open up, challenging me to expose myself to her, but I had to go first before she'd consider making it mutual.

In other words, I was fascinated and confused, and my mind started to wander twenty minutes into our discussion of *To the Lighthouse*.

Letitia was saying, "The writing itself, as writing, expresses a theme that's diametrically opposed to the theme as it appears to the characters within the story, and that's what makes it so specifically a *woman's* story, don't you think, Terry? I mean, here, where Lily calls out to the dead Mrs. Ramsey...."

She read the passage aloud, drawing out the words with hidden meanings. Eerie, it seemed to me, calling a dead woman's name: *It was strange how clearly she saw her, stepping with her usual quickness across fields among whose folds, pur-plish and soft, among whose flowers, hyacinths or lilies, she vanished.*

Creepy, right? But I knew Letitia was reading it to me for a purpose. From the way she looked at me and the way she read, from the kind of silence in the room when she finished reading, I knew I was supposed to react in some specific way. She was waiting for me to say...what? And meanwhile, half my mind is on the clouds outside the window (purplish and soft), half is on not looking at Letitia's lips (purplish and soft), with some other fraction saying, But you're not that kind of person, Terr, to get hung up on an isolated body-part like that—and of a straight woman, too, how crass. And all I could think of to say about *To the Lighthouse* was what I had told Letitia already: "I still don't think it's fair for her to kill off Mrs. Ramsey in a parenthesis like that."

Something's going on here, Terr, I said to myself instead. And that's when Frances slammed into the house shouting blue murder.

Letitia and I froze. She looked like she was trying to figure out if this kind of thing might be considered normal in a place like Everywhere House. I wasn't sure myself how to react, but when feet came pounding up the stairs, my curiosity took over. "Excuse me a minute, 'Titia," I said and scrambled to my feet.

Out on the landing, women were pouring out of every room and Frances was talking a mile a minute at the top of her lungs. No one could hear a word she said, until, "...arrested her!" she hollered.

"Arrested!?" Toni and Jeanne screamed in reply.

"Yeah, as in busted. Locked up. Incarcerated. They went right in to Athena House and took her off to jail."

"But who, Fran? *Who* got busted?"

"Barb!"

"Barb who?"

Suddenly Peg's ear-splitting whistle shut us all down. "Let's have some order here, women," she ordered with mock ferocity into the silence her whistle had created, "so we can find out what the fuck's going on, okay? Okay. So now, Frances, tell us what—and who—the hell you're talking about."

"It's Barb, I told you. You know. One of the Furies from Athena House. They say she killed somebody—a man. Jan's on the phone about it right now."

Like a treasure-hunt team, we immediately wheeled as a group and poured ourselves thunderously down the old wooden stairs. Jan was just hanging up the phone as we reached the kitchen door. She turned somberly to face us. "It's murder all right."

There was a minute of shocked silence, and then the pack of us started to break up from our clog in the kitchen doorway. We drifted automatically towards the living room and settled in bright-eyed clumps, as if for one of Everywhere's marathon house meetings.

Letitia was standing in the doorway to the hall. I'd forgotten all about her in the excitement, and now I felt uncomfortable about that, and about the way she suddenly stood out as not-one-of-us. I didn't want to hurt her feelings, but I also really wanted to be free to join my housemates now. She'd probably never even heard of the Furies, I realized. Not these Furies, anyway, although she might know about the famous East Coast group by the same name, women who helped get the second wave of feminism rolling in the late Sixties and early Seventies. As far as I know, this local sect of virulent lesbian separatists had nothing in common with that earlier group besides the name. They were intent on policing the "political correctness" of the lesbian community in Seattle long before PC became an issue for straight people. Like many dykes I knew, I felt a mixture of admiration for their radical daring and fear that the next target of their righteous fury might turn out to be me.

As I walked up to Letitia, I was surprised to see a sort of panic in her eyes. "I'll see you tomorrow, Terry," she said quickly, and was gone.

"What are we doing to *do*?" Jeanne burst out immediately.

"Wait, the questions is, why should we do *anything*?" Toni countered.

"Are you kidding? She's a dyke, isn't she, and—"

"She's not just a dyke, Jeanne, she's a goddamn Fury. Do you think she'd raise a finger to help one of us if *we* got busted? You remember that anti-boychild leaflet they put out when they picketed that fund-raiser for Lesbian Mothers' National Defense fund—"

"Yes, but this is different, Toni," Connie broke in. "She's in jail, after all. And besides, it's sure to be in the newspaper and—"

"All the more reason to *not* get involved, then," Toni insisted. "I mean, that's just what we need, right? More bad publicity. On top of New Haven and the lesbian-baiting around the SLA, and that other group of separatists spray-painting 'Kill Men' graffiti all over town, a murder is exactly what we need right now, right? What I say is—"

"Geez louise, Toni, I know you're upset," Fran objected, "but really, you can't just list those things like they're all the same and then draw some kind of line that says that's them over there and all of us over here on this side, we're the *good* lesbians. I mean, who's going to believe that, even if it didn't totally suck politically?"

"And who'd want to, anyway? I mean, just look at where you're living, Toni," Jeanne demanded. "Have you forgotten already? Everywhere House is called that because *We Are Everywhere*. It's the oldest dyke slogan there is, and it means we are *together*, right? We are a community!"

"Yeah, but wait a minute," insisted Fran. "What's important right now is for us to be *ready*. It's happened again and again—I mean, just look at New Haven, like Toni said. They had lesbians in jail for over a year because they wouldn't talk to the grand jury about other women in the community. When the cops decide they have an excuse to pick on lesbians, we're all at risk. And this business about Barb could be just the excuse they need. There could be a cop at the door any minute now, and what the hell are we going to *say*?"

She was scaring us, and Toni scared us even more when she added, "We don't just need to decide what we'll say about Barb, you know. Hell, what *could* we say? Most of us don't even know her. But they won't stop there. What are we going to say when they ask about meetings we've been to, other women we've seen at lesbian events, that whole guilt-by-association trip?"

A shiver ran round the room, and some of us glanced toward the dark hallway

4

leading to the front door, half expecting to hear the rat-a-tat-tat of a billyclub. Up to then, our only contact with lesbians being jailed for their associations with radical politics had been reading in the local lesbian newsletter about women we didn't know. I looked at Fran's tense face and tried to make some sense out of the thoughts ricocheting around in my brain.

"We need to think about self-defense," I said haltingly, "but political integrity and solidarity are important, too. Just as important, I guess…. Or *more* important?" I looked around, hoping for an answer, hoping I'd like the answer I got, but the room was full of silence and uncertainty. No eyes met mine as I looked from friend to friend, so I dropped my own eyes to the hole in the rug where some previous tenant's magic-making had gotten a little too intense. A candle flame is made of fire, and fires have to be watched, even when they're dedicated to the Goddess. "We're so vulnerable," I heard myself thinking aloud and, afraid of my own fear, looked up and found Peg's eyes.

As if drawing comfort from my gaze, she smiled and her strong, deep, lovely voice broke the silence. "Hey, ladies, let's get real here, OK?" The Voice of Reason we called her, because she always sounded reasonable, whether she was or not. Peg was the closest to a butch in our group of political lesbians, but ninety-five percent of it was sheer play. She was a big woman, she was comfortable in overalls, and if some people's assumptions led them to take her for a stereotypical bulldagger, well, she was not about to tailor her wardrobe just to make bigots feel more comfortable. She had a sense of humor from here all the way to tomorrow, and she was kind; despite her size, she wouldn't push you if you didn't push her first.

"Let's not waste our time agonizing until we know what it is we're agonizing about, okay?" she went on. "I mean, if Barb offed a rapist, that's one thing." Hoots and shouts of agreement. "But if she just went out and bumped somebody off for being male, well, that might be a different story—for me, anyway."

"What do you think, Jan?" Connie asked. Jan had lived at Everywhere House longer than anyone—the only survivor of the Great Schism of 1976 when the women of Everywhere House turned separatist in two different directions and split with a mighty thunder. That split, goddess bless it, is why I got to move so quickly from the moldy little room in the basement up to my cushy room on the second floor; but even when I was stuck underground I still knew I was lucky to live in the same house with Jan. Chronologically, Jan was three or four years older than the rest of us. In brain-years, she was almost a different generation. Connie said it was a class difference: we middle-class types could afford to prolong our adolescence, whereas a lower-class woman like Jan had to grow up fast. That may have been right, but as far as I've heard, no one knows why most people—lower-class, middle-class, or whatever class—grow up normal and a handful, like Jan, grow up wise. You just naturally *trusted* her, if you were honest and you had any sense.

Jan usually didn't talk a whole lot, and when she did it took her a while to get started. Now, she rubbed a long forefinger up along her nose and pushed back the lock of straight blond hair that fell forward over her face whenever she relaxed her usual backwards-slanting posture. "I think," she said slowly, "it's time for dinner." And when we all reacted with groans and started working at her to go on, she said, "No, I mean it. I mean, think about it. What do we know so far?" We thought about it. "We know the cops got Barb in jail because they say she killed some man. And that's it, right?" We couldn't disagree. "Well, that don't give us damn-all to go on, you know. I mean, you do what you want, but here's one girl who don't go running off making plans based on what the policeman say—specially not what he say about a woman, and even more specially, not what he say about a dyke."

Jan's words bled the energy from our inflated impatience to act, and left us a bit resentful. Not a fair reaction, of course, because we depended on Jan for exactly that kind of deflationary common sense. But still, you can't always help feeling what you feel.

"So what do we do now?" asked Jeanne again, "Besides dinner, I mean."

"Well, I guess the place to start is the Furies," Jan answered thoughtfully. We groaned collectively. "I'll get ahold of Anne in the morning," Jan went on. "I can make it there and back during class break." Jan didn't hang around with the Furies as a group, but she and Anne had been friends a long time and refused to let ideology get in the way.

And that's where we left it Sunday night. We had to; Jan wouldn't budge, despite all our pleas and bribes and wheedlings. "Not on the phone," she said, "and not tonight. Let it cool down a few hours. Nothing we can do till morning, anyway." And we had to accept her decision. Oh, we continued to kick it around while we pulled dinner together, and while we ate, and for the rest of the evening, but we all knew Jan was right: we couldn't make any plans until we had more facts to go on. The phone was busy until midnight, but none of the dozens of women who called knew any more than we did, so finally we all just went to bed.

Monday, you better believe it, was a drag. Letitia eyed me invitingly from across the Women's Novels class, but I felt too Monday-ish and unsettled to go over and talk, especially to someone I knew wouldn't be able to give me any answers. Besides, I was late because I'd overslept. For no good reason, I was running late all day, to every class and to my work-study job in the library. All day I kept realizing I was late again and dashing off to the next class or whatever, and then when I got there I'd sit down and go blank until it was time to arrive late for the next scheduled activity. I thought about going home for lunch, but it didn't seem worth the effort. Jan wouldn't be home till after four, and more inane discussion was not what I needed to lift my dragging spirits.

What I did do during lunch was search through the morning paper. It seemed odd to have to hunt. As wound up as I was, as all of us were, I expected to see the murder announced in screaming banner headlines: *Lesbian Slays Innocent Male, Decent Citizens Demand Death Penalty*. All there was, though, was a blurb in the *Police Blotter* column on page eight, section C:

Police responding to calls from residents of a University of Washington dormitory at two-thirty a.m. Sunday morning found a wounded man outside the UW's Applied Physics Laboratory located just north of University Bridge. He died two hours later at Harborview Hospital without regaining consciousness. Identity of the victim is being withheld pending notification of relatives. Cause of death will not be made public until completion of the autopsy, but police are initially ruling the death a homicide. Seattle Police Department spokesman Bill Lockton told reporters early this morning that a suspect has been arrested and scheduled for arraignment later today.

The Applied Physics Lab, by goddess! The APL is only about a quarter mile from Everywhere House. All of sudden my grilled-cheese-and-pickle sandwich didn't look too appealing anymore; I didn't think I'd be able to force it down past the knot in my stomach.

What kind of "community" is this, anyway?, I asked myself. We talk about "the Seattle lesbian community" like it's something real, something that actually exists, as if we're all just one big happy non-nuclear family. And we make jokes about how we all know each other, maybe even too well. 'There's really only seven dykes in Seattle,' we say; 'the rest is done with mirrors.' Just one big not-so-happy family, all right, and there I was in bed Saturday night, sleeping peacefully, while a bare quarter mile away a woman, a lesbian, someone I'd met and talked to, a woman I'd thought of with friendship in my mind, was fighting for her life all alone.

At least, I supposed she was alone, and I supposed she was fighting for her life. I mean, calling themselves man-haters is one thing, I assured myself, but that's just talk, right? They may talk about how much better the world would get along without men, but they wouldn't really…would they?

I positively *itched* for the day to be over so I could get home and find out what Jan had learned from her Fury friend Anne. By the time I got to my one-thirty class, I heard people talking about the murder. The victim, they said, was a professor right there at the University, somebody named Simpson. I stopped by the English office after class and looked him up in the Faculty/Staff Directory. And there he was: Theodore A. Simpson, Assistant Professor, Philosophy.

By three-forty I was on my way home, drawn irresistibly to the route that would take me past the APL. There was a cop car parked right there by the building, its left-side tires on the sidewalk, and a man in police uniform leaning against the car, looking bored. I immediately felt guilty as hell. If I'd been the only civilian on the street, I probably would've turned and run, at which point

I would have *looked* guilty, too, and the cop might even have noticed me. There was the usual flow of students, though, as I headed west past the highrise ugliness of Terry-Lander dorm. I tried to imagine what the students there had seen from their windows so early on Sunday morning. Did they hear a woman—Barb— scream? Or was it Professor Simpson, the victim, who screamed? *Her* victim? Maybe. Somebody's victim, for sure. I decided the students couldn't have seen much, or not very clearly, because even the lower-floor dorm rooms were high above the sidewalk by the APL. In between, Campus Parkway maintained its width as it deadended into the offramp from University Bridge. Anyone looking from Terry-Lander would've seen no more than puppet-figures way down here by the APL, where I looked queasily around me for evidence of murder.

I don't know what I thought I'd see. Pools of blood? A chalk outline of the body? Fingerprint powder drifting like week-old snow? Wide yellow ribbons strung between sawhorses kept me too far away to see whether any of those TV cop-show staples were actually present. But nothing shielded me from the most shocking evidence of all: the graffiti newly painted on the building's cement wall.

It's true, then, was my first horrified reaction. Because there was the sign of the Furies, a labyris—the two-headed axe of the Amazons—in black spraypaint, and under it, in red, a typical Fury slogan. *All men rape. Womyn, fight back!* The words were a selection from the mild end of their slogan-spectrum, but still recognizably Fury, and nobody else in the city would have used the labyris then. The Furies had made it their own special symbol, and it identified the graffiti on the APL as reliably as a signature or a fingerprint. I stood there gaping for half a minute and then took off up the hill for home.

2.

The first time I ever saw Barb was at the Lesbian Resource Center about a month after I moved to Seattle. The LRC had two little rooms then in a suite leased by several feminist groups over an office supply store on "The Ave," as University Way is known. I'd only been to the LRC once before and was headed there that day to check the "Roommates Wanted" board. Had I known how soon the separatists in Everywhere House were going to split and free-up the upstairs rooms, I wouldn't have bothered. The dampness and the big hairy spiders in the basement were really getting me down, though, and that's how I came to meet Barb.

It wasn't exactly a formal introduction. She'd have knocked me down if I hadn't hopped back out of the way. As steep and narrow as those stairs were, there was no room for anyone but Barb—and she was coming down them as fast as anyone could without flat out falling. She looked huge coming towards me, and she sounded huge, too, an avalanche of blue denim and blue language. "Fucking, half-assed, cock-sucking feminist creeps!" she roared, and was gone.

I was impressed. The wind of her passing almost blew me out of the corner I'd huddled myself into at the bottom of the stairs. Recovering, bemused, I turned again to climb the stairs and, looking up, saw a halo of pale faces staring silently down. They seemed to be in shock.

By the time I reached the top, the spell had broken and one of the women was proclaiming resentfully to the world at large, "I was only trying to be friendly."

"Of course you were, Carol," another woman responded. "Don't pay any attention to her. Barb's got a chip on her shoulder as big as a tree."

"And she's sure got the shoulder for it," snickered a third woman.

"I really thought she was Deb," protested Carol earnestly. "I mean, I only met her once, and she and Deb were together, and I just got them mixed up, that's all."

"What's the problem?" I asked.

"Well, she...she attacked me," Carol replied, with anger beginning to replace the anxious self-justification in her voice. "I mean, all I said was, 'hello, Deb,' just to be friendly, and she started *yelling* at me. 'All fat women look alike to you, you can't even be bothered to tell us apart, seen one you've seen 'em all.' On and on, just literally screaming at me. She must be crazy."

That was my introduction to Barb. Later on I'd learn that, according to Barb herself, she wasn't crazy, she was Furious. A lot of people said, "Well, her *furious* looks an awful lot like anyone else's *crazy*," and I guess they were right. That's how it *looked*, I mean; but until this murder business came up, I didn't think that was how it really *was*.

The second time I met Barb was at the Furies' Fat Oppression Workshop. When I mentioned to Fran that I was going to the workshop she said, "You're kidding!" and then, "Hey! Why don't we all go!"—meaning, all of us from Everywhere House.

"Hey, Peg!" she called out to The Voice of Reason in the kitchen, "let's all go to the Furies' fat oppression workshop tonight. Wouldn't that be a howl?"

"Naw," drawled Peg, leaning in the doorway, "they're so far out it's no fun even ribbing them. They don't get righteous, they just get nasty, and nasty's no fun at all."

"Did you guys know them when they lived here?" I asked. I knew that three of the Furies had lived in Everywhere House before the big split, out of which the Furies were born.

"Shit yes," Fran answered. "I mean, everybody in the city knew them, more or less. I never worked with them or anything. They 'do not care to associate' with low-consciousness dykes like me." The dainty sarcasm in her voice put quote marks around that disdainful phrase. "About a year ago," she went on, "Fennel saw me wearing a skirt at an LRC dance, and none of the Furies have deigned to speak to me since."

"Oh come on, Fran, 'fess up," said Peg, laughing. "You don't have to exaggerate when you talk about the Furies, they've already exaggerated themselves to the limit. You know it wasn't just the skirt. You were wearing fucking eye shadow and lipstick that night, you closet femme you."

Fran giggled and turned stage-British. "Theatre, my dear, purely Theatre," she said.

That conversation was still in my mind as I sat down on one of the metal folding chairs provided by the Furies for participants in their Fat Oppression Workshop. Even though there were only about twenty of us, they'd rented a room—it looked like half a former gym—in a community center. "Private Meeting. WOMEN ONLY" read a hand-lettered sign on the door to the room.

The five Furies in attendance stayed caucused in a corner until ten minutes past the appointed hour. The rest of us had straggled in by ones and twos, some of us shy and unsure, others with that special at-home-in-the-world air that Peg called "the lesbian feminist prance." Before feminism, she says, dykes who dared to be out used to swagger, a proud strut that said, "You can hate me, world, but you can't break me." The way lesbian feminists of the '70s walked, on the other hand, said: "Yup, I'm a woman-loving-woman, people, and if you don't like it it's because you're jealous, poor repressed hets that you are." When the Furies broke out of their huddle to join us, I'd decided I could report to Peg that the workshop group consisted of one old-fashioned swaggerer, nine new-age prancers, and about ten quiet-walking women in various stages of coming out.

Barb started the workshop by directing our attention to the schedule-cum-outline on the first page of the stapled packet we'd each picked up from the chair we sat down on. Conspicuous by its absence was the usual "check-in" period to start things off—no going around the circle for introductions and "tell us a little bit about how you're feeling this morning" for this bunch, as had become almost compulsory for any group aspiring to feminist political standards. I was seriously dabbling with the possibility of asking why, but just then Barb concluded her opening remarks by answering my unasked question.

"The purpose of this workshop," she said, "is educational." She glanced at each of the other Furies, as if for confirmation—or for support? I wondered; what is she feeling? I couldn't tell anything by looking at her; or by listening to her, for that matter. She droned when she talked, like someone reading a text book. Fixing her eyes on a point above our heads, she continued, "We worked hard putting this information together for you. Helen will present the information, Karen and Lil will analyze the information, and then we'll divide into two groups. Clove will lead the group for thin lesbians, and Fennel will lead the group for fat lesbians." And suddenly she stopped, ending as abruptly as if a switch had been thrown, sending her into suspended animation until further notice.

I was fascinated. What's going on behind this woman's face? I wondered. Half hiding behind my copy of the information packet, I watched Barb study her own copy of the packet as Helen began to read its second page out loud. Barb was a big woman for sure, looking even bigger in her loosely-fitting overalls and baggy shirt. Even her head looked unusually large, despite the familiar "dyke cut" hairstyle that made many women in the community looked pin-headed. Barb's head looked square and solid, and her large face was flat and inexpressive. A description I'd read more than once in British novels arose in my mind and seemed to fit Barb better than anyone I could remember: "She's got a face like the back of a bus." And just about as expressive. I've been drawn to large-size women ever since my first pre-teen crush (on Gertrude Stein), though, and there was something about Barb that intrigued the hell out of me. When Alice Toklas met Gertrude Stein, a bell rang inside her and she knew she was in the presence of genius. That's not quite how I felt about Barb; I wasn't at all sure I'd recognize genius when I saw it, for one thing. On the other hand, I *was* sure that I was in the presence of a woman who was more—who was other—than she made herself appear to be. And, *why?*, I kept asking myself. *Why, why, and why?*

Throughout the presentation and the analysis, Barb remained silent and almost motionless. I'd already read most of the information we were being spoon-fed, and read it in more interesting articles, written by feminists, so I felt free to let my mind wander a bit. The contents of the packet Helen read to us were mostly scholarly articles from medical and psychology journals; very odd sources for a lesbian-feminist workshop, I thought, and quite amazingly boring, in my opinion. Even the analysis wasn't much improvement, because we were not given a chance to participate. Karen and Lil simply read out the Furies' interpretation of "fat oppression as a tool of patriarchal oppression." Fat is healthy, they said, but the Patriarchy makes people believe it's unhealthy in order to keep women, and especially lesbians, oppressed and under control. Dieting weakens women, so patriarchy brain-washes women into being so afraid of being fat that most of us are on diets all the time. Plus we're tricked into doing the patriarchy's work when we oppress ourselves and other women who are fat.

By the time we reached the 'Groups' part of the program, I was both impressed and disappointed. Impressed by the Furies' hard work gathering all this information and setting up the workshop. Disappointed, because we were not allowed to question or participate. And besides, their analysis sounded woefully over-simplified to me. You were either fat or you were thin, you either oppressed or you were oppressed, you either believed the Furies' party line or you were a "collaborator" and a functioning arm of "The Enemy." Well, I couldn't speak for anybody else, but *my* life just wasn't like that—though how *much* not like that, I was only beginning to learn. So as much as I agreed with the basic information on which the Furies based their analysis, I was getting pretty damned itchy just sitting there in silence.

What's more, I'd come to a decision: one of my major goals in life, from that moment on, would be to evoke some recognizable trace of emotion—preferrably joy—on the massive face of Barb-the-Stone-Faced-Fury. I mean, hey, the contradiction was just too much for me. Here was a woman who allied herself openly with a heavy-duty my-politics-are-my-life group called The *Furies*, and yet there she sat, allowing no trace of emotion to appear on the surface of her skin. I thought back to our first "meeting," the near collision on the stairs up to the LRC, an occasion when Barb's feelings came through loud and clear. And I said to myself, Terr, this woman needs help. It's gonna be deadly for her if the only emotion she allows herself to feel is fury. As we divided ourselves into two groups under the steely eyes of the five Furies, I entertained myself by trying to imagine what Barb would sound like if she giggled.

I didn't get a chance to begin my campaign during the rest of the workshop, of course, because Barb went to Fennel's "fat" group and I was relegated to the "thins." If you took a poll at just about any shopping mall in the country, I bet at least eighty percent of the people asked would describe me as "overweight." That's not the same as fat, though, so I didn't mind being lumped in with the thin group. What I did mind was the way Clove "led" the group. We were allowed to acknowledge our own pain, the years we spent hating ourselves for being "too fat," the punishments we doled out to ourselves for eating "too much," but only if each pain statement was quickly followed by a confession. As "thin" lesbians, Clove said, we were guilty of oppressing fat lesbians, and the purpose of the "thin group" was self-criticism and repentance. I did try to present my point of view, that the point was what were we going to *do* in order to change things. Clove obviously had her orders, though. As the only Fury in the "thin" group, she was determined to keep us criminally-thin dykes in line. Every time I suggested talking about how we could change what we've been brought up to think and feel, Clove slapped me down with some statement like, "Fat lesbians are dying, and we are complicit." Beating my head against the wall couldn't have felt much worse.

The workshop ended exactly on time, thank goddess, and I was the first one out the door—but not by much. I had a couple blocks to walk to the bus stop, and when I noticed another workshop participant heading in the same direction, I slowed down and let her catch up to me. With ulterior motives, I admit. I'd seen this woman several times at the Slipper, the only good women's dance bar in town, and I hoped maybe chatting with her about the workshop would give me nerve enough to ask her to dance next time we both turned up at the Slipper on the same night. Not that I was cruising her or anything, you understand. Just that she's a fabulous dancer and, who knows, it could only be fun, right? "How'd you like the workshop?" I asked as she drew level with me.

"Shit." She sounded thoroughly disgusted. "That damn Barb. Telling me that *I* am oppressing her! Telling me my *thoughts* oppress her—" She glanced quickly at me and broke off into an inaudible mutter.

Because I'm white, I said to myself. *Damn.* I'd seen her look around when she first came into the workshop room and seem to debate with herself whether or not to stay. Everyone else there was white. I felt sad and awkward, but also intensely curious. "How did she know your thoughts were oppressing her?" I asked.

"Because I made a mistake, that's why. Because I made the mistake of saying I think life would be easier on me if I was to lose a hundred pounds. And she's there with her 'you're oppressing me with your internalized hatred of your own fat,' which I did *not* say that I hate my own fat or my own self or my own *nothing*—you understand what I'm saying?—but she sit there and talk about *me* oppressing *her*, big-ass fool that she is, because I say I'd have it easier if I weighed one-twenty instead of two-twenty. And what she think she know about my life, anyway? Her and Fennel sitting there telling me 'the black culture this' and 'the black culture that.' Supposed to be more tolerant of fat than white culture. *Always* supposed to be better than white culture, listen to some of you white women tell it, even though you'd sooner die than live in it your own selves. So what I say is it's one thing to look from the outside and say 'ooo, black culture is so this' and 'black culture is so that,' and I ain't saying otherwise, you dig? Hell, I wouldn't be nothing else *but* black even if I could. I love my black culture and my black womanhood. But don't you go be telling me what it's like being a fat black dyke, because I know more about that than you *ever* want to know, believe me!"

"I believe you!" I said, laughing. "And I can just imagine Barb saying that to you, too. She's got the one-track mind to end all one-track minds, apparently."

"One track," she smiled back, "and narrow gauge, at that."

We'd reached 23rd Avenue by then, and she was headed south so we had to split up, her on one side of the street and me on the other. I didn't quite have the nerve to say, "See you at the Slipper sometime," as we parted, but I tucked the thought away in my mind like a promise and didn't think of Barb again till I got home. And then, as soon as I walked in the door, there was Fran saying, "Hey, Terr! They let you go! You surrendered yourself to the Furies, and they let you go again! What's the matter, not a big enough catch for 'em, so they threw you back?"

I laid a finger to my lips, tiptoed with elaborate precaution to her side, and whispered in her ear, "Promise you won't tell anyone, Fran, but Barb and I are secretly engaged." When I looked back at her from halfway up the stairs, she actually didn't seem one hundred percent sure I was joking.

3.

Despite my dawdling at the murder scene, I beat Jan home. She arrived a scant twenty minutes later, but that gave me plenty of time to get thoroughly irritated by the fight going on in the kitchen. Ordinarily the seven of us who lived in Everywhere House weren't that easy to get together. We almost always managed near-perfect attendance at the monthly house meeting, but sometimes only after rescheduling it two or three times. The excitement of the murder brought us all together, though; in our shock and uncertainty, we huddled like baby foxes in a den. The taken-for-granted politics of lesbian solidarity—an easy, if superficial, stance to assume in good times—turned scary when just being part of the community might bring the attention of the police down upon us. I don't think we were as frightened about what the police might do to us as we were unsure of our ability to fulfill the politically sophisticated role we'd so casually assigned ourselves as radical lesbian feminists. We knew of lesbian feminists who'd been jailed for non-cooperation with the justice system, and each of us wondered how well she'd play the part of political heroine if called upon to do so. It seemed deeply unfair that this threat to our peace of mind should come from a member of a group whose hard-line separatist politics and apparent contempt for anyone who disagreed with them tested the concept of lesbian solidarity to the limit.

Toni and Jeanne were going at it hot and heavy when I arrived, "discussing the situation" as fiercely as only ex-lovers can.

"The Furies are part of this community, that's all I'm saying, and—."

"If you're so concerned about the community, Jeanne, why do you insist on imposing your politics on every other lesbian in the city? Sounds like fascism-of-the-left to me, and it sounds pretty damn familiar, too."

"Fascism!" Jeanne turned her rhetoric to the room at large. "Did you hear that?! Now she's calling me a fascist! Do you believe this woman? We've got a real crisis on our hands, and she reacts by calling *me* a fascist! And you know, it's so unprincipled, Toni, typical but unprincipled, for you to—"

"Oh yeah?" Toni spat back. "Well, if you wanna talk about unprincipled, let's just not forget about that dance last year when you—"

I could tell by the minimal reaction on the part of the other women in the kitchen that this argument had been going on long enough to inspire complete apathy, despite the inflammatory language being thrown around. As the new-comer I had a choice: take sides and prolong the general boredom, or try to short out the argument by ignoring it altogether. "Any news?" I asked, "or are we still picking over the same old hash?"

"It's lentil stew, actually," said Peg, stirring the contents of a big sauce pan on the stove. "I couldn't find any canned tomatos so I put in some tomato paste instead. What do you think?"

"We could always have it on spaghetti," yawned Fran, lifting her head six inches off the table. "Assuming there *is* any spaghetti."

"I'm sure it'll be fine, Peg," said Connie. Sitting tidy and composed across the wide table from Fran's sprawl, she was sewing steadily away at the baby clothes she made for a crafts booth at the Public Market. Everyone in the house secretly admired Connie's discipline; you could tell by how loudly we all proclaimed our inability to tolerate such a tedious, femmy activity.

Fortunately, Jan walked in just then, so Toni and Jeanne didn't have a chance to pick up their argument where I'd interrupted. She looked tired and depressed; there were strain lines in her face and the slump of weariness in her shoulders. Even her corn-colored hair looked dim and discouraged as she accepted a cup of coffee and turned to face us, leaning back with her elbows on the counter.

Fran hitched her stool over to the counter and leaned against Jan in a comforting way as the rest of us waited for her to begin. "So," Jan said, patting Fran's curly hair softly. "I guess you all been waiting to hear my report, right?" She smiled, sort of, which made her look even more depressed.

"Okay," she went on. "I'll tell you what I been able to find out so far. The first thing is, there's gonna be big trouble for the Furies. The second thing is, it ain't gonna be that bad for the rest of us. Far as I can tell."

Connie looked up from her handwork to say, "Are all the Furies involved?"

"No. Not in the murder. Only Barb."

"What do you mean, then?" Fran asked her, tilting her head back to look up at Jan. "How is it going to be bad for the Furies, and how do you know it won't be bad for the rest of us?"

"Guess I better tell it all the way it happened," was Jan's answer. "Starting from when I called up Anne this morning from school." Jan was in a program at Seattle Central Community College up on Capitol Hill, not too far from the Furies' Athena House.

"She wouldn't even come to the phone." Jan's mouth pulled down on one side in what looked to me like anger. "So I went on over there at lunch time. Took me fifteen minutes to talk my way through the goddamn door, and then I thought for a while I'd have to lay Lil and Karen out before they'd let me talk to Anne. 'We're not ready to talk to outsiders,' they were saying. 'She don't wanna talk to you today.' Bullshit. I've known Anne since before any of them come to this town, and they go telling me she don't wanna talk to me. They had her scared, that's all."

The room was silent, spellbound, as Jan paused for another angry sip of coffee, and then went on with her story. "Finally I get 'em to let me stay. They decide they can 'trust' me. So everybody goes in the living room and sits down, and that's when I notice something's going on with Clove. She's the little, young-looking one, you know?"

We knew.

"Okay, so everybody's sitting around in sort of a circle, except for Clove is off in a corner. Off away from everybody. And they're all acting like she ain't even there. Don't talk to her, don't look at her, nothing. Turns out the other women think Clove went and split to the cops, told 'em something about 'We never went near the APL, we never hit the APL,' something like that. And that's how the cops know it was just Barb, not the Furies but just Barb that was there, and all the rest of 'em trying to decide if they're gonna cut out Clove for talking to the cops or Barb for bringing the cops down on 'em in the first place. This business gonna bust the Furies clean apart for sure. Sure as shit."

I couldn't hold back another second. "Geez, Jan, just a minute! How did the police know to go to Athena House at all? And how did they know it was Barb, if it was, and what does she have to say about it?" As Jan talked, the vague mental image of myself under police interrogation had been replaced by a clearer vision of Barb's large, sullen face, and my formal posture of lesbian solidarity gained sudden vitality from the shiver of sympathy I felt for her isolation.

Jan grinned a little at me, which I was glad to see even as I itched with impatience to understand what the hell had happened Saturday night at the APL and today at Athena House. "Well, the way it looks, the police recognized the spray-painting—you remember that time Lil got caught doing that wall on Tenth Avenue?" We all did, of course, there'd been a big story about it in the Gay News. "Same slogan, so the police figured it was the Furies again. And then they had the spray can and the knife"—a tremor passed through the room—"that they say got Barb's fingerprints on. But the cops didn't have her prints, of course, until they showed up at Athena House with a warrant, five o'clock Sunday morning. Woke 'em all up, took 'em downtown, got everybody's fingerprints.... That's when Clove up and told 'em about 'we was out, but we didn't do the APL.'"

"You mean she told the police they'd all been out spraypainting?" Jeanne's incredulity spoke for us all.

"Yeah, well, you gotta understand," Jan responded. "I don't say she should of, but you can understand it, the way these things go. I mean, there you are, asleep in your bed, and then there's the police taking you in and talking about murder.... Before I left I did get Anne alone for five minutes, and she says, soon as the cops seen how scared Clove was they took her off by herself and got her to talk. Seems they was all out spray-painting Saturday night real late, all seven of 'em, in three cars. Then about one o'clock everybody but Barb decides they wanna call it a night and go for a blow-out at the Clock"—that's a twenty-four-hour restaurant near downtown—"and Barb goes and gets all righteous on 'em, saying they're supposed to be overthrowing the patriarchy, trying to trip 'em into staying out all night. So there's sort of a scene, Anne tells me, and then the rest of 'em say, 'the hell with you, Barb, we've had enough, we're going to the Clock.'"

Hardly moving, Jan brought the scene to life for us: the six big and one small-sized Furies, hiding from the streetlights at one o'clock in the morning, fighting with each other in whispers over whether to overthrow the patriarchy now or later.

"Anne had left her wallet in Barb's car," Jan continued, "so she had to walk back with her to get it before they broke up. On the way, Barb told her she was gonna hit at least one more place before she went home, probably the APL. So then Anne goes and gets in the car with Helen and Lil to go to the Clock, and she tells 'em Barb's gonna do the APL. But the thing is, they don't none of 'em tell the others; you dig? So that's how come Clove goes and tells the cops, 'But we never went near the APL.' Because she never knew Barb had meant to go on there alone. And the Furies now, they're calling Clove a traitor for talking to the cops about dyke business, plus the whole lot of 'em are scared shitless because they don't know nothing about what Barb might've done aside from painting. They don't know if they oughta call her their hero or cut her off for a fool, and until they get it figured out, they're gonna be one scared, nasty bunch of women."

There was silence after Jan finished her story. Eventually Peg spoke up. "You say they found a can of spray paint and…a knife, both with Barb's fingerprints?"

"Yup." Jan was cradling her coffee cup in both hands now as if for warmth, though there couldn't be much warmth left in the cup or the coffee anymore.

"But, so who is this guy that she…that was killed?" was Peg's next question.

"Theodore J. Simpson," I sighed and all eyes turned to me. "Assistant prof." Another sigh. "Philosophy."

"What I can't figure out," I said when being the silent center of attention got to be a burden, "is why she'd leave her fingerprints at the scene like that. If she meant to kill him, I mean, as a political statement or something."

A few pairs of eyes drifted off to consider that puzzle, and then somebody said, "Maybe he tried to stop her from spray painting. Maybe he attacked her, even. So she panicked and ran…?"

We stayed pretty quiet after that while we finished putting things together for dinner. Jan went off to wash and change, and Connie tactfully separated Toni and Jeanne by asking Toni to help her shift the big rubber plant in the living room. She kept moving it around to different places every few weeks, trying to achieve the highest possible ratio of green to yellow in its five or six sad leaves. About an hour later, the discussion picked up again, and then it all went haywire even faster than usual. Everywhere House women had always been renowned for intense arguments, but they usually were of the long, slow-burning, analytical variety, and they never before—or since—achieved the thrilling climax of a temper tantrum by yours truly.

What finally got to me, amid all the predictable pro- and anti-Fury argumentation and the "but the real issue is…" calls for clarity and reason, what finally really lit my fuse was the way Barb somehow seemed to disappear in the verbiage.

Feminism, murder, a woman's right to self-defense, oppression, community—the discussion started out fairly rational. The longer it went on, though, the more abstract it got. After fifteen minutes I began to feel like I was disappearing into another dimension and nobody noticed but me. There was an awful lot of distance in that room all of a sudden, and all of it was between me and my intently arguing housemates. It was like having a high fever when you're a child. Or looking through the wrong end of a telescope. Even their voices sounded distant and strange, and it got harder and harder to believe that any of them knew what the hell they were talking about.

"Well, shit, Jeanne, I'm pretty sick of all this loose talk about community," Toni was charging as I struggled to get my ears back in focus. "Just what the hell is this 'lesbian community' you talk so much about? Does it mean every woman who's ever slept with a woman, or what? Or is it political? And however you define it," she concluded, raising her voice above Jeanne's attempted interruption, "I'd sure like to see you explain how come it means we've got to support the Furies but they don't have to support us."

And they were off. What is community. What does support mean. Is every oppressed group automatically a community and, if so, does that mean community cannot exist without oppression. And from another angle, can you even call it a "community" if oppression is the only thing a group of people has in common. They went on and on and on, eventually sinking to the level of questions like "what is lesbianism" and "are human beings basically good or basically evil" before hitting rock-bottom with the inevitable recitation of that fine old feminist koan, "the personal is political," and its endlessly answerable corollary, "yes, but what does that *mean?*"

Next thing I knew, I was on my feet making a speech. "This is a *person* we're talking about," I told them, furiously. "Or rather, this is a person we're *not* talking about. But we damn well ought to be talking about her, because she's…she's a person, dammit, an individual human being, with feelings and fears, and she's sitting in jail right this very minute, maybe scared half to death, and we sit here talking as if she didn't even exist. It makes me sick."

I was almost yelling by the end of that peroration, which I basically never do, so we were all taken by surprise. Even Fran was too astonished to interrupt, although at one point I could see in her eyes that she was thinking sarcastically, "Barb has feelings? Barb is scared?" We'd all gotten into the habit of accepting Barb the way she apparently wanted us to see her, like some kind of super-dyke, impervious to normal human weakness or emotion. The Furies stuck so tight together they never gave the rest of us a chance to know them one at a time, and they almost seemed to compete among themselves to come across as the toughest one of a very tough bunch. So part of me could understand Fran's skepticism. Another part of me, though, kept wondering what Barb might be hiding from the world behind her fiercely dead-pan public persona.

4.

I woke muddle-headed at seven o'clock Tuesday morning, the alarm clock bleating in my ear, and me with an eight o'clock class. As I dashed madly about the house getting myself ready for the day, my brain kept trying to tell me something. "Hey, don't you remember, Terr?" it said, "you were going to be sure to—" And suddenly there'd be Connie yawning in my ear and opening the mirrored cabinet above the sink to get the toothpaste, making it necessary for me to bob and weave like the wide-awake person I definitely was not in order to continue the complex task of making sure the top button on my shirt was inserted into the correct buttonhole. I don't even want to think about how often I've arrived places with my shirt buttoned à la Picasso.

Not until seven-thirty-five, when I was already on my way out the door, did my brain manage to force the complete message through to consciousness: I wanted to be sure to leave a message for Jan this morning. I grabbed the message pad from the phone stand, scribbled, *Jan. I need to talk to you ASAP. It's important. Terry*, stuck the slip of paper to the hook Jan had put on her door for that purpose and was gone.

Two hours later, Letitia glommed onto me outside the door of the classroom where our Women's Novels class was about to meet. She looked intense. In fact, she looked very intense, and all that intensity was aimed straight at me. I almost tripped over a crack in the linoleum walking the last few yards to the door where she was waiting. Feeling inadequate tends to make me clumsy, and I just knew I didn't have it in me to respond adequately to whatever it was Letitia had found to be so intense about. Not right then, anyway.

Luckily for me, before I had a chance to drop my books on Letitia's feet or in any other manner demonstrate my suavity and general couthness, the prof swirled by on her way through the classroom door and we knew it was time to go in. "Talk to me after class," Letitia all but demanded as we settled into adjacent tablet-arm chairs. I nodded my "yes," along with a little shrug meant to convey "for a few minutes anyway." If I weren't firm with myself (and Letitia) about taking some time to go over my notes before my eleven o'clock botany class, I was sure to have trouble with the quiz. And besides, I had too many other things on my mind to feel much interest in extra-curricular discussions of Virginia Woolf—and what else could Letitia want to talk to me about?

Fifty-five minutes later, I was wondering if Letitia herself knew what it was she wanted to talk about. She'd scooped me up as soon as class was over and ferried me off to an isolated bench among some baby rhododendrons behind the Engineering Library. The intensity was still there, but she seemed to be having trouble putting her thoughts into words. "I haven't talked to you since Sunday," she said finally, after a silence long enough to notice.

"Hmmm," I said, not being able to think of anything more polite or meaningful. We'd only met that quarter, after all, and weren't close friends. Letitia looked at me steadily, as if waiting for me to go on. "I heard somebody in my eight o'clock class say there might be snow showers today," I improvised. "Pretty weird, what with the crocuses being out already."

Letitia dropped her eyes and we sat wordlessly though another long silence before she inquired, "Is your friend still in jail?" She said it quietly, but she was looking at me, right in the eye, like some kind of all-knowing lie detector.

Well, hell, I said to myself, I don't want to talk about it with her, I really don't. She probably doesn't know anything about us, and it's really just too complicated to explain to someone who doesn't... who probably can't even... well, hell, I just really don't want to talk to her about it right now. But I had to say something, of course. "Say something, Terr," ordered my id. I'm sure I sighed, giving in to my own better nature, though a substantial part of my reason for giving in was considerably less than altruistic. As much as I did not want to talk to her—or any other straight woman—about Barb and the murder right then, Letitia still intrigued the hell out of me, even while making me freeze my ass off on a bench for no good reason. I kept feeling like she wanted something from me, something really special, and I couldn't help hoping she'd find it eventually, whatever it was. So I compromised. "Yeah," I said, "so far as I know." And then quickly, with the classic welsher's gesture of a shot cuff and a flash of wristwatch: "Hey, look at the time! Gotta run, Letitia. Botany quiz this morning. Maybe we could get together some other time."

Within a minute or two I'd made good my escape, leaving behind a promise to "really talk" on Friday at the latest. That meant, I figured, that I wouldn't have to start getting nervous about it till Thursday at the earliest. A social klutz's life is not a happy one.

My lunch that day was enlivened by a copy of the morning's newspaper I found abandoned on a crumby table in the HUB cafeteria. "Patty's Ammo Testimony Contradicted," screamed the headline like some distorted echo of the headline I'd expected to see a couple days earlier about Barb. According to the story under the headline, the prosecution in the Patty Hearst trial had begun to call rebuttal witnesses following the completion of the defense attorney's case. Was she a willing participant in the bank robbery, a "real" terrorist, a willing adherent of the Symbionese Liberation Army's "armed struggle" tactics? Or was she a poor little rich girl, the victim of a terrorist plot, forced to participate in the robbery for propaganda purposes by the "evil" SLA members who had kidnapped her? Those were the questions the mainstream papers raised again and again. Meanwhile, the other papers—the feminist, lesbian, or leftist papers—printed poetry written by the lesbian members of the SLA, and some of us fell a little bit in love then with the beauty of the words and the glamor of a political commitment strong enough to die for.

I stared at Patty's pale, thin face on the front page as I munched my fries. What does it feel like, I wondered, to hold a machine gun. From her pictures, Patty Hearst hardly looked strong enough to lift one; but she'd done it. Would I do it? I wondered. Would there ever be a cause compelling enough to take me out into the streets with a gun in my hands? Is that where my political beliefs would lead me if I let them? Or were all of the "armed struggle" groups in the U.S. victims of a kind of brainwashing brought on by wishful thinking? There was one in Seattle, even, called the George Jackson Brigade, and some of its members were said to be lesbians, too. Did the GJB rob banks because they were at the forefront of a real revolution? Or did they do it because they needed so much for the revolution to be real that they were willing to sacrifice their lives to create that illusion? And where, I silently asked Ms. Hearst's picture in the paper, does Barb fit in to all this? Is she acting out her own version of the revolution against the patriarchy? I tried to picture a jail-cell conversation between Patty and Barb, but I didn't know enough about either of them—or about a jail cell—to make it go anywhere.

I was in danger of serious depression by the time I finished the fries, so I flipped through the paper looking for a good-news story to mull over while putting in my work-study hours that afternoon. As luck would have it, the first story to catch my eye was a follow-up on the previous day's conviction of Ted Bundy in Salt Lake City. Bundy, the story reminded me unnecessarily, was a suspect in the disappearance of eight young women in the Seattle area. Did they think I'd be able to forget that this nice-young-man creepola had most likely charmed and murdered all of those women and who knows how many more? So which is more dangerous to a woman like me, I challenged the newspaper to answer, a committed revolutionary like the lesbians of the SLA (or like Barb, added a little voice from the back of my mind) or a thoroughly respectable young heterosexual chap like Bundy?

A ripple of laughter was the only answer; I looked up to see a covey of young women passing my table in a cloud of face powder and perfume. Sorority sisters, most likely, I thought, and then suddenly realized, looking at their trim, identical young bodies as they disappeared around a corner, how they, too, formed a group, an organization, a "brigade," maybe even a community. What kind of reality did they invent for themselves every day, I wondered as I left the cafeteria. And would it shock them if they knew that, according to my reality, an accurate title for their collectivity might be: The Future Female Victims of America, Inc.? I couldn't picture any of them using a machine gun, but I sure as hell could picture each of them walking sweetly off to her death with a Bundy clone. And smiling all the way.

That evening, Jan came to my room with my note in her hand. "What's up?"

I took a deep breath and let myself wait while Jan folded herself down on the foot of the bed—"all arms and legs," like C.S. Lewis' morosely lovable Marshwiggle. Then I got up, turned my desk chair around to face her, sat down again, crossed my legs, straightened my back, uncrossed my legs, got up, twisted my hands into a knot, dropped myself down onto the foot of the bed next to Jan and said, "I want to go see Barb."

Jan made a noise halfway between a snort and a chuckle that expressed her surprise very well. "Oh you do!" she said. "Why's that?"

For some reason I was feeling sort of defiant. Maybe I was expecting Jan to say I shouldn't. Or maybe I just didn't think I could explain myself very well and therefore didn't want to have to try. At any rate, I found myself answering Jan's question by saying nothing more than, "I promised myself a long time ago that some day I'd see Barb smile."

Jan's eyebrows went up about six inches, but she didn't actually laugh in my face. For all I know, she didn't see anything funny in my answer, though it clearly wasn't anything she'd expected to hear. She sat looking thoughtful for a few seconds and then said, "OK. Lemme make a call."

A few minutes later she was back. And I was still sitting motionless on the foot of the bed, waiting for her. "Her visiting hours are Wednesday, seven to nine. Wanna go tomorrow?"

I nodded, speechless with the number of questions I had to ask. I'd never visited anybody in jail before and had no idea at all how to go about it, much less where to find the jail. Jan didn't wait for any questions, though. "Meet you here at six-forty-five, then. OK?" she said.

"You're going with me?" I practically shouted it at her in my relief.

"Sure," she said. "See you then." And she left me alone with my women's novels, my leaf cross-sections, my Spanish stem-changing verbs, and almost twenty-four hours to get myself through before the adventure would begin.

5.

The weather forecast Wednesday morning was for "rain turning to showers." Geez, only in Seattle: rain turning to rain. And anyway, it didn't. Turn to showers, I mean.

By six-forty-five, the whole world was wet and dark. I was shivering, despite the sweatshirt under my rain slicker, either from the chill in the air or from the chill of anticipation in my mind. All day I'd been realizing and denying, realizing and denying. I was going to jail—"Go to Jail. Go directly to jail. Do not pass Go...."—but what's more, I was...aw shucks, it was too corny to even think about Terry Barber, Girl Detective. Yeah, sure.

I'm still not sure how or why I'd decided to appoint myself the Hercule Poirot of the case. Maybe it had something to do with how I felt when I walked by the APL, the Scene of the Crime, and pictured Barb in my mind. My Mom used to tell me, "Terry, you can't always be for the underdog; just because someone is getting the worst of it doesn't mean he's always right." I guess she didn't think a tendency to root for the underdog was really such a bad character trait, though, because she never tried very hard to break me of the habit. Being married to a high school English teacher may have something to do with it, I suspect; high school teachers are underdogs by definition. Anyway, I was riding a crest of crusader energy when Jan popped her head around the kitchen door and said, "Ready to roll?"

Jan had a beat-up old tank of a Chevy stationwagon back then. She'd ease it down to the south end almost every weekend, where she had some mechanic friends who'd work on it with her. With their help, she kept it roaring its exhaust-laden way around town from week to week, even though she never got much chance to use it herself. Almost every day somebody'd be asking to borrow it, and I never heard her say no unless she'd already lent it to somebody else.

That night, though, the car—she called it Rosie—was parked across the street in front of the house. Jan opened the passenger door for me from the inside (no handle on the outside), I climbed in, and we were off. We didn't talk much on the way. Jan had already checked that I had my ID with me—"and nothing else." ("Will they search us?" I'd exclaimed, and she'd said, "Probably not," in a way that told me she wouldn't ever trust any of them as far as she could throw them, so why take chances.) I was burning to ask for descriptive details about the jail, but I didn't want to interrupt Jan's concentration on her driving.

The windshield wipers went "swaap...pause...swaap...pause...swaap," with about a hundred gallons of rain pouring over the windshield between each "swaap," and Jan kept having to wipe the fog off the inside of the window with a rag she kept on the seat. What with the rain on the outside and the oil (from the rag) on the inside, I figured we had about as much visibility as a deep-sea diver in one of those old-fashioned diving suits. The kind that's got a big metal helmet with a tiny window of thick glass set into it. Except, of course, that the deep-sea diver wouldn't be moving at thirty-five miles an hour through a sea crowded with other, equally speedy and metallic moving objects. Finally, Jan slipped Rosie into a parking space I wouldn't even have tried and we were there.

The lobby of the Public Safety Building was deserted, except for a couple of men muttering angrily in a corner. Our footsteps sounded loud as I followed Jan to the elevators. There was a grim, wary expression on her face. Shoulders hunched, she tilted her chin up to stare at the two arrows above the elevator door, waiting for the "up" arrow to light. "I fuckin' hate this place," she said.

The elevator, when it came, was empty. And dirty. We got in, and Jan plugged button number six with her thumb. I was holding my breath when the doors opened again, and I clenched my teeth to keep the shiver running up my spine from turning into a total-body shudder. This was the jail.

We got off the elevator into a small, poorly-lit room. The wall ahead of us was about five feet away, with only about ten feet of space between the walls to the right and left. Obviously, the elevator was the only way we'd ever get out of there again. The other two doors in the room were set behind bars, little cages that reached out into the room. Over the cage on the left was a sign saying, "Men." Over the cage on the right a sign said, "Women."

Jan moved directly to the cage on the right and pushed a button set into a corner of it. Nothing happened. I shifted from foot to foot and felt like hundreds of hidden eyes were watching me. Suddenly something went "Ping!" behind me. I jumped a yard and whirled around in mid air. It was the elevator, arriving on the sixth floor again after another trip down to Third Avenue. A woman got off carrying a baby; a toddler scampered out after her and clung to the edge of her jacket. Impatiently, the woman stooped and hurried the child along with a hand flat on his back as she moved from the elevator to the cage on the left and pushed the button. Nothing happened.

Looking around some more, I saw that the room had an extension on each side, two stubby little arms, one on each side of the elevator shaft. The outside wall of each arm was lined with dark windows, eight to a side, with about two feet of room between that wall and the elevator shaft. I tip-toed up to one of the windows and peeked in, but I couldn't see anything through the thick, dirty glass except darkness and, dimly, another wall a couple feet away.

Jan, meanwhile, had found a half-sheet of pink paper and was writing something on it. "Visiting form," she told me in answer to my enquiring look. "Over there." She nodded in the direction of a little ledge projecting out from the wall.

I picked up a copy of the form and read it while Jan finished filling hers out. "Name. Address. Relationship. Date. Time." Jan handed me her pen and, as I started filling in the form, went back to push the button again.

And then, suddenly, everything started happening at once. The elevator arrived again and disgorged a group of about eight people, all talking, at the same time as an incredibly bored voice crackled out from a speaker above the door marked "Women."

"Yes?" it said.

"Visitors for Barbara Randall," Jan shouted up at it.

I strained my ears trying to hear over all the folks milling around and talking, but it was at least thirty full seconds before the voice spoke again. "Fill out visiting forms and have ID ready," it recited without enthusiasm.

"We did," Jan hollered back. "We're ready now."

She got no answer, but by that time there were other people ready to push the button—both buttons, the Men's and the Women's—and announce their presence to the voice behind the bars. From then until we left to go home an hour later, it seemed like the elevator was delivering another load of people into that crowded little room about every ninety seconds. And all of us were wet from the rain. Before long, the air itself was almost too wet to breathe. Wet and sticky hot, like being under water in a big, dirty bathtub.

Jan and I waited for over half an hour. I usually like to watch people, and there sure were plenty of people in the waiting area for me to watch, but pretty soon it seemed like they were all too close, somehow. There were more women than men visiting; most of the women had children with them and were visiting someone on the men's side. Over on our side there were, among others, two young men who seemed to know each other but were visiting different women, a woman who looked to be about sixty and had three young kids with her (somebody's grandmother, I supposed), a middle-aged man with sad eyes and a teenaged boy who looked like he'd come along under protest, and a large family (I never did managed to figure out exactly how many of them there were) whose cheerfulness I admired, under the circumstances, even as I regretted their communal tendency to shriek. More than half the visitors, on both sides, were black. As far as I could tell, I was the only first-timer in the room.

Finally the slowly moving gears of the system began to grind out the prisoners we had come to see. One by one, or family by family, the visitors were drawn to the grimy windows by the sudden appearance of a friend's face, a mother's, a father's, a son or daughter's face behind one of the eight thick panes of glass. Some of the windows were separated by little partitions sticking out from the wall, so I found myself cruising nervously up and down, worried that Barb might show up at a window partially hidden by a partition and we'd miss her.

When she appeared, however, it was at one of the stand-up windows, the ones with no partitions, no place to sit down, and no illusion of privacy. Her big face seemed to be floating, detached, behind the greasy, thick glass of the window, like an ailing fish in an aquarium that hasn't been cleaned in weeks. Fish die in an aquarium if it isn't cleaned and refilled regularly, because after a while there isn't any oxygen in the water. Barb looked like her own oxygen supply had reached the critical level a couple days since.

Oh my god, I thought. What the hell am I doing here.

Patiently, Jan lifted the telephone receiver off its hook and put it into my hand. Barb, like a delayed-action mirror image, did the same on the other side of the glass.

"Hello, Barb," I said. "Remember me? I was at the fat oppression workshop, and we talked once at the Slipper." No response showed on Barb's face. "Terry Barber," I prompted. But still there was no reply.

"Tch," said Jan behind me. She knocked on the glass and gestured for Barb to look down and to her right. Barb's eyes obediently slid downwards. Jan knocked again, and this time, when Barb looked up, she made pushing motions with her thumb, the same as she'd done to call the elevator. "You gotta hold in the button, girl," she muttered, knowing Barb couldn't possibly hear her.

A couple seconds later, a burst of static made me jerk the receiver away from my ear. "Go on," Jan told me, "she oughta be able to hear you now."

"Hello, Barb," I ventured. "Can you hear me?" She nodded slowly, but her lips, though slightly open, produced no sound that I could hear. Okay, I said to myself, this is it, Terry. Get a grip on yourself and start all over.

So I did. I introduced myself and reminded Barb of where we'd met. Then I said, "I wanted to be sure you were okay and, you know, ask if you need anything."

Speak to me, Barb, I was crying inside, but all she did was stare and stare and stare. She looked hypnotized, dazed, stunned, totally out of it.

Jan nudged my shoulder. "You better say whatever it is you come down here to say. There's other people here want to visit, and besides, you can't count on being able to visit more'n ten, fifteen minutes at a time."

Well, hell, I said to myself. And then, to Barb, "Say something, Barb! Are you all right?" By now I was speaking very slowly and enunciating very clearly, as if I weren't sure Barb and I spoke the same language. "Are you all right?" I repeated with a few more decibels.

Barb closed her eyes and took a deep breath. "Yes," she mumbled.

"Are there any messages you'd like me to take to anybody?" I asked.

She looked at me with something like fright in her eyes. It could have just been surprise, I guess.

"Jan, here, knows your friend Anne," I told her, hoping that would encourage her to think of us as trusty messengers. "Is there anything you need to have done?

Or anyone you'd like us or your friends to call? Your family, maybe?"

As soon as I said "family," Barb began to shake her head "no, no, no," and a tear was shaken out of her eye by the movement of her head.

"Well, can you tell me a little bit about all this, Barb?" I asked her. "I really want to hear your side of it, and as far as I know, you're the only one who knows your side, so far."

Barb raised a shoulder to hold the receiver for a minute, wiped at her cheek with the back of her hand, and looked at me with less of a glaze in her eyes than she had up till then. "I didn't..." she muttered haltingly, "I didn't ... I was there, but I didn't...I only...I had to get away, I had to...he grabbed my arm and I had to—"

Suddenly she turned away and I let out my pent breath in a gust of frustration. You didn't *what?* You only *what?* You had to *what?*

"I gotta go now," she said, stonily, as she turned back to face me. "They say I gotta go now."

She began to remove the receiver from her ear and I yelled into my end of the fragile linkage, "Wait, Barb! Wait! Do you have a lawyer? Do you want me to find one for you?"

Her arm froze for a split second, suspending the receiver about two inches from her ear, and then she carried the action through, hanging up on me. I threw myself against that little bit of grungy glass, straining to catch a glimpse of her as she was led away. Was she shaking her head "no"? And even if she was, did that mean she was answering "no" to one of my questions and, if so, which one? Had she even heard my questions? I flung the receiver onto its rest and, spinning on my heel, accidentally flung myself into Jan's arms.

"Whoa," she said. "Don't be in such a hurry. That's one thing you'll have to learn if you're gonna go through with this: jail time is slow time. No point wearing your head out smashing it against *this* damn wall. Whaddya say we get Rosie to take us back home now, maybe pick up some fries on the way and see what pieces of the puzzle we got so far."

I squeezed her so tight I felt my shoulders creak. Getting out of that horrible place was exactly what I wanted to do, the sooner the better. But even more delightful than the relief of stepping out of that hellish building into the cold, wet night air was the comforting realization that Jan seemed to know why I'd wanted to come there in the first place. But how did she know? I'd never told her I was determined to stick by Barb and investigate the murder on her behalf. Hell, I'd barely told myself. So how in the world did Jan know?

The question was on the tip of my tongue—"Jan," I started to say, "how did you know—" and then I stepped off the curb into six inches of cold dirty water. "Well fuck a flying duck," I said in disgust.

Jan laughed. "Better not let Fran hear you talk like that." Fran was a fanatical vegetarian and friend-of-all-the-animals, among other things.

"If I had long legs like you, I'd miss all those puddles automatically," I grumbled. "You'd think a city that gets as much rain as Seattle does would figure out how to keep gutters from clogging up all the time."

By the time we got to Rosie, all I could think about was dry clothes and a hot drink. There'd be time later to ask Jan all the questions I wanted to, I decided; so I just huddled myself down in the seat and felt clammy, rousing only to pull a dollar out of my jeans as we pulled into Dicks Drive-In. The smell of the fries revived me, and by the time we got home I was really looking forward to that hot cup of tea and a long, quiet talk with Jan. If anybody could help me pull my thoughts and feelings about the murder—and about Barb—into some kind of order, she would be the one.

The minute we walked through the front door, "They're back!" somebody yelled, and the living room filled instantaneously. Bodies rained down from upstairs, erupted from the basement, and rolled in from the kitchen. A crowd, in other words, gathered rapidly. And all of them focused on me and Jan.

"Did you see her?" several voices demanded. "What did she say? What did she say?"

Jan put her arm around my shoulders and, bouyed by that gesture, I answered, "Uh, well, yeah, we saw her, but—"

"Is it true?" someone yelped. "Is it true?"

"Geez, you guys, I don't know what all the excitement's about," I complained. "I mean, it happened four whole days ago, so why all the uproar now?"

There was a beat of silence and then, from Toni, "You mean you don't know? You haven't heard?"

Oh my god, I thought, another murder. But, "Heard what?" I asked, and almost everyone in the room was happy to provide the answer.

"It was her husband!" "The dead guy!" "She was married to him!"

I felt the shock hit Jan a good ten seconds before my own brain kicked into gear. "You mean..." I stuttered, "You mean Barb. . .?"

"Yes, of course we mean Barb," said Jeanne. "Kinda don't know whether to laugh or cry, right?"

She was right. Barb, the Separatist to end all Separatists, uncontested winner of the Man-Hater-of-the-Year award, was Mrs. Theodore J. Simpson, faculty wife. Downright unbelievable. "I don't believe it," I said.

"Believe it, Terr." Peg sounded grim. "We heard it on the radio news and again on the tube. The police had a copy of the marriage certificate sent in from Montana."

"So I guess that means Barb didn't say anything about it to you guys," said Toni, disappointed. "We were hoping you'd come back with all the inside skinny."

Jan sighed. "All we got is some fries, and they getting old fast. Come on, girl, let's eat." And then, as she started us walking towards the kitchen door she said very softly in my ear, "Barb's got visiting hours again Saturday afternoon, Terry. You wanna go back and try it again?"

The "yes" burst out of me with a force that made me realize, all of a sudden, how furious I felt. "Yes, goddamn it. And goddamn her," I added for good measure.

Jan just nudged me towards a chair and fetched a plate for the fries.

Naturally, everyone in the house followed us into the kitchen, but it didn't take them long to give up on me and Jan after we answered their questions about the jail. After that, they returned to the discussion that obviously had begun long before our arrival.

"I guess you were on the right track, Jeanne," said Connie, "talking about Yvonne Wanrow's case the other day. This is starting to sound more like self-defense. I mean, when we were assuming the man was a stranger—"

"Well, geez, talk about assumptions!" interrupted Toni. "I can't believe we're going to assume it's okay for a woman to kill a man, just as long as she knows him. Or is it only husbands who deserve to be killed?" She cut off Connie's attempted protest and continued self-righteously, "I've said all along that feminism and murder don't mix, whether you call the killing political or not."

"But Toni!" Jeanne exclaimed as she snitched another fry, "That's a false dichotomy! Women's self-defense *is* political."

"I bet that's her motive, right there," said Fran maliciously; "she was afraid we'd find out she's married."

Peg snorted. "She's not stupid, Fran," she said. "Off the wall, I grant you, but not stupid."

"So?" Fran didn't get it.

"So, it didn't work, did it?" said The Voice of Reason, reasonably. "We probably never would have known, if she—or somebody—hadn't bumped the dude off."

"Well, it doesn't surprise me, really." Connie sounded as calm as usual, even when her statement was met with hoots of disbelief. "Oh, I was shocked at first," she continued, "but not when I'd had a few minutes to think about it. I mean, why would she be such a hard-line separatist if she didn't have something like that—like a failed marriage—to be separating from?"

"Dammit, Connie," said Jeanne, "now you're doing it, too. Just because the personal is political doesn't mean a woman's politics is nothing but a reflection of her personal history. I may not agree with the Furies, but as a feminist I can't sit by and let you trivialize their politics."

Oh lord, I thought, here we go again. My anger was draining away into depression under the influence of my housemates' palaver and the inability of our two orders of fries to feed the multitudes. Something tapped against my ankle under the table, and I looked up to see Jan speaking to me with her eyes.

"Let's go," they said, and my spirits lifted a tad.

We got up simultaneously and headed for the door.

"Hey, where are you two going?" called Peg.

"Got to go change our socks," I said. I liked Peg a lot, but it was Jan I needed to talk to right then.

She led the way up to my room, and we settled onto cushions on the floor, me pulling my wet socks and shoes off as soon as I hit the floor. Jan sat cross-legged rubbing her eyes with the heels of her hands.

"So," I began, "you figured out I want to, uh, investigate, right?"

"Yeah," she said without looking up. But then she rested her elbows on her knees, dangling her hands in her lap, and looked me in the eye. "I don't know why, though."

Aargh. That was the toughie. "Well...." I tried to find some words that would bring my feelings into focus. "It's just that, the way everybody's been acting, I feel like somebody has to try to stand back and, like, look at it objectively. Know what I mean?"

"Mmmm. Not really," said Jan.

"Well, it's like—everybody assumes she did it, right? Nobody talks about 'did she do it or not,' it's all just 'how will this affect us,' 'how could she do this to us.' I mean, I know Barb isn't the most lovable person in the world, but she isn't stupid, so why would she commit what looks like a really stupid murder—fingerprints all over the place—unless she had no choice? This business about her being married really blows my mind, though. Talk about hypocritical! But still, she deserves a chance to tell her side. And I hate how everybody's so self-centered about it. Why don't they talk about how all this affects Barb for a change?"

Jan nodded and looked down at her hands for a minute before she said anything. "I think maybe I can understand that, in a way. Ever since I come up here to live"—she meant, up to the U District from the south end of the city, where she used to live—"ever since I've been living with these 'political' lesbians, I been noticing...about this 'community' business."

I guess I must have groaned involuntarily, because Jan grinned at me before she went on. "Yeah," she said, "everybody's always talking about community. Gets so you hardly want to hear it anymore." She paused again and went on more seriously. "But it do mean something, Terry. You know what Jeanne's always saying about how lesbians don't have no role models?"

I nodded.

"Well, that ain't exactly true for me," Jan said, "because I wasn't never a 'political' lesbian, I was always just a dyke, from way back. But I can understand it, though, what she means. And I think she's right, too."

I was fascinated. Jan had never before talked before, in my presence, about the differences between her and the rest of us in Everywhere House.

"Because..." Jan hesitated and then went on, "...you women're really trying something new. Sometimes I think you're all crazy. But mostly I think...I think you just might be on to something. This house here. Lotta time it seems to me like some kinda kindergarten, everybody playing games all the time. No," she said in response to my frown, "I don't mean games like that, not like you're running games on each other. I mean...you're living like *life* is a game, almost, like you can make up the rules your own selves as you go along. All this 'process' you got. And 'community.' Now, where I come from, there's community, all right, but it's...it just *is*. You got the folks you hang with, and then there's all the others, and they got people they hang with, and that's communities. I mean, communities is what you're born to, or you grow up to. Not something you 'create.' Not where I come from, anyways."

I was fascinated. Jan had never before talked, in my presence, about the differences between her and the rest of us in Everywhere House. "Where do you come from Jan?" I ventured.

'Tacoma, mostly," she said. "I thought you knew that."

"Yes, but besides that. I mean, Connie's from Tacoma, too, and, well, the two of you sure don't talk the same, for one thing." A couple of times new visitors to Everywhere House had expressed surprise upon meeting Jan. Was this the same Jan who'd answered the phone when they called last week, they wanted to know, because on the phone she sounded...well, Black.

Jan laughed. "Girl, you right about that. Connie's nice and all, but for damn sure she ain't never been to my Tacoma. And I ain't never been welcome in hers, neither. I know I don't fit most people's categories, most middle-class white people's anyways. That's probably because there wasn't never many white folks around where I grew up. And not a one of 'em middle-class. Most of my family ain't white, comes to that. But we was talking about you, not me. About you and your communities."

"Okay," I agreed, "go on with what you were saying before. You said we make ourselves up?"

"Yeah. And that makes you.... I dunno. What is it Peg says when Fran goes all weepy? 'Needy,' that's it. You all that way, all the time, but you mostly don't see it, do you?"

I felt a bit lost at that point, and maybe a bit offended, too. "No," I said, "and I don't see it now. What do you mean we're 'needy'? Weak, you mean?"

Her voice had a considering tone. "No, not weak, exactly. Just needy. You need each other all the time, because it's like, while you're busy creating your community, you're also creating yourselves at the same time. The two things go together, right?"

The light dawned. "Riiiiiiight!" I exclaimed.

"Yeah," said Jan. "So that's why whatever Barb mighta done to that dead man, she done it to all you women, too. Barb's one of you, so whatever she is, that's *you*. Unless you all decide to kick her ass outta this community you're creating."

I sighed. Jan was grinning at me again, I realized. I smiled more happily back as she said, "Okay, so what's your next step, besides going to see Barb Saturday?"

"I think I better do some work on the other end, don't you? We need to know more about the victim. I spend most of my life at the University these days, so it shouldn't be too hard for me to find out what this Simpson guy was like."

Jan was looking down at her hands again and looked up to say, "You be careful, girl. Could be Barb killed that man; could be she didn't. If she didn't...."

"Then somebody else did." I nodded. "I'll be careful. I've got an idea, though. I know somebody who's doing work-study in the Philosophy department. Maybe I can get her to show me some of this Simpson's class lists, and then I could talk to some of his students."

"Well, take it easy, take it slow. Don't go getting yourself noticed." Jan stood up and stretched herself back to her complete five-feet ten-inches. "I gotta go; got a date. We can talk more Saturday, anyway, if we don't get a chance before. Visiting starts at four."

"Okay, thanks," I said, and I wished I could think of something else to say, something that would keep her with me, keep her from walking on out my door. There wasn't anything, though, so I watched her go. Then I felt lonely, so I called Ellie, the woman I was lovers with then, and made a date for Friday night. That wasn't exactly what I wanted, somehow, but it would have to do.

6.

My first Thursday class wasn't till nine-thirty, and I was in the Philosophy office at eight forty-five. By that time I'd succeeded in dredging up from my memory the name of the work-study student I aimed to suborn there. She was a ditsy-looking blonde named Cherri who'd been in my Intro to Western Civ quiz section the previous quarter. We'd run into each other by chance in the work-study office back at the beginning of March and compared notes on our Winter Quarter jobs. As we chatted, I'd been reminded of my earlier conclusion: Cherri's surface of flaky femininity covered a very capable brain. Like a lot of well-socialized women, however, her surface went fairly deep, and I was pretty sure I could get what I wanted from her without waking up the mind below.

I found her standing almost motionless, facing a waist-high cabinet in a deserted corner of the department's main office. Resting on the surface of the cabinet were ten stacks of paper and one of those collapsible metal collators. I watched for a minute as Cherri's right hand gently, almost tenderly, transferred one sheet of paper from stack A to slot 1 of the collator, then one sheet to slot two, then one sheet to slot three, and so on. It was mesmerizing. I intruded myself into her consciousness just as she was about to begin all over again with stack B. "Hi, Cherri. Got a minute?"

"Oh…hi," she said, obviously groping her way back from daydream to reality at the same time as she tried to remember my name.

"I remembered you were working here this quarter, so I've stopped by to ask a small favor." Her eyebrows lifted a fraction of an inch. "I'm considering taking a Philosophy class next quarter, but I'm not sure, really, if it's my kinda thing. So I thought, before I register I oughta talk to somebody who's already taken the class and get a first-hand report." I gave her no room to reply. "Turns out, no one I know has taken intro Philosophy classes yet, so what I want to do is look at the class lists for this quarter's classes and jot down a couple names of students to call."

My hope was that Simpson, being a lowly untenured Assistant Prof, would have been teaching at least one of the entry level courses. And I didn't want to ask for his class list specifically, because Cherri was bound to have heard about the murder—you couldn't be on campus that week and not hear about it—and might wonder what I was up to if I mentioned his name.

"You could ask the secretary," Cherri said. She wasn't lazy, she just didn't see any reason to expend energy on a project that wouldn't provide any dividends for her.

"They're always so busy," I temporized, my mind working furiously. If I went to a secretary, she'd be sure to ask me lots of questions, maybe tell me to go see an advisor instead. There wasn't anything wrong with what I was asking Cherri to do, but that didn't mean it might not be against the rules. "If you want, I could finish up this collating for you while you photocopy the lists from the 100-level classes...."

Apparently the energy balance between collating and photocopying weighed out in my favor. "All right," Cherri said after a few seconds of silence, and she drifted off towards a file cabinet across the room. I was nervous enough to welcome a mindless task like collating. My fingers flew, and I was just neatening the edges of the last completed document when Cherri returned with five pages of names for me.

"Gee, thanks a lot!" I told her as I relieved her of her burden. "You're a real pal."

"I don't want this to come back on me in any way," she said sternly.

"You'll never hear a word, from me or anybody else. Thanks again." And I dashed off.

It was misting outside. "Misting" is when it's not raining and yet you're filmed with moisture the minute you step out the door. For newcomers, it can be a nasty surprise to discover that after just a short walk through this non-rain they're soaked to the bone. I stuffed the class lists into my backpack and ran for Loew Hall, praying that Simpson had been teaching one of the classes I now had the lists for. What would I do if he hadn't? I refused to think about it until absolutely necessary. And as it turned out, that necessity never arose. The third of the five lists was for Philosophy 102: Contemporary Moral Problems, and there was his name at the top of the page. It was one of those classes with a big three-times-a-week lecture section, presided over by Assistant Proffessor Simpson, and twice-weekly quiz sections, smaller divisions of the larger class, where graduate students got a chance to test their nascent tutorial skills. Of course in a large lecture section the students would have less contact with Simpson. But on the other hand, I consoled myself, a lecture section gave me a much longer list of students to work with. The success of my plan thus far went to my head like champagne.

When I looked up from the class list finally, I had a huge grin on my face. Letitia, just then coming in the door, smiled back somewhat uncertainly, surprised, I suppose, by the sudden change in the intensity of my response to her. I'd been friendly to her right along, the way you are to classmates, but I'm sure I'd never before seemed so hugely delighted to see her. And of course, the fact that I wasn't smiling at her at all was not something I felt capable of explaining, especially given that the class was beginning that very minute. Ah well, I decided, no harm done. I hope.

I hurried out of the classroom as soon as the fifty-minute hour was up, waving acknowledgment to Letitia's reminder of the "talk" we'd agreed to have the next day. Across the street in the HUB cafeteria, I whipped out Simpson's class list again, along with a granola bar and a pencil, all set to start picking out the students I'd call.

There's only so much you can tell from a list of names, of course. Gender, primarily. With a computerized class list, you can't even tell what name a person actually uses. The computer has me down as Barber, Theresa Alexandra, of all things, because my father's mother was named Theresa and my mom was going through a Russian literature phase at the time. No way to know ahead of time who these Jacquelines and Elizabeth Roses would turn out to be. And come to think of it, I reminded myself, I still hadn't decided exactly what approach I was going to take. Did I want to find uncurious types who would answer my questions about their Philosophy 102 prof without wondering why I asked them? Or was I looking for someone with keen insight into human psychology, someone who'd know immediately why I was interested in Simpson and be able to suggest all sorts of reasons for murdering the guy?

I wasted the rest of my only free hour of the day coming up with questions like that and finding answers for none of them. When the time came to leave for class, all my bright satisfaction in the morning's accomplishment had faded into drab determination. It was beginning to feel as if detective work, like feminism, was a long-term commitment, with plenty of hard work separating the brief, precious moments of revelation.

The afternoon stretched ahead of me like an expanse of desert. The only oasis in sight was the fact that, since my work-study job was in the library, I'd probably be able to sneak in a few minutes with the student directory, looking up some of the names on Simpson's class list. On the other hand, I was pretty sure I wouldn't have the kind of time I needed to come up with the questions I wanted to ask, and the need to get those questions clear in my mind seemed more urgent all the time. Even though I told myself it was just a coincidence, and not such a surprising one, either, really, I was still a bit in shock from my discovery that the seventh name from the bottom of the fifth section of Simpson's class list was Letitia's. And my appointment with her was less than twenty-four hours away.

7.

I spent some study time in the library after work, so it was about eight by the time I got home and found Peg sitting alone in the kitchen. The inch-long hair that usually jutted out over her forehead like a miniature visor was sticking straight up in the air, a sure sign of aggravation. Never the less, she looked reassuringly solid, planted there with her wide bottom on the chair and her two strong arms propped before her on the table. She looked up as I came in, and there were patches of red on her cheeks from where she'd been resting her head on her hands. The contrast made her high, pale cheekbones more evident than usual, so that she looked more than ever like the hearty, healthy Nords she descended from. Laughing in the snow. Herding reindeer. Chewing tough deerhide into baby-soft leather.

"Hi," I said. "Know if Jan's around?"

"Nope." A pause, and then, "I mean, yes, I do know. She's not. Just Connie, I think."

In fact, I could hear Connie's record player softly in the background—the kind of breathy instrumental record I think of as moon music.

"So what's with you?" I said. Peg was looking kind of glum.

She stretched her arms out in a full-body yawn before she answered. "Nothing. Don't pay any attention to me; I'm just going through one of those dumb days that happen to everybody once in a while."

"What kind of dumb?" I asked absentmindedly as I foraged through the fridge for sandwich makings.

"Oh, just your typical, ordinary, everyday kind of dumb, I guess. Spent two hours at the bookstore this morning trying to straighten out the back orders. Without noticeable success." Peg was one of the handful of women whose hard work kept the local women's bookstore open for years as its financial condition passed from grave to terminal. "Then I opened at eleven, as advertised, after which I sat there alone for two more hours. And from then until Katy relieved me at four—she was supposed to relieve me at three, you understand—I had four, count 'em four whole customers. One of whom actually bought something. The other three: two of them read every newspaper and magazine in the store and put none of them back in the racks, and the other one lectured me for ten minutes about how feminism is destroying the potential for socialist revolution in America."

I snickered as I dripped honey onto the tahini I'd spread on two pieces of bread. "Oh yeah, it was a bundle of laughs," said Peg. "And then my good friend Terry walks in and says, 'Why, hello, Peg! Wonderful to see you! You sure are a sight for sore eyes!' And the cares of the day are lifted from my heart as the sun lifts the dew from the roses."

"Geez, Peg, I'm sorry," says I. "You know I'm always glad to see you."

A muffled "humph" was her only reply. I sat down with my sandwich and reached out to grab her wrist with my free hand. "Listen, don't tell the others, but you're probably my favorite housemate. Ever."

That last word got me a smile. Peg had heard at length about the women I'd lived with for two years in Milwaukee, between home and high school in Brookfield and then the big move to Seattle and the University. Suffice it to say that being favored over that group of women (or over my stories about them, anyway) was not exactly the dyke equivalent of the Nobel Peace Prize. "No, but really, Peg, I'm sorry. It's just I've had a lot on my mind lately."

"Haven't we all." There was companionable silence for a minute as I ate, my teeth pleasantly glued with tahini. Then Peg startled me by asking, "What are you and Jan up to, Terry?"

"Mmph, nnrmph," I said, and pointed to my glued-together mouth.

"Something to do with the murder, right?" she went on.

Thanks to some strenuous tongue work, I managed to swallow the mouthful and respond. "It's not Jan, really, Peg, just me. And hey, don't go, you know, talking about it, okay? I feel weird enough about it already. If everybody in the house started bugging me, I wouldn't be able to stand it."

"Okay," said Peg thoughtfully, "but do you mind telling me about it? I don't want to come on like Mom here, but I care about you, Terr, and it worries me to think of you off looking for murderers. Not that I doubt your many admirable abilities, you understand, but.... What if you actually caught up with some creep—always assuming that Barb isn't the only creep in the case—and he didn't like you nosing around? And for that matter, what if the police don't like you nosing around?" Interesting question, that last one. It made me realize I hadn't given much attention to the police so far.

"I don't think you need to worry, Peg. I haven't done anything yet, and I don't intend to do anything dangerous. I just want to find out what the hell happened. At first it was, well, because I'm interested in Barb anyway, because I've never been able to figure out what makes her tick. She's such a dyke, isn't she? I mean, you look at her and you see what maybe straight people see when they look at any of us. What she is—or what she seems to be, or tries to be, anyway—is what we're all supposed to be, right? A big, tough, man-hating, plain-as-a-pikestaff, shit-kicker. And now we know that she was married to this murdered guy, well.... I just gotta try to find out what's going on: who is this woman, and how did she wind up married to a man somebody hated enough to kill."

I bit off another hunk of sandwich, effectively putting my mouth out of action for the duration of the chew, and Peg had a chance to tell me that she hated to say it but, "When you look at the facts, there's a very good chance that what happened is exactly what it looks like. Barb married this guy back in Montana before she realized she was a lesbian; then she leaves him and comes to Seattle and becomes a dyke. When he pops up in her face again, she lashes out at him in— I don't know—anger, or fear that he'll blow her cover as the compleat lesbian. Or maybe hatred for something he did to her back when they were together. You know what they say, Terry: the spouse is always the top suspect. And look at what we've got here. An estranged wife—and a pretty strange wife, too—whose fingerprints are on the knife that killed her husband. It's probably what they'd call a classic open-and-shut case."

I swallowed and sighed. "Peg, you are depressing the hell outta me." She tried to speak but I motioned her to silence. "No, it's okay. I know what you're saying is probably true, and whatever little nosing around I do won't change anything. But still, I feel like I gotta try, if only so there's somebody out here who's willing to try looking at things from Barb's point of view." If only I can manage to *get* her point of view, I added to myself.

Peg didn't seem one hundred percent convinced, but she decided not to argue. "So what are you going to do, exactly?" she asked instead.

"Well, tomorrow I'm going to talk to at least one of the students who was in Simpson's class this quarter. You remember that woman who was here, in my room, when Fran came busting in and told us Barb had been arrested?"

"Oh ho!" said Peg. "So she was a student in the victim's class, eh? What an interesting coincidence!"

"Yeah. Kinda weird, but it probably really is just a coincidence. The thing that gets me is that she's been trying to…make up to me or something. Even before the murder, I think. It was her idea for her to come over here, I mean. And ever since then she's been bugging me to 'talk' to her, and I don't know why."

Peg leaned back in her chair, laughing her deep, infectious laugh. "Okay," I said, "I'll bite. What the hell's so hilarious?" I'd started to grin automatically, although I had no idea what was funny.

"You are!" She indulged in a bout of luxurious eye-wiping with the back of her hand as the guffaws toned down into chuckles. "You really mean to sit there and tell me you have no idea what that woman's up to, Terry?"

"Letitia?" I said. "What do you mean, 'what she's up to'? You don't even know her, do you?"

"Good goddess, girl, I don't need to know a person to recognize flirtation when I see it."

"Flir— You mean Letitia is flirting with me?!" I was astounded. Not only was I not the kind of woman who got flirted with, but the lesbian feminists I hung out with then didn't flirt. We had meaningful relationships. Flirting, the theory went, was a manifestation of sexism, a misdemeanor committed only by men or "male-identified" lesbians. For a straight woman to initiate such "male" behavior was even more mind-bogling.

"Sure she's flirting with you," Peg said. "It's plain as plain."

"But...why?" I still couldn't believe it.

"What do you mean 'why'? What kind of reason does a woman need to flirt? She's attracted to you, that's all."

"But she's straight, Peg," I protested.

"So what?" The Voice of Reason at her most ultra-reasonable. "There's a first time for everybody, right? Or maybe she's just out for a test drive, looking to see if a lesbian affair would be better than whatever she's got now."

The last bite of my sandwich gave me time to consider Peg's analysis of the situation. "Well, if that's what's going on," I said, at length, "then: yuck."

"Oh, I don't know. I think it's kind of cute." Peg's laughter had left her in a teasing frame of mind. "Who knows? Maybe you've got a fine career ahead of you. I can see it now: Terry Barber's 'Create-a-Lesbian.' Overnight service." That last quip set her off again, and she left the kitchen still booming with laughter.

Up in my room, I started to think again about tomorrow, and about what I'd just been saying to Peg. It's weird, but sometimes I don't even know what's in my mind until I hear myself saying it to somebody. According to my own conversation, Barb exemplified the straight stereotype of a lesbian. Or was it really my own stereotype she fit?

A mere eighteen or twenty-four months ago, I hadn't been sure Terry Barber had what it took to be accepted as a lesbian by the dykes I looked up to as "real lesbians." Was I still looking for a stamp of approval by some mythical lesbian board of standards? Was that buried uneasiness part of the fascination Barb held for me? I didn't like to think of myself as that insecure, but even less did I like the strenuously repressed fear that the more radically lesbian I let myself become, the more I'd be like Barb: a bitter, vengeful woman, so profoundly alone she couldn't relax even within the community she claimed as her own.

Fifteen minutes and no homework later, here came Toni knocking at my door. "Hey, Terry," she said, "I'm on a recruiting drive. Can you come up to 4017 for an hour or so and help us get a mailing out?"

"Sure." I followed her down the stairs. "What's the mailing for?"

"It's a combined effort," Toni told me as we trotted up the hill to the nearby house we called, because of its address, simply 4017. "The Susan Finch Defense Committee is having a benefit dance to raise money for legal fees"—Susan Finch was a battered woman on trial for killing her husband—"and the women's co-op is putting on a rummage sale to raise money for a coffee house—you know, for an alternative to the bars. Plus, a couple of the leftist bookstores are sending some percent of some day's sales to a defense committee for some Black Revolutionary Something back east, and the George Jackson Brigade Defense Committee is doing an educational on armed struggle."

In the front room at 4017, a woman was reading aloud from a newspaper as I joined the line of collators. "Patty depicted as SLA Queen," she read, "…joined enthusiastically in sex with her captors. 'Miss Hearst was ripe for conversion to an exciting new lifestyle,' says prosecutor."

A chorus of bronx cheers greeted each phrase, and a woman I vaguely recognized from somewhere said, "Typical! If there's one thing the media can't stand it's politics."

My collating speed picked up as I got into it: one cherry-red sheet, one chrome-yellow sheet, one day-glo-green sheet, one anemic-looking beige. Tap on the table to get them aligned, fold, fold, staple, and toss onto the pile for the labelers. As I worked, I read the yellow sheet in snatches and decided I'd definitely try to get to the armed struggle workshop. And maybe the benefit dance (cherry-red sheet), too.

"Hey, Gina!" somebody at the table called out. I felt a waft of cold, damp air on my back and turned to see a new volunteer coming in, a woman I recognized as part of the collective of the local lesbian-feminist newsletter. "I heard you got a letter from one of the GJB women. Is it true? Are you going to publish it?"

Gina looked tired and rain-weary. "Who told you that, Vickie?" she snapped angrily. "Nobody's supposed to know. For chrisssake, I'm beginning to believe it's true women can't keep their mouths shut for a minute."

"Keep your shirt on, Gina," the other woman said. "We're all okay here. And you couldn't expect Allie not to tell *me*."

Gina might have had something to say about that, but she didn't get a chance. Instead, the woman who'd been standing at the end of the table rubber-stamping the bulk mail permit stamp on each batch of leaflets suddenly broke her silence with a harangue that set us all back on our heels. I'd noticed she'd been wielding the stamper like a weapon, whumping it down hard enough to shake the table, but I hadn't drawn any conclusions. After all, maybe the ink pad was drying out; or maybe she was channeling her aggressions away from an irritating employer, or building up her arm muscles; who could know.

She was a painfully thin woman with wispy blondish hair cut short and urgent protruding bones in her face. "It's not a game," she said. "It's not a party. These people are risking their lives. They are out there making the revolution." (She said it with capital letters: The Revolution.) "They are underground. They need our help to communicate with the communities they left behind when they accepted the revolutionary duty to act as the vanguard. And when they entrust their message to us, it is our responsibility to make sure we do not add to the danger they already face. They take a big risk when they reach out like that. Can't you understand how hard it is for them to isolate themselves from their communities? How much they want us to understand what they're doing and why?" She'd wound herself up to a peak of repressed emotion, and she teetered right on the edge of that peak as she clenched her hands into fists and challenged us: "Don't any of you supposedly political women know what *happened* today?"

The rest of us stood motionless as statues. We felt guilty as hell, of course; that was automatic. And we also felt ashamed of ourselves for having fun, for being safe, for "being political" instead of living out our politics like the members of the George Jackson Brigade did.

No more than a second passed before the tightly strung woman at the end of the table collapsed in upon herself, her thin body concaving as she bent at the waist, her bare arms raising her hands to her mouth. I have a treacherous habit of flashing back to poetry at times; a psychologist would say it's a mechanism by which I detach myself emotionally from what's going on around me. From my point of view, it's often how I understand what's going on. At that precise moment, my flashback was to Millay's, "An Ancient Gesture," her poem about Penelope.

> I thought, as I wiped my eyes on the corner of my apron:
> Penelope did this too.
> And more than once: you can't keep weaving all day
> And undoing it all through the night;
> Your arms get tired, and the back of your neck gets tight;
> And along towards morning, when you think it will never be light,
> And your husband has been gone, and you don't know where, for years,
> Suddenly you burst into tears;
> There is simply nothing else to do.
>
> And I thought, as I wiped my eyes on the corner of my apron:
> This is an ancient gesture, authentic, antique,
> In the very best tradition, classic, Greek;
> Ulysses did this too.
> But only as a gesture,— a gesture which implied
> To the assembled throng that he was much too moved to speak.
> He learned it from Penelope...
> Penelope, who really cried.

I don't claim the whole poem passed in measured cadence through my conscious mind as she turned and ran, her hands still over her mouth, her back still bent. But it was all there, that poem, in some part of my mind, and the feeling of it was truer than ever before. She sounds so angry, I said to myself, but what she is feeling is grief. She's been working and working, and caring so very much. · The rest of us care, too. Intellectually. But she is like Penelope. Penelope who really cried.

Somebody said something then about how "she's been under a strain," and we started to do our work again. Nobody brought up the letter from the GJB member again, but somebody did pick up the newspaper off the floor and read us the front-page article about how the GJB had rescued one of their captured comrades from the police that afternoon. One policeman was shot, but he was expected to recover.

I left for home an hour later in a thoughtful, not to say morbidly depressed, state of mind. The state of my room was pretty depressing, too, littered as it was with the detritus of educational effort. As I crawled into bed, I realized what I really wanted to do more than anything right then was have a long talk with Roger Krueger, my best buddy since eighth grade. In high school, he'd just about saved my life by being male. No one could make remarks about me (especially what I later could see as my "butchier" aspects), because everybody knew I had a boyfriend. What they didn't know, of course, is that he really was my friend, not my "date." It was some kind of miracle, I guess, that we found each other—an adolescent girl and an adolescent boy who wanted a friend more than a boyfriend or girlfriend. We talked and talked, working our way together towards the beginnings of who we were in the world and what we might be able to do about it. For five very important years we were inseparable, and for five years after that I clung to the idea of our friendship as a kind of personal guarantee, as if any changes between us would undo what had gone before. Our friendship was the solid rock on which I began to build a sense of myself as a person rather than the child of my parents, and much of my ability to risk change in myself was based on my confidence in that foundation, artificially perserved as it was.

If only Roger had turned out to be gay, everything would have been perfect. But alas, he's as naturally straight as I am naturally curly, and that made it all the more important for me to maintain our friendship unchanged. After all, no matter how far I allowed the interaction of my nature and my politics to lead me toward the margin of the world I was born to, as long as the unit of "Roger and Terry" still existed I had a reliable tow-line connecting me back to my past. Roger, meanwhile, had his own reasons for continuing our friendship, beyond the fact that I'd been as important to him as he'd been to me. Genuine friendship with an "out" lesbian feminist confirmed for him that he was still part of the world where politics means accepting the challenge of personal change and the risk of being different. He accepted my lesbianism with bland curiosity, but he never got over being offended by any and everything he perceived as separatist. Mostly, though, his willingness to stick with me was the result of his stubborn goodness. It was from Roger I learned most of what I know about friendship, and for better or worse, friendship means not letting go until you have to.

Most people, of course, would have let go a hell of a lot sooner than Roger did. For example, when I moved into Everywhere House, I called him up one night from a pay phone on the street. We'd been talking for about ten horrendously expensive minutes when I said to him, "You better not call me here, okay? I'll call you, though, I promise."

There was a pause that made my pulse race and then he said, "Why, Terry?"

Goddess do I hate this, I said to myself before I stammered out my answer. "It's, well, a women's house, Roger. You know. We've talked about it, about women's space. How women need to have spaces of our own to recover in. From sexism. And patriarchy. You know."

"And a fucking phone call from a man who happens to be a friend is an invasion of that space?" He sounded more than skeptical.

"Well, yeah. I mean, everybody in the house agrees not to bring any men in, and what if you call someday when I'm not there—or even when I am there but I'm down in my room—and one of the other women answers the phone? I mean, to me you're Roger, but to her you're just a man demanding her attention, right there in her own home. I'm sure they'd consider it an invasion." This had happened pre-schism, when the house was still full of separatists, and I knew damn well they'd consider it an invasion. Some of them, I was sure, would consider it no less than a violation.

"Either you're living with a bunch of oversensitive weirdos, Terry, or you're telling me we're not really friends any more," Roger told me then. "Or both, come to think of it."

"What do you mean?!" I protested. "Of course we're still friends. I said I'd call you. The phone at Everywhere House is a shared phone, after all, and I don't think you should blame me for the restrictions. For that matter, I don't think you should call people you don't understand 'over-sensitive weirdos.' What's with you, Roger? Why are you making such a big deal over this?"

"Oh, I see. It's not such a big deal. Okay. If I have a problem and need to talk but I can't call you because my voice would pollute your house, no big deal, right? If I get busted or run over by a truck or the doc tells me I've got a fifty percent chance of living three months if I survive the surgery, or if I read something really fantastic and just have to tell you about it, no big deal. I'll send a postcard, that's all. Only take about a week, maybe two. No big deal."

I tried to interrupt his manic flow, without any idea what I'd say if I succeeded, but his anger overrode me. "You say we're still friends, Terry? Well, I have to wonder what the hell that means to you. In fact, I have to wonder if maybe the reason you don't want me to call is because you don't want those women to know you have me for a friend. You're embarrassed to admit you actually like a human being who happens to be a man. Isn't that what's really in your mind?"

I denied it. I even cried and denied it. But of course I wasn't really altogether sure. And our friendship, although it survived the argument, had never been as free and easy after that. He didn't call me, and I called him from the house only on those few occasions when I could be sure nobody would overhear me. Sometimes, when I heard how he had to make an effort every time to get over feeling angry at me all over again, I'd think, maybe I shouldn't call him anymore.

Maybe I shouldn't try to keep him as a friend. But I couldn't bring myself to make the break. We'd gone through some important changes together, Roger and me, and we had some wonderful times in common. More selfishly, I guess it was important to me to know there was a man—a straight man—who could be friends with a lesbian, as hard as it was for both of us at times.

I couldn't call Roger that night after the mailing party, but I fell asleep thinking about him, and the dream I woke up from the next morning left his voice ringing in my ears. In the dream, I was in my room at Everywhere House, and Roger came knocking at the front door. Somebody let him in to the front hall, and I heard him say, "I've come to see Terry." I was frozen; I couldn't move, couldn't call out to him. "She doesn't want to see you," I heard Clove's voice say. "But I need to talk to her," said Roger. He sounded close to tears. "I need to talk to her." "She doesn't want to see you. She doesn't want to see you. She doesn't want to see you," said Clove. I do, I do! I tried to shout, but I woke up with Clove's tinny voice shrill in my ear: "She doesn't want to see you, you, yooooooooou."

I slapped off the alarm and got up, gratefully shaking the littlest Fury's phantom voice out of my ears. Today was the day I was talking with Letitia, and I had a date with Ellie for dinner and dancing later on. But somewhere in there, I promised myself, I'd get together a pile of change and call Roger. I definitely would.

8.

Friday woke up gorgeous. That's how it is in Seattle. It rains till you think you can't stand it anymore and you wonder whether there really is any color but gray left in the natural world. And then all of a sudden the sun comes out and you remember why you decided you wanted to live there after all. Naturally, as soon as the sun is visible everybody under sixty—and a third of everyone else—takes off as much clothing as they can get away with, never mind that the thermometer's stuck at forty-nine degrees.

As I headed towards the brick plaza called Red Square, I had to pick my way over and around a multitude of student bodies sunning themselves on the shallow steps in front of Kane Hall. There's another flight of steps heading out the other side of the Square towards the fountain where I was due to meet Letitia. On a clear day, the view from the top of those stairs is fantastic. First there's the fountain, a plain man-made pond with a single gush of water rising high into the air. With any amount of wind, the column of water becomes a big white feather dancing in the sky. And behind it rises the huge white cone of Mount Rainier, looking good enough, and almost close enough, to eat—or to worship, depending on my mood. The shadows on the mountain are blue like the shadows on the moon.

I walked briskly down the steps from Red Square, exactly on time, admiring the mountain's jaunty beret—a single cloud snagged on the fourteen-thousand four-hundred-forty-foot crest—full of a determined confidence that the appropriate words for the upcoming talk with Letitia would appear in my brain at the appropriate time. Or else they wouldn't, but so what, right? Too late to do anything about it now, I reminded myself cheerfully. And then I saw her.

She was standing at the edge of the fountain with her face towards the west wind and her long brown hair fluffing out behind her. But she wasn't alone. A man was there, too. I slowed my approach to watch them talk. With her head tilted upwards, the woman became a child again. I saw her look up to him for approval as she listened, as she talked, then duck her head modestly as approval came. When she smiled up at him again, it was with a slight twist of the body that brought her shoulders tilting down and back, her chest moving not-too-crudely out and up. I'm a good girl, her body language said, but sexy, too.

I was close enough then to hear her laugh. She laughed not freely, the way Peg laughs, but with her mouth only half-way open, her hand moving up to hide her lips when it was time for the laughter to end. It made me sad to see her going through those ritual motions of femininity, and it made me selfishly glad to be a dyke. We've all got internalized shit to work through, goddess knows, but at least my friends and I don't have to put on little femininity plays for each other every time we want to have a conversation. I was starting to feel less than enthusiastic about talking with Letitia, and that probably made me look sort of fierce as I strode the final few yards in her direction.

"Okay, sure," I heard the man say. "Tell Jim I'll be calling him soon for the phone number for those cabins." And with a so-long flip of the hand he turned on his heel and was gone by the time I reached Letitia's side.

The shutters flicked down inside her eyes when she saw me. We stood there a bit awkwardly for a few seconds, adjusting to each other's presence, and then she totally blew me away by saying, "I'm so glad you came."

"Oh," I said. "Me too. So...you wanna go eat, or what?"

"It's such a beautiful day. Why don't we just sit in the sun and talk for a while? That's what I've been missing so much, ever since I came to Seattle. Not the sun," and she smiled, "the talking." She must have seen the perplexity in my eyes, because she went on to say, "We could get some food at the HUB and eat out-side, if you're hungry. It's just...I feel like I haven't had anybody to talk to—really talk to—since high school. Know what I mean? Remember that friend from high school you talked to for hours and hours about everything?"

I laughed my relief. "Funny you should say that. When I fell asleep last night I was thinking about my best buddy from high school and missing all those hours of working out the meaning of the world with him." Letitia smiled and nodded, but I saw a tremor in the delicate muscles near her eyes and thought, How weird! Her best buddy probably was a girl. No wonder I'm confusing her, especially if Peg's right about this flirting business. "I'm starved," I told her. "Let's go see what the HUB can offer us today."

I picked up a bagel and some yogurt in the cafeteria, and by the time I got through the check-out line Letitia was waiting for me at the other end with an orange in her hand. We headed up the stairs and out to the metal chairs and tables set in the sun on the balcony overlooking the downward sloping east side of campus and the blue of Lake Washington beyond.

"Listen, Letitia," I all but demanded. "I've got a problem I need your help with. Will you help me?"

She looked guarded but said, "What do you want me to do?"

"Tell me everything you know about Professor Simpson."

"Ted?"

She calls him *Ted?!*, shrieked a closed circuit in my mind.

"Why do you want to know about him?"

"I'm trying to find out what happened to him, and I've always heard that the first step in solving a murder is to find out as much as you can about the victim.

48

You're an insightful person," I wheedled, "and I know you had at least one class with him, so I figure you might be able to tell me a lot. If you're willing."

She concentrated on peeling her orange for a minute as she thought it over, and then said, "I heard his wife did it. Your friend."

The lesbian, she did not add, though we both knew it was there in her mind. "Well," I said, "it's hard to explain, but...well, if you're a lesbian, it's like...."

Letitia was concentrating on separating the sections of her orange; it seemed to be a delicate operation requiring all her attention. Even breathing would be a distraction, so she was holding her breath. I sighed in frustration and tried to think of how to make this woman understand.

"Okay," I said finally and fell back on the most common experience I could think of. "Remember when you were in high school and there were always little cliques? Different kids would get lumped together, either by choice or because everybody else always saw them a certain way, even if they didn't like each other all that much or agree about politics or whatever?" Letitia was frowning at a section of orange; it glowed in the sunlight but gave me no specific assistance, and neither did she. "Well, imagine being in that situation yourself, okay? Say, you and another girl in the class are always seen as 'the smart ones' in the class, or the 'teacher's pets,' or 'the rebels,' or—"

"Or 'the Jews,'" Letitia said calmly, and slipped a piece of orange into her mouth.

Eureka! A handle! Letitia might not have a lesbian consciousness, or even much of a feminist consciousness; but that didn't mean she had no consciousness. I felt cheered by the first real bit of herself Letitia had been willing to share. Maybe there was hope for friendship in our futures after all.

But meanwhile, Barb was still in jail. So, "Exactly!" I said. "And say the other girl was accused of murder, and you knew that from now on 'murderer' and 'Jewish' would be linked in people's minds. Say you knew that when people talk about this girl and say 'murderer' they're really thinking 'murdering Jew.' And say you also have a suspicion that maybe the case against her will be handled a bit differently than it might be if she weren't Jewish, maybe people's assumptions will make certain evidence look more damning, or maybe the cops won't bother to investigate other possible leads as much as they might if she weren't Jewish...."

Letitia had her remaining orange sections laid out in a circle on the table. "Okay," she said and looked at me fully, seriously. "What is it you want to know?"

"Everything you can tell me," I said. Whew! What a relief! "Anything that will help me get some idea of who he was. I never even saw the man, so anything you tell me will be useful. Even what he looked like, for example."

She paused to marshal her thoughts. Despite her tentative openings to me, she was still cautious and controlled in every word and gesture. I watched the sun sprinkling glints of light within the smokey darkness of her hair and turning the tiny hairs along the margins of her face into gold patina. I marveled again at the soft fullness of her deep rose lips, and I wondered: Is she mannered and self-conscious because of how people—even me—always look at her? Or do we look at her because of the way she handles herself, the impression she gives of gracefully walking a tightrope where the least loss of control, the tiniest slip, can mean a fall. A fall from grace.

"He's—he was," Letitia began, corrected herself, paused, and went on. "He was about thirty-five, I think. Five-ten or so. Wavy brown hair cut fairly short, a small beard. Medium build." She gave me a small frown of apology. "There really was nothing special about him physically. A fairly typical young faculty type; tweed jacket with suede patches on the elbows, you know what I mean. I always thought he probably went out and bought himself a pipe the day he got accepted into graduate school. To celebrate."

"Sounds like maybe you knew him from more than that one lecture section," I ventured.

"I met him first at a party. A beginning-of-the-year party for faculty and grad students in Philosophy." She saw my wrinkled brow and added, "I have a friend in the department. He was.... Well, you know how those parties are." I didn't, as a matter of fact. "The chairman has his secretary send out invitations for 'drinks and hors d'oeuvres from two-thirty to five-thirty,' and everybody who doesn't have tenure yet feels obligated to put in an appearance. By three-thirty, there are thirty-five people milling around in the chairman's house, drinking. By five, all the grad students are lining up to shake his hand and go have a pizza and say mean things about the assistant professors, and at five-thirty the assistant professors and their wives say what a wonderful time they had and what a beautiful house the chairman has and how much they're looking forward to the coming academic year, and then they all go home and say mean things about everybody with tenure."

"And what about the ones who have tenure?" I couldn't help but ask.

"Oh, they drop by about three," she said, "just to gloat."

We watched the sailboats for a minute, tiny on the distant blue of the water, and then she picked up the thread of her description again.

"I was with...my friend and a group of people at the party who were talking about how much it costs to be in politics these days, arguing about whether you get better congressmen or not when the candidates all have to have their own money to begin with. Then Ted wandered up. He heard somebody say that college professors don't earn enough to run for office, and that set him off on a tirade about how unfair the whole university system is to younger teachers. To himself, mostly, it seemed. He was pretty bitter about it, but I didn't really pay much attention to him until he started talking about students. Because..." Letitia stopped for a few seconds, as if looking for the right words to say exactly what she meant. "…It sounded almost like he had someone specific in mind. Not that he mentioned any names, but he sounded really vicious. And you don't get that vicious, do you, unless you've been hurt yourself."

"What was it he was bitter about?" I asked. "About students, you said?"

"About students with more money than their professors. About women students with money: 'rich bitches playing at being college students, who don't give a fuck about the academic process.' Something like that."

"Sounds like a real charmer," I said.

"Oh, he could be charming. One of the full professors came up right about then, and Ted turned off his anger just like that. Of course, then he came on a little too…servile. Trying to flatter the prof and come on like a colleague at the same time. When the group broke up, Ted sort of guided me into a corner—you know, the hand on the elbow bit—and started coming on to me. He didn't get very far, though, because my friend saw us and came over. As soon as Ted found out I was…I had a friend in the department, he just…switched himself off again."

Letitia's dark eyebrows moved down in a frown of concentration. "It's like he had a certain way of relating to female students, but when he found out you didn't exactly fit in that role—that you weren't 'just' a student by his criteria—well, he had a whole different way of relating to you. Especially if you were connected to the department in any way, because he'd always be thinking: 'how will this affect my position when the tenure committee meets?'"

"Sounds yucky," I commented. "But you chose to take a class with him."

Letitia tilted her head back for a challenging glance, then nodded silently.

"So what was he like as a teacher?" I asked, wishing I could think of some inoffensive way to add: and why did you choose the one section of Philosophy 102 that you *knew* was taught by an asshole?

"Pretty much what you'd expect," she answered. "Pompous, self-important, pedantic…. It's funny, though."

"What?"

Her upper lip was caught and held by her lower teeth for a long minute as she rummaged through her mind for the words she wanted. Meanwhile my psyche ached from the static battle between my better judgement and my overwhelming desire to reach out and gently release that full, beautiful, dark pink lip. I could almost feel the silky softness of it on my fingertips, but I wrenched my attention back to Ted Simpson as soon as she began to speak again.

"He played up to the women in the class," she said, "just like you'd expect him to. But it was…different. At the party, before he found out I was 'more than a student,' he'd come on like a real Don Juan. Straight sex. With an intellectual edge to it, of course. I mean, you got the impression he'd quote highclass French pornography in bed instead of *Hustler*, but his whole line was based on assuming you were interested in him—and he was interested in you—for sex. You know

51

how they say, 'that guy thinks he's God's gift to women'?"

"Yeah."

"Well, that was Ted, believe it or not. You couldn't help but think, 'my God does this guy have an inflated idea of himself.' I suppose it must have worked for him with some women or he wouldn't have kept it up. But that's why I was so surprised to see how he was with the women in his class."

"And how was that?"

"I've been trying to think how to describe it. It wasn't really paternalistic, but it sure wasn't his usual hard sexual sell either. It was sort of like a cross between a big brother and a favorite uncle. But that doesn't quite get it, either. He talked to his students a lot after class, especially the women, and he was always offering to give them extra reading or time outside class."

I interrupted her. "Did you ever get any of that extra reading or tutoring?"

"No." Her negative was instantaneous and definite, as if she was throwing up a wall between Simpson and herself in her mind—or in mine. "I think there were probably only about two or three women he sort of concentrated on. He'd make a point of asking them if they had any questions or problems they wanted to discuss, and in a few weeks, they were down there at the front of the room after class every day. But I'd swear he never laid a hand on them. The sexual thing just seemed to be...gone."

"Maybe he thought it would be too risky, having an affair with a student. Until he got tenure, anyway."

"Hmmmm. Maybe."

I had the feeling there was something missing from Letitia's account, but I wasn't sure enough of myself, or of the nascent friendship between us, to winkle it out of her yet. So instead I asked, "Could you tell me who those two or three women were? His 'pets'? I'd like to talk to them, too."

Letitia looked faintly annoyed; she did it by dropping her eyelids a certain way and pulling her mouth a tiny bit tight. "I don't know their names," she said. "It was a big class, you know."

I pulled my precious class list out of my backpack and nudged it to her across the table. "How about taking a look at this? Maybe one of the names will jog your memory."

A minute or so later, "Jennifer," she said aloud. "Jennifer Stone. I think she was one of them." She put the list back on the table, turning it to face in my direction and pointing to the name. "And that was kind of funny, too. She seemed to me like exactly the kind of student he'd been bitching about at the party. Very upper-middle class WASP; very daddy's-little-girl-deserves-the-best."

"You've been a terrific help, Letitia," I said, "and I can't thank you enough. I mean it." She looked dubious, no doubt because my thank-you was a pretty obvious lead in to good-bye. "You understand, don't you, how wound up I am in this murder business right now. That doesn't mean I haven't enjoyed talking to you, though. I really have."

She was looking more and more dubious with every word, and I began to feel perspiration evaporating clammily off my forehead in the light breeze from the lake.

"No, look, I'm not just saying it to be polite. You're somebody I find...very interesting"—it flashed through my mind to wonder whether that was enough of an understatement (or did I mean euphemism) to qualify as a lie—"and as soon as I get this other business straightened out...."

"It's all right," she said, looking more relaxed. "I'm interested in the case, too, after all." We were looking at each other as clearly and honestly at that moment as we ever had, and she said, "I didn't like Ted very much, Terry, but...."

"But...?"

"He's dead," she said.

And oddly enough, I felt I knew exactly what she meant. It wasn't the sappy "don't speak ill of the dead" routine. It was the sense of irretrievability. The soul has left the body, and that's it. He gets no more chances, no more little pleasures or griefs. Whatever he was, whatever he might someday have become, it's over. As Kenneth Patchen put it,

> This is a man. He has a poor time in the world.
> You are not to kill him.
> This is a man. There is a purpose in his being here.
> You are not to kill him.

I'd never told any of my lesbian friends about that poem, because I was afraid they'd laugh at it. Or at me. Looking into Letitia's caramel-brown eyes, though, I thought maybe I would be able to share that poem with her. Maybe we could be the kind of friends we both missed from our high school days. If I could manage to cool out the sexual attraction I still felt for her, that is.

I jumped up from my chair, stuffing the class list back in my pack and slinging it over my shoulder as I headed for the door. "I'll see you Monday, buddy," I said, and the reflection of her beautiful and, for once, uncomplicated smile came out to meet me in the dark glass of the door as I swung it open and headed for a telephone. -

9.

Luckily, Jennifer Stone was one of the names I'd found in the student directory and written in on Simpson's class list. She lived in one of the dorms, so I dialed free from a campus phone in the HUB. Seventeen rings later, "Greetings!" boomed a hearty male voice, yanking me abruptly back from a daydream of blue sky glimpsed through a window in the stairwell.

"Is Jennifer Stone there?" I asked.

"Never heard of her."

"This is Hansee Hall, isn't it?"

"So they tell me!" He just had to be a jock. Or a clown. Or both.

I sighed and tried again. "Look, I've got to locate Jennifer Stone. It's an emergency. According to the directory, she lives in Hansee Hall. Is there some way you could help me get through to her?"

The word "emergency" sobered him. "I'll see what I can do," he said; "hold on." I heard the clunk as he put the receiver down, and then, distantly, his voice receding down a hallway. "Calling Jennifer Stone. Calling Jennifer Stone. Emergency phone call for Jennifer Stone." And then silence. Just as I was about to give up and go away, I began to detect sounds of life again in Hansee Hall. Voices. Faint and far away at first, growing louder, gradually nearing, turning into. . ."But I don't know." The woman's voice was petulant. "I don't kno-o-ow where she went."

There was a brief, unpleasant scraping sound as the receiver rasped on wood, and then the man was back on the line. "I found a friend of Jennifer's for you," he said.

The voice in the background objected, "We weren't really friends," but she took the phone and spoke sharply in my ear. "Jennifer doesn't live here anymore. She moved out a couple weeks ago, and I don't know where she went."

"Do you have any idea how I could find her?" I asked. "Any friends I could call who might be in touch?"

"She went with Bob Farris for a while. You could ask him, I guess."

She didn't sound hopeful about it. But then, she didn't sound like she cared a jot one way or the other. And at least I had another name to try. "Bob Farris," I repeated. "Does he live in Hansee?"

"No, he was at McCarty last quarter, maybe still is. I heard he and some other guys were moving off campus, though, so I don't know...."

"Well, thanks for your help," I said and hung up, thinking, What a downer. Here I'd been all set to talk with Jennifer Stone and really get to know what Simpson was all about, and where is she? Vanished, with just enough time before my one-thirty class to look up Bob Farris in the student directory at the HUB information desk.

At four forty-five, I sneaked away from my chores to use the phone tucked away by the ladies' room on the third floor of the graduate library. "Is Bob Farris there?" I asked, ready to hear he'd moved to Mongolia and left no forwarding address.

"Hey, Bob!" the voice immediately hollered into my ear. "Phone for you!"

"Bob Farris here," a new voice told me a few seconds later.

"Wow, I can't believe I really got you!"—it burst out of me without premeditation.

"Oh?" Already he sounded like a man with independently movable—and deliberately trained—eyebrows. "Who is this?"

"I'm trying to locate Jennifer Stone. It's kind of an emergency, and—"

"Oh, her," he spoke across my stammering. "She's crazy."

"Can you tell me how to get in touch with her?" I asked.

"Try the airport," he said scornfully. "Wait till someone tries to sell you a flower and then mention her name."

"You mean she became a Moonie?" My heart sank.

"One of those, anyway. Moonie, Loony, whatever they call themselves. Can't tell one bunch of nuts from another, myself."

"Look, can you possibly be more specific? I have to get a message to her and—"

"They've got a house at Forty-Third and Fourth. Just look for the one with the crazies going in and out." He banged down the receiver.

Damn. My best Simpson lead so far, gone to Moonie-dom. What a low blow. What a drag.

As soon as I could justify it, I stumped off the job and out of the library, still undecided about what to do next. I had to meet Ellie on the Hill at seven. Should I race off to look for Jennifer first? Or should I go no further than the basement of the undergrad library and call Roger from a pay phone amongst the junkfood vending machines? The weight of coins in my pocket, thunking against my thigh with every step, decided for me. Tonight I'd call Roger. Tomorrow—or someday very soon—I'd go in search of Jennifer Stone.

The beautiful day had become a blusterous evening. As I crossed Red Square, the wind blew straight and hard into my face from the west. Somebody'd slipped the sky into fast forward, and clouds raced from west to east in ones and threes, so fast they looked symbolic of something very dramatic. The end of the world, maybe. Those clouds had made it over the Olympic Mountains to the west. No

55

doubt the first of them had already hit the next major obstacle, the Cascade range just fifty or sixty miles east of the city. When enough of them had log-jammed themselves up against that mountain wall, the sky would be one solid mass of darkening grey, and then the rain would begin.

Almost an hour later, I caught a bus up the Hill and ran the seven blocks from the bus stop, arriving at Ellie's apartment in a burst of speed and sweat. A quick look at my watch assured me that I was only eight minutes late when I rat-tat-a-tatted on her door, so I wasn't prepared for the faintly annoyed look on Ellie's heart-shaped face. She's always been a more serious-minded person than I am. No doubt you have to be more serious if you want to be a lawyer the way she did, commuting between Seattle and the U of Puget Sound in Tacoma four or five days a week. And she'd already made it clear that tardiness was a serious offense in her personal statute book. But what the hell, eight minutes isn't such a big deal.

Looking back on Ellie and me from a distance of years, I can see a lot now that was invisible to me then. Take that evening, for example. I got annoyed because I thought she was annoyed by my being eight minutes late. Whereas in fact, it wasn't the eight minutes that bothered her at all. The way she saw things, we were supposed to be "going out on a date." And if I'd had the smarts to look at her then and know what I was seeing, that expectation should have been obvious to me. Ellie was about two inches taller than me that evening, which meant she was wearing her "dress" shoes, the ones she'd chosen because they were "dressy" and yet didn't emphasize the one-inch height advantage she had over me when barefoot. With her medium aqua blue slacks—not jeans, but tailored slacks with little pleats at the waist and, of course, no back pockets—she was wearing a blouse that was very definite about being a blouse, not a shirt. Her shiny brown hair was cut so it hung just right around her face and shingled higher in back to show off her long white neck. All in all, an elegant package. To me, she looked like she hadn't bothered to change since she got home from playing lawyer-to-be, but naturally I was too generous to hold that against her.

And what did Ellie see when she opened the door to her "date" for the evening, her "steady," her "significant other"? I was a somewhat sweaty, somewhat chubby little dyke in Salvation Army jeans, a tee-shirt from the co-op's free box worn under an old plaid flannel shirt, hair cut by the local appearances-are-not-important dyke barber, and ancient gym shoes with loud, mismatched laces. It's a wonder she didn't claim a headache and invite me quickly out the door.

We were lovers and friends for almost a year, Ellie and I, and we neither of us caught on, during all that time, to the fact that we were doing something absolutely miraculous; we were maintaining a fairly close and, at its best, truly intimate relationship despite the fact that we lived in two different worlds and spoke two entirely different languages. If the two languages had been different the way

English and Spanish are different, at least we'd have had a dictionary to help us out. As it was, though, we used the same words to mean completely different things. I thought we were friends who were lovers. For her, being somebody's lover was so different from being a friend that the two kinds of relationships simply couldn't be combined in one person. I assumed "lesbian" was a political category as well as a personal identity; for me, lesbians were women who chose to challenge patriarchy by living out our love for women and our commitment to women's lives. For Ellie, lesbians were indistinguishable from other women except that they happened to fall in love with a woman instead of a man. The only social change she was interested in, as far as gay rights were concerned, was to promote into general public consciousness her own opinion that lesbians are just as "normal" as anyone else.

Why in the world did she put up with me as long as she did? Probably because she didn't want to admit, after we met and she almost immediately "fell in love," that the relationship was a failure. I think she fell in love with me because she wanted to be in love in order to feel loved and not lonely, because we had a good time together and became lovers, and because she'd grown up assuming she'd be in love with anyone she had a sexual relationship with. For me, the relationship lasted because I assumed we were friends and you don't give up on your friends, especially your lesbian friends. And because we did have good times together, and I did enjoy making love with her, and I did (and do) find it much easier to stay lovers with someone than to become lovers with anyone else. It pains me now, though, to think of how insulting it must have felt to her when I showed up for our "date" that evening looking so grungy. If I wasn't interested in playing her games, I should have left her alone. But of course I was blithely unaware of our language differences at the time.

So that evening proceeded according to an already familiar pattern. We went to Mama's Mexican Kitchen for dinner. Mama's wasn't a gay place, but it always had a large gay clientele. At Ellie's request, we waited an extra five minutes so we could have one of the booths instead of a table. It didn't make any difference to me where we sat, but Ellie liked the feeling of seclusion and privacy she got from a booth. Even so, I couldn't help but see and be seen by several friends and acquaintances as they passed by on their way to or from their own tables, and Ellie's irritation irritated me all over again every time I irritated her by interrupting what she saw as our intimate dinner for two in order to say "hi" to some passer-by.

We did manage to talk, though, in between the interruptions. Not about what was bothering us about one another, of course; we never talked about that unless we were too upset to be rational. Instead, Ellie told me the latest from law school. Other law-student dykes I knew were always complaining. "It's so boring," they'd cry, "and it's not what I'm into at all. All this corporation stuff they make you take, it's like they're trying to weed out all the radicals by boring us to death."

Ellie, on the other hand, was stimulated by the intellectual challenge. When I commented one time that it all sounded like intellectual game-playing to me, she responded, "Of course it is. It's all a game. But it's a game designed to sharpen our minds. It's tough, but you'll never win if you don't take it seriously."

If you'd told me then that the woman I danced and slept with would go on to become a prosecuting attorney intent on working her way up through the increasingly powerful levels of judgeship, I'd have said you were crazy. Every other law student I knew was a political dyke trying to learn a skill with which she could help the poor and oppressed. Life didn't turn out that way for a lot of them, but that's what they thought they were about then. So I guess it's no wonder I could sit and listen to Ellie talk and still not really hear a thing she was telling me about herself. It's a good thing she didn't realize what was going on either; she'd have felt so very lonely sitting there alone with me in that high-backed booth at Mama's.

About the time we were scraping the last of the enchilada sauce off our plates, I started telling Ellie about the murder.

"Oh yes, I heard about that," she said. "Sounds like an open-and-shut case. I suppose her attorney might be able to bargain for a reduced charge, though."

"What does that mean?" I asked.

"Well, if she alleges diminished capacity or self-defense—depending on the actual details of the crime and how much the prosecution is able to prove—the court might go for a plea of guilty to second degree, or even involuntary manslaughter, if her attorney's any good and plays his cards right."

"And what would that do for Barb?"

"She'd probably get fifteen to twenty years if it's second degree, maybe as low as five to ten for manslaughter. She could be out in two-and-a-half years. Even sooner if she's got any backing. Maybe even get off with some sort of treatment approach, who knows."

"Backing...?"

"Family, usually. You know, tearful but highly respectable parents in court. That kind of thing. And a top-of-the-line attorney, of course."

"That's terrible!" I said. "That kind of thing isn't supposed to make any difference. And anyway, what if she didn't do it?"

Ellie looked at me blankly. "Didn't do it? Oh. Well, I don't know the details, of course, only what I read in the paper, but it sounded like a pretty tight case to me." She nudged the check suggestively in my direction and said brightly, "Shall we go?"

We got to the Slipper about nine, and the place was already on its way to being full. I spotted some friends on the dance floor and would have joined them, but Ellie steered me to a table of her own friends. They found a couple chairs for us from somewhere, and Ellie settled down to chat while I set off across the room for a pitcher.

When I wriggled my way through the crowd piled up against the bar, I was delighted to find myself standing next to Jan. "Hi!" I said.

"Hey," she answered, her usual greeting.

"Been here long?" I asked. "I didn't see you when I came in a minute ago."

"But I saw you, though," she said. "You and...."

"Ellie."

"Yeah."

I felt uncomfortable suddenly. "I guess you never really met Ellie, right?, maybe just passed her in the hall at home. Want to come over and get introduced?"

"Naw," she said, "never mind." Stew the bardyke set my pitcher on the counter. "I'll see you tomorrow afternoon."

"Right," I said, "see you then." And as I picked up the pitcher and started to turn away, "Hey, Jan, can you tell me the name of that woman dancing over there? The one in the blue and purple shirt?" I gestured with my chin towards the woman I'd talked to after the Fat Oppression Workshop.

Jan turned and leaned with her left elbow on the bar, her eyes puckering to see through the smoky gloom. "That's Dru," she said. "Who wants to know?"

"Just me, that's all. I'm trying to work up the nerve to ask her to dance."

"Hell, why not?" Jan laughed. She reached her arm out along the surface of the bar and gave the back of my neck a quick squeeze. "Dru's alright, and she sure does like to dance."

Naturally, I just happened to pass close to Dru on my way back to Ellie, and took the opportunity to say, "Hi, Dru!" and smile.

"Hey," she said, too polite to be obvious about not remembering who I was.

Ellie and her friends were gossiping happily when I reached the table and put the pitcher down. The first time I sensed a break in the conversation, I pulled gently on Ellie's hand and said, "Wanna dance?"

We danced three or four fast ones in a row, then a slow one, then another fast one, and Ellie pulled me to the edge of the floor saying, "Gotta go to the Ladies."

I watched her zig-zag her way across the room and around the corner to the toilet line, and then I made my move. Dru was sitting with her back to the dance floor, so I came up behind her and waited there for a minute until she'd finished what she was saying to the other women at the table. Then, with my pulse racing and my face flushing hot, I tapped her softly on the shoulder and said, "Hi again, Dru. We met at the Fat Oppression Workshop, remember? Wanna dance?"

She thinks I'm crazy, my brain was grieving, she's wondering why in the world I'd think she'd want to dance with me. Luckily, the jukebox chose that moment to start in on an old Motown hit you could see she just didn't want to miss, so she decided to take a chance on me.

It took a few seconds for us to adjust to each other once we hit the dance floor, but after that it was great. It was fabulous. Dancing with Ellie was fun, but dancing with Dru was *dancing*. And given that physical coordination has never been among my outstanding characteristics, I knew I had been granted an experience that wasn't likely to happen very often in my life. When I was a kid, I went through a phase of dreaming about dancing—or skating, depending on the season. It felt like flying in my day dreams, the swooping, swirling, unfettered-by-gravity gracefulness of it. Needless to say, dancing to Motown in the Slipper, even with Dru, didn't have quite the same feeling to it as a dream of waltzing in a Viennese ballroom. What did match the dream was the feeling of being united with my partner by the music, both of us being the muscles for the physical expression of the distant musicians' inspiration. I forgot about feeling foolish, forgot to worry about whether anybody was looking at me and saying to themselves, "Geez, even I dance better than she does." Unselfconsciously, I followed Dru's moves, not as imitation or constraint, but just because she held me with her eyes and brought me into the music with her.

We were both laughing when the music ended, and I was panting a little, too, when I said to her, "You should be a teacher, you know that?"

She laughed again and gave a little bow. "Maybe someday, baby. Be cool." And she headed back for her table with a farewell wave of her hand.

I caught a glimpse of Jan as I turned off the dance floor, sitting at a table now, sideways, sloping back from the edge of the chair with her long legs stretched out into the crowded room. I thought I saw her grin, maybe even at me, and I would have gone over to her except that the next thing I saw was Ellie.

Ellie standing by the corner around which she'd disappeared on her way to the Ladies Room. Ellie looking angry. Ellie gone all stiff again and turning quickly away, once she was sure I had seen her, to go gather up her jacket, speak quickly to her friends, and march resolutely towards the exit door. Oh hell.

I caught up with her in the middle of the steep flight of stairs down to the street door. "Ellie," I cried, "where are you going? What's wrong?" As if I didn't know.

She refused to speak to me all the way back to where she'd parked her car, and for a minute I thought she'd get in and drive away without me. She sat behind the wheel, motionless, for all of thirty seconds before reaching over to unlock the door on the passenger side.

I wore out my "what's wrong?" variations during the first five minutes, so we rode in silence the rest of the way back up the hill, and the silence continued through the parking of the car, the unlocking of the street door, the climbing of the stairs, and the entrance into Ellie's third-floor apartment. Once inside, she threw her purse on the couch, took off her jacket and flung it over the back of a chair, and started to pace.

Oh lord, I said to myself as I sank down into the couch, it's one of those. I hated these humiliating scenes that made me feel like an actress uncomfortably forced into playing a male role in a play, that forced me to wonder whether there really was some truth to the old male stereotypes of women as emotionally manipulative and controlling. No matter how I tried to break us out of the routine, no matter how reasonable and loving or angry and outrageous I tried to be in order to break the pattern and bring us through to something more real, Ellie always seemed able to twist my words back into part of the same old script. Eventually I would decide, every time, well, this is just something we have to get through, I guess, so I'd give in and play along, hoping to get it over with as quickly as possible. "Why are you angry, Ellie?"

"You know why!"

"Is it because I danced with Dru?"

Angry silence, angry pacing.

"If that's it, Ellie, I don't really see why it should make you angry. I mean, you were out of the room at the time, and it was just one dance...."

"I thought," she said, coming to a halt in front of me, "I thought we were together. I thought you invited me out because you wanted to be with me. But I guess I was mistaken."

"Oh, Ellie, of course I wanted to be with you. And I was with you. It was just one dance, and you weren't even there, and—"

"And you couldn't even wait one minute, not even one little minute, while I was in the Ladies. The minute I turn my back, the very minute I am out of the room, you are suddenly overcome with the need to dance. Never mind that if you'd been willing to wait just one little minute I'd have been back."

I couldn't help it. I covered my face with my hands and groaned.

Ellie burst into tears and fled, leaving me feeling cruel and horrible on her bottle-green couch.

I followed her into the bedroom, expecting to find her dissolved on the bed. But no, we still had one more act before the final scene. Instead of a weeping heap I found a blazing brand.

"I don't believe you!" she raged as I entered the room.

"Wha...?"

"You wanted to dance with her, that other woman. You wanted to dance with her, not with me."

"Well, sure I wanted to dance with her, Ellie, but—" And that did it. Howling with despair, she launched herself across the bed in a full bellyflop onto the neat, beige-and-brick-colored bedspread. I sighed deeply and lay down beside her. Why does she have to make herself so unhappy? I asked myself again. Isn't she too smart for this? I was irritated, but I was deeply unhappy, too. Ellie was my friend, and I wanted her to be happy, I wanted us to be able to be happy together. I couldn't believe she enjoyed these emotional storms, but I couldn't figure out why she seemed unable to avoid them, either. Ellie and I were both lesbians, for heaven's sake. We were sisters.

Gradually, I insinuated myself around her, holding her and stroking her hair and making the cooing nonsense noises meant to comfort. She turned to me, finally, and cried out the last few tears into my shirt. Then we held each other for awhile, and then we quietly took off our clothes and crawled into bed. I'd already known for an hour that any verbal or physical move on my part that even vaguely hinted of sex would lead to nothing but more grief and, on my part at least, guilt, so I sighed again and spooned myself around my friend's warm back as she drifted off to sleep.

In the morning she was awake before I was, humming cheerily along with the radio in the kitchen as she fixed me breakfast. Life is strange, I said to myself, and I got up to take a shower. We had a fine time all the rest of the short morning, although I felt as if the ground beneath us might turn into ice and break at any moment. Soon after breakfast we took a walk over to her friends Mona and Stacey's house for lunch. I played Lego in the living room with their two kids while Ellie looked at their paint chips and wallpaper samples in the kitchen.

"Mona and Stacey are doing the whole house over room-by-room," she told me when I brought the kids in for juice about two o'clock. "Isn't this wallpaper lovely? That's for the living room, once they get the old paint off the woodwork and refinish it." She sounded wistful, and I thought back to the careful touches of color in her own small, modern, wall-to-wall-shag apartment. I sat down and tried to feel interested in interior decorating for almost half an hour, but then I'd suddenly had enough and decided it was time to go.

"Thanks for the lunch, Mona, Stacey. I'll give you a call, Ellie, okay?"

"You're leaving? But—"

"Yeah, I told you, Ellie, remember? I'm visiting Barb at the jail this afternoon."

I kissed her and saw her roll her eyes at Mona and Stacey as if to say, Didn't I tell you? as I turned toward the door.

10.

It only takes about twenty minutes to walk from the top of Capitol Hill to the Pike Place Market downtown. Even in March, a Saturday brings the arts and crafts vendors out in large numbers, and I scanned the motley collection of brass belt buckles, silver earrings, chunky pottery, ceramic toothbrush holders, and the odd old-fashioned yarn octopus before passing through the double row of produce and seafood stalls on my way to Soup and Salad. The small, collectively-run restaurant hung out over Western Avenue and the then unrenovated "hill climb"—a series of dilapidated wooden stairways—leading down to the Elliott Bay waterfront. As I paid for my small pot of peppermint tea, I shared a smile with the bearded guy at the cash register. I didn't know him, but I knew he'd be part of the approving collective consensus next time the Lesbian Mothers National Defense Fund or the Anti-Racism Organizing Committee asked to use the restaurant for a fund-raiser, and he knew I'd be one of the grass-roots attendees. That didn't exactly make us friends, but it did make the restaurant a comfortable place for me to be.

I took my thick, white mug and my dented tin teapot over to the counter running along the outside wall of the place, and perched there on one of the high wooden stools. The view was not to be sneered at, even under a sky going increasingly saggy with impending rain. Sternly, however, I tore my eyes away from the curve of the Bay with the green lump of West Seattle on the south and the islands of Puget Sound fading into mist straight ahead of me. I had work to do: it was time to don my Sherlock Holmes cap (or my Jane Marple shawl) and exercise the little gray cells again.

"What happened?" I wrote in the notebook I'd pulled from my backpack. That's what I wanted to ask Barb that afternoon. What the hell happened down there by the APL, leaving Ted Simpson dead and Barb's fingerprints on the murder weapon.

My attention drifted up again and snagged on one of the big white Washington State ferries heading slowly out from the downtown ferry terminal. Usually when I see a ferry I react by wanting to race right down and take the next one out. I can almost feel the wind blasting against my body as I stand at the forward rail on the upper deck, pointing myself into the open water ahead and feeling ridiculously adventurous even though I know that for lots of people the ferry system is no more exotic than the city's bus system. It's just transportation, after all.

That day, though, the ferry I saw headed out across the Sound to Bremerton or Winslow looked different to me. It looked sealed, somehow. Cut off. A world unto itself, and there it went, sliding easily across the surface of the water, as remote as a spaceship slipping through the emptiness of outer space. The ship seemed serenely indifferent to its own isolation, the temporary community of its passengers unaware of the huge distance separating them from me and all of my world as I perched there on a wooden stool looking out over the edge of the city.

With a sigh, I forced my mind back to the notebook on the counter. "TS: any enemies?" I wrote.

Several moody sips of tea later, I was thinking about Dru, remembering how great it felt to dance with her, how easy it was to laugh with her. I remembered her indignation about Barb after the fat oppression workshop. Yes, she definitely seemed like an interesting woman to know. But mostly, I had to admit, I was intrigued by the way she danced. Not just that she danced well but that she seemed to be creating the dance as she danced it. When she danced, it was her dance, not just her version of a dance everybody else was into at the time.

I started a mental review of my other friends and acquaintances to see if I could find any other match like that—any person who could so completely own a particular activity or art as she performed it.

And then it came to me. "They tell me, You play like a man," said a voice in my memory; "and I say that's the best compliment anyone could give me." Mrs. Goodman, my violin teacher when I was in eighth grade, my last violin teacher, in fact, because of her tendency to say things like that. "Don't be so stiff!" she scolded again and again, "Don't be so dainty! You must learn to play like a man or you'll never be a violinist, only a girl who plays the violin." I never answered her back, but only because I couldn't find any words to say how angry she made me feel. Why was it so bad to be "a girl who plays the violin"?

But that was old history. Old, sad history, given that I let my irritation with Mrs. Goodman drive me into quitting violin before I figured out how to translate what she was trying to tell me into a language I was able to understand. And it seemed sad to me, too, that I could think of no one else in my life but Mrs. Goodman (as violinist, not as teacher) who came close to matching the integrity I felt in Dru as a dancer. The grace, in a metaphysical as well as physical sense, the centered self without self-consciousness, the fully emerged woman who was the woman-inside-the-woman in Marge Piercy's poem, the woman who "laughs uproariously from the belly /…a woman peppery as curry, /…compounded of acid and sweet like a pineapple, / like a handgrenade set to explode, / like goldenrod ready to bloom."

I savored the words of the poem in my mind, and wondered. Was Peg that woman, maybe, when she laughed? Or maybe she was Jan…only, when? Definitely not Letitia, ever. As much as I liked Letitia, I couldn't help but see how different her kind of grace was from Dru's. Like the difference between a tight-rope walker and the hard-won but apparently effortless flight of a ballerina.

A spear of astonishing sunlight pierced the heavy clouds over the Bay and drew a circle of dancing gold on the dull silver of the water. It was time to go, time for me to get myself on down to the jail and ask Barb some questions. When I dutifully trotted my teapot and mug over to the dirty-dish station, there was a well-worn copy of Thursday's evening paper on the rack next to the trays. "Suspect Arraigned in UW Slaying," read the headline staring up at me from page three. I grabbed the paper and headed out the door with my pulse racing.

According to the paper, Barb had been arraigned on Thursday morning and her attorney had asked for a continuance. Reading between the lines, I got the impression that the lawyer—"retained by the defendant's family in Montana"—hadn't even met Barb until they found themselves in court together. I thought of what Ellie had told me and wondered if this lawyer guy was already bargaining with the prosecution for a lesser charge. And would Barb go for it if he did? It was hard for me to picture Barb, the Barb of the Furies, as the client of a male attorney. Would she really be willing to let a man do the talking for her? I shivered, crossing Marion Street, at the cold wind off the water. It blows up those east/west streets in a gale and smacks you every time you get to an intersection: just one more example of being vulnerable in an exposed position.

I was shivering all over by the time I spotted Jan, her long back propping up a wall across the street from the Public Safety Building. Partly it was the cold wind, but at least a third of the goose bumps were how I felt about going up to the jail again. The sight of the barred and security-screened windows made my stomach churn, and I remembered a picture I'd seen in a feminist pamphlet about medieval witch killings. It was a picture of a cage, like an oversized bird cage, hanging in a public square. There was a woman in the cage, and being hung there was part of her punishment. These days, the cage takes up the whole floor of a building, I thought, wondering how many women were in there right now, hanging in a steel cage six stories up.

Jan saw me coming. "You hear the latest?" she asked.

"I just now saw in the paper about the arraignment," I said. "She's got a lawyer."

"Yeah, but about the Furies."

"The Furies? No, what—don't tell me they've all been arrested!"

Jan smiled grimly. "Naw. Don't take no police to make trouble for 'em, those women make their own. What I'm talking about, they cut Barb loose—and they're all leaving outta here, too. All but Fennel."

I could see now that Jan was really angry. "Is Anne going with them?" I asked.

"Yeah. Damn fool. Won't listen to a thing I— she scared, that's all. Scared they'll cut her loose, too, like they done Barb."

We started across the street to the Public Safety Building, Jan tense and heated by my side. "So.... Where are they going?" I said, and she snorted.

"Won't say. Better be someplace I can't get at that shithead Lil."

Wow, Jan was really burning. I could imagine what must have happened: she'd tried to talk Anne out of leaving and gotten thoroughly trounced by the other Furies. I wished I was brave enough to take Jan's hand as we walked through the lobby.

The elevator dinged us upwards, along with several other people who also got out at the sixth floor. Unlike the first time, my fingers hardly shook at all as I filled out the little pink form. Jan, after she got the attention of the Voice and hollered out Barb's name, leaned her back against the wall beside the elevator and slid down a ways, bringing her mouth down to the level of my ear.

"Seem like Barb's been doing a helluva lotta lying, Terry," she said. Although the airless room was crowded with people already, including an infant crying most desperately, I could hear Jan's soft voice very clearly. It's like she's used to this, I thought, and knows how to be in...this kind of place. I thought vaguely of actors trained to project their voices to the back rows, even when the script called for a whisper.

"What do you mean?" I asked her.

"You know she's suppose to be working at that bag factory down in the south end?" I nodded and she went on, "Turns out she never did. Turns out she never had no job at all. Applied, maybe, but never got hired. And every day she'd be coming home saying, They put up the quota again, and That foreman's so mean, and all. But it's all in her mind, it's all just a lie. She never was working at all, she's been getting money from daddy back home in Montana. And all the time talking about how she's working class. Sheee-it."

"But—" I was stunned. "But why? Why would she lie like that, Jan?"

"Because she's a liar, I guess," was Jan's unforgiving reply.

"Uh, I get money from my folks, too, you know, Jan." My heart beat harder than usual for a second as I waited for her to confirm that the tuition money my parents had been saving up since I was five didn't put me in the same disdained category as Barb.

Jan just looked at me, and then said crossly, "You know that ain't the same. Kids that got parents, their parents help 'em out. I ain't saying it's fair on kids that ain't got, but that's the way it is. Barb can go ahead and be rich as hell, for all I care, long as she don't lie about it and run games on the women she's suppose to be tight with. Almost makes you feel sorry for 'em, don't it, to see how Barb's been putting it over on 'em. And besides that, it makes me mad as hell when somebody who ain't anywhere near working class starts mouthing off about how it feels to be working class. Like we can't even talk for our own damn selves, you see what I mean?"

I did see. "Thanks for being willing to come here with me," I told her, "feeling like that about Barb."

Jan's voice sounded warmer, finally, as she responded, "I'm here because I said I'd be here, and because you're my friend. All right?"

Before I could put my smile into words, one of the women waiting nearby tapped me on the shoulder and gestured towards the row of windows along the wall on the women's side of the room. "That the one you come to visit, honey?" she asked. I looked over at the first sit-down window in the row and saw Barb's white face mouthing silently at me behind the glass. "Thanks," I said, and went to have my talk with Barb.

She looked all there this time, and ready to talk. Sitting down made it seem more natural, too, even if I was sitting on a metal stool bolted to the cement floor, with graffiti-etched wings of painted metal sticking out past me from either side of the visiting window. I picked up the receiver and immediately had Barb's breath in my ear. By now she was sitting back from the window as far as she could and still keep her finger pressed on the button that made the phones work. Her face looked dim and fluid behind the thick glass.

"Hi, I hear you got a lawyer," I said, trying to sound upbeat and friendly.

Barb merely shrugged my words away. "Tell me—" she said, and her voice broke into silence.

"Tell you...what?" I asked

"When you were here before, it sounded like you meant to...look into it." Anyone else, under similar circumstances, might have said that wistfully or hopefully or pleadingly. But not Barb. She said it accusingly.

"That's what I'm here for," I retorted. "You're the one who knows most about it, and you told me damn-all the last time I came."

The light was so dim in there that I couldn't be sure, but I had the feeling Barb's eyeballs had gone as flat and hard as the pane of glass between us. "What do you want to know," she said.

I took a deep breath and let her have it. "Okay. I want to know exactly what happened between you and Ted Simpson the night he was killed. I want to know about Simpson—who can I talk to who knew him, what was your relationship with him like, who else might have killed him. Assuming you didn't. I want to know what your lawyer plans to do, and what you plan to do about it. And I want to know the truth about any other lies you've been telling that it might be important for me to know."

We stared at each other for a minute before my irritation spontaneously added, "And if you've decided you want me to help you, Barb, I'd like to know why the fuck you think I should." That wasn't really fair, given that the investigation was all my own idea, but Barb had the unfortunate ability to provoke anger and then make me feel resentfully guilty for feeling it.

Several dead seconds later, a tremor ran through her body and shook her finger off the telephone button. She had to hunch herself forward a bit on the stool, closer to me, in order to reestablish contact. With her large head turned to avoid my eyes she said, in a much softer voice, almost a whisper, "They expelled me."

"They—oh, you mean the Furies. Yeah, I know."

She tipped her head slightly, as if peeking out from behind some invisible barrier to read the expression on my face. "They gave Mr. Winterstone a letter for me. They said...."

Her voice trailed off and gave me time to remember that Winterstone was the lawyer mentioned in the newspaper. When Barb failed to continue her sentence, I felt my quick surge of empathy begin to ebb, leaving behind a more abrasive response. "Look, Barb," I told her. "I'm sure it's hard on you, being rejected by your friends when you're in trouble like this. But we don't have time to fool around now. Who knows how long they'll let this visit last? So come on and talk to me, okay? Answer my questions, dammit."

Her head came front and center again and her body slid back to the full extent of her arm. It was freaky, in a way. She seemed to have only two emotional modes at this point, and for each of them she had a corresponding posture. With nothing in between.

"Start where the other Furies left you that night," I instructed. "I already know about before that." The news seemed to shock her a bit, but after a few seconds she picked up her story readily enough. You couldn't say she spoke matter-of-factly, though; that would be implying a higher emotional level than she allowed her voice to show.

"I went to do the APL. I did it, and then I was putting the cans back in the bag and he came walking up on me. From the campus side. I would have just gone but"—her finger half slipped off the telephone button, and I saw that her other hand was clenched, dead white and trembling, on the receiver.

"He called my name and I recognized his voice. Up till then I thought he was just a man, just any man. But then I knew it was him. He called me and came up and said things about me, about how I look. He called me a fat, stupid slob and then he laughed at me and I sprayed him in the face with the paint. The black paint. Then he grabbed my arm and twisted it and I dropped the can. He let go. I dropped the bag and pulled out my knife. I pulled out my knife and I opened it."

I was holding my breath and the telephone receiver in my hand was clammy with sweat. When I tried to speak, my voice got stuck halfway. What if it had been me there that night? I cleared my throat and croaked, as calmingly as possible, "Okay, Barb, you're doing fine. This is exactly what I need to know. Go on."

Her tongue flicked out to wet her lips. "I thought he was going to hit me. It was self-defense. Except he didn't. All he did was take the knife away and tell me to get the fuck out of there before he beat the shit out of me. That's what he said—and then he—I thought he made a move at me with the knife. So I ran away."

She stopped speaking and any words I might have thought to say myself were temporarily blown away by the blast of anger she finally let me see in her eyes. No, it wasn't anger, exactly; it was fury. Fury and deep, deep shame. She had run away. She had let a man taunt her and take away her knife, and then she had run away. With all the mocked flesh of her body bouncing under her jacket, her big thighs rasping the denim of one leg against the other with every step, she ran away as he watched her and despised her all the more. Just as her sister Furies would despise her, she must have feared, for her failure to use the self-defense techniques they'd practiced together so many times.

I sighed. Hearing Barb's story didn't seem to bring me any closer to knowing what happened to Ted. "Did you see anyone else around, Barb?"

She shook her head no.

"Think," I urged her. "Imagine yourself back there. I know it's hard, but I've got to have some kind of clue. Isn't there anything, anything at all, you can see or hear or smell when you imagine yourself back in that time and place?"

A noticeable frown creased Barb's wide, smooth forehead, and I felt a prickle of hope. "I don't know," she started slowly, "but I think maybe there was something. I think maybe he might have heard someone coming. It's just an impression, but right after he grabbed the knife, he sort of turned away for a second, sort of looked off over his shoulder, just for a second. And then after that is when he told me to get out."

"Were you surprised that he did that? Told you to leave, I mean?"

She thought about it briefly. "Yes. I'd expect him to want to hurt me more than that."

Her eyes were softer, more inward than before. Thoughtful would describe them; or considering. Meanwhile, I'm sitting there thinking: And this kind of pain is going on all over the world all the time. I swear, sometimes I wish we could just give up on this human-being effort and go be otters instead.

"What else?" asked Barb flatly. "I left. That's all I know." Her momentary gentleness was back to armor.

"Who can I talk to about Simpson? I've got a lead on one of his students, but I need someone who knew him better and longer."

"You better write this down," she responded finally, after a blank minute of thought or resistance. I waggled my pen and notebook at her through the window. She gave me a phone number and the name Carolyn Enderly. "Don't call except between eight and five weekdays. Tell her I gave you the number. She'll tell you when you can go talk to her."

Sounds weird, I was thinking, but I said, "Anyone else?"

She shook her head, and I sighed at her stubbornness, her loneliness.

"Did he have a girlfriend, do you know?" She didn't react, so I repeated the question.

"I guess," she said.

"You mean he was the kind of guy who probably would? Or do you have some reason to think he definitely did?"

"He did."

"I should talk to her. Do you know her name?"

"No."

"Did you ever see her?"

A pause, and then she turned her head woodenly from side to side in a slow-motion mime of no.

"So how do you know she exists?" I challenged her.

"He sent a picture."

The sentence came out of her mouth like a kid peels a band-aid from an unhealed sore. Again, pity vied with impatience in my mind. "That's great!" I exclaimed, deliberately hearty. "Where can I find it?"

"I burned it," she said, and her mouth snapped shut. I tried for several minutes to get more out of her on the subject of the photo, but she simply wouldn't play. No, she couldn't remember when he'd sent it. No, she didn't remember what the woman looked like. No, she didn't know anything at all. The very last bit of information I managed to pry out of her that day—and then I half wished I hadn't—was that she admitted having chosen the APL as her personal target that night for two reasons. Because any physics lab must be a bastion of evil male energy. And because she knew, I finally got her to concede, that Ted would be likely to see her slogan painted there. "Yeah," she mumbled, eyes averted. "I guess I figured he'd see it. On his way to work." A shrug of her shoulders tried to add, so what?, and I had no idea how to calculate the importance of the fact that she clearly hadn't eliminated Ted Simpson completely from the life of her mind.

"Okay," I sighed finally. "So now why don't you tell me why you've been lying to everybody all this time."

Her eyes narrowed slightly and her lower jaw moved a fraction to the right. As if she were clenching her teeth so hard they slipped. "That's not relevant," she growled.

"Not relevant to the investigation, maybe," I shot back, "but relevant as hell to the investigator. I know it was me came to you and not the other way around. But still, you can't expect me to go on even wanting to figure this mess out if you're not willing to loosen up a little and talk to me. And be honest. I mean, it's your life, right? But I do want to help you if I can. If you'll let me. And I'd like to think we might get to know each other a little along the way. Who knows, we might even turn out to be friends some day."

As I talked, Barb's large white face gradually lost its rigidity, taking on that fluid look I'd noticed when I first sat down at the window. It scared me to see her like that, as if there was suddenly nobody home inside that big body, nobody in charge of the muscles twitching painfully in her face. In a nightmare or a horror movie, I thought, the flesh would begin to melt now and run globbily down off the bones underneath, the very substance of her changing into something else altogether. Something over which she had no control.

The melting lasted all through my nervous harangue, right up till I said we might be friends. At that exact point, the meltdown stopped and the big freeze was back full strength. "I'm going to Montana," she said. Full stop. I was still sitting there with my mouth hung open, trying to figure out how to tell her what an inadequate response that was, when a shadow hit the wall behind her. She glanced back and to her right, then looked at me and said, "I have to go now."

"But—"

"I have to go." Suddenly she was pushing herself towards me, almost pressing herself against the glass. "Talk to Carolyn," she said almost pleadingly. "Talk to her, and...let me know what—"

The looming shadow must have spoken again, because Barb suddenly shrugged her shoulders, put the receiver back on its hook and, without another look at me, disappeared into the gloom of the jail.

"Wanna go get something to eat?" I asked Jan as I shivered in the cold outside the Public Safety Building. The rain hadn't started falling yet, but there was a definite misty moistness in the air.

"Not a question of wanna," she said. "I gotta go to a meeting now. Another time, hey?"

"Sure, no problem," I told her, and turned to see what had attracted her attention behind me. "Hey, that's Rosie!" And sure enough, the big old car pulling up to a stop in the Load and Unload Zone was none other than Jan's battered Chevy.

"Oh, shit, forgot I wanted to tell you—hold it a minute, Terry," Jan said as three long strides took her to Rosie's side. She bent down to the window for a minute, and I could just make out a figure inside leaning over to roll the window down. Then she turned back and waved me to join her. "We're going up the Hill, Terry. Wanna ride?"

"Sure. Thanks." Anything to get out of the wind.

Jan yanked the rear door open for me and I climbed in, shoving over a heavy box on the seat. The woman in the driver's seat was just an anonymous head of short dark hair; she could have been any of fifty women I knew in the community—or knew about , anyway. Jan was sitting with her left arm stretched out along the back of the front seat, her hand almost certainly touching the other woman's neck in the near darkness of the car. With some women, that would suggest a relationship; with Jan, I wasn't so sure.

Almost as soon as the car pulled away from the curb, Jan spoke over her shoulder in my general direction. "Got a friend to call and find out the cop in charge of Barb's case, Terry. Name is White. Lieutenant White."

"Great, Jan, thanks," I said to the dim one-quarter view of her pale face in the darkness. "Are you going with me if I get an appointment with him?"

She snorted. "No way. You're on your own for that one. I don't mess with no police."

My sigh was inaudible, I hope, and the only sounds for a minute were the rain that finally got around to falling and the rheumatic flap of the windshield wipers. I tried to settle myself more comfortably in the slot of space available to me, and in the process noticed for the first time the contents of the box into which I'd placed, of necessity, my left arm.

"Hey," I said, picking up one of the yellow sheets of paper in the box, "I helped mail out a bunch of these the other day." It was the flyer advertising the GJB Support Committee's workshop on armed struggle.

"Yeah?" Jan grinned at me in the rearview mirror. "We appreciate the help."

The implication took a second or two to sink in. "We?" I repeated in surprise. "You mean you're involved with this, Jan?"

"Yeah. That's what this meeting's about tonight. You coming to the workshop?"

"I've been planning to. But, Jan...."

"Yeah?"

"I'm surprised. I mean, I had no idea you were into this kind of politics."

Jan exchanged a quick glance with the woman in the driver's seat. "What kind of politics you mean?"

"Well.... I mean, you're not GJB. Are you?"

Another look passed between the two of them. "No. But I am GJB Support Committee. Part of it, anyways. Any reason why I shouldn't be?"

I had to say something. But what? I said the only thing I could think of: "No." And then a minute later I was able to add, "It's just I didn't think of you as someone who'd be in favor of the kind of things the GJB is into."

"Like what?" she prodded.

"Oh, like...guns and bank robbery and bombs."

"Self-defense. Expropriations. Armed struggle." The driver spoke for the first time, her voice carefully cool and neutral.

My body seemed to be getting smaller, especially my throat. The streets outside were wet now, and shiny with reflected car lights and neon. Looking out at the lights from the back seat, I felt like a child again. In the front seat, my parents would be discussing something I couldn't understand, and it scared me. I wanted us to have arrived already. I wanted to be home, safe and warm and dry at the kitchen table with a cup of hot lemon and honey.

A movement from the front seat brought me back to the present. Jan was twisting herself around in my direction again. "You're a smart woman, Terry," she said, "you just ain't thought it through yet. You think for a minute about where I'm coming from, you won't be surprised about where I'm headed. The way it was for me, I always knew who my enemies was. That's one thing you get, being poor: there's some things so clear you just *know*. You know who's your friend, and who it is that's keeping you down. And if you don't know from the get-go, you sure find out quick, the first time they put you in the institution." Jan had untwisted gradually as she talked, and her voice got softer the more she faced away from me. I had to lean forward as far as I could to catch her last words.

"So then when you come to think political," she said, "well, you just naturally hook up with other folks that you can tell has got the same idea. Like they say, the enemy of my enemy is my friend."

There was a shooosh of water against the belly of the car as it splashed into the puddle by the curb at Fourteenth and Howell. Jan exchanged another look with the driver. "This okay for you?" she asked, and I realized her eyes had moved to mine in the rearview mirror.

"Oh. Sure, this is fine. Thanks for the ride. And…can we talk more about this some time, Jan?"

"Don't see why not," she said. "And you come to that workshop too, hear?"

"I will," I promised, and climbed out of the car. "Thanks again." The car door slammed. They were gone.

Okay, Terry, what the hell are you gonna do now? I spoke sternly to myself in order to keep from feeling lost in the dark. Get out of the rain, I responded. Okay, good plan.

A phone booth is out of the rain, so it seemed a logical place to start. The quarter sang in the slot, and there was Ellie at the other end of the line. "Hi, I'm in the neighborhood," I said, trying to keep the chattering of my teeth unobtrusive. "How about I pick up some food and come keep you company for a while?"

That sounded fine to her, so I did. We had take-home burritos and listened to Cris Williamson, and then she invited Trudi over for a few games of three-handed Scrabble. Trudi lived in the same building as Ellie, and the two of them were Scrabble fanatics. Funny thing, though, they neither of them could bring themselves to give up their own assumptions about what makes a perfect game of Scrabble, so they almost always set me up beautifully at least once a game to hit on one of those fabulous triple-word-score boxes. As a result, they never beat me as badly as they should have, given their emotional investment and my happy-go-lucky indifference.

And I enjoyed watching the two of them play. Their eyes would narrow as they examined their tiles, carefully inscrutable until, flash! An inspiration would go off inside them like a flare, and you could see them exerting all their mental energy in an effort to keep the other players from changing the one word on the board that they needed to remain the same until their turn came around again. Because with that one word they would be able to spell out one of those words only a Scrabble player can love—because only a Scrabble player knows them. I wonder if anyone has ever done a master's thesis on it: "Tracing the Movement of Obscure Words through Unrelated Populations by Means of the Individuated Interchange of Scrabble Participants."

"That's not a word!" hooted Ellie. "I challenge! I challenge."

"Challenge away," grinned Trudi smugly.

And sure enough, the word existed. Mansuetude: mildness, gentleness. "Got that one from a freaky little sergeant in Omaha," Trudi boasted. "Hot as the blazes, the barracks looks like a disaster area, the platoon commander is due any damn minute for inspection, and the woman up and hits me with mansuetude. I'll never forget it." Trudi had been in the army, and she never ran out of stories.

That night, my words kept coming out loaded with hidden significance. Plot. Dumb. Fail. The other two didn't notice, of course, partly because they just expected me to produce easy four-letter words like that, and partly because they weren't aware of how bound-up I felt in the world of Ted Simpson's murder and Barb and the Furies and the GJB. Even though all three of us were lesbians, my lesbian community seemed invisible to Ellie and Trudi. As invisible to them, come to think of it, as Trudi's had been to me, until I'd found myself in the middle of it at an ex-Army-dykes' party one time.

Scrabble always left Ellie in a very cheerful mood. After Trudi went home about eleven, we played some more music, softly, and slow-danced our way into the bedroom. I always loved making love to Ellie when she was happy. It was the sort of blissful experience that makes you furious later on, when you realize how seldom it's possible for a person like Ellie, living in a world like this, to be that kind of happy.

11.

The next day, Sunday, it was Jeanne's and my turn to go shopping for the house. As far as shopping went, Jeanne wasn't a bad partner. I didn't have to pry her out of bed, because she was one of the two "morning people" in the house. And she stuck to the list, with no tedious sidetracking into things like is it more politically correct to eat free-range eggs (from liberated, happy chickens) or regular eggs (cheap protein for the masses).

We had the food all bought and put away by eleven-fifteen and I found myself faced with the eternal student dilemma—can I force myself to sit in my room and study in the middle of the day when it's not even raining? The answer, that day, turned out to be No.

Ever since I'd gotten myself involved in investigating Ted Simpson's murder, my mind had been full of seemingly irrelevant questions. Why did I feel so attached to Barb somehow, even when I was furious with her? Why did Letitia want to be my friend, even though I seemed to make her nervous? Was it me she was interested in, or was it me-as-a-lesbian? Was there a me besides the me-as-a-lesbian? Why did I think nothing of helping mail out a million leaflets for the GJB Support Committee and yet feel totally zapped when I found out Jan was out there organizing support for the GJB's armed struggle?

If Roger'd been there, he'd have sat down and tugged back his hair and said, "Whoa, slow down to my speed, Terry." And I'd have sat down, too, knowing that talking things through with Roger would do me good. But alas, Roger was in Wisconsin, so I pulled a few unnecessary weights out of my backpack and set off instead for the house of alleged cult-member Jennifer Stone. Letitia had identified her as one of Ted Simpson's pets, so Jennifer might be able to tell me quite a lot about the man.

Forty-third and Fourth, the guy at McCarty Hall had said. Practically my neighbors—just three blocks up and three blocks over from Everywhere House. The block, when I got there, proved to be no surprise. Just your usual Seattle neighborhood, slightly modified by proximity to the University. Some of the bigger houses had been transformed into dingy rooming houses for students; a few of the smaller ones probably still were home to regular working-class families. And one of them, I'd been told, was now the center of a religious cult. But which one?

I strolled up and down from Forty-second to Forty-fourth a couple times trying to figure it out. Not the one with a tricycle and a kid-sized plastic bucket in the front yard. Probably not the one with clean white pebbles replacing the grass around a couple of immaculately tended rose bushes. Eventually I narrowed my candidates down to the three. One of them I then excluded because there was a mailbox on the railing of the front porch with the name Larsen painted on it, and the second of the three, upon closer inspection, proved to have kindergarten-style construction-paper Easter eggs taped to the inside front windows. So the third one had to be it, and I geared myself up to put my deductive powers to the test.

The doorbell hung down three inches on a very moth-eaten wire; it probably hadn't worked in years. Unlike lots of Seattle houses, the front door here was solid. No discreetly curtained window, not even a spy-hole. My knuckles sounded pitiful on the solid wood, so I switched to a fist. *Bunk, bunk, bunk.* And then I waited.

I couldn't see a thing inside the house—the blinds were pulled all the way down on both front windows. *Bunk, bunk, bunk.* I tried it again. And suddenly the door was opening. It opened about three inches, and then it stopped. I could see the face of a tall white man peering out at me. He didn't speak.

"I'm looking for Jennifer Stone," I said.

He did not reply. The door did not move.

"I want to talk to Jennifer Stone," I told him, more loudly this time.

"Why," he said. His voice sounded too heavy to turn up at the end of a sentence, the way most people's do when they ask a question.

"I need some information from her," I said.

"No interviews." The door started shut.

"Wait!" I blurted. "It's not about her, or about…this group. It's about someone she used to know. And it'll only take a minute. Or two. Really. It's not a big deal, as far as she's concerned, or you, but I know she's here, and I need to talk to her. It's important."

The man leaned a little bit away from the door for a second, and I had the impression of someone else in motion behind him. Did I hear a whisper? I couldn't be sure.

"She doesn't want to talk to you," he said, and shut the door.

Damn. I thought about banging on the door again, but there didn't seem to be much point. Discouraged and irritable, I slouched across the street and down a few houses to some concrete steps set into a cut in the bank of a front yard. The unpruned hedges on either side gave me a place to sit and pout out of the wind.

This wasn't what I'd expected at all, and it left me feeling put down hard. From past experience with Moony-type people, what I'd expected was to be welcomed, even enveloped, not shut out and shut down. I thought my problem would be to get away, to pry myself out of their recruit-hungry hands, and here

I was with my own nightmare's mantra ringing in my ears: She doesn't want to talk to you.

I'd been huddled in my hedge-and-concrete shelter for no more than four minutes, I suppose, when I heard a door open. Peeking through the scratchy tangle of the bush to my left, I saw two men emerge from Jennifer's house. Was one of them my reluctant conversationalist? Could be. And the other one, perhaps, the shadow behind the door.

Invisible in my hideyhole, I saw one of the men stick something on the door before joining his comrade en route to a black sedan parked at the curb. Both of them looked up and down the street before getting in the car, but I could tell they hadn't seen me.

As soon as the car was out of sight, I was back on quest. *Bunk, bunk, bunk* went my fist against the door, and *bunk, bunk, bunk* yet again, right in the middle of the hand-written sign: "Meditation in progress. Do not disturb."

No response. Nothing at all. I shivered and considered my options.

The front of the house obviously had nothing to offer, so I decided to try my luck at the back. The cracked cement walkway circling the house from the left side of the front door was under sustained attack by grass, dandelions, and assorted other growing things whose names I didn't know. Only the riotous success of various non-grass-like weeds showed there used to be a strip of garden along the fence. Whoever these people are, their religion clearly is not based on caring for the world around us, I deduced to myself, just to keep my spirits up. Something about the tall man's heavy voice made me distinctly reluctant to be discovered by anyone of his ilk in the backyard of a house to which I'd already been refused admission.

At first sight, the back of the house didn't look any more hopeful than the front. The slope of the yard made the house stick up half a story or so above ground level in back, placing the two windows almost out of reach. An abbreviated back porch with a short flight of unfinished wooden steps looked promising, though, and I climbed them as quietly as I could. But no, the windows were set just far enough from the door to keep me from peeking in, even if there hadn't been curtains. They were "café curtains," the kind that have a short ruffle at the top of the window, then an open space, and then a set of pull-together curtains hanging from a second rod in the window's middle. If I could get high enough, I'd be able to look in between the ruffle at the top and the closed curtains at the bottom. A big if it was, however; I'd need more than a leap off the porch to get me up and over there. I'd need a ladder, is what it amounted to.

Fortunately, my mom always had exactly that kind of curtains in the kitchen at home, and I knew that no matter how firmly they were closed, they always left a little gap open at the bottom. As a result, I must have got up at least three hundred days of my life to find our cat Lenore stubbornly and unmovably reclined on the least convenient square of linoleum in the kitchen floor. She would deign to move only when the sun had shifted far enough to miss the gap where those equally stubborn café curtains adamantly refused to meet.

Thanks, Lenore, I said silently to the sleek black memory of her, and tip-toed back down the wooden steps to the ground. Sure enough, the curtains in the window to the right of the back door displayed that same characteristic gap at the bottom. When I stretched up on my toes, the gap made a perfect eye-level peephole and a thrill ran up my spine as I detected movement in the room beyond the dirty pane of glass. There were two of them, I decided, two light-blue shadows in motion. And because the two ominous men were dressed in dark business suits, light-blue looked hopeful to me.

I took a deep breath and rapped on the window with my knuckles.

The movement in the room jerked to a stop, and I imagined two heads turning in my direction. A minute later, two eyes were peering through the gap at me, one eye from each of two faces. And then they were gone. So I rapped again.

This time, the curtains were pulled apart a few inches, giving me a much better view of the people in the room now revealed to be the kitchen. They were about my age or a few years younger; one male, one female, both wearing what looked like identical garage-mechanic jumpsuits of clean, light-blue cloth.

"Open the window." I pantomimed the action, not daring to yell loud enough to make them hear me through the pane of glass.

The two of them looked at each other interrogatively but did nothing.

Rap, rap, rap, I went again, and again pantomimed the effort of hoisting open a window as I smiled reassuringly at them. I just want to talk to you, idiots, open the goddamn window, I muttered to myself.

After another long look at each other and a few words I couldn't hear, the young man finally grabbed hold of the little handle at the bottom and tugged it jerkily upwards. Shrii-iitch, kerchunk!, went the window, the first sound being the squeal of disuse, and the second being the impact with something in the window frame—nails, I suppose—that kept the window from opening more than about four inches. Damn. But it would have to do. The people inside looked at each other again and then, in unison, bent over to peer at me through the four-inch gap.

"Hi!" I said brightly. "My name's Terry." Something about their wide eyes, seen clearly now for the first time, made them look much younger than they otherwise appeared. "I'm looking for Jennifer Stone," I added and then, seeing a flash of fear, "I just want to talk to her about someone she used to know. Not about herself or this place or anything like that."

The two of them straightened up a bit to look at each other again. I was beginning to get awfully tired of that response. When they bent down to eye level again, I suddenly flashed on what this situation reminded me of. It was like they were on an elevator that had gotten stuck between floors. The door opened up and down instead of sideways, but otherwise it was exactly the same. "Wouldn't it be easier to talk if you opened the back door?" I suggested.

"Oh, we couldn't do that!" exclaimed the boy.

"We're not supposed to let anyone in," the girl added. "And besides, we don't have the key." She spoke placidly, apparently undisturbed at being locked in. "I suppose we shouldn't even be talking to you at all," she went on, with the slightest of worry-lines appearing on her young, untroubled brow, "but you look all right...."

"Oh, I am," I said. "You don't have to worry about me. All I want is to talk for a few minutes with Jennifer. She is here, isn't she?"

The girl giggled. "That's me," she said. "I'm Jennifer, but my last name is peaceful now."

"Uh...your last name is...?"

"Peaceful," she repeated. "And this is Gary Peaceful. We're all Peaceful here." They broke into a merry little laugh that chilled the hairs on the back of my neck.

"Fine," I said. "So, Jennifer, what I want to talk to you about is Professor Simpson."

"Ooooh," she glowed, "do you know Professor Simpson? He's my eff eff!"

"Your....?"

"My eff eff. My First Follower. He's the one who brought me to walk the Peaceful Way."

"Before me peaceful, behind me peaceful, under me peaceful, over me peaceful, all around me peaceful," the boy broke in with a smug smile on his face.

I recognized the Navajo chant from my many thousand childhood readings of *The Family of Man*, but coming out of Gary Peaceful's mouth the words sounded like an advertising slogan.

Jennifer beamed at her companion and then, turning back to me, confided, "He's our newest Walker in the Peaceful Way."

"Uh, yeah." My mind was reeling. Could this really be the same Jennifer Stone that Letitia described as one of Simpson's hated "rich bitches," and that Letitia herself considered "very WASP, very daddy's-girl-deserves-the-best"? I'd been expecting a self-centered, sophisticated snob, and instead here I was with Dorothy and Toto. "But about Professor Simpson, Jennifer?"

"Isn't he wonderful?" she gushed. "And you'd never expect it, would you, to find an FF in a place like that, although it's true we most of us do seem to find our FF's in college.... But I guess that's because of the age thing, isn't it?"

"Uh...." I seemed to be saying that a lot in this conversation. "What exactly is an FF, Jennifer?"

"Why, a First Follower, of course." And Toto nodded: I knew that.

"A First Follower of what?" I prodded.

"A First Follower of the Leader," she answered patiently, as if I should have been able to figure it out for myself. "There's only one Leader, of course, but there are quite a few First Followers. I'm not sure how many exactly; not a whole lot, but quite a few. And then there's The Generation. That's us. The Generation of the Peaceful Way."

The two of them beamed at each other, proud and silly as peacocks in a garden. "We'll all be walking the Peaceful Way before we die," said Toto—uh, Gary—earnestly. "You too!" He seemed to offer me that reassurance as a gift and, when he got no response, added, "The generation of the Sixties failed, because they turned to false leaders and the way of violence."

"And That's Not the Way," chimed in Jennifer, the capital letters clear in her voice.

"There is no way to Peace," chanted Gary in response, and then the two of them in unison: "Peace Is The Way."

Now that bit of ritualized dogma I recognized as a quotation from A. J. Muste, one of my parents' heros. Not that anything I'd seen or heard so far about this Peaceful Way of the Leader and his First Followers and a decaying little house with children locked inside by menacing men in business suits seemed to have any connection whatsoever with the work of Muste and the other nonviolent activists I'd grown up admiring.

"So who are those guys in suits who wouldn't let me talk to you, and locked you in when they went away?"

"Oh, they're The Guardians of the Peaceful Way," Jennifer said with nothing but naive sincerity in her voice.

Gary, however, suddenly twitched at her side and muttered, so low I could barely hear, "We're not supposed to talk about it, Jenny."

Jennifer blushed and hung her head at his rebuke.

"Were you a UW student, too, Gary?" I asked.

"No," he replied cautiously, "I was at Eastern." That meant Eastern Washington University on the other side of the state in Cheney.

I wanted to ask about his "eff eff," but his face was beginning to look altogether too reluctant about the whole business. And goddess forbid he should scare Jennifer off before I had a chance to find out more about Simpson. After all, it was Simpson I was investigating, not the Peaceful Way.

"So Jennifer," I said with feigned good cheer, "let's talk about Professor Simpson."

"Okay," she responded, her face lighting up like a Christmas tree. "Isn't he just the nicest man?"

"You used to talk to him after class, didn't you?"

"Oh, yes. He was such a big help to me. At first I thought"—she blushed again—"he was, you know, coming on to me, but it wasn't that at all, not at all. He really wanted to help me, he could see how lost and confused I was, not knowing why I was there or where I was going, and my values all confused, and he just, you know, listened to me, at first, and then he started to talk to me.

Really gradual at first, asking me about myself, what my family's like, my plans for the future, just everything about me. He was so caring, you know? Really interested in me—not as a student or a girlfriend, just me as me, as a human being. It was wonderful." She sighed at the memory.

"And then?" I encouraged.

"And then he showed me the Peaceful Way," she said. "No more confusion, no more questions about what am I doing here, what am I going to do with my life. Because there's nothing more important than world peace, right? I mean, when you come right down to it, what else matters? I could never really get into it before, but that's because everybody always talked about it like it was something political, and I thought, 'What a drag,' right?" She giggled again. "Some of the other kids used to put me down for not being into all that political stuff, and now it turns out I was right all along. It really is a drag, all that arguing and fact-chasing and blaming people, all that political stuff. Because the Peaceful Way is the Way to Peace, and the Peaceful Way is spiritual, not political. It's all so obvious once you see it, but I bet I never would have," she finished fondly, "without my wonderful F.F." And then she added eagerly, "Have you seen him lately?"

"No, actually, I…." Geez, she doesn't even know he's dead! " Tell me, Jennifer, was it Professor Simpson who suggested that you move in here?"

"Oh, yes. He helped me so much, like suggesting I get a post office box so my parents couldn't track me down. They aren't so bad, really, but they're the wrong generation, and I know they'd never understand about the Way."

"So they think you're still in school?"

"Of course. They'd never keep sending me money, otherwise. They'd be out here in a flash and make me go back home. You see, they just wouldn't understand how important this is. So it's not lying, really, it's doing them a favor, making them part of something wonderful that otherwise there's no way in the world they could ever get into. Especially daddy!"

I sternly denied myself the satisfaction of pointing out her illogic, and instead asked, "Did you give the money from your parents to Professor Simpson?" And then silently cursed myself for that accidental past tense. It slipped right by Jennifer, though.

"Oh, no!," she said. "Never! That's not the Way. The money all goes to the Leader. The Leader knows the Way."

"How many of you were shown the way by Professor Simpson?"

"I don't know," she said, with a reversion to her isn't it obvious? tone of voice.

"Don't you talk about it?"

"Who?"

"You. The people in the house. The whatta-ya-callums, the Generation."

"Oh, well, there's only me and Gary right now. When I first came, there was another girl, Chris, but she walked a week ago, right before Gary came."

"She walked? You mean she got away?"

Jennifer looked blank, as if the words "got away" meant nothing to her. "She walked further on the Peaceful Way. It's what we do when we're ready. I'll probably be walking pretty soon."

"Uh huh. And where do you go, exactly."

"California, I think," she said indifferently. "Wherever the Leader leads."

"So you don't expect to see your FF again?"

"No," she sounded sorry but resigned. "They're First Followers because they were the first to follow The Leader, but also because they're the ones you follow first." She saw my confusion and added kindly, "You don't keep following your First Follower. Once you find the Peaceful Way, you follow the Leader. Naturally."

"Naturally," I echoed. This was all getting just too bizarre—the two giggly kids trapped above me in their elevator to Nirvana, and me creeping illegally into a weedy Seattle backyard to listen to their litany of borrowed chants and banal slogans of salvation. The Peaceful Way sounded horribly sad, not to mention criminal and scary, but it was perfectly possible that none of it had anything to do with Simpson's murder. On the other hand, though, I told myself with a slight lifting of spirit, this Peaceful Way racket sounded phony enough to provide an alternative motive. Simpson had lured at least one money-bearing child into the scam, and if he got greedy, maybe got on the wrong side of one of those Guardians—

The sound of a car door slamming brought me out of myself with a start. Jennifer and Gary, I could see, were beginning to tire of crouching at the window, and I was beginning to wonder whether that car door might indicate the return of the Terrible Two. "I guess I better go now," I said, looking up into their faces again.

"Okay," they said, not really caring. And then Gary asked, "You aren't going to tell anyone you talked to us, are you?"

"No. At least, if I do any talking, I won't use any names." They looked worried at that, whether at the thought of their parents or out of fear for the Guardians, I had no way to tell. I didn't want them to be so worried they'd talk about me, though, so I did my best to reassure them. "I'm part of the Generation, too, like you said. Who knows, maybe I'll run into an FF of my own one of these days. But meanwhile, it'll just be our secret that I was here at all, okay? Unless there's anyone you want me to call for you, friends or family or...?" I let my voice trail off suggestively, but the response I got was the one I pretty much expected.

"No!" they both exclaimed, and Jennifer, in a serious big sister voice, said for the two of them, "It's not a good idea just now, thanks."

"Okay. Well, thanks for talking to me," I told them. "Take care of yourselves, you two." The window was down by the time I reached the corner of the house, and as I crept unobserved to the street, I promised myself I'd do something—heaven only knows what, but something—to blow open the locked doors of the Peaceful Way and subject the First Followers to a healthy dose of public third degree.

And if you weren't already dead, Ted Simpson, I vowed to the cloudy skies, I'd get you for this, too.

12.

It was my turn to cook dinner for Everywhere House that week—it was strictly do-it-yourself every night but Sunday—so I headed back to the house with my thoughts all a-roil. I'd heard about cults but never actually spoken to any cult members before, and it left a distinctly nasty taste in my mouth. Theoretically, I believed everyone had a right to make her or his own choices, including her or his own mistakes. If a person wanted to be a Moonie or a Catholic or a Buddhist or a Way of Peacer, well, that was their business, not mine. So why did I find myself wanting to break down the door and carry Jennifer kicking and screaming out of the Way of Peace and back into the Way of Reality? Was it my business if she was happier giving her parents' money to a so-called spiritual Leader, no matter how phony he seemed to me, instead of to the University? For all I knew, her parents might feel worse if Jennifer had left the U to find happiness and personal liberation in a lesbian commune like Everywhere House instead of to save the world as part of the Generation. Granted, that wasn't a fair comparison. We had no Leader sucking up our money, no ominous Guardians at our doors. Getting out of Everywhere House was easy. Getting in, on the other hand.... I was peeling an onion for the soup by that time, and through a haze of tears I flashed back to my dream of Roger at the door, trying to get in.

"Oh, the hell with it!" I said crossly as I dumped a can of tomatoes into the soup pot. Jennifer was not the point here; Barb was the point, the murder was the point. I'd tell the police about Simpson's involvement in the cult, I decided, as a possible source for an alternate motive. And maybe I'd try to talk to Jennifer again, just in case it turned out she did need a friend on the outside. But it wasn't up to me to decide what was best for the woman. It was her life to live, not mine.

I put everything reasonable I could find into the soup pot, shook in some pepper and sea salt, and stumped grouchily off to the bathroom to piss. "Hi," I said shortly, finding Peg on her hands and knees scrubbing out the tub.

She grunted in reply and then, as I sat on the toilet, leaned back, wiping her forehead with the back of her hand, for a rest. She looked comfortably settled there, against the tub, so after I pulled up my pants and flushed, I closed the lid and sat down again. "Peg, did you know Jan is part of the George Jackson Brigade Support Committee?" I asked her.

"No, is she?"

"Yeah, she told me so last night. She's helping put on that workshop about armed struggle." Peg nodded but didn't seem to have anything to say about it, so I prodded her into responding by asking, "Aren't you surprised?"

She thought about it. "Don't seem to be."

"Why not? I mean, I was."

"Well.... She hasn't always been political, I guess, but she decided to move in here, after all, knowing it was a political house, so it's not surprising she's taken up being political herself."

"Yes," I tried to object, "but—"

"And what other kind of political work would interest her? Maybe crisis work, in a shelter for battered women or something like that. But I doubt she sees herself as a counselor; doesn't talk enough, usually. Yeah," she reflected, clearly thinking it out as she went along, "Jan doesn't talk a whole lot, and she doesn't read as much as the rest of us do. Which says to me that maybe she's the kind of person who isn't so comfortable with words. She's more an action kind of person. So maybe that's why I'm not surprised to hear she's GJB SC."

"But," I sputtered, "she's not a bomber, Peg! She's not a violent person, she's not a bank robber!"

"Yeah, but the GJB doesn't call themselves violent. Or nonviolent either, of course. They call it self defense. And they say they've always been careful not to hurt people—or as careful as you can be, once you arm yourselves to the teeth and vow to defend yourselves and your comrades by all means necessary. They did shoot that one policeman, but he shot at them, too, as I remember, and they didn't kill him."

I felt like I was falling back down the same hole I'd fallen through the night before, when Jan first told me she was part of the GJB SC. "I can't believe this, Peg," I said. "You're a Support Committee member, too?"

"No, but that doesn't mean I can't tell the difference between a mad bomber on the loose and a carefully planned action by a group of dedicated radicals."

"You mean you aren't a member of the Committee but you do support what the GJB does?"

"No, actually, I don't. I think their analysis is way off base, and because of that they do stupid things and take unnecessary risks—and put at risk the communities they identify with, one of which happens to be the lesbian community. They seem to think the revolution is just around the corner, and that they're the ones that are going to make it happen. If they were right, they'd be heroes. I just don't happen to think they're right." She shifted her back a bit against the side of the tub before she went on, and draped her right arm over the tub, scrubbing idly at the bathtub ring with the sponge she still held. "On the other hand, maybe they're right and I'm wrong, in which case I am a bourgeois obstructionist who'll be stood up against the wall and shot, come the Day."

I leaned myself back to think but had to jerk myself forward again as soon as the back of my shirt came in contact with the clammy layer of condensation that always coated the toilet tank. "And you think Jan's analysis of the situation is like that? That the revolution is just around the corner?"

"I don't know, Terry. What did she have to say about it."

"She said.... I can't remember her exact words, but she said she'd always been poor, and if you're poor you always know who your enemies are, and that the enemy of your enemy is your friend."

"Well, there you are, then," said Peg. "The GJB is about the only political group in town that, A," she ticked off the points with her sponge, "has out lesbians in it, and B, actually does more than just talk, and C, is willing to come right out and say that rich people are the enemy. No wonder Jan supports them. 'We should support whatever the enemy opposes and oppose whatever the enemy supports,' as Mao always tells us." She smiled sadly, probably remembering the days when she was a longhaired leftist groupie, always on a diet and always ready to argue which male leader was the most right-on. She'd told us all about it one night when Toni scored a big stash of dope and we all got silly together. It was a howl to hear her tell it, and to see her imitate her femmy former self. But when I sobered up, what I remembered was her saying, very softly, towards the end, "I guess I'll always hate myself for letting them fool me into living that lie so long."

"Okay, Peg," I said, "now that you've cleared that up for me, are you ready for another one?"

She laughed. "As long as you leave me enough time to finish this tub before dinner," she said.

"Right. Here goes: There's this woman I see a lot at the Slipper. She's a really good dancer—I mean, really extraordinarily good—and I've always wanted to try dancing with her but been too shy to ask." Peg's eyebrows were beginning to rise and I felt an assumption coming on, so I hurried to head it off. "No, it's not about monogamy."

"Oh, good; I'm tired of that one already."

"I saw this woman at the Furies' fat oppression workshop," I went on, "and I had a chance to talk to her for a minute afterwards. Nothing substantial, really, but at least we chatted. Then on Friday night I saw her at the Slipper again, and I asked her to dance, and it was wonderful. Her name is Dru, by the way. Jan knows her. Okay so far?"

Another nod.

"All right, so here's the question: Am I a racist?"

Peg did a dramatic double-take at the suddenness of the it, chuckled, and said, "Dru is black, I take it."

"Right," I said. "And the thing is.... Well, you know that stereotype about how all black people are good dancers, so what I wonder is, is it racist of me to

86

be interested in this woman, who is black, primarily on the basis of the fact that she's a good dancer. Especially considering I don't know any other black women in Seattle, which maybe in itself means I'm racist, anyway." Sometimes these things simmered in the back of my mind for days and then erupted without my having been aware they were on their way to a boil.

"And now," Peg said, "you want to know whether it would be racist for you to try to get to know this woman, right?" I nodded uncertainly. "Because if wanting to get to know her means you're racist," she continued, "I guess you'd be willing to promise never to speak to her again, eh?" Peg managed to keep her voice serious, but a grin split her face as she finished speaking.

"Oh, for heaven's sake, Peg," I objected, nudging her knee with my foot, "you make it sound so silly!"

She leaned forward to pat me on the knee. "Okay, Terry, I'll be serious. But really, don't you think you're maybe worrying about a problem that doesn't exist except in your mind?" She saw the doubt in my face and said, "I'm not saying racism doesn't exist, or racist stereotypes, or that it's not a problem that you don't know any black lesbians. But listen, think about how you met the women you already know. Ellie, for instance. How did you meet her?"

"At the Slipper," I admitted. "Dancing."

"You danced with her, and then you got to talking, and then...one thing led to another, right?"

"Right."

"So why is it necessarily any different with Dru?"

I pondered the question and started feeling cheerful about it already. "Maybe it isn't any different, really."

"Not for you, maybe," said Peg. "Of course, we don't know how Dru might feel about it."

"What do you mean?"

"Well, just think about it. Think about what it would be like for Dru."

"Because I'm white, you mean?"

"Right. Or rather, not because your skin is pink and hers is brown, but because you come from a different culture than she does."

"We're both lesbians," I said defensively, "we're both women."

"Yeah, but...well, it's sort of like you and that straight woman, the one you don't want to think is flirting with you."

"Letitia?"

"Right. There's nothing wrong with her, is there?" I shook my head. "And yet...." Peg looked at me expectantly.

"Okay, I see what you mean. There is sort of a barrier there. It does seem like a lot more work to be friends with her than with a lesbian."

"Yeah, with straight women you've always got to be watching what you say so you don't shock them."

"And they never understand what's funny, either," said a new voice, and Peg and I looked up to see Toni leaning in the doorway. "You can never tell a joke without explaining it for ten minutes, plus they're so defensive about men. It's like, they can complain about their boyfriends, but the minute a dyke gets critical it's 'man-hating.' Makes me want to puke. And speaking of bodily functions, Terry, how about you shit or get off the pot, hey?"

"Oh, sure, Toni, sorry," I said, vacating the toilet and taking Toni's place in the doorway. "But that makes it sound so hopeless, somehow," I told them both. "If we're not willing to put up with straight women, and black lesbians aren't willing to put up with white lesbians...."

"I didn't say it isn't possible, Terry," Peg replied, "it's just I think there's a reality there you shouldn't ignore if you do have a chance to get friendly with this woman at the Slipper."

"Hey, this sounds interesting," Toni said. "What woman at the Slipper? Not a straight woman, I hope."

"No, Terry's interested in a black woman she's been dancing with—"

"Hey!" yelled Fran at the bottom of the stairs, "is somebody gonna do anything about whatever it is that's boiling all over the stove?"

"Oh shit, the soup," I cried and rushed down to salvage what I could of the household's dinner.

13.

On Monday, I got to class a few minutes early and made a beeline for the chair next to Letitia's. "Hi," I greeted her. "If you're not busy tonight, want to walk up to Phinney Ridge for the sunset? Weather's supposed to be pretty good, I hear."

She looked a bit taken aback, as if wondering what hidden messages might be lurking in my simple invitation. It could have been all over between us right there, but instead she rose to the occasion beautifully. "Okay, Terry. That sounds really nice, in fact. I love to walk, but somehow I haven't been doing it as much since I moved to Seattle. You'll have to tell me where Phinney Ridge is, though. I'm sure I've heard of it, but...."

"I thought we could meet on campus someplace," I told her. "I have to work till five, but if you could meet me near Suzzallo we could set right out and get there in plenty of time." The prof came in just then, so we finished our conversation quickly and under our breath. We'd meet at the George Washington statue at five-o-five.

Fifty minutes later I was out of there, deliberately not noticing what looked like a deep pink flush of nervous anticipation on Letitia's cheeks. It was hard enough maintaining my vow of equal treatment without being reminded, simultaneously, of the two main factors threatening to get in the way of my integrity. To wit: Number one, the way Letitia continued to give off signals of uneasiness around me, signals that read to me like fear, on her part, of lesbianism. And, number two, the way my body continued to give off signals of deep and abiding interest in kissing those soft, pink lips and holding that warm, blushing body next to mine.

Geez, talk about stereotypes, I rebuked myself sternly. But really, I responded in my own behalf, it wasn't my fault I was so inexperienced about flirting. Peg probably wouldn't believe it, given her own unhappy experience as an active participant in heterosexual role-playing, but if anybody'd ever flirted with me before, I hadn't been conscious of the fact. I'd just never considered myself flirtation material. Maybe Letitia was the only person who'd ever looked at me and—because of some hangup about lesbians—thought 'sex,' so then I picked up on her vibes somehow, and that's why I got all hot and bothered with her when I didn't around other women I liked but wasn't involved with sexually. Or maybe, I had to admit, I was just digging myself deeper into a pit of rationalizations. I wonder how she'd react to Barb, I thought, and then felt intensely disloyal, whether to Barb or to Letitia, I wasn't sure. But if I sometimes saw Barb, despite my better intentions, as the prototypical lesbian, and Letitia, it seemed, saw me as.... Ah well, I had two more classes and three and a half hours of work to get through before I'd have to meet her again and face the challenge of figuring her out.

By five the air was misty with unfallen rain, and I wouldn't have been surprised to find Letitia prepared to suggest a postponement of our walk. She looked cold, standing there by base of the statue at five after five, but she smiled when she saw me and said, "I brought along a thermos of tea to drink while we watch the sunset—if we can find the sunset through the clouds." Her cheerful acceptance of the deteriorating weather made me feel cheerful, too, cheerful and adventurous and friendly. Within fifteen minutes we both of us stripped off our jackets, warmed by the climb up the Fortieth Street hill despite the fact that it had begun to rain for real.

I don't know what it is that makes the difference, but sometimes I huddle from the rain and other times I glory in feeling it as intimately against my body as the laws of public nudity allow. That afternoon was one of the glorious times. By the time we reached Phinney Ridge, both of us were thoroughly wet but glowing inside from the walk. I guided us north a bit and a block west of the crest to a tiny triangular park created by the intersection of several streets that seemed to have encountered one another pretty much by accident. Just as we got there, the sky announced that, yes, on further consideration, the sunset show would go on tonight after all.

Looking out over the lowlands of Ballard to the dark waters of Puget Sound beyond, we saw the end of the squall approaching us. Behind it, the sky opened up blue over the islands of the Sound and the mountains of the Olympic Penninsula. We sank down on the park's one bench and put our jackets on again. Letitia got out her thermos, and we passed the cup of hot tea back and forth wordlessly for a few minutes as the moving storm uncovered a corner of the sun and a bright fan of light backlit the last of the approaching rain.

" 'A last long line of silver rain....' " I murmured, and was thrilled to hear Letitia's voice softly add, " 'A sky grown clear and blue again.' "

"Are you an Edna St. Vincent Millay fan, too?" I asked, turning to her in my delight.

She smiled but kept her eyes on the sky as she answered me by quoting further from Millay's "Renascence."

> The world stands out on either side
> No wider than the heart is wide;
> Above the world is stretched the sky, —
> No higher than the soul is high.

The heart can push the sea and land
Farther away on either hand;
The soul can split the sky in two,
And let the face of God shine through.
But East and West will pinch the heart
That can not keep them pushed apart;
And he whose soul is flat — the sky
Will cave in on him by and by.

"I've loved Millay ever since I discovered her when I was about nine or ten,"
I told her after a minute of savoring silence. "We'd just moved into the house
my parents still live in, and I found a whole treasure trove of old stuff up in the
attic, including an old copy of Millay's *Renascence,* all warped and water-
spotted. Later on, if I tried to read Millay to my friends in high school, they'd
just laugh and make fun of her. They thought her poetry was corny because it
rhymed and had rhythm." Even Roger, I remembered sadly, confessed he considered Millay a very "minor" poet. "Some of her short poems are clever," he
admitted, "but...."

"For me it was the basement," said Letitia suddenly, her eyes still fixed on
the scenery. "My parents divided things up into 'okay' and 'not okay,' and all
the 'not okay' stuff was stored in the basement rec room. That's where I found
Millay."

"How did they decide what was okay?" I asked.

"What was safe was okay, what wouldn't compromise them if the neighbors
saw it, or...whoever." She was biting her lower lip again, I noticed. "My parents
were radicals in the thirties and forties. They never actually joined the Party,
but they went to meetings and demonstrations and handed out socialist leaflets. All the usual stuff for first generation Russian-Jews in those days. And
then came McCarthy, and they got scared. They got terrified, actually," she
said, bitterly, "and they never got over it. From then on, they wanted to be
'safe.' And that's all they wanted, for themselves and their children."

"Mmmm," I ventured, "and is that so terrible? To want your kids to be
safe?"

But, "It's not their concern that bothers me, it's their hypocrisy. I mean,
they never really changed their beliefs—which I admit is to their credit,
because a lot of people did—but they hid them so. It's not just that they
became politically inactive, they became politically neutral. Politically dead and
buried. Literally. Anything they considered the least bit tainted by political
content or political implications was hidden away in the basement as if it were
pornography. I spent hours during high school down in the basement listening
to their Lenny Bruce records, and that's when he was still considered a dirty
comic. They never forbid me from learning whatever there was to learn, they

e feel like I'd die if I ever did anything about it. The police would
the house, or there'd be a pogrom, I don't know." She shrugged.
it clear that even if I wanted to be a martyr myself, it would be
y selfish of me to expose them and my little sister to the risk of
My father would be fired and my mother would be an outcast and
my sister would get beat up at school... And it would all be my fault for not
behaving, for not being careful enough."

"Did they come right out and say that?"

"They said, 'Jews have to be careful,' " she answered flatly. "Don't stick your
neck out even when it seems safest, even when everyone else is doing it,
because when the reaction comes, it's always the Jews who get the worst of it."

"And were they right about that?"

She looked at me as if in surprise and then laughed. "Yes, I suppose they
were."

We sat in thoughtful silence for a minute as the darkness grew, and then my
wandering brain reverted to the last topic but one. "Why was Millay on the
'not okay' list?" I asked.

"Because she was a bohemian and lived in Greenwich Village with a lot of
leftists and had affairs with women," Letitia answered readily. As soon as the
last words were out of her mouth, she took a quick look at me over her shoulder. We were sitting close enough that our jacket sleeves touched, if not our
arms, so it wasn't easy to look each other in the eye at that point.

"And is that why you were...interested in her?" I carefully neglected to spec-
ify which "that" I had in mind.

"Because she seemed so free," was Letitia's answer. "Just like you."

"Like me?" I was surprised. "How am I more free than you are?"

She didn't answer right away, and when I shifted myself around to look at
her, her face was slanted down and frowning. "You can do anything you want
to, can't you?" she said finally. "There isn't any plan laid out for you that you
have to either follow or fight against. You can be a lesbian, for example," and
her arms crossed to clasp across her body, "without it being a betrayal of your
duty."

"How does duty come into it?"

She sighed. "Well, to start with, if I don't have children, Hitler won."

My reaction—mouth hanging open, eyebrows peaked in bewilderment—
made it obvious that she'd have to do some explaining.

"It's my duty as a Jew to reproduce, to help ensure the continued existence
of the Jewish people in the face of genocide and anti-Semitism. Besides which,
it's my duty to my parents to provide grandchildren. Sometimes it seems like
the only reason they had me was so they could have grandchildren some day.
And it's not just that they want me to have kids. It's everything. My parents
aren't religious, but they want me to be more Jewish than they are. They

taught my sister and me all sorts of things we ought to do, as Jews, that they never bother with themselves. We're supposed to be more successful than they are and more devout, too. They've sacrificed their lives to bring us up with all these advantages so we could get a good education and marry well and have careers and bring up our children with vacations in Israel and Hebrew school once a week and a respected position in the local Jewish community. I just feel so pressured sometimes. So hemmed in by expectations and traditions and rules. Sometimes I even hate being Jewish. If I were like you, I would be free to live any kind of life I wanted to without all this—"

"Hey, Letitia!" I broke in. "Something came to me just now, from what you've been saying. Let me tell you about Jennifer."

"Who? Oh, her." The lack of enthusiasm was overwhelming.

"No, I'm not changing the subject, Really. Just listen for a minute, you'll see. Remember what you told me about her? She was a spoiled kid, right? A WASP with a rich daddy. Exactly the kind of person you envy sometimes, am I right? The kind of person you think of as being so free."

Letitia shrugged.

"Well, believe me, you oughta see her now. Turns out she hated that freedom so much she gave it away." I described the grungy house with the locked doors and the Guardians who ordered Jennifer to talk to no one. I described the pleasure Jennifer seemed to take from the ritualized repetition of trite credos, and how she'd turned over all control over her own life to the Leader.

"And she's so happy, Letitia," I concluded. "She's so happy she looks sort of foolish. When you look at her face, it's like you're talking to a child, but she's not a child. She's a woman who's blissfully happy because she doesn't have to think for herself any more. From now on, there will be an automatic answer for any question that might arise. She won't have to decide what she ought to do, because she'll always be told what to do, and what she's told will always be 'right' because it comes from the Leader. It's too bad freedom isn't transferrable; I'm sure Jennifer would've been glad to give you hers."

There was a pause, and then, "Jesus!" blurted Letitia, as heart-felt as I'd ever heard her, "what a waste!" She turned towards me on the bench. "What did you find out? Anything that might help you solve the murder case?"

I told her about Simpson being Jennifer's "eff eff."

"I knew I didn't like him," she said, "but that's really disgusting. I bet the whole thing's nothing but a racket. And it sure opens things up as far as motive goes. With people like that, anything could happen. Even one of the recruits might have killed Simpson—somebody who got away from the cult and was afraid Simpson might make him go back. A lot of the people who go into a thing like that must be pretty unstable to begin with."

I had to admit she was right, but it depressed me to think that in order to clear Barb I might have to implicate someone like Jennifer.

"So what's your next step?" Letitia asked.

"Tomorrow I'll call this woman Barb wants me to talk to. Other than that, I guess I need to think about talking to the cop in charge of the case. All I know about him is his name, Lieutenant White, and I have no idea whether he'll be willing to talk to me at all. Not to mention the fact that I get goosebumps just thinking about it."

Letitia looked at me curiously. "You're not afraid of the police, are you?" she asked.

"No. I'm not afraid, exactly, but to picture myself walking all by myself into the police station to interview a Lieutenant about a murder.... Especially now, and as a lesbian."

"Why would that make a difference?" Letitia still avoided saying the word.

"Lesbians are considered suspect these days," I told her. "Back east, a couple communities of lesbian feminists have been raided by police political squads—and in California now, too, what with the SLA—that's the Symbionese Liberation Army, the group that kidnapped Patty Hearst. Some of them are lesbians. The cops say they're looking for evidence of links between radical lesbians and other kinds of radicals, but they always seem to get pretty general about it. Women get put on the spot—even women who aren't very political—just because they're part of the community. All of a sudden there's a cop in their face asking who all was at the newsletter meeting last week, and who danced with who at the benefit dance for political prisoners, and what lesbian house have you ever heard there's a gun in. Things like that, things you might think it wouldn't hurt to talk about, but once they start writing it down.... Say you innocently tell them that you saw X dancing with Y, and the cops associate Y with Z and Z with some bombing case they're working on. You may have landed X in big trouble, even though she probably never even met Z in her life and didn't know Y except to dance with. There are women—lesbians—who've spent more than a year in jail for refusing to answer questions like that for a grand jury," I concluded with gloomy relish.

"So why, then?" Letitia burst out with a shudder. "Why are you getting mixed up in this on purpose?"

I sucked thoughtfully on the inside of my lower lip for a minute before trying out my answer on the both of us. "Because Barb is a lesbian, for one thing, and because she happens to be a lesbian who—for various reasons—doesn't have much support from other lesbians at the moment. She's also the most radical lesbian I know, I guess, the one who's gone furthest with her lesbian politics in some ways. Following out the hardest implications of radical feminist analysis and really letting it change her life. Letting herself feel the consequences of that analysis. Giving up on trying to fit in. Letting herself feel all the way angry—furious—at things that really ought to make all of us angry."

As I spoke, I felt myself gaining in clarity and warmth, and I rushed on with even greater passion. "People don't like radicalism because they don't want to be challenged about the things that would make us angry if we were willing to think about them clearly. Right? People don't like being angry. They don't like angry people. Angry equals 'mad,' crazy, ugly. Most everyone thinks Barb is ugly, but to me she's...she's a work of political art, in a way. She's what I might be—maybe—if I let go of my 'nice-ness' and just let myself go, out to the edge of where my politics ought to be leading me."

A car turned the corner to the southwest of us and Letitia's face, slightly bowed in thought, flashed ivory in its sweeping headlights. Suddenly the dark and the cold were all around me. I wasn't really sure of any of what I was saying, after all. Was I? Did I really know anything about Barb, or was I just making her up as I went along?

"Or at least," I finished lamely, "at least I know I want to get to know her. I want to know if she's on the right track, I guess. And if she is, I want her to be able to be happy, so I'll know it's possible to be radical and be happy at the same time. Because if it's not...."

The silence stretched for half a minute before Letitia turned toward me and said, calmly, "Would it help if I came with you to see the police?"

"Hey, would you really?! That would be great!"

"I'll telephone for an appointment tomorrow. When would be a good time for you?"

Letitia's efficiency sort of took me aback, but I think I managed to react as if planning ahead came more or less natural to me. I pulled some paper and a pen out of my pack and said, "Here, I'll write down my class schedule and my work hours for you." She took the hastily scribbled notes from my hand and read them over before tucking them carefully into a pocket of her canvas carryall. "That's my home phone number at the bottom," I said. "Why don't you give me yours, too, so we can be sure to get in touch with each other as soon as possible. That might be important if it turns out to be hard to schedule the appointment with White."

I had my pen poised over the paper, waiting for Letitia to recite her number for me, but she didn't seem to want to.

"Why don't I call you," she said after a long fifteen seconds of silence had rolled by.

In a flash, I knew the reason for her reluctance. "Don't worry, I'll be discreet," I said, unable to keep quite every trace of sarcasm out of my voice. "I won't say, 'Hi, Jim, this is Letitia's lesbian girlfriend calling.' "

She blushed deep rose. "How did you know...?"

"When I met you at the fountain that day I heard the man you were talking to say 'Say hello to Jim,' or something like that. So I just assumed you probably lived with a man named Jim. No big deal. Right?"

"Right," she said faintly, and gave me her number.

After that, I felt like a heel, of course, but I wasn't sure how to get us back to the easiness we'd had a minute before. Fortunately, Letitia had something else on her mind.

It was fully dark now, and getting colder. Obviously time to go. Letitia was headed for the number Five bus, she said, so we were walking up towards Phinney Avenue when she suddenly said, "I wanted to tell you, Terry. You might want to talk to a woman named Compton. Frances Compton. She's an associate professor in Philosophy, and I think she must have known Simpson pretty well."

"Do you know her yourself?" I asked.

"I've met her a few times. She seems like a really nice person. And I think she'd be sympathetic with what you're doing. She's been at the U for years and years, and finally a couple months ago they decided to give her tenure. The department's been very resistant to women professors, and Frances, well, she's sort of a feminist. Sort of…unorthodox in some ways. I think you'll like her."

We didn't talk about the case anymore after I'd jotted down Compton's name in my notebook, but I felt relieved to have regained the easy friendliness we'd had before the incident of the phone number. In fact, I felt downright giddy with happiness, walking with Letitia through the dark and shiny streets. We heard a cat mew at one point, and both of us turned automatically to look for it. "You like cats?" I asked her.

"I love cats," she answered.

"You should have met Lenore," I told her. "Lenore was the best cat there ever was."

"I never heard of a cat named Lenore before."

And that is why, when the bus pulled up to the stop twenty minutes later, its passengers were treated to the conclusion of my dramatic recitation of Poe's "The Raven." Letitia was laughing so hard she almost dropped her bus fare, and we waved like the oldest of friends as the bus pulled away.

As soon as the bus was out of sight I tore off home and up to my room. "Dear Roger," I wrote. "Here is my phone number. Please forgive me for being such an idiot. I hope you'll give me a call me some time. I miss you. Much love, Terry."

14.

Mailing that letter was the first item on my agenda Tuesday morning. The second item was the call to Carolyn Enderly. "Call between eight and five," Barb had said. It was eight-o-five when I started to dial.

She answered after the fifth ring, just when I was about to give up. "Hello?" she panted anxiously into the phone.

"Is this Carolyn Enderly?" I asked.

"Yes." Her high, breathy voice sounded uncertain.

"My name is Terry Barber, and I'm calling because Barb Randall gave me your name."

"Barbara?" she exclaimed. "Oh!"

I couldn't tell whether that "Oh!" meant "Oh, good!" or "Oh, no!" so I forged ahead regardless. "I'm trying to help Barb—Barbara—by finding out what really happened to Simp—to her ex-husband, and she suggested you as someone who could help fill me in on the background."

"No! Stop that!" she cried, but before I could draw any conclusions she added, "Put that down this minute, Robert. Carefully! You know your daddy would be very angry if his beautiful kachina got broken. Now go get Louisa, please, and bring her in to Mommy. Nicely, Robert. She's just a very little girl, remember, and she can't walk as fast as you."

There was a pause and then, apparently, she became aware again of the telephone receiver in her hand. "Oh," she said. "Oh, yes. What was it you wanted? About Barbara? How is she?"

The last question was spoken with real affection and concern, with real attention, and I warmed towards this unknown Carolyn Enderly. "She's doing okay," I told her, "under the circumstances. She's in big trouble, though, and that's why I'd like to come see you as soon as possible. You're the only one she could think of who might be able to help me help her. Is there a time today or tomorrow when we could have a talk?"

"Oh." It seemed to be her favorite word. "Oh, well, of course I want to help. If I can. Of course. I'm sure there's been some kind of mistake, because Barbara would never—" A loud child's wail cut her off and I heard the receiver clunk against some hard surface. "Oh, Robert, for heaven's sake!" came a cry in the distance.

Approximately five minutes later, as my chances of arriving on time for my first class of the day all but vanished, even if I ran and there was no traffic to hold me up crossing Roosevelt Way, Carolyn returned, more breathless than ever.

"I'm sorry," she said. "They're such a handful. Are you there?"

"Yes," I assured her, "I'm here, but I do have to leave very soon. Can we set up a time for me to come see you?"

"If you think it might help...though I can't quite see...but a friend of Barbara's...." She was having a conversation with herself, obviously, and all I could do was wait for the outcome and hope for the best. "Well, I think...if it's for Barbara...," she decided finally. "Robert will be going to pre-school at ten every morning this week,"—thank god, the tone of her voice implied—"so it would be easier for us to talk if you could come between ten and two."

"Fine," I said, "I could make it today, in fact. Some time between eleven and eleven-thirty—depending on the buses, and on where you live, of course. Is that okay?"

"Oh. Oh, yes. I'll be here."

The background noise level began to rise again, but before she got distracted I managed to elicit her address, thank her, and say "Goodbye till later, then."

I ran like crazy to my first class, the miscellaneous contents of my backpack clunking and thunking rudely all the way, and slid breathlessly into the seat closest to the door just as the class began.

"What happened?" asked Letitia anxiously at fifty minutes plus two-point-five seconds.

"What do you mean?" I asked her anxiously back.

"You were so upset, I thought something must have happened."

"I wasn't upset, I was just late, had to run all the way from home. That's all."

"Well, good. I guess." She smiled ruefully. "I've been sitting here all this time worrying, trying to figure out what might have gone wrong."

"I was on the phone to that friend of Barb's," I told her as we left the classroom together, "and...well, it's a longer story than we've got time for now, but I did arrange to see her later today. Any luck with Lieutenant White?"

"No, but I left a message for him. If he hasn't returned my call by three, I'll call him again. Shall I call you tonight to let you know?"

"Yes, please! I'll be studying for a Spanish quiz so I may not be very coherent, but I'll definitely appreciate a call."

It felt good to be talking to Letitia so much more naturally, and I managed to stay focused on that good feeling until I got off the bus on Capitol Hill and spotted the address Carolyn Enderly had given me that morning. That's when the old what the hell do I think I'm doing here feeling returned, full force.

The house was one of the more impressive ones on the Hill, a well-maintained two-and-a-half stories that had never suffered the indignity of being sectioned into apartments. A house Ellie would die for, I thought, walking slowly up the cement path dividing the rich green of the lawn. A well-to-do house. A respectable, cultivated house. A house befitting the benign power of a family patriarch, and about as far from the Barb of the Furies and Athena House as it was possible to imagine.

I pushed the doorbell button and heard mellow chimes ring out, muffled by the solid wood of the front door. A minute later, the door opened and I found myself staring into the anxious eyes of a woman a few years older than me. Everything about her looked expensive but in slight disarray. Her dressing gown—it looked too silky and fine to be called a housecoat—hung off her right shoulder, and her feathery mules seemed headed in a different direction than her feet. Slightly above my five-feet-four, a tousle of soft, medium-long, medium-blond hair surrounded a face that seemed to have six different things on its mind without being able to concentrate on any of them.

"Oh," she said, so I knew right away she had to be Carolyn Enderly.

"Hi," I said, "I'm Terry Barber. Here to talk about Barb—ara, remember?"

"Oh, yes," she said, "come in. I was just.... I mean, of course, please come in."

She led me across the polished tiles of the entryway and into a living room that resembled her uncannily. All the ingredients of the room looked carefully chosen and expensive, and they should have blended into a harmonious, luxurious whole. The furnishings were either modular and matched or had an air of being chosen to complement some other "feature" of the room, the way the muted brocade of the drapery picked up the pale colors of the Chinese rug filling the center of the floor. Around the edges of the rug, the blond wood of the floor was smooth and unmarked. As Carolyn awkwardly gestured me toward the L-shaped sofa, I was realizing I'd never lived in a house with a room like this, where everything had been bought all at the same time and with a specific room in mind.

It would have looked like a photo in a magazine, except for the film of disorder that covered the room's immaculate self-image like dew on a morning meadow. Bits of children's clothing clung to the back of a chair or peeked from behind the sofa. A large metal fire engine with real rubber wheels lay upside down in the empty fireplace. The lefthand side of the drapes bulged out around a huge, brightly-colored beach ball. And bits of paper, the kind of scraps you get from cutting out paperdolls or snowflakes, seasoned the geometric austerity of the rug.

"We'd have preferred to have the living room in the back of the house, of course," Carolyn said uneasily as she perched on the edge of a chair with wooden arms and pale blue upholstery. She looked around the room anxiously, as if afraid it might not meet with my approval. "...with the French windows onto the garden," she continued, "and...but of course with the kitchen back there, and the stairwell...."

"It's very nice," I dutifully said, and was glad to see her relax into my approval. I was benefiting even then from the aura of ordinariness that, I realized years later, I carry about with me despite my sexual preference, an air of inoffensiveness that renders me unthreatening to a surprising variety of people.

Carolyn pulled a raggedy superhero out from behind her on the chair and settled back to talk. "You're a friend of Barbara's," she said wistfully.

"Yes, but I haven't known her very long. That's why I've come to talk to you."

I paused to shuffle through some questions in my mind, but Carolyn started to speak without any prompting. "She used to come here almost every day, you know. Around nine, usually. She needed a place to work, and that upstairs room was just sitting there, so...."

"She has a room here?" Good grief, Barb was turning out to be one big bundle of surprises.

"It's my sewing room, really," Carolyn explained. "Supposedly. We mostly just stored things there, until Barbara asked if she could use it. Bill doesn't know, of course." The last sentence tacitly swore me to secrecy.

"And she came here every day?"

"Mm hmm." Carolyn smiled gently to herself. "She always brought cocoa, and we'd sneak a cup when she took her morning break. Robert is at preschool then, and Louisa is usually with Virginia, like she is now"—she gestured toward the faint roar of a vacuum cleaner upstairs—"so there didn't seem to be any harm. I never kept any here in the house, of course. Oh, but Bill wouldn't like it anyway; he wouldn't like it at all. And of course, he'd be absolutely right."

The absolute rightness of her husband seemed to make her sad.

"What's wrong with cocoa?" I couldn't help but ask.

"Oh, it's not the sort of dietary habit one wants to encourage in one's children," she responded seriously. "Bill and I talked it all out before Robert was born, and we decided what would be good for them—for our children—and about discipline and, oh, everything. Parenting is a very important job, after all. And of course Bill doesn't have time to.... So it's my responsibility to implement the child-rearing guidelines we agreed upon...."—he says, I added mentally as the flow of her words guttered out again. "But I do love cocoa," she added, with a fast, conspiratorial smile. "And I do miss Barbara so much! All the talking we'd do—and we always have. Talked, I mean. Ever since seventh grade." The wistful note was back in her voice.

"You went to school together?"

"Yes, back in Butte. That's in Montana. I don't know why we got to be such good friends." Carolyn leaned against one wing of the chair's high back and twisted a honey-colored strand of hair around her right index finger. "Her father's really rich, you know. And mine, well, my dad did get to be a shift supervisor, but still…. Barbara's dad is Mr. Randall, the man who owns the mines. So you'd think she could have been best friends with anybody she wanted to. Except…."

"Except?"

"Oh, well, you know. Barbara's always been…different. Her parents said she was difficult, and they were always nagging at her. 'Do this, do that, act like this, act like that.' And she never really looked the way they wanted her to. Even when she lost all that weight our senior year. And then she married Ted, of course, and dropped out of college…." I was about to interrupt the silence with a question when she murmured, "Poor Ted…."

"Because he was murdered, you mean?" I asked, switching gears to take advantage of this new opening.

"Oh…that, too. But…. He was such a jerk, really, and I guess he was pretty hard on Barbara towards the end. The end of their marriage, I mean. She wouldn't talk about him at all any more. Not even with me. But he was kind of pathetic, too. He had such big ideas, and nothing ever worked out for him. Nothing ever worked for him the way he thought it should."

"How did they meet?"

"Oh, he was a junior already at the University—"

"In Butte?"

"Yes, that's right. Bill and Barbara and I are all from Butte. Well, Bill's family's from Missoula, but they've lived in Butte for years now."

"And Ted?"

"Oh, Ted. No, he came just to go to the University. Which tells you something right away, of course. Everybody knows an easterner doesn't go to college in Montana if he's got any choice. They're really prejudiced that way. They'll go to eastern schools first, then west coast, then south. But the plains states are always the bottom of the barrel, as far as easterners are concerned."

"Do you know anything about Ted's background before he came to Montana?"

"Not really. Oh, he told some stories and did a lot of name-dropping. The usual easterner stuff. But nothing specific. Nothing you could be sure was true."

"How did you and Barbara meet him?" After fifteen minutes with Carolyn, the Barbara was starting to sound downright natural to me. Barb, as I knew her, existed on some other plane of existence than that inhabited by the cocoa-loving Carolyn Enderly.

"Oh, well, I guess it was Bill that introduced us, really. The two of them worked at the mine that summer—that would be the summer after Barbara and I graduated from high school. Bill and Ted were between their sophomore and junior years. A lot of the kids from the college worked at the mines during the summer. It was good PR for them, for Barbara's dad, I mean. He always set aside a certain number of jobs for the college kids. And most of us needed the money, of course." The sound of something hitting the floor upstairs drew her eyes to the ceiling briefly, but her mind didn't seem to follow them.

"It was a macho thing for the guys, too," she continued. "You know, proving they were man enough to make it in the mines. Like their dads, some of them. Even though they weren't going to be miners themselves. Because you didn't go to college if you planned to be a miner. A mining engineer, maybe, or some kind of scientist in the industry, but not a miner. You went to college to get away from that. But it was a big deal anyway, for a lot of the guys, to last out the summer down in the pit. Bill did it that year—because they paid good money, he said, but you could tell he was proud of himself, too. And I guess that's why he asked me to find a date for Ted so we could double-date some time. Because he was sorry for Ted, because Ted didn't make it. He didn't last out the summer, poor guy."

"A blow to his masculine ego, eh?" I mused.

"Yes, and being an outsider made it worse, of course. There were plenty of kids ready to make fun of him as a mamby-pamby easterner and all that. Can't hold their own in a real man's world, and so on. The truth is, Ted just wasn't cut out to be a he-man like that. And he'd be a lot better off if he didn't feel like he had to 'make up for it' all the time. In my opinion, of course."

There it was again, that gleam of intelligence followed by a coy expression of self-doubt. Please excuse me if I sound too sure of myself, said her shy little smile every time she accidentally made a statement that didn't curl up into a question at the end.

"So you double-dated," I said, "and then what?"

"Oh, Ted really made a play for Barbara, right from the beginning. Everybody said it was because he knew who she was, who her father was, and maybe they were right, I don't know. He was lovely to her then, though. Charming and thoughtful, giving her flowers he'd picked himself, giving her books to read, helping her study, oh, a real Prince Charming. He said they were—what was it?—oh, yes, intellectually compatible, that's what it was. That old 'I love you for your mind' routine. And Barbara just bloomed. She really did."

"She loved him?" I found myself feeling sorry to hear it.

"Oh, yes. He was her knight in shining armor, the smartest man in the world, the bravest man in the world. He could do no wrong, as far as she was concerned. He was only two or three years older than Barbara, but in some ways it was like a father-daughter relationship. Because Ted liked to be her teacher, but he loved her and seemed to accept her the way she was, whereas her real father was always finding fault. Oh, yes, she loved Ted all right; no doubt about that."

I sighed. "Do you know why they split up?"

"Not exactly, but it was Barbara's idea. The last thing Ted wanted was a

divorce, even though the marriage hadn't helped him as much as he expected."
Carolyn could see by my face how little I understood about Barb's marriage, so she kindly filled me in. "Ted always thought being married to Barbara would help him in his career. Being married to Mr. Randall's daughter, I mean. Being married to all that money. It doesn't really make sense, I know, but that's just how he felt about it. If he was part of the Randall family, he should be treated like, oh, like aristocracy, I guess. He should have an 'in' with the people at the top, and all that kind of thing. All the doors to a brilliant academic career should magically open before him. And they should have money, of course, he and Barbara."

"And they didn't?"

"Oh, Barbara had some for herself. Her parents were never mean to her or anything like that. They love her, in their way. But they thought, if Ted was going to marry her, he should support her. If he'd been a good husband to Barbara, and the marriage had lasted, I'm sure they would have gotten some of the family money eventually. But Ted didn't want 'eventually,' he wanted right now. He always wanted right now."

"When did they move to Seattle?"

"Oh, that was right after Ted graduated. They got married—the Randalls wanted them to wait until he got his M.A., but Ted said they couldn't stand to be separated for so long—and he'd been accepted here at the University, so they came here in...seventy-one?"

"Was Barbara happy about that?"

"Oh, yes! She was very happy to get away from Butte, away from her parents. And she—well, Bill and I went to Chicago then; that's where he went to law school—but she told me before she left how wonderful it would be to be living with Ted, and him going to school, her keeping house and being the hostess for deep philosophical discussions lasting way into the night. It was like a dream for her. She loved it. I'd never seen her so happy."

"So what happened?" Dammit, I knew that woman was capable of happiness.

"Oh, the usual things I guess." Carolyn looked sad, but she looked hurt, too, and I wondered how much of "the usual" she recognized in her own marriage to that paragon of correct thinking, Mr. Bill Enderly, Esquire. "Not enough money, too little space, Ted going out to the University every day, Barbara stuck in a dinky little grad student apartment, Ted feeling resentful of their poverty, Barbara feeling ignored and abandoned. They started to pick at each other, you know, the way it happens when you're just starting out."

The two of us stared bleakly at the rug for a minute before she went on.

"But then he started trying to get her to get money from her family, and that's where she dug her heels in. She'd rather put up with ugly furniture and boring food than ask her dad for money. Of course, Ted took that to mean that she was ashamed of him, that she thought if he was a 'real man' he'd be making enough money and she wouldn't have to ask her parents. But he was wrong. That wasn't what was in Barbara's mind. She just didn't want to have that much to do with her parents. She wanted them to be independent, that's all, no matter what.

"But.... Oh, Ted was feeling inadequate about himself and so he started yelling at Barbara about 'if you were a good wife, you'd be more supportive, I thought I'd married an intellectual equal, not a housewife who can't even keep house.' And he went on from there to everything else. Her looks, her weight, her clothes, her nagging him to spend more time at home, her being bored because she was stupid.... It was pitiful. She'd write me these long letters full of everything he'd said, trying to figure out how much of it was true."

I snorted my disgust, but Carolyn seemed too absorbed in her memories to notice. "Oh, some of it was true," she said. "Barbara wasn't a very good housekeeper, but then, it's hard when you live in a depressing place like that, with so little money, and she'd never really done much housework before, of course. And she did tend to let herself go a bit, I'm sure, because she always did except when Ted was right there being Mr. Right; but blaming her was sure no way to help her feel better about herself. And—oh, it was just a mess, just a mess, with no 'bad guy,' really, when you look at it objectively. They neither of them got what they wanted out of the marriage. That's all. So eventually Barbara decided to get out." Carolyn's eyes focused speculatively on my face as she added, "Of course, I didn't know then about this other...interest she'd developed here in Seattle. And I supposed that must have had something to do with it."

Her last sentence was almost a question, clearly inviting me to explain Barb's lesbianism to her, a task for which I felt monumentally unprepared. "Was it a friendly divorce?" I asked with feigned innocence.

"Oh, no. Not at all. Ted did everything but slit his wrists to get her back. But Barbara wouldn't budge. She came out to see me in Chicago once during that time. That must be about three years ago now. In fact, that was the first time Bill was...critical of her. Not to her face, of course, but to me, after she'd left. He said she seemed 'unbalanced.' Even though," she hurried to add, "he did say it seemed to him that what Ted really wanted was to stay connected to the Randalls and all that money."

"But Barbara stuck to her guns," I said thoughtfully, and Carolyn laughed.

"She certainly did. She didn't want to talk about what was behind the divorce, but she seemed proud of herself for doing it all on her own without asking anybody's advice. And even if she was unbalanced, like Bill said, well, we had a lot of fun those few days she was in Chicago."

"Was she afraid of Ted?" I asked abruptly.

Carolyn's smile faded into a worried frown. "No, I don't think so. Not afraid of him. Not physically. At least, I don't think so." The tone of her voice and the expression on her face said, At least, I hope not.

"Barbara said he sent her a picture of his new girlfriend," I began again after a short pause.

"Oh?" She sounded surprised, but then, "Oh, it must have been in that letter he sent her here."

"Did you read it?" I asked eagerly.

"No." We both clearly regretted the fact. "I wondered, though, what he could have said in it to make Barbara so upset. She opened it right away, but then she hadn't done more than peek into the envelope before she was all of a sudden cramming it into her pocket and running off upstairs with such an expression on her face. If there was a picture of his girlfriend, I suppose that could explain it, although...." Carolyn gave a little shake of the head, as if giving up on that puzzle, and mused, "Maybe she's the one we saw in the restaurant that time. Do you have the picture with you?"

"No, Barbara burned it, she says. But tell me about this woman in the restaurant," I urged. "When was this?"

"Oh, I don't remember, really. A year ago, maybe? Bill was entertaining a client and his wife, and they wanted to try the local salmon so we took them to one of those places at Shilshole Bay. I was quite surprised to see Ted there. I wouldn't have thought that restaurant was his sort of place, really. Too pretentious, I'd expect him to say.

"He didn't see me, fortunately. I didn't really have anything to say to him at that point, but of course I'd be polite to him if we met. We used to be friends once, after all. I didn't speak to him in the restaurant, though, because I wasn't sure how he would react. And with the client there...." Carolyn looked at me with an entirely unnecessary apology in her eyes. Ted Simpson wasn't anybody I'd go out of my way to converse with under any circumstances.

"So what did the woman he was with look like?" I asked.

"Oh, very attractive."

"Beautiful?" I probed dismally.

"No, I wouldn't say she was beautiful. But definitely very attractive. She was wearing a wonderful dress, a deep emeraldy turquiose color with a sheen like real satin." Carolyn sighed. "I wish I could be more helpful, but I only saw her that one time, and from across the room."

I thought of a few more questions to ask about Ted, but nothing emerged that seemed to shed any light on his murder. After the divorce, he'd called Carolyn a few times, trying to get her to tell him where Barbara was. Barbara had sworn her to secrecy, though, so Carolyn never told him anything, and as far as she knew, except for the one letter than came addressed to Barb in care of Carolyn, there'd been no further contact between them. Until the night he died.

"What did Barbara do when she came here every day?" I asked to disipate the chill of that thought.

"Oh, she was studying. She said by the time she went back for her graduate degrees, she'd have her thesis already written." Another wistful sigh. "I used to envy her and wish I could concentrate like that, get back to studying again, but...."

"Could I take a look?"

"At her work, you mean? Well...I don't...."

"She sent me to you," I reminded her, "and there must be a reason. There must be something here that can help get her out of trouble."

Carolyn looked both doubtful and perplexed. "Well, since she sent you...."

Just then the calm isolation of our living room dialogue was interrupted by a series of bumps and whoops from the stairs out in the hall.

"Oh," said Carolyn, looking vaguely in that direction. Seconds later, a woman who looked disconcertingly like my mother was standing in the doorway. She had an upright vacuum cleaner in one hand, carrying it as easily as if it were a broom, and behind her was little Louisa, a blond two-year old, carrying the farther end of the hose-and-nozzle attachment as if were the hem of a princess' train. "Whoop!" she said. "Whoop, whoop!"

"Want I should do this room now, Missus?" the woman asked. Her voice and face remained bland and indifferent, but I could have sworn there was a hint of mischief in the mind behind them. Inside, maybe she too was going whoop! whoop!

"Oh," said Carolyn looking around insecurely. "Would you mind taking Louisa into the kitchen, Mrs. Adams? I'll just show Ms. Barber upstairs, and then I'll be down to fix Louisa's lunch. All right?"

"Fine with me," Mrs. Adams said and then, to Louisa, "Come on, kid, time for a coffee break."

"Cookie," Louisa instantly replied, and the two of them disappeared from the doorway, leaving the vacuum cleaner to await their return.

As with many three-story houses in Seattle, the gracious living stopped after the second story. Carolyn led me to a door at the end of the upstairs hall, and when she opened it I saw a flight of steep, uncarpeted stairs, dimly lit by a bulb in the ceiling. "We don't really use this space much," Carolyn repeated apologetically, "so we've never made any improvements. But Barbara didn't seem to mind. She said it was just what she needed. I won't go up, if you don't mind."

"Thanks," I said, and my obvious sincerity seemed to allay her remaining doubts.

"I'll be in the kitchen if you want me. The room you want is on the left at the top of the stairs."

I stood there alone for a minute trying to guess what I'd find up there in Barbara's room. My imagination wouldn't play, though, so I shut the door behind me and climbed the wooden stairs.

The room at the top of the stairs was small, stuffy, and crowded. Beside the sewing machine, which peered out from under a pile of clothing and fabric scraps, and against the opposite wall where the ceiling sloped down to shoulder level were stacks of cardboard boxes. Each carried a scribbled notation like "extra dishes" and "books—misc."

At the far end of the room was a dinette table. It looked, at first glance, as unused and forgotten as the sewing machine; miscellaneous piles of old magazines and dusty shoeboxes littered its surface, and several articles of clothing hung from its single chair. On closer inspection, though, the table did look more promising than anything else in the room. It's surface wasn't as fully covered with stuff as it appeared from the doorway, and what's more, it was clear from the pattern in the dust that some of the piles on the table had been moved in the not too distant past. I did some experimental rearranging and quickly had a quite usable space cleared. But cleared for what? The light from the window would make the spot perfect for doing homework, for example, but Barb wasn't a student. As far as I knew. Nor did anything on the surface of the table look likely to interest either my Barb or Carolyn's Barbara. The two shoeboxes I peeked into contained, alas, merely shoes. It wasn't until I'd exhausted the top of the table and pulled out the chair so I could sit down and think about what to do next that I hit the jackpot.

Crammed in among more cartons of miscellaneous unneeded assets under the table was one of those ugly plastic laundry baskets, this one in poisoned-lime green with both handles torn half-way loose. I raised one corner of the old flannel nightgown lying on top and there it was. Barb's secret stash: three library books and six of those old-fashioned composition notebooks with the stiff, black-and-white marbled covers and "Barbara Randall" written in blue ink on the black line in the white box on the front of each one.

I was shivering as I hunkered down in the cramped little space and laboriously transferred the contents of the basket to the top of the table. Did Barb know when she gave me Carolyn's name and phone number that she was giving me access to her private notebooks? As soon as I had everything on the table, I tiptoed back across the room to shut the door. Then I put on two of the sweaters hanging from the back of the chair, and settled down to read in the chilly pool of sunlight falling on the array of Barb's secret life.

First the books, I decided, on the "save the best for last" principle. It was disappointing, nevertheless, to find that the books seemed to bear out Barb's story to Carolyn about working on her thesis. All three of them were from the public library and wore the uninviting solid blue or green of the long-ago re-bound. *Labor Management: A Study in the Day-to-Day Dynamics of Human Interaction in the Industrial Setting. The Paper Industries of the Pacific Northwest: A Report, 1960-1970.* And last but not least, *Life on the Line: Coping Mechanisms of Low-*

and Medium-Skilled Industrial Workers. Whoopee. I set the books one on top of the other and pushed them aside. On to the notebooks, then.

They were numbered, I noticed, from one to six, so I opened number one and started to read. "Paperworks Plus," read the first line in the firm but child-ish-looking hand that must be Barb's, "specialty paperbags of all sizes and imprints." An address in the southern end of the city followed, and then: "Oct. 1, 1975, I am hired. $3.25/hr. Line supervisor Mr. Jennings—white, tall & thin, receding brown hair, blue eyes, carries clipboard w/workorders, office w/ glass wall behind backs of workers on line. Other workers:"—I ran my eyes down the rest of the page and flipped to the next. Both pages carried a list of names, mostly women's, with a brief description of each named person. On the third page was a crude drawing, a row of stick figures each labeled with one of the names in the list; the third stick from the right was labeled "me." Another figure, this one labeled "Margie," had an X drawn across it and a note saying, "see p. 50." Sure enough, I discovered, Barb had hand-numbered each page in the notebook. I turned to page fifty and found a paragraph headed *Margie.* On November thirty, according to Barb, Margie had been fired for staying home to care for a sick child. The child's name was Pete, and he was three years old.

Great, I told myself in perplexed exasperation. I come here to find out about Barb and Ted, and instead I get the scoop on Margie and Pete.

It took about twenty minutes of leafing through the six notebooks for their full meaning to begin to sink in. At first, I took the notations as a regular journal, but then I remembered what Jan had told me: "Turns out she never had no job at all." Barb was living off money from her parents, at the same time as she was going home to the Furies in Athena house every day with stories about her hard day's work in the factory. And now here I was in the room where she *really* came every day, and....

Hardly believing my own thoughts yet, I dove back into the library books; there, in three sheets of closely-written paper folded into *Life on the Line,* I found a briefly annotated list of the books Barb had checked out of the library during the past two-and-a-half years. "Gd descrip of emot reality, no gd re: current tech," she'd written for a book called *My 15 Years as a Factory Hand* by Susanna Emerson Bradley. I flipped to the end of the bibliography and sure enough, there were the three books now sitting on the table before me. The Paper Industries book, she'd written, was "excel tech info, esp re: curr market tendcy."

The sun slanted through the window at a different angle than when I'd started, bathing only the extreme right side of the table in its warm yellow light, and I was definitely cold as I leaned back finally to marvel at the magnitude and audacity of Barb's creation. It was a circle, I realized, a recycling of information from real-life to the half-life of academically refined data and then back to quasi-real-life again. Instead of turning her field work into a thesis,

Barb was using other people's theses to create a fictitious reality that she recorded as if she were a social scientist recording her observations in the field. Her five-and-a-half notebooks-worth of notes were a daily journal of those "observations," an elaborate aide de memoire to ensure accuracy and consistency when she reported to the other Furies the day-to-day events in her made-up world.

The woman was a world-maker. A genius. Of a sort. I made a mental note to myself to find out, somehow, just why the hell her genius had been channeled into this particular endeavor, even if it meant tracking down the Furies and submitting my questions into the furnace of their incessant rage.

I thought it unlikely there'd be anything about Simpson in the notebooks, but with so little else to go on I couldn't see letting them pass unread anyway. On the other hand, I'd be late to work even if I left right that minute. The obvious solution was to take the notebooks with me, so I gathered them up and trotted down the two flights of stairs to ask Carolyn if she had any objection.

The vacuum cleaner roared in the living room as I passed by, and I found Carolyn alone in the kitchen amid the detritus of her daughter's mid-day meal. When she heard my step in the doorway, she guiltily dropped the crust of a peanut-butter-and-jelly sandwich back on the table and stood up with the brisk air of someone who was just about to get something done.

"Do you mind if I take these notebooks with me?" I asked. "I'll give them back to Barbara when she gets out, of course, but I need to read them and I don't have time to do it now."

"Oh sure, of course." She paused as if something new and not entirely agreeable had occurred to her and added reluctantly, "In fact, I'd really appreciate it if you would take everything of Barbara's. For the time being, I mean." It obviously made her sad to be clearing Barb out of her house, out of her life, and it made me sad to wonder whether she'd ever get mad enough or confident enough to stand up to her husband.

"Besides these, there's just some library books," I said. "Do you want me to return them?"

"Yes, please. That would be a big help," ashamed and relieved at once.

I panted my way back up the two flights for the books, and to make sure the room was rearranged back to its original state, and then hurried down again. Carolyn met me at the bottom of the stairs and walked with me to the front door. "Will you let me know if...?" She left the question unfinished, but I knew what she wanted.

"I'll call you if I find out anything definite," I assured her, "and meanwhile, try not to worry. Barbara will be glad to know you wanted to help, and we'll just have to trust that the truth will out, sooner or later."

She smiled sadly, gratefully, as she opened the door, and I suddenly thought to ask her, "You said you and Barbara talked a lot, Carolyn. What did you talk about? Her thesis?"

"Oh, no." She seemed to find the thought faintly ridiculous. "We just, you know, talked. Chatted. About, oh, everything. Butte, things we did together there, people we used to know, places we'd like to go...and food, too. Did you ever have s'mores?"

The wistful look on her face was almost unbearable, and I fled from it with no more than a "thank you very much" and a clown-like smile.

A bus caught up with me half-way down the hill, and I rode the rest of the way back to campus with my mind running in idle. Traffic was light in the early afternoon, both in the street and on the sidewalks. Every time my wandering eyes touched on someone walking in the chilly sunlight, I saw them as separate—not just distinct from one another, but as if separated—set apart—by the light they walked in. By walls of space, said the voice in my brain, and as soon as I got to the library and signed in for work I took myself off to the poetry shelves to read the rest of the Howard Nemerov poem.

They were so amply beautiful, the maps,
With their blue rivers winding to the sea,
So calmly beautiful, who could have blamed
Us for believing, bowed to our drawing boards,
In one large and ultimate equivalence,
One map that challenged and replaced the world?

Our punishment? To stand here, on these ladders,
Dizzy with fear, not daring to look down,
Glue on our fingers, in our hair and eyes,
Piecing together the crackling, sticky sheets
We hope may paper yet the walls of space
With pictures any child can understand.

Yes, I told myself after reading the words several times. My memory had been accurate: the poet's image did evoke the kind of terror I felt while riding on the bus, thinking of Barb. What I hadn't remembered, and what gave an extra edge to the eery relevance of the poem, was its title. The poem was called "Projection."

15.

Letitia did call me that evening, as promised. I was deep into a review of tense sequences in Spanish when the phone rang and, ten seconds later, Fran was hollering my name up the stairs.

"¿Como está?" Letitia said in response to my hello.

"So wound up in cramming for this quiz that I feel like I should answer that in the past subjunctive," I told her, "if I could only figure out how."

"Okay, forget Spanish for a minute," she said with a laugh. "I talked to Lieutenant White this afternoon."

"Great!"

"I'm not sure *he* thought so, but he did agree to see us. Is Thursday afternoon at 3:30 okay for you?"

"I'll make it okay," I declared. "What was it like talking to a police lieutenant?"

"It wasn't the easiest conversation of my life. He seemed suspicious of our motives, wanted to know who we were and why he should devote any of his time to us."

"What did you say that persuaded him to see us?"

"First I said we were citizens with information relevant to the Simpson murder case. When he wanted more than that, I said I was a student of Professor Simpson and knew things about his private life that the police might not have a chance to find out."

"Wow." I said soberly. "That's...brave of you, putting yourself out there like that, when it's not even your case, I mean. Not even as much as it's mine."

Her next words sounded a little hesitant. Embarrassed, maybe, I thought. "Well, anyway, it did the trick. He agreed to see us. For what that's worth."

"To me it's worth a lot," I assured her. "Even if we don't get anywhere with him, I really appreciate your taking this on."

We agreed on a time and place to meet Thursday afternoon, and all too soon it was time for me to start thinking Spanish again. I postponed the inevitable for a further ten minutes by calling Ellie, but she was hard at work (as usual) on her law school studies. No matter how happy she was that I called—and judging by what she said and how she said it, my voice was to her like water in the desert—she never lost sight of the three-year clock she'd bet her life on. A time for everything, and everything kept strictly to its time. I told her I'd be busy during the day on Saturday, what with the armed struggle workshop and then maybe visiting Barb again, so she suggested I come by for dinner on Saturday and we'd take it from there. Next thing I knew, her "See you then, lover" was followed by the clunk-( )-dialtone of procrastination ended too soon.

Stretching myself reluctantly back upright, I ambled towards the stairs.

"Still detecting, eh, Terry?" came Peg's wry voice from the living room.

Startled I peeped around the archway. "Hi, Peg. I didn't know you were there." There was a stack of papers on the coffee table in front of her, and a much bigger stack of books on the floor at her feet. Work brought home from the bookstore, I assumed.

"Poor me." She heaved a burlesque sigh. "So easily overlooked. Why don't you come on in and tell me all about it?"

I didn't take much persuading. As soon as I got in the room, though, I was taken-aback to discover that the unidentified scratchy noise I'd been hearing without hearing ever since I came downstairs was one of Connie's moon-music records playing very softly on her horrible little portable record player. She was sitting in a dilapidated easy chair in a corner of the room, a pool of light from a floor lamp focused on the sewing in her lap. So now Connie would know about my detective business, too, dammit.

"I didn't mean to eavesdrop, Terry," Connie said looking up from her sewing. "I hope you won't mind if I don't get up and leave right now, though. This batch has to be delivered tomorrow, and it's taking me longer than I expected. But don't worry: I promise not to blab."

She sounded so reasonable I couldn't very well complain. "Sure, Connie, "I said. "It's not like I don't trust you or anything, it's just that I don't want it to be a topic of general conversation around here. Not yet, anyway. But the way people keep finding out by accident...."

"Aw, come on, Terry, don't keep us in suspense. How goes the investigation?" That was Peg again, of course.

"Well, I guess you heard I'm about to pay a visit to the police. On Thursday."

"Yeah, but why? Are you trying to get something out of them, or do you have something to report?"

"Both," I answered firmly. "I think I may have found another motive for the murder."

Peg and Connie were gratifyingly impressed, so I went on to tell them about the Peaceful Way and Simpson's role as eff eff. Inevitably, the details of the cult struck Peg as ludicrous and laughable, but Connie's response was to worry. "Those poor kids. That's despicable, to take advantage of their vulnerability like that!"

"Yeah," said Peg. "It's hard to believe anybody's that stupid"—Connie tut-

tutted in a reproachful kind of way—"but even so, it's wrong to take advantage of them. And you think it might be dangerous, too. Right, Terry?"

"If you'd seen those Guardians...." I rolled my eyes. "Does anybody act that threatening without being willing to back it up with force at some point?" I gave them the run-down on my scant discoveries thus far, and made the mistake of ending with: "So it seems to me there's a good chance of another motive in this cult business, even if Barb's marriage does look more like a motive the more I find out about it."

Naturally, then they—well, Peg, to be precise—wanted to hear all about Barb and Ted. I was hesitating, reluctant to share her secrets with anyone else yet, even with Peg and Connie, when I heard the front door open and close. It was Jan. "Jan, hi!" I called to her as she crossed the hall. "Haven't seen you for ages!"

"Hey, Terry," she said with a smile as she returned to lean in the wide arched doorway. And "hey," she added, nodding to Connie and Peg.

She looked so good to me, her long body curved against the scuffed-up woodwork, blonde hair gleaming dully over her forehead. Her eyes, I noticed again, were wide and direct when she looked at me, but there was almost always something guarded about the set of her mouth and chin. In general, her body language said to all of us in Everywhere House, I trust you—but just so far. With me, though, lately, I thought maybe I detected a willingness to go a bit farther than that. I wanted to draw her in, to keep her with us for a while. "How's the planning going for the workshop?" I asked her.

"Pretty good," she replied. "Hell of a lotta work, though, and only three days to go."

"You know, Terry and I were talking about it, Jan," said Peg, "and we wondered why you got involved with the GJB."

Jan shrugged herself away from the doorframe in an irritated sort of way and looked from Peg to me. "I don't know as I'd say I'm 'involved' with the GJB. What I do know is I don't like nobody going around saying I am."

"Point taken," Peg said easily. "I haven't and I won't. What Terry's getting at, though, is why you decided to work on this armed struggle workshop instead of doing some other kind of political work."

Jan didn't look very reassured by what Peg said, and in fact there was starting to be a definite feeling of strain in the air. Out of the corner of my eye, I saw Connie look up from her needlework and measure the two of them with her eyes before returning to the delicate stitching of lace on peach-colored satin.

"Two reasons," Jan said finally, after she'd gazed silently at Peg for a minute, her mouth a tight line. "Maybe three. One is, I got respect for the Brigade. They're putting their ass on the line more'n anybody in this city, far's I can see."

"But isn't there a better way than armed struggle?" Peg asked. "I mean, violence is self-perpetuating, isn't it? And—"

"And for reason two," Jan interrupted her, "because most of the white people in this town that call themselves political don't know a damn thing about what's real. They read in the paper, GJB terrorist brigade, and they think, I hope the police catch 'em quick and lock those nasty, violent people away. They say they want change, but they can't do without their precious police to take care of 'em, and they don't never notice that it's the police who're doing the violence, the police who're the terrorists for anybody that's not white skinned and upper-middle class in this world. Anybody like me, for instance."

There wasn't much any of us could say to that, and after a short silence Jan continued, "That's for two. And for three, because before people can get active, they gotta know how. They gotta know the possibilities. And for that, if we don't educate 'em, sure ain't nobody else gonna do it for us."

"Maybe," Peg said, obviously unpersuaded, "but why do you call it an 'Armed Struggle Workshop'? Don't you think that weakens it? I mean, how many of the people you want to educate are going to be attracted by a title like that and how many of them are going to be scared off? Maybe if you'd called it—"

"Fuck that shit, Peg!" Jan suddenly exploded. She was leaning forward slightly now, her arms down at her sides but her fists clenched. "Where'd you get off telling me how we oughta educate? You and that sad-ass excuse for a bookstore! Who the hell ever goes there, huh? Nobody, that's who. Nobody but you and your tight-ass little group of middle-class book-heads. And you trying to tell me about education. Shee-it, ain't nothing in that store of yours worth reading, even if anybody could afford to buy it, which mostly they can't. Nothing in there but books *by* college professors *for* college professors. So who the fucking hell you think *you* educating, girl?"

Peg was leaning back, as if blown against the back of the couch by the force of Jan's anger, and Connie had let her hands go idle as she looked from woman to woman across the room, her eyes narrowed in consideration.

"Well, christ on a crutch!" Peg shouted back. "What a bunch of self-serving balony! No, I mean it, Terry," she told me as she motioned a half-formed protest back into my open mouth. "Maybe you deserve a chance to spout off like that, Jan, and I'm not gonna tell you you're wrong about how you feel. But I'll be damned if I'll sit here and let you get away unchallenged when you defend tactics like the GJB's as a response to the mess this country's in. I mean, my god, just look at the results! How many women have been endangered by those tactics already? How many new police files have been opened on lesbians who don't know shit about what they're doing? How many—"

Again Jan cut her off. "One fucking hell of a lot, I hope," she yelled, and then, at a volume more suited to the shocked silence, "Don't you think it's about time some of you-all got a taste of what it's like?"

"Not if it means supporting murder, I don't!" was Peg's stout reply.

"Murder?" Jan's incredulity was too big for her slender body to contain or control, and it propelled her out into the middle of the room. "Here I come talking about serving the people, about leading the people in resistance, and here *you* go talking about murder. If that ain't just—"

Peg bounced up from the couch, and the two women stood face to face on either side of the coffee table, the air hot and electric between them. "Damn it," she spit, "we're on the same side, Jan. We are. But I can't stand to see you throwing yourself away for the sake of some make-believe revolution that'll only get you and a lot of other women hurt, dead, or in jail."

Jan's elbows were cocked, her long legs bent as if to spring—whether forward or away, I couldn't guess. A moment later she shook herself loose and said quietly, bitterly, "Sometimes you just gotta do something, girl. Something big, you know? Sometimes you gotta go with what you've got; you gotta decide: are you gonna be with the ones who are out there fighting, the ones who have some kinda plan anyways, some kinda answers. Or are you gonna let them go down alone and everything stay the same as always. Your life going by, and getting smaller every fucking day." She paused, and the light from the lamp flashed yellow off her hair as she turned to go. "Sometimes you just gotta hit back and to hell with it," she said. We heard the door of her room open and close in the silence.

Peg fell back onto the couch and buried her face in her hands. "So much for reasoned political dialogue," she said a minute later, looking up with an unhappy half grin. She looked wearily at the piles of papers and books in front of her. "Shit. Guess I'll call it a day."

The three of us told each other goodnight, and Connie obviously didn't share my surprise that when Peg left the room she turned, not right and up the stairs to her room, but left and out the front door of the house.

"Do you think she'll be all right?" I asked.

Her calm but none too comforting reply was: "Which one?"

16.

When the alarm clock buzzed me awake on Wednesday, the wind was smashing rain against my bedroom windows, and the floor felt cold as winter on my bare feet. I was the only one in the house who got up; everybody else must have heard the wind and the rain and decided to sleep in. Ordinarily that made me feel virtuous and hardy; but that particular Wednesday it just made me grouchy. And this was another of Barb's visiting days at the jail. I knew I had to go. It was the only responsible choice, the only decision consistent with feminist integrity. But boy oh boy did I hate the thought of it.

The rain had tapered off a bit by the time I left the house, but it was too late. I was already depressed. My first class was the one with Letitia, as usual, and that should have been some help. Maybe she'd be free for lunch, I suggested to myself with forced cheeriness; wouldn't that be nice? For the first time ever, though, Letitia wasn't there when I reached the classroom, and by the time she arrived the class was already starting. So ask her afterwards, said my inner Pollyanna. Sure. Except that as soon as the class ended some other woman latched onto Letitia and locked her into a discussion of some point the prof had made. I hung around as long as I could without being late for my next class, and then took off even grouchier than before.

By the time I plodded up the hill to Everywhere House after work that afternoon, I was not a very nice example of the species. My only accomplishment for the whole day was to make a Thursday lunch-time appointment with Frances Compton, the Philosophy prof Letitia had recommended. I'd called her office from a campus phone at the HUB, and her deep, rich voice should have been a balm to my spirit. Instead, it made me feel about twelve years old in comparison, and I felt like I was babbling as I tried to explain why I wanted to see her. After I hung up I decided she probably gave me the appointment just to get me off the phone. I thought about buying myself some special treat on the way home to make up for having to go down to the jail later. But it was raining still, and the mere thought of how I felt in that jail visiting area made me feel too tired to walk out of my way, even for something as thrillingly illicit as a Cadbury chocolate bar. Besides, I told myself with the defiant pessimism of a woman rubbing salt in her own wounds, the way things are going for me today, they'd be all sold out of the kind with hazelnuts, anyway.

I dropped my front door key in a puddle where the roof of the porch leaked, fished it out with a frigid hand, and clomped gloomily into an apparently deserted house. The kitchen would be too depressing, I decided, empty, nothing interesting to eat, so I headed up the stairs to my room. At least I could change to dry socks—if I had any clean ones on hand. The door to my room was standing ajar, though I was sure I'd closed it when I left that morning. Oh well, as long as it's not my last pair of dry socks, they're welcome to it.

But it wasn't a borrower that had entered my room, it was a communicator. Tossed casually on the surface of my desk was a non-narcotic anti-depressant to rival all of those over-prescribed pills the mind doctors love giving to women. The note said, in Fran's wandering script: "Barb called (from jail!!). Don't come today, come Saturday. (I told Jan. She said she'd talk to you later.)"

I did a little dance with myself between the end of the bed and the dresser as the whole day's worth of dread was transformed instantaneously from a bellyful of puddle water into a headful of steam. I don't have to go, I don't have to go, sang the steam as it whistled out my ears.

Once I was through dancing, though, and had dry socks on, I found myself faced with the need to, after all, do something with the evening that lay ahead. Final exams were imminent, so studying was always an option. But first I'd have something to eat.

The house was absolutely silent as I creaked my way downstairs; with the rustle of Fran's note in my pocket the only sign of life. Cold rain still blew intermittently against the dark windows, and I was feeling downright spooky by the time I'd crept through the dusty cave of the living room and flipped the light on in the kitchen. Welcome to Everywhere House, I told myself with a return of the grouchies, the empty heart of the Lesbian Nation.

The refrigerator and I both sighed aloud. "So what's your problem?" I said, just to hear myself speak. The sound of my own voice made me feel more at home, but not a half-inch more cheerful. In fact, by the time I hauled out a chair to sit on and slapped my tahini sandwich—made with the heels of the last vanished loaf—down on the table, I had reached the point where the only way out of grouchy is through a good bout of mad. "Come Saturday," indeed! What nerve! As if I were at her beck and call. Well, I'd show her. I'd show her I could be just as furious as she could. And I promptly set out to do so.

I unlocked some door deep in my heart, a door I usually tried to pretend wasn't even there, and let the anger pour out, pushing against the edges of my mind, looking for something or someone to aim itself against. My memory had no trouble providing targets.

There were Marianne and Brenda, and even my "best friend" Melinda, giggling in the locker room, sneering and pretend-retching over the dirty details of the female body. Brenda had found and brought to school a magazine belonging to her older brother, and all that week the thing for seventh-grade girls to do was chant "ooo, sicko, sicko, sicko," ritualistically purifying themselves from the taint of the so-called lesbian sex featured in the magazine. They didn't know about me. Hell, *I* hardly knew about me. But it hurt me, it hurt me bad, and after that the world was a different place for me.

The world was where the high school boys hid and flaunted their own magazines, and the high school girls still sneered but devoted their lives to becoming those women I could never be. The world was where Janice, the summer after we graduated, was raped by a man she met at a midnight rock concert and even Roger, after he said, "That's terrible," said, "She should have known better." The world was all the teachers I ever had, including my last quarter English prof, who believed real life was only for men because a woman "can always get married," as if marriage was any guarantee of security, or even of safety, for most of the women in the world.

As I let myself fill up with anger, I felt myself growing stronger. I felt myself expanding, my body taking on weight and mass, my face growing bigger and rounder and flatter, my eyes going flat and hard. In a way, it was scary being so angry, but it made me feel a lot bigger than usual and it made me feel closer to Barb, too. You see, Barb?, I sent a grimly triumphant thought wave towards her cell. You see, I can be furious, too.

I was leering like a maniac at my empty glass when Jeanne wheeled in through the kitchen door with her friend Gretchen. "Hi, Terry," she said, and then, "Hey, what's wrong? You look kind of…. Are you okay?"

"Sure," I said, and it was immediately true. "Kind of bummed out by coming home and finding nobody around, that's all. Been one of those days, you know?"

"Do I know!" She handed Gretchen the glass of water she'd just poured and rolled her eyes at the both of us. "Try being a printer, if you really want to know about 'one of those days'! And this weather, yuck, it's enough to make you think about changing planets."

"'There's a hell of a good universe next door,'" said Gretchen unexpectedly.

I laughed, delighted, and gave her, "'He spoke. And drank rapidly a glass of water.'"

"Hey, all right! Another secret cummings fan in the community!" Gretchen had reddish brown hair like fluffy wire and reddish brown freckles across her broad, light-brown nose. "We're running our lines from different poems, but at least we're coming out of the same collection, eh?"

"Somebody wanna tell me what's going on here?" Jeanne said.

"e e cummings, you philistine Franklin-ette," Gretchen answered her.

"Oh, that again," grumbled Jeanne with a grin, just as I opened my mouth to say, "Okay, now I'm the philistine. What's 'Franklin-ette' signify?"

Jeanne and Gretchen chuckled and bumped hips. "That's our Secret Sorority," Jeanne told me. "Dyke Daughters of Franklin. As in Benjamin. So many lesbian printers around, stands to reason we need our own professional networking association. And you got to admit, there's no more respectable sponsor than good old Ben-boy."

"Our motto," said Gretchen, her mock-serious tone barely masking a giggle, "is: Every dyke printer as high as Franklin's kite."

"Oh, so that's it!" I said, finally catching on. "You've been smoking yourselves a little end-of-the-day relief, huh?"

"Just a little," admitted Jeanne, still laughing. "Just a little, little, bit. Butt. Just a little, little butt."

That set them both off again, and made me wish I'd been around for the joint as well as the aftermath. Ah well, I consoled myself, even stoned they make better company than you do tonight. So when the two of them asked if I wanted to go along to the Crescent with them, I didn't hesitate—except to ask whether they had a car to go in. They did, so we got in it and, giggling madly, drove off into the night.

The Crescent was one of those "discreet" women's taverns. From the outside it looked like a largish storage shed propped up against the blank end wall of a block-sized building containing storefronts below and cheap apartments above. The dull yellow door opened not on stored boxes and bales but jukebox music, the salty smell of beer, and waves of cigarette smoke that caught and complicated the meager light. Bars have never been my major hangout, but the Crescent was as familiar to me as any and I felt comfortable there. Gretchen found a place to park across the street, and the three of us dashed through the rain and piled on in.

"Mmm, listen to that!" Jeanne exclaimed the minute we were through the door. "They're playing our song, lover—come on!" She put her arm around Gretchen and tried to pull her off towards the little dance floor hiding in an alcove off the main room of the tavern.

"Just let's pick up some suds first," Gretchen replied. "My throat's so dry."

We each collected a glass of draft from Laurie behind the bar and when the two of them turned toward the dance floor again, they spotted a friend of theirs sitting back against the wall behind the door. "Hey, Sarah!" they chorused, and then Jeanne said to me, "You know Sarah, Terry?" I shook my head, and Jeanne hooked her arm through mine to pull me along. "How's it going?" she asked the woman sitting alone at the table and, without waiting for an answer, "Sarah, this is Terry Barber, one of my housemates, Terry, meet Sarah Nakasuma, one of my workmates."

"One of *our* workmates," Gretchen corrected her as soon as she'd swallowed the first third of her beer and deposited her glass next to Jeanne's on the table. "Talk to ya later, you guys. Right now, we got some dancing to do."

I felt awkward standing there with a glass of beer in my hand staring at somebody I didn't know, so I sat down and added my glass to the collection on the table. Sarah was a slender woman about my own age, with straight, firm eyebrows, a nose just big enough to escape my bias against the too-small variety, and a fairly wide, pensive mouth. "You're a printer," I said, hoping that would sound enough like a question to start a conversation.

"Yeah," she answered. "At least, I'm on my way to being." The way she said it wasn't quite reluctant, but she didn't sound overjoyed to have my company, either. I was just beginning to think about how to remove myself as gracefully as possible when she shifted herself forward a bit in her seat, as if she'd made up her mind to accept my presence, and told me more. "The women at the press have taken me on as an apprentice. It's what I really want to do, but I can't hack the Community College program, even if I could afford it, which I can't, so they're letting me learn it from them instead." Now that she was talking I could see that my first impression of her was wrong. It wasn't that she didn't want to talk, it was just that she'd been alone and needed a few seconds to readjust.

"That's neat!" I said, meaning it.

"Yeah." She grinned wryly. "It's also not so easy. I work nine-to-five downtown every day, then race up the hill and put in two or three more hours at the press, not to mention Saturday. Doesn't leave me much time and energy for anything else. But I love the work. I love the paste-up, I love the camera work and the darkroom, and I love to see the pages coming off the press." She was leaning forward now, her arms flat against the table from the elbows on down, and a bubble of red from the light behind the bar shone in her short black hair.

"How long have you been doing it?" I asked, and then, "Is it something you've always been interested in?" She didn't need much from me to keep her talking, and I was fascinated by her fascination with the process of printing, if not by the details of the process themselves.

"Do you think you'll stay on at the press as a paid worker after you're through being trained?" I inquired after she'd taken me step by step from mock-up to final product.

She paused and frowned, folding her hands together on the table and studying the inside of her joined palms. "I don't know. Maybe. I really appreciate the training, but I don't always agree with their politics. What I'd really like would be to have my own press. But...." She shrugged her hands apart, and neither of us needed to say it: Money. Always a downer.

I cast my mind around for a less fraught subject, and my eyes lit on the familiar Armed Struggle Workshop leaflet lying on the table. "Did you work on this?" I asked.

She gave it no more than a glance and said, "Yeah. They got a break on the price, too, even though it's not an expensive job: just one color, no paste-up or anything."

"Are you going to the workshop?"

"I don't know. Haven't decided."

"I know one of the women who's putting it on," I told her, "but I think I'd go anyway. I have a lot of questions about armed struggle—because I basically know nothing about it, I guess."

"Yeah, well, I'm pretty tight with my time these days," Sarah said. She hesitated for a few seconds, watching herself draw swirls on the table with the wet bottom of her beer glass. "And besides, no offense to your friend, but I'm not sure this workshop would have the kind of answers I'm looking for." She smiled a little shyly, a little shrewdly, and added, "Hell, I'm not even sure they're asking the right questions."

"What do you mean?"

"Well.... I have my own separatist perspective on things and—" she broke off when she noticed my gaping jaw, and her expression hardened. "Surprised, eh?" she said with a challenge in her voice. "Okay, which is it? You thought all separatists were white, or you never thought a dainty little 'oriental' woman would ever be anything as tough and pushy as a separatist?"

It was obvious this was a scene she'd been through before, and I was very glad to be able to tell her, with complete honesty: "Neither, as a matter of fact." She looked skeptical, if not incredulous, so I hastened to explain. "I admit I was surprised to find out you're a separatist. And I admit that part of the reason is... well, you probably won't like it: I was surprised because you're so friendly and reasonable. And because a separatist is exactly what I need right now."

Now it was her turn to be surprised. "What's that supposed to mean?" she demanded with wary curiosity.

I took a deep breath. "You know Barb Randall, from the Furies?" Sarah nodded cautiously. "Well, she's in jail charged with murder, you know"—another grudging nod—"and I'm trying to help her. I'm trying to find out who might have killed the guy she's charged with killing." Sarah's eyebrows had been rising steadily and were now totally hidden behind her bangs. "Well, one of the main people who's helping me is a straight woman. Letitia's okay—I mean, I like her, and she's not homophobic—but she's...straight. She doesn't really know that much about lesbians and lesbian culture, not to mention lesbian politics."

"Why should she?" interjected Sarah almost belligerently.

"Well, no reason, really. Except she does seem interested. I mean, personally interested. As in: most lesbians start out thinking they're straight, right?" Sarah merely shrugged. "But anyway, she is helping me, and Barb is a separatist, and I just know that one of these days I'll need to explain to her—to Letitia—just exactly what separatism is all about. She's bound to be curious. And the trouble is, I'm not sure I really know myself. What separatism is all about. And that," I concluded raggedly, "is why I really need to talk to a separatist right now, and why I was surprised to find out I already was."

About three sentence fragments from the end of that little speech, Sarah's right hand had risen from the table, palm out, and started waving back and forth a little bit as if to say, Hey, hold on there, hold on. "Whoa," she said, "you can't go around explaining separatism to people by Barb. That would be like me introducing you to my family by explaining the DAR." It took a minute for me to recognize her "you" as meaning me-as-white-woman, and it would have taken a lot longer than that for me to work through the analogy. For better or worse, Sarah didn't give me time to think about it. "There are extremes in every political sector—just look at the left and the GJB, for example—but those extremes don't invalidate the whole sector."

Now it was my turn to say Whoa. "Wait a minute," I said, "you're going too fast for me." I could see her decide to cut me some slack as she consciously relaxed back into her chair. "Are you saying Barb isn't a separatist?"

She opened her mouth for an immediate answer but then stopped short, the thinking she was doing pulling together the inside corners of her eyebrows. "I don't know," she eventually replied. "I guess there isn't any reason she can't call herself a separatist if she wants to. What's important, though, is that you know there's more to separatism than the kind of sound and fury you get from someone like Barb."

"I find it attractive, in a way," I admitted. "The sheer power of all that anger. And the Furies *have* done some work in the community. They were the first ones to talk about fat oppression as far as I know, and their stuff on self-defense is interesting, even if I'm not ready to go out and buy a gun like they recommend."

Sarah looked at me speculatively. "Is that why you're trying to help Barb?" she asked, "Because you like her politics?"

"No, that's not it. In fact, like I said, I don't feel like I even know her politics. I mean, I know what the Furies say about fat oppression and guns and a couple other topics, but I don't have any feel for what it means when a woman calls herself a separatist. It's got to mean more than just 'I don't work with men,' right? By itself, that's just a preference, not a political analysis."

The shy, clever smile crept sideways onto Sarah's face. "A preference can play a mighty powerful role in putting together an analysis," she said, and I grinned back at her in recognition. "You're right, though. There is a lot more to separatism than that. For me, it's basically a tactic, but it's the essential tactic. Given the dynamics of sexism in this society, the way it reinforces the dynamics of sexism in minority communities, and the way racism works to keep women locked up inside communities defined by aspects other than gender, I just don't believe women can develop an autonomous politics without autonomous organizations. And without autonomous organizations—without separatism, in other words—we'll never be able to construct truly woman-centered analyses on which to base our work against either sexism or racism as experienced by women of color. As experienced by me, for instance."

She looked at me inquiringly, as if to say Are you with me so far?, and I sighed. "You make it sound so reasonable," I told her, and she laughed.

"It is reasonable," she declared, "and that's why it's so frustrating to see things like this taking up so many lesbians' time." She tapped her fingers against the leaflet lying on the table. "Why can't they bring themselves to put our concerns first? Why is it always male-led movements and male analysis that get most women's support—even most feminists' and lesbians' support?" She looked at me in silence for a minute and then said, "Well? I explained separatism to you, now it's your turn to explain non-separatism to me. You're going to this workshop on Saturday, you said. Can you tell me why?"

My brain felt the size of a pea as I struggled to find some words that would sound as reasonable as Sarah's.

"I don't mean to put you on the spot here," she added kindly when she saw the state I was in. "One thing about calling yourself a separatist, you get used to challenges so you tend to clarify your politics in self defense. I didn't used to be able to lay it all out like that—which is my Readers' Digest Condensed Version, you understand, sort of 'Intro to Separatism 101'—until I got jumped on a few times by anti-separatists and didn't have anything to come back at them with. That's one of the advantages of separatism, I guess, or one more proof that it's the right way to go. I mean, no offense, but look at you. You're a political lesbian, right?" I nodded weakly. "Yet you've never gotten your analysis together enough so you can use it to explain the basis for your political decisions. Now, doesn't that tell you something? Don't you think maybe it's indicative of some flaw in your process that your own politics—the politics you assume are your own—aren't accessible to you as a reasoning tool?"

"You mean I wouldn't feel this stupid if I were a separatist?" was all I could think of to say.

"Oh, no! Wait! I didn't mean to do that, really!" Sarah reached out towards me across the table. "Damn. I'm sorry to come on so heavy and—" She broke off in confusion and then resolutely admitted: "And I'm sorry, but I can't remember your name."

"Terry," I told her.

"I didn't mean to make you feel stupid, Terry. Just the opposite, in fact. I mean, what I meant was the opposite. Can you see what I mean?" She ran her hand through her hair, and the red blob of light became a many-legged star. "It's this kind of politics"—tapping the leaflet again—"that keeps women thinking they're stupid, because this kind of politics isn't our kind. It isn't the way we think. It isn't the way we live our lives. It's not shaped the way we are. So no wonder women who want to be political and have only this kind of politics to follow wind up thinking they're stupid. As far as women are concerned, this"—tap, tap—"is stupid politics. That's what I meant to say."

In my mind, images of Jan mingled with the blare of the jukebox and the memory of Barb's white face behind the visiting-room window at the jail. I'd expected to be seeing her tonight, I remembered, and instead here I am listening to this intense, shy, friendly, prickly woman named Sarah who expects me to hurt her but can't stand the thought that she might hurt me. What a world. If Roger were here, I said to myself.... But, no. I couldn't be sure of that anymore. We'd been apart too much and too long for me to be sure we'd be on the same wavelength all the time. But if Letitia had been there, I might have said, "Are you a James Baldwin fan?" And I would have recited his words: "The moment we cease to hold each other, the moment we break faith with one another, the sea engulfs us and the light goes out."

Instead, "Sarah," I said, "I guess about the only thing I'm sure I really do understand right now is that you didn't mean to hurt my feelings." She looked a little bit comforted by that but not enough. "It's okay," I told her. "I'm used to being confused."

We were polished off the last dregs of our beer, when suddenly there were Jeanne and Gretchen again. "Time for us to be heading home, Terry," Jeanne said after sliding the rest of her beer down her throat. "Are you about ready to go? Or would you rather wait and catch a ride with Jan?"

"Jan's here?" I asked in surprise. It felt strange to think of Jan walking in and my not knowing she was there.

"It's time for me to get out of here, anyway." Sarah scooched back her chair and stood up. "I won't be able to keep my eyes open at work tomorrow, and I don't want to miss that three-color run you promised to save for me afterwards."

"You'll be there by five-thirty, right?" asked Gretchen. "If we can get started by quarter to six...."

Sarah and Gretchen had started towards the door, still talking three-color run, when Sarah looked back to say goodnight. "I enjoyed talking to you," she said politely, with a resurgence of her original shyness. "Good luck with your... project."

"Thanks," I said, "...for the explanation. Hope I'll see you again some time." She smiled and turned back towards the door.

Whew! I said—or felt—to myself, and then Jeanne was asking me again, "Are you coming with us or not, Terry?"

"I am, but I want to ask Jan something first, okay?"

"Long as you're quick about it," was her answer, so I blitzed off as fast as possible through the increasingly crowded tavern.

Jan saw me coming and greeted me with a nod and her usual "Hey."

"Excuse me for interrupting," I told her and the other two women at the table. "My ride is waiting so I've only got a minute."

"No problem," said one of the women, and the other one spread her arms in a shrug that carried the same message.

Whether for reasons of her own or because she could tell I felt shy about asking my question in public, Jan immediately stood up and said, "Come on, Terry. My turn to buy a round." She put her hand on my arm to steer me back to the bar.

"Can you get me in to talk to Fennel," I asked as soon as we got there. "She's the one of the Furies who didn't leave town, right?"

Jan leaned her back against the bar and stared down at me thoughtfully. "She's still here all right, but it won't do no good to have me fronting for you. Fennel'd sooner talk to you than me. Sooner talk to almost anybody. What d'you want with her, though?"

"Just to find out more about Barb, and about that night. I'd tell you all about it—about the investigation, I mean—but I can't right now. Jeanne and Gretchen are waiting for me."

She was silent for a minute, still looking at me as if trying to solve a faintly perplexing puzzle, and then turned to the bar. "Hey, Laurie, let me use your pencil," she called to the bartender. Laurie flipped the pencil from behind her right ear and sent it skidding down the surface of the bar. "This's the number where Fennel's staying," Jan told me as she wrote with Laurie's pencil on a handy napkin. "Might's well call yourself as ask me to. All right?"

"Sure," I said. "Thanks, Jan. Will I get a chance to talk to you soon?"

Her breath went pfooo, meaning roughly Damned if I know, but she smiled. "After Saturday for sure," she said.

I hugged her quickly, silently, and left the bar, the napkin clutched in my hand.

By the time we got back to Everywhere House it was after ten, almost too late to try calling Fennel. Peg was passing through the front hall when we came in. "Want to join me in some tea and popcorn?" she asked as Jeanne and Gretchen disappeared up the stairs.

"Sure," I replied. "Just let me make this one phone call and I'll be right with you." She ambled on into the living room, and I settled down by the phone for a few deep breaths before dialing. "May I speak to Fennel?" I said when I heard a gruff H'lo at the other end.

"Who's this?" the voice wanted to know.

"My name is Terry, Terry Barber. I live at Everywhere House. I've been down to see Barb, and she asked me to—"

"Right," she interrupted me. "What do you want?"

"I'd like to talk to you," I said, holding on to my patience with both hands. Now that I knew separatists didn't have to be rude, relating with Furies seemed even harder than before. "In person, if possible."

There was a long silence and then, "Okay. Friday. Evening. Seven o'clock. You come here. Alone."

There wasn't room for me to argue, so I didn't. "Okay, what's the address?"

She gave me an address on Capitol Hill and hung up.

Well, up yours, too, Fennel, I fumed silently as I put down the receiver, tucked the more fully annotated napkin back in the pocket of my pants and went to join Peg in the living room.

She looked up from her book as she heard me come in. "I thought you told me you didn't know any black women in Seattle?"

I stopped dead in my tracks and stared at her. What is it with the world today?, I asked myself silently, rhetorically. "So?" I said out loud.

"So Gretchen doesn't count?"

For a minute I wavered on the triple brink of guilty explanation, angry frustration, and total blank overload. Then I focused on Peg's familiar smirk and knew everything would be all right after all. I picked up the nearest pillow, threw it at her head, and launched myself after it for a messy tussle over the popcorn bowl.

Fifteen face-stuffing minutes later, we turned to each other and said with perfect simultaneity: "She's Jeanne's friend; you can't really say I 'know' her." and, "So you're going to go get yourself involved with another one of the Furies, huh?"

It was a perfect standoff and both of us were tired, so we rinsed out the empty popcorn bowl and went upstairs to bed.

Wouldn't you know, the next day Letitia asked me right before class if I'd have lunch with her. I had to tell her 'No,' of course, because I already had a twelve o'clock appointment with Professor Compton. It occurred to me that maybe Letitia would offer to go along and introduce me to the Philosophy prof, but she didn't.

Several hours later I was knocking on Professor Compton's open office door. She was a large-framed woman in early middle-age with an abundance of grey-streaked chestnut hair pulled into a knot at the back. When she heard my knock and looked up from her desk, I saw serious chestnut eyes over the edges of her half-lens glasses. "Professor Compton?" I said.

"Yes. And you're..." she glanced at a note on the desk "...Terry Barber, I imagine."

"Right. Thank you for seeing me." I took a few steps into the office and then followed her gesture to a chair by the desk. "Letitia Vedermann suggested I talk to you," I began. "About Professor Simpson."

"And your interest is?" inquired Professor Compton, her voice sounding just as rich and evocative as it had over the phone the day before.

"I'm a friend of the woman who's accused of killing him," I blurted, "and I'm trying to find out more about him because I'm trying to find out who really did it."

Professor Compton took off her glasses and tapped them thoughtfully on her desk blotter. When she looked up at me again, her gaze was frankly appraising. "You believe your friend is innocent," she said.

"Well, yes. She says she didn't do it, and...the thing is, she and I are both lesbians—" Her steady gaze did not waver. "—and it seems to me the police just might be taking the easy way out here, figuring a lesbian ex-wife is such a perfect suspect that they don't need to bother looking any further." The push of her lips and the tilt of her head admitted the theoretical plausibility of my argument. "So I've been trying to find out who else might have wanted Simpson dead. I never even met the man myself, but from what I've heard so far he doesn't sound universally beloved."

A warm chuckle—toasted chestnuts were the words that came to mind—prefaced the Professor's response. "Not even hemispherically beloved, I'll wager," she said. She spent the next two minutes checking me out, trying to make sure, I think, that I wasn't about to go tearing off in some mad crusade with whatever she told me and get myself hurt or in trouble. Not to mention that I wouldn't misuse anything she might tell me, that I wouldn't gossip or go around bleating But Professor Compton told me....

I passed inspection, but she did have some conditions. "As long as you intend simply to do research, as it were, and turn the resulting data over to the authorities, Terry, I am willing to contribute information to your endeavor, for the sake of seeing justice done with respect to your friend. Not least because I too, as you may or may not have guessed, am gay and have some personal knowledge of discrimination."

I was delighted to hear it. "Maybe that's what Letitia meant when she said she thought you'd be sympathetic."

"Did she? I try to be sympathetic more or less equally to everyone, actually. But perhaps she was speaking in a sort of code. People often do."

"What's it like being a gay professor?" I asked, easily deflected, as always, by my curiosity.

"I'm not sure I know the answer to that question yet," she responded. "If you had come to see me last quarter, for example, we could not have had this conversation."

"You weren't out, you mean?"

Her shoulders moved slightly, as if repressing a shudder. "Let's just say I was not tenured. In this department, as in others, many prefer not to know officially that which they certainly do know unofficially. It would be easier to live with that preference for dual reality, of course, if the unofficial knowledge weren't so often allowed to influence official decisions on matters such as tenure."

"Well, I'm happy for you anyway," I told her, and she smiled gently.

"Thank you. I am happy for me, too. But now: what exactly do you wish to know?"

"Anything you can tell me, really. Your impressions of Simpson, what you know about his life and his friends—especially his girlfriend, any changes you noticed in him lately...."

After giving the matter some thought, she started to speak. "I would not usually feel free to pass judgment on my colleagues—and certainly not to anyone outside the department. Keeping in mind the situation, however, and the fact that the man is, after all, dead.... Simpson impressed me as immature and ambitious. He was more eager to 'win points,' as they say, than perhaps anyone else I ever knew. I was the recipient of a great deal of condescension from him, because I am female and because he wanted our male colleagues to see that he knew how to relate 'collegially' with a woman. At the same time, however, I was always aware that he fully expected to receive tenure before I did—not because he understood the sexism institutionalized in departmental politics, but because he simply assumed that he, a male, was more worthy of tenure than I, a female. I suspect he was sincere in that assumption, by the way, which could almost have been endearing. It's much more the fashion around here to be insincere in one's attitudes towards women and sexism.

"About his life and his friends I know very little. He was an avid and irritating amateur photographer; we all heard many times about his boyhood ambitions in that direction, and we all got thoroughly tired of his popping off flash bulbs at every opportunity. As far as I know, he didn't socialize a great deal outside the academic community, and the girlfriend you mentioned is unknown to me. I did meet his wife—your friend Barbara—once, at a cocktail party soon after he joined us. He introduced her as if she were a particularly noteworthy member of an object class—a Sheraton sofa or an Adams fireplace, something of that sort. 'One of the Montana Randalls,' he said. She is the woman who has been charged with his murder, correct?" I nodded, trying to imagine Barb at a faculty cocktail party. "I felt sorry for her," Professor Compton said quietly. "She seemed to be trying so hard."

Both of us were silent for a minute, both of us, I imagine, contemplating a different image of the same woman in our minds' eye.

"You asked about recent changes," she said, and I felt my hopes lift. "Ted was no ascetic, as you may know; he put a high value on the things money can buy. I heard him once, talking to another junior member of the department, describe his own philosophical orientation as 'progressive pragmatism,' if you can believe it. Apparently he had in mind some variation on the 'self-interest is the proper basis for all ethical behavior' school. Most adherents to that doctrine, in academic circles anyway, speak of 'enlightened self-interest,' but I can't recall that Ted ever found it necessary to use that adjective.

"But I digress. I had noticed recently that Ted seemed to be...anticipating something greatly to his benefit. For years now we have been given to understand that he is—or rather, was—a man hard done by, a victim of fate or circumstance, a man cheated of what was rightfully his. He tended to go around being stricken. Whenever Ted wasn't morose or celebrating some minor triumph of his own imagining, he was invariably being noble and long-suffering." She paused, tightened her lips for a second and said, "To be fair, he usually was quite cordial to me, as I've said. Condescendingly so, but constant in his cordiality. This strain of 'nobility' I have described did emerge occasionally, but usually it was hidden beneath a layer of 'collegiality.' Of course," she told me with a smile that transformed her face, "I could be imagining the whole thing. It could be nothing more than projected hostility on the part of a middle-aged lady."

"Do you have any idea what he was anticipating?" I asked her.

"Not really. He was quite lavishly mysterious about it. You'd have thought a chair was about to be endowed in his honor. Whatever it was, I suspect it had a great deal to do with money. He had become studiously casual about his climb up the academic ladder. At a departmental meeting just a few weeks ago, he volunteered to take an extra class, saying, 'If I'm still here next year, that is.' When someone asked him about it, he equivocated and wriggled away."

"Do you know anything about his religious beliefs?"

Her eyes widened briefly and then narrowed in thought. "No. I shouldn't have thought he had any."

"Well, it's just that the most interesting thing I've found out about him so far—the thing that seems most likely to have something to do with his murder—is that he's been involved with a group called the Peaceful Way. It's...well, there's a Leader, a sort of guru, the members all wear blue coveralls, and—"

"What you're describing sounds more like a cult than a religion," broke in Professor Compton, the skin over her strong nose wrinkling in distaste.

"I'm not sure it's even a cult," I told her. "I mean, some cults, however other people might feel about them, really are the expression of somebody's beliefs about how to live a good life. This one, though, I'm not so sure about. Some of the details don't add up." My mind's eye flashed back to the ominous Guardians. "And I know for a fact there's money involved."

"Ah. In that case, assuming for the sake of discussion a broad enough definition of 'religion,' I presume you may in fact have stumbled onto the focus of Ted's religious life. Such as it was." Her intelligent voice was dryer than summer in the Sahara.

"Can you think of anything Professor Simpson said or did that might be a link between the Peaceful Way and whatever it was he was anticipating?"

Professor Compton shook her head decisively. "Nothing at all. I'm quite sure he never mentioned that group to anyone here in the department. That sort of thing would spread like wild fire through the gossip network, especially with an already unpopular fellow like Ted." Professor Compton looked at her watch. "I have a student conference scheduled for one o'clock."

"I have to be at work by one anyway," I said. "Thank you, Professor Compton. I really appreciate your taking the time to talk to me."

"You're quite welcome," she said rising from her chair and reaching for the briefcase on the far edge of her desk. "All I ask in return is that you remember what you told me: that you will act sensibly and not take undue risks. I can't imagine, for one thing, that the police would look favorably on any attempt to conduct an investigation paralleling their own."

I reassured her again about my limited intentions, suppressing with a sigh an automatic impulse to fret against the parental tone she kept slipping into. As I left her office, I was wondering whether I'd ever be adult enough to feel socially equal to an intelligent, self-possessed woman like Professor Compton. Was it my sense of childish inadequacy, I wondered, or her sense of adult authority that determined the tone—and seemed to set the limits—of our interaction? I did like her, after all, so why was it so hard for me to imagine us being friends?

I was halfway down the hall when I heard her call my name. "I've just remembered something," she said, as I retraced my steps. "Ted did have a friend outside the department. In Linguistics, I'm almost sure. A rather unpleasant-looking chap. The one time I saw the two of them together I remember thinking 'Tweedledum and Tweedledee'—not that either of them was fat, you understand, but because they seemed like rather nasty mirror images of one another. Ted called him Ellis, I believe, but whether that was the family name or a given name I'm afraid I can't tell you."

"Thanks!" I said. "I'm sure I'll be able to track him down. Just to talk to, of course."

We smiled at each other, friends of a sort after all, and I muttered Ellis, Ellis, Linguistics, Ellis to myself all the way to the library.

Letitia and I had arranged to meet at the bus stop at two, and as I approached from the east I saw her approaching from the west. "Good timing!" I called out to her as soon as we were in hearing range. Around her neck, just visible between the open lapels of her coat, was a fine gold chain bearing a gold Star of David. She'd never worn it before that I could remember, and I'd been seeing her almost every day for the whole quarter.

"It's sort of like a good-luck charm," she said, and then I really did blush.

"I didn't mean to stare," I apologized. "It's just I never saw you wear it before."

"Sometimes it helps me feel braver."

"The best defense is a good offense?" I suggested.

"Exactly."

The bus pulled up at the stop, and I spoke to her back as I followed her up the stairs. "Yeah. In the long-run, passing is not a mentally healthy lifestyle." We found aisle seats across from each other about half-way back, and I leaned towards her in order to say, as softly as I could and still have her hear me,

"How do you feel about being taken for a lesbian, though?"

"By Lieutenant White, you mean? Doesn't bother me."

Chewing over the complexity of Letitia's relationship to identity would have kept me busy for the rest of the ride, but I didn't get more than a second or two before Letitia changed the subject. "Did you talk to Professor Compton?" she asked. We were discussing various ways to approach Simpson's friend in Linguistics when the bus arrived at Third and James. A look at the directory in the lobby of the Public Safety Building directed us to an office two floors below the jail, and I felt the weight of Barb's cell pressing down on me as the elevator pushed us up to our rendezvous with Lieutenant White.

After we'd made our presence known, we sat for five minutes on rickety old wooden chairs in a waiting area that couldn't really claim to be a room. It was odd to see so many policemen "at home," as it were, clomping in and out, acting much more at ease than they do out on the street. Occasionally one of them would be a woman, and it may have been my imagination, or projection, but the women didn't seem to feel as much at ease there as the men did.

Lieutenant White turned out to be a middle-aged black man in a business suit. "Ms. Vedermann? Ms. Barber?" he inquired and gestured for us to follow him down the partition-sided interior hallway. Fifteen steps later he opened a door marked "Witness Interrogation." The room was completely bare except for a beat-up metal desk and three chairs, two on this side, one over there. Lieutenant White circled the desk and in the split second before we all sat down, I saw Letitia's Star of David register on his mind, just as it had registered on mine forty minutes before. His eyes were hard to read after that, because he kept his eyelids half-way down, a habit that accentuated the long, wrinkle-rumpled expanse of skin sweeping up past sparse eyebrows to the receding edge of his short-cropped hair. A pencil in his right hand flickered rapidly up and down, up and down, barely failing to connect with the desktop each time it oscillated downward. His version of a worry stone, I supposed. "You had some information you wanted to give us?" he said in a courteous but neutral tone of voice. When the only response was a furtive glance between me and Letitia, he prodded, "You knew the victim, I believe."

"I was in his class," Letitia responded, her voice remarkably matter-of-fact, "and I had met him once or twice at departmental functions. Then last week, after Terry—Ms. Barber—and I talked, she met a classmate of mine from Professor Simpson's class. A woman named Jennifer Stone."

That was my cue, but I didn't have any idea how to begin. I cleared my throat. "*Hummkra.* I—excuse me—I tried to call her because Letitia—Ms. Vedermann—said she, Jennifer Stone that is, had been spending extra time with Professor Simpson so I thought she might be able to tell me something about him. But when I called her dorm, she'd moved out. I managed to track down her boyfriend"—the Lieutenant's pencil was moving at a nice, medium speed—"and he said she'd gone to live in a cult house. Well, he said she'd become a Moonie, which turned out not to be true, exactly, but he did tell me where the house was where she was living."

As I talked, the pencil moved slower and slower. Is that a good sign? I asked myself, and just then Lieutenant White gave me the answer. In the negative. "Ms. Barber," he said, sliding it in too smoothly to sound like an interruption, "I wonder whether you might start by telling me the relevance of this...story of yours." The pencil was motionless between his fingers.

"I'll try," I sighed. "So.... I found out from Jennifer Stone that Professor Simpson, the victim, was part of this cult called the Peaceful Way. He was a recruiter, in fact." Waggle-waggle went the pencil, moving slowly, but moving once again. "He talked Jennifer into joining, and now she gives all the money she gets from her parents—the money for her tuition at the University—to the Peaceful Way leaders."

"And you draw some conclusion from that fact that you believe is relevant to Mr. Simpson's death?"

"Well, yeah! I mean, it's such an obvious scam! I went there to talk to Jennifer, and some big goons in dark suits wouldn't let me in the door. They wouldn't even let me talk to her. I had to sneak around the back after they left, and even then I had to talk to her through a barely open window because the goons locked her in when they went away." My revived indignation at the memory of that conversation with Jennifer evoked no echo in Lieutenant White's impassive face. "Doesn't that tell you something?" I insisted.

"Not in relation to my investigation, no."

"But he was a recruiter, don't you get it? He was involved up to his eyeballs in this cult scam, talking naive kids like Jennifer into turning over their tuition money to a phony religion and then, once they're really hooked, shipping them off to California or someplace where nobody knows them and—"

"Shipping them off?" inquired Lieutenant White sharply, the pencil vibrating with life once again.

"Jennifer says they never stay in the house for long. The group, or maybe even Simpson himself, sets up a P.O. box for them so they'll keep receiving their checks, and then the kids get taken off somewhere. Jennifer didn't know where, but they had her so fuzzy-headed that she didn't even care."

The Lieutenant tapped the desktop soundlessly once with the eraser end of the pencil and said decisively, "Thank you for bringing this to our attention. I'll pass along your information to the appropriate section of the department, and they may be getting in touch with you if they need verification." He had both hands flat on the desk now and was shifting his weight forward as if to stand up as he added, "If there's nothing else...?"

I couldn't believe it. "Nothing else?" I exploded. "How much more do you need? You've got Simpson connected with a bunch of thugs who are brainwashing people and stealing their money, and you need more?!"

"I need," the Lieutenant explained with strained patience, "some indication that these people you mention have anything to do with the investigation into the violent death of Theodore Simpson."

He was still on the edge of his chair, poised to stand and end the interview, when both of us were startled by Letitia's unexpected reentry into the conversation. "Those who can make you believe absurdities can make you commit atrocities." In response to our blank stares she added, "Voltaire," and then subsided back into silence.

"Exactly." I proclaimed as soon as her words had sunk in. "Just think of the possibilities, Lieutenant. You've got those strong-arm goons who must be making a mint out of this cult, and who knows how far they'd go to protect their racket? But you've also got all those brainwashed kids, and believe me, they really have been made to believe absurdities. Who knows what they'd be willing to do to protect their religion? Plus the parents of the kids in the cult when they find out how their kids have been brainwashed and milked for all they're worth."

"Thank you, Ms. Barber, for laying it all out for me like that." His sarcasm was so carefully polite it was almost invisible. "As I said, I'll pass your information along to the appropriate—"

"But *you're* the appropriate person, and I can't believe you don't see what a wide field of suspects we've opened up here. Surely you mean to investigate all of this. You're not going to sit back and let Barb Randall be an easy way out."

Lieutenant White laid his pencil on the desk, carefully adjusting it into parallel with the edge. "Ms. Barber," he said, using the voice he must have learned in police school for calming hysterical women. "Like many members of the public, you seem to be under a misapprehension about the nature and responsibilities of my duties as the officer in charge of the investigation into a homicide." Both of us were controlling ourselves with a visible effort, but my effort had sound effects, too—uneven breathing and the intermittent gulping of swallowed words. He watched me swallow a big one and then continued. "My role is to gather evidence at the scene of the crime and, when necessary, additional corroborative evidence including the interviewing of any witnesses. As soon as I have gathered sufficient evidence, I turn that evidence over to the district attorney. It is the district attorney's responsibility to determine whether the evidence makes a strong enough case to take to court, and it is the court's responsibility—the judge's and the jury's—to decide whether the evidence presented by the district attorney proves the guilt of the defendant beyond a reasonable doubt. You will note, Ms. Barber, that my job is over once I have handed over the evidence to the district attorney. In this case, the district attorney did decide that the evidence was sufficient to bring formal charges against Ms. Randall, and now it is up to the judge and the jury to decide, when the case

goes to trial, whether the defendant is guilty as charged. If she is not guilty"—
he held his pencil vertically in the air above the desk to ward off the words he
could tell were about to erupt from my mouth—"we can be confident that the
court will find the evidence inconclusive. In that case, the district attorney will
instruct me to reopen the case. But until that time"—he raised his voice, realizing that the pencil alone was about to prove insufficient—"I would be derelict
in my duty if I spent any more time on this case. There are plenty of other
cases that require my attention, believe me."

He stopped speaking and watched me closely from under his half-closed eyelids.

"I talked to another professor in the Philosophy department a few hours
ago," I insisted, "and she told me Simpson was all excited about something
lately. He probably expected to come into a lot of money, she said. Now
doesn't that—"

He sighed and then twitched his lips tight for a second, as if rebuking himself for that small sign of impatience. "I suggest you go home now, Ms. Barber,
and think about what I've said. When the case comes up in court—"

"But it doesn't have to even get that far!" I almost pleaded with him and
then, as he took the pencil firmly in his fist and started to rise once again,
blurted, "Wait! There's something more." He hesitated briefly in a half-way
position between sitting and standing before subsiding once again and resign-
edly nodding for me to continue. "It's about Barb. Barbara Randall. I know
her, and—" was that a smug look of 'I thought so' I detected in Lieutenant
White's face?—"and I believe her when she says she didn't do it. Okay, so what
I think doesn't carry any weight with you"—he tried to look politely bland—
"but even so, I think you owe it to, to *justice* to think about what I have to
say."

The Lieutenant slid the sleeve of his suit jacket back and looked at his watch.
"I can give you two more minutes," he said.

I took a deep breath and began my spiel. "You know Barb is a lesbian"—his
face didn't change—"but you may not know, or understand, what that means,
really. It means she's a member of a particular subculture, and it's not always
easy for someone outside a subculture to understand what they see when they
look at what's inside the subculture. A subculture is—"

"I know what a subculture is, Ms. Barber." The Lieutenant's cheeks looked
harder than before, as if he was sucking them in, showing more of the bone.

"Okay, well, in the case of the lesbian subculture, there's a lot of misunder-
standing on the part of outsiders, and it's possible that some of that misunder-
standing might make it hard for you to really see Barb without prejudice. I
mean, all this stuff about 'man-hating,' for example, that a lot of straights—
heterosexuals—think of when they think about lesbians, that could really cloud
someone's objectivity in a case like this. What most people don't understand is

that, aside from not being true at all for a lot of lesbians, a lot of what looks to outsiders like 'man-hating' is really a form of, well, propaganda, a way of making words work to change the way people think."

I couldn't tell if my own words were making any impression at all, and my reckless improvisation threatened to get hung up on the lump in my throat. "Listen," I said, groping desperately for a way to get through to him, "do you have any children?"

That certainly got his attention, even if it did almost cost the pencil its life. "We will leave my personal life out of this," he said coldly, definitively.

"Okay. I didn't mean to.... But how can I explain it to you if you don't let me see what you think and feel about things? I mean, you say I should just wait till the case against Barb goes to court. But from my point of view, that's not as... dependable as you seem to think it is. From my point of view, Barb will be judged by straight people according to their prejudices about lesbians. You say all you do is give the evidence to the D.A., but you know there isn't really anything objective about a process like that. What you see depends on how you look, and where you look, and what you expect to find. If you see a pervert, a man-hater, and you perceive certain aspects of her subculture to mean something different than they mean to her—" Very much in my mind were the Furies' 'kill men' graffiti, but I didn't want to risk worsening the Lieutenant's prejudice by bringing up anything too specific.

Lieutenant White quickly took advantage of my brief silence and stood up. "I understand what you are saying, Ms. Barber." He sounded almost gracious in his relief. "And I can assure you that the case against Ms. Randall rests on factual evidence, not prejudice. Now if you will excuse me—"

"But all I'm asking is that you consider the alternatives!" I repeated as I stood up, accepting the finality of his decision to end the interview. "All I'm asking is that you recognize the possibility that somebody else might have wanted Simpson out of the way, somebody else might have had a motive even better than the one you think Barb Randall had."

As I spoke, I followed Letitia out the door the Lieutenant was holding pointedly open for us. He stood solidly in the middle of the narrow hall, heading us firmly back towards the exit door. "I think we've both made our positions clear, Ms. Barber," he said. "Ms. Vedermann. Good afternoon."

Defeated but rebellious, I turned and marched away, grumbling, "Well, *somebody's* got to investigate it."

"Ms. Barber," he called to me sharply and I stopped in my tracks. In three strides he was at my side. "There are laws," he said, "against private citizens interfering in police business. Those laws are strictly enforced. What's more, that kind of amateur meddling can be dangerous. Do you understand me? I am warning you to stay out of this."

I looked up into his dark brown eyes, now fully open and looking down at me intently. Maybe he does have a daughter, I thought. He was a hard man to read, for sure.

"I understand," I said, and kept the rest of my answer to myself.

17.

The sky was twice as dark when we left the building as it had been when we went in, and a stiff wind was fighting with the rain. It wasn't heavy rain, but determined.

"Yuck!" I said as Letitia and I shivered down the sidewalk to the bus stop in the next block. Without a word, we headed for the high-roofed entryway of the County Courthouse and joined the dozen other people already sheltering there. It was a squeeze, but we managed to fit both of us into a cranny out of the wind and rain but still with a view of the buses pulling up. Crammed together like that, I could feel Letitia's trembling through her coat and mine. "Are you okay?" I asked her. "Want to wait inside where it's warmer? I could dash in and get you when the bus comes."

"I'm okay," she said very softly, almost whispering it in my ear. The next thing I knew, there were two hands in my pocket. One of them was hers. "I'm not that cold," she said as her thin fingers wrapped into mine. "I think maybe I'm in shock." She laughed a little and then shuddered and gripped my hand like a vise for several painful seconds.

I pressed myself comfortingly against her, thankful for the dark and the sheltering corner. "What do you mean?"

"How did you dare talk to him like that! My god, to a cop! I couldn't believe how you kept pressing him."

I was astounded. To me it hadn't felt much different from the many talks I'd had with the principal back in high school. I used to be in there arguing with him about something at least once month. Indignation over some other student's problems carried me easily over the threshold of his office, sometimes without even waiting to be announced. "Hmm," I said, trying to think how to put it. It's not that I didn't like Letitia's hand in mine, but I didn't much like the idea that she might be giving me credit for a bravery I didn't think I possessed.

"Here's our bus," she said, and her hand went away.

The bus was fairly crowded; the two of us and ten or twelve other people stood in the aisle. "Are you going to try to talk to the district attorney?" Letitia asked as the bus groaned to its next stop.

"Probably not," I told her. "Doesn't seem like it would do a lot of good."

"Good," Letitia said firmly. "I didn't like the sound of that threat at the end." She shivered again.

A few blocks later, a man squeezed past us down the aisle carrying a tabloid newspaper with a headline saying "Patty Hearst: Rebel in Search of a Cause?" I groaned and glanced at Letitia to share it with her, but she apparently hadn't even noticed the headline going by. *What does she think of all that?* I wondered. *How strange that I wind up going to see a policeman with the one friend I've got that I've never talked to about that kind of politics, the kind that puts some lesbians at the wrong end of hostile policemen's guns.*

"Are you going to the Armed Struggle Workshop on Saturday?" I asked her out of the blue.

"The...? I don't know. What is it?"

When I explained, she seemed vaguely interested but unwilling or unable to be definite one way or the other. In fact, all the way to the U District, she seemed very much absorbed in mulling over something else, and very distant with it.

"See you Monday," I said after thanking her again at the bus stop where we both got off. "Or at the workshop on Saturday, if you decide to go."

Letitia had been staring moodily at the sidewalk, already half turned to walk away towards the east as I prepared to head west, but she looked up at me sideways, sort of oddly, I thought, as I thanked her. Without a word, she nodded, raised one hand in half a wave, and walked thoughtfully off with the wind tugging and snatching at the loose strands of hair working their way free of her braid.

The rain had stopped while we were on the bus; perversely, it started again as I headed up the hill for home. Shivering, I thrust my balled-up hands into the pockets of my jacket—and the left-over warmth they found there made my heart jump into my throat. I could feel Letitia's hand even more clearly than when I'd had it there to hold. I could feel the heat of it, and the way the bones were alive under the skin. Half an hour ago, sheltering in the drafty Courthouse entryway, I'd been distracted by her voice close to my ear, the powdery smell of her hair. Now, undistracted, I let the miracle of that brief contact come alive again through the memory I hadn't even realized my hand was capable of. "Truly amazing," I said to an orange-sherbet cat crouched statue-like on the retaining wall I happened to be passing. The cat studied with deep suspicion the wacky grin I felt on my face.

As soon as I got home I ran up to my room, to my well-thumbed copy of e. e. cumming's 100 selected poems. There it was, a poem I'd always loved for the sound of it, not guessing I'd ever read it again for the sense it made of my own experience. I was reading selected verses over and over to myself—

> your slightest look easily will unclose me
> though i have closed myself as fingers,...

(...the voice of your eyes is deeper than all roses)
nobody, not even the rain, has such small hands

—when the phone rang and Fran called my name.

"Teeeerrrry, it's for yooooou," she was hollering again as I reached the top of the stairs. When I got near enough for her to me hand the receiver, she added in a dramatic hiss, "It's a man!"

"Hello?" I said to the telephone, making a face at Fran and her rabid curiosity.

"It's a Roger, in fact." He sounded a bit tentative—and who wouldn't? Being hissed *about* is only a hair less unpleasant than being hissed *at*, even long distance.

"Hiya, Roger!" My glad cry was perfectly sincere, but I couldn't help seeing it as a political act, too. If my housemates had a problem with my getting phone calls from a man, they'd have to tackle me about it, that's all. I wasn't willing to keep my friendship with Roger in the closet any more.

After the usual preliminaries, I gave him a run-down on the murder investigation. Letitia's name came up a lot, of course, but by the time I finished my report I was wondering if it didn't come up just a few times too often. And if so, why? Was I unconsciously trying to reassure Roger that I still was friendly towards straight people? The fact that Letitia lived with a philosophy TA was relevant to my story, but I could have told Roger that in some other way than how it came out of my mouth: "She lives with a man who is...", as if it was his gender, not his job, that mattered. On the other hand, maybe it was my own life Letitia was becoming more central to, not the murder investigation at all.

Meanwhile, Roger was sounding distracted—which is not among his usual characteristics.

"Are you okay, Roger?" I asked finally. "Sounds like you've got something on your mind."

"Yeah," he sighed, "I guess I do. It was great to get your note the other day. Just when I needed it."

"Does Sandie mind your calling me?" I hoped the question was a tactful way to give him an opening if the problem on his mind had something to do with trouble in their relationship.

"She's gone to a meeting," he said, and then came a soft snort of amusement as we both realized how that sounded. "But no, she doesn't mind." He paused and then pushed himself into the heart of the matter. "The thing is, Terry, Sandie and I are talking about getting married."

Married, I said to myself. Oh.

"It's just—Sandie's getting to a point now, in her career, where it probably makes a difference. Not the morality thing," he hastened to add. "At least, probably more for women than for men, even now, although a couple of teachers have told me it's not good for a teacher of young kids to not be married. You can get away with it on the east coast, they say, or on the west coast, but not in the midwest. But even aside from that, what Sandie says is true: people just don't take you as seriously when they find out you're living with somebody, even if you're in a committed, long-term relationship. You're just not considered an adult unless you're married. And…we're pretty sure we do want kids some day, and being married is…. Everybody says you owe it to your kids, right? So…."

Married, I said to myself. And then: Well, why not?

"So, why not?" I asked him. "What's the problem? Besides marriage being an out-moded and discriminatory form of social control, I mean."

"I know, it's shitty that you can't get married even if you want to, just because the other person wouldn't be a man. But that's…political. It's an issue. What's bugging me is a lot more personal than that.

"It just seems like there's a whole lot of shit that goes along with getting married. And with being an 'adult' in that sense. It doesn't just mean buying a legal document and telling the judge 'I do.' It means…. Oh hell, I don't know how to explain this! Just a minute, let me think."

I let him think.

"It's like the minute some people get married they all of a sudden buy into those roles." He said the word with horror in his voice. "All of a sudden it's 'the little woman' and 'boys' night out.' Fucking Ozzie and Harriet time. They talk to each other differently; hell, they talk *about* each other differently. It's crazy."

"Everybody assumes that, once you're married, you'll automatically turn into what they think is a normal adult, right? And you're not ready to settle for that—you want to be at least a little bit better than normal—but you're afraid the transformation may take place whether you want it to or not. Am I reading you right?"

He sighed his relief. "Yeah, you got it. Feels good to have somebody understand what I'm talking about finally. Even Sandie doesn't seem to catch on completely. I was starting to think maybe I wasn't operating on all cylinders on this one."

I laughed, recognizing a cliché he'd adopted from my mom. "Well, you know you'll never be normal to me, Roger. I just plain won't let you."

When I finally put down my botany text and went to bed that night, I discovered a question lurking in my brain. If getting married was what would make Roger a fully-accredited adult, what did it mean for me and all my lesbian friends that we weren't allowed to be married? The issues raised by that question seemed worthy of serious analysis, but I wasn't in the mood and fell quickly into a mossy dream.

18.

None of my classes met on Friday, so all I had in mind to do that day, aside from work in the afternoon and my evening appointment with Fennel, was study. Ordinarily, being only one week of classes away from final exams is more than enough to concentrate my mind. I'd never been involved in a murder case before, though.

Perversely, everyone was gone by the time I dragged myself out of bed that morning. "What is it with this house these days?" I asked the pathetic rubber plant in the living room. "Either every dyke in town is here, or nobody's here."

I spent the morning alternately studying and doing chores. "Who the hell made this mess, anyway?" I muttered viciously as I sacrificed a perfectly good sponge to the removal of an incredibly sticky substance from the floor under the kitchen table. I'd have been surprised and hurt, of course, if anyone else in the house expressed anger over my neglected spills when it was their turn to clean the floor. "Oh, lighten up, Terry," I told myself at last, and went to take a shower before heading for campus. Somewhere between the Spanish subjunctive and the kitchen floor, I'd come up with a plan.

The Philosophy office was in a campus building that lay on my route to the library, so I stopped in there to use the directory. I had no idea where the Linguistics office might be, and I'd decided it was high time I follow up Professor Compton's tip about Ted Simpson's friend. With luck, I'd have a phone number for him before I had to be at work.

I was returning the directory to the woman behind the front desk in the Philosophy office when I heard my name. The beautiful voice was unmistakable.

"I'm glad to run into you, Terry," Professor Compton said. "Would you have time to join me in my office for a moment now?"

Once inside her office, she closed the door and turned to face me. "I won't take up much of your time," she said, "but privacy did seem in order."

I was intrigued, needless to say.

"Assuming our agreements still hold..." She looked to me for confirmation and got it . "...I will tell you that I now know the identity of Ted Simpson's girlfriend."

Sensation in court! as my father would say.

"You must use this information very discreetly," she warned me, "if you use it at all, because the woman in question is a graduate student in this department." Professor Compton frowned. "As you probably know, it is considered highly unethical for faculty to establish relationships with thir students. Relationships of that type, that is to say."

"I won't tell anybody," I promised eagerly.

"Her name—and again, I count on your discretion, Terry—is Heidi Bascom. An excellent student, by all accounts." She seemed about to add something else but decided against it.

"Thanks, Professor. I really appreciate your help. And don't worry, I'll be careful." And I was off.

An optimistic glance at my watch said there was still time for a visit to Linguistics, so I headed east at a trot. "Heidi Bascom, Heidi Bascom," I muttered to myself. When I got to Linguistics, the first thing I did was whip a pen out of my pack so I could register the precious new clue somewhere more reliable than my memory. The woman behind the only occupied desk in the office was staring at me as I looked up from my task.

"Hi!" I said brightly. "I'm looking for David Ellis." None of the linguists in the directory had the first initial E., so the David Ellis I found in the University catalog seemed a safe bet to try.

"Dave's not here anymore," she said.

She looked bored, so I tried the chatty approach. "Not here!" I exclaimed. "My goodness! Where has he disappeared to, and when will he be back?"

"He's not coming back," she said with a complacent smile. "Not even if he wanted to. The Chair is not too happy with Dave Ellis these days, believe you me. Here it is almost the end of the quarter, and pfft! He's gone."

"You don't mean literally disappeared, do you? Like kidnapped, or something?"

"Oh, no, I mean, that could be forgiven, right? Like an act of God. But his mother has been sick forever, know what I mean? He never even went to see her very often, and now all of a sudden he can't stand to be away from her bedside? I mean, reeel-ly!" She smirked. "If you ask me, it's nothing to do with his mother, anyway."

"What do you mean?" I asked as encouragingly as possible.

"Well, if it was an emergency, they'd've called the office, right? The doctors or whatever? At the very least, she'd be in the hospital. But she's not. I know she's not, because of this."

With a triumphant flip of the wrist she handed me a small sheet of paper filled with rows of numbers. It was a telephone bill, I realized, from the University's telecommunications unit, and she'd run a yellow highlighter over one line near the end of the page.

"That, believe it or not," she smirked, "is the number for Mrs. Ellis's home. I know because I checked. And just look at the date: he made that call standing right by this very desk just last week. We wouldn't even get a prelim billing statement like this ordinarily," she told me confidentially, "but the Chair's got a bee in his bonnet about unauthorized use of the line, so he asked Telecommunications to do a special run." The thought of the male Chair of Linguistics wearing a bonnet, with or without a bee in it, almost made me lose track of the story, but not so my informant.

"He was standing right there," she said, pointing dramatically at the floor by my side, "and I heard him with my very own ears. 'I'll come up right away, Mother,' he said, 'No, of course it's not a problem. I'll be there this evening, so just sit tight and wait for me. Don't even think about going to the grocery store,' that's what he said, 'I'll pick up some supplies on my way into town.' So there. That proves it. He was talking to his mother, and she was at home, not in the hospital, and not too sick to answer the phone, either."

"So he's gone to...Bellingham?" I read from the bill in my hand.

"Yes," she sniffed. "His father used to be a big noise on the faculty up there, you know." She clearly considered a big noise on the faculty of Western Washington University almost inaudible compared to the faculty here at the UW.

"Well, I guess since I'm this close, I might as well call him, anyway," I said, trying to project the aura of a visiting out-of-town friend without really lying. "I'll just jot down this number...."

A very small frown began to gather in her face, so I wrote quickly, handed over the bill, and got out before she had a chance to decide she had a duty to keep the information confidential. "I'll tell him you send your regards," I said as I hightailed it out the door.

Nobody said anything about the ten minutes I'd accidentally taken off the top of my work shift. During my mid-shift break I looked up Heidi Bascom in the phone book and found a Bascom, H. listed on Eastlake. Nobody answered at that number, but I wasn't too disappointed. Things were really picking up. Running into Professor Compton was a real stroke of luck, and locating David Ellis had gone much more smoothly than I had any right to expect. And now it looked like I could plan on stopping by to see if I had the right address for Simpson's elusive girlfriend on my way up Capitol Hill to interview Fennel that evening. There wouldn't really be time to talk, even assuming the H. Bascom listed in the phone book was the Heidi Bascom I was after and she happened to be home; but at least I could hope to find out for sure and maybe even set something up for later. All in all, I was starting to feel like I'd reached the point in the case where—in books, anyway—things start to shake loose and get interesting. It didn't occur to me then quite how shaky things could get.

19.

Most of us were home, for a change, at dinner time that Friday evening. Jan wasn't, of course. We were all looking forward to the Armed Struggle Workshop the next day, and to having Jan spend more time at home after the workshop was over. "Maybe we should have a celebration for her," suggested Connie, and the others—Fran, Toni, Jeanne (and the visiting Gretchen)—immediately jumped on the bandwagon. By the time Peg arrived, they'd formed two camps: the small-and-intimate advocates, and the big-blast-with-lots-of-beer band. I'd have loved to hear Peg, doing her Voice of Reason schtick, hammering consensus out of the controversy, but my appointment with Fennel was seven and I wanted to stop by Heidi Bascom's on the way.

I wanted to do some thinking about David Ellis, too. Was there any connection between his sudden departure from Seattle and his friend Simpson's murder? The fact that he'd lied, apparently, about his reason for leaving seemed to point towards an affirmative. Wouldn't the police have talked to him already, though? Well, no, probably not, given how stuck they were on Barb as the guilty party. So that meant I should go talk to him myself, right? Bellingham is a long ways off, though; almost to the Canadian border. How would I get there? On the bus? That would be a real drag, especially if it turned out he had nothing significant to tell me. The thing to do, I realized with a sinking feeling, was to ask Barb about it when I visited her at the jail on Saturday. Sure will be glad when she's outta there, I admitted to myself, knowing that my pleasure at her release would be partly due to my own release from the obligation to visit her.

The bus let me off on Eastlake into a light drizzle of misty rain. To the west, small apartment buildings covered the slope down to Lake Union. To the east, more apartments and some left-over houses blanketed the hill up to the swath of the freeway, already on stilts as it headed south around Capitol Hill. Heidi Bascom's apartment turned out to be in one of the ugliest buildings in the area: a clumsy concrete-block affair that looked more like a motel than a place to live. I climbed the outside stairway to the second floor walkway and studied the door of apartment two-nineteen. "H. Bascom P. Smythe," read a card on the door. I took a few deep breaths to steady my nerves, and knocked.

Instantaneously, the door flew open and a red-headed woman in a svelte navy-blue raincoat was telling me, "Yes?"

"Uh, Heidi Bascom?" I stammered.

She stared at me with narrowed eyes. "You're not a reporter, are you?" she said, her voice implying that the news media were really scraping the bottom of the barrel if they'd hired me.

"No, no. My name's Terry Barber, I'm a student at the U, and—"

"She's had enough hassle from reporters already, just because some fool in the office handed out a résumé showing Simpson on her thesis committee, and she's still kind of shaky, but—Heidi!" she hollered back over her shoulder, "it's for you!" She dropped her voice again to say, "Don't upset her. She's got enough on her plate right now. I've got to leave right this minute or I'll be late." And she was off, pushing past me onto the walkway and heading for the stairs as fast as her high heels would go.

I stepped inside the apartment and shut the door behind me. The concrete blocks were as dominant inside as out. For middle-class housing, which it obviously was by its pretensions and location, the poky, cold little rooms were as depressing and uninviting as any I'd ever seen. I felt a shiver run up my spine as I surveyed the dinette and kitchen from the living room where I was standing. Everywhere House was maddening sometimes, but at least it felt like home. This place is only fit to exist in, I said to myself; you couldn't really live here.

As if to contradict my thoughts, a woman emerged at that instant from the darkness of the short hall leading back, I assumed, to the bedrooms and bath. She looked awful, but it was a kind of awful that's undeniably alive. She looked like pain, like a walking wound. She also seemed to be on the point of going out, wearing an unbuttoned peacoat with a black scarf around her neck. The black slacks and a black sweater I glimpsed beneath the coat emphasized the extreme pallor of her face. Against the dull whiteness of her skin, her features looked distorted, exaggerated, extreme. She was very, very thin.

"Uhhh," I said, "I'm sorry to bother you...." Goddess!, I was moaning to myself, why didn't I realize she'd be like this. The grief-stricken widow, even if she wasn't his wife. I'd never interviewed a bereaved person and had no idea how to make it any easier on either of us.

"What do you want?" Her voice was slightly hoarse, and she didn't seem to have the energy to care much about her own question.

"I'd like to talk to you about Ted Simpson," I said baldly. Her only response was the continued fumbling at the buttons of her coat, her right hand moving slowly from button to button as if counting them by touch. "I know you were... going with him, and I'd like to offer my condolences." She folded slowly onto a chair by the entryway to the dinette area, folding down and down until her head was almost between her knees. By the time I'd taken two steps in her direction, I could hear that she was crying softly, wearily.

"Nobody was supposed to know," she said, lifting her bony face slightly. I couldn't tell if she was angry, upset, or just sad to find out her secret had been exposed.

"I won't tell anybody," I assured her. Her face was too far down again for me to guess at her reaction. "I need to find out more about him...to help a friend," I said as gently as I could, "and it looks like you're one of the very few people who might be able to help me. You and maybe David Ellis, but he's—"

"You talked to him?" Again, I wasn't sure what emotion lay behind her words. Whatever it was, it was strong enough to bring her upright in the chair, and urgent enough to interrupt me.

"No, he's left town. Gone to Bellingham, I think. I haven't made up my mind yet about going up there."

"Don't. He's a—he's not important. I can tell you anything you need to know."

Mysteriouser and mysteriouser, I said to myself. Heidi hadn't even asked me why yet. I checked my watch. "Damn, I've got to be on the Hill in twenty minutes. And it looks like you were going out, anyway. Could we set another time to get together?" Heidi sat looking blank. "It would be a big help," I added, "if I could check out with you some of the things other people have told me about—"

Suddenly, she pulled herself together. "I'll give you a ride," she said, to my astonishment. She stood up, buttoned her coat, and headed for the door.

Any doubts I'd had about Heidi's ability to concentrate well enough to drive had vanished by the time we reached her car in the row of carports that took up most of the building's ground floor. Although she still looked like a refugee from famine, plague, and grief, she was obviously well in control of herself as she unlocked the car door and got us on our way.

"I really appreciate the ride," I told her tentatively as she pulled her dark green Honda out onto Eastlake. I couldn't tell if she was intensely concentrated on the traffic or on something completely removed from the here-and-now. I wasn't even sure she'd heard me until, half a minute later, she said, calmly, "No problem. I was going out anyway. What is it you want to know?"

"I'm assuming, for personal reasons, that the woman who's been charged with killing Ted didn't do it." No reaction. "Can you tell me who else might have had a reason to?"

A pause, and then: "No one."

"Did he seem any different the last week or so before... ?"

The car stopped at a red light, but her hands stayed clenched, knuckles white, on the steering wheel. "No. The same." She glanced quickly at me, moving her head so fast I expected to hear the bones rattle. "Why?"

"Well, I've been hearing things. That he seemed excited about something. And then his involvement in this Peaceful Way business...."

"I had nothing to do with that." She didn't sound defensive about it, merely matter of fact. "I wasn't interested. I'm not interested."

"So.... What did bring you and Ted together?"

"Our work." The way she said it sounded almost noble. "We were preparing a series of articles for publication. Together. And he helped me with my thesis." A weird edge crept into her voice. When I leaned forward a bit and glimpsed her face in the glow of a passing streetlight, I saw that her mouth was twisted in a taut grimace.

Oh hell, I silently exclaimed. Oh hell and damnation! This woman obviously loved the creep, and now she was falling to pieces without him.

She went on, though. "That's why," she said, forming the words slowly and carefully with her stiff lips, "I think I might...go away." She glanced at me again, as if to check on my reaction. "I might...go elsewhere. To finish my degree. Because...we were working so closely...our work was so intertwined that...."

"Yeah," I said, trying to make my voice carry some of the sympathy I felt without sounding condescending or superficial. "I can see that would be really tough, to try and carry on as if—"

"Is this anywhere near where you wanted to go?" Her voice was calmer again, and she looked at me carefully, as if examining me from a much greater distance than the width of her diminutive car.

Surprised by the abruptness of it, I looked up and found that she'd pulled the car over to the curb near an intersection just three blocks from Fennel's address. "Yes, this is great. Thanks. I'll get out here, then."

She sat motionless, waiting for me to go.

"Could we arrange another time to get together," I inquired hopefully, "for another talk?"

She frowned, and I was struck by how little flesh she had to frown with. "I don't know," she said finally. "I don't know that I have anything more to say to you."

"Oh, but—"

"Give me your telephone number," she said. "And your address, and we'll see."

Well, it seemed pretty weird to me, but I wasn't exactly in a position to insist. And besides, I had her address and phone number, so it seemed only fair for her to have mine, too. "Terry Barber," I wrote carefully on a sheet of paper pulled from my pack, and then my address and phone number. I handed her the paper, said my thank-you-and-goodbye into her silence, and left the car. When I'd walked a few paces ahead, something made me turn around and look back. A streetlight shone through the windshield of the little car, and Heidi's face floated white and rain-distorted above the steering wheel. *My god!* I gasped silently.

For a second, something about the expression on her face made her look so much like Barb that I couldn't believe my eyes.

Heidi's car passed me by the time I reached the end of the next block. As far as I could tell, she didn't even glance in my direction.

Okay, I told myself. Now on to Fennel. It didn't seem like the upcoming interview could possibly be much worse than the one I'd just been through. But I wasn't expecting it to resemble a bed of roses, either. Except maybe with regard to the thorns.

The address Fennel had given me turned out to be the top floor of a house stuck in behind another house. Capitol Hill is like that. Exactly at seven I was reaching for the doorbell labeled "up" when the door edged open into darkness.

"Fennel?" I ventured.

"Quick," she said, opening the door just wide enough for me to enter.

"Upstairs," she muttered. As I followed her up, I thought back sympathetically to the woman at the LRC who'd mistaken Barb for one of the other Furies, the day Barb almost knocked me over on her way down the stairs. It's not that Fennel really looked like Barb; not when you took her feature by feature. Her nose was much sharper, for one thing, and in fact her entire face and figure were constructed on a smaller scale than Barb's. Nevertheless, despite her relative delicacy, she managed to project virtually the same general impression: blue denim straining to contain a surging mass of big, angry woman.

The stairs ended at a door that opened into a kitchen considerably smaller than the one at Everywhere House. As soon as Fennel shut the door behind us, she moved quickly to the room's one window and peered out. "Were you followed?" she asked, keeping her gruff voice almost a whisper.

I had to stifle a nervous giggle. "Are you serious?"

Her answer was an angry glare. "In here," she said.

I could see a reflection of lamplight and hear a television playing in a room to my right, but Fennel led me through a different door and into the darkness of a short hallway. At the end of the hall she turned us into a room lit by a shaded, low-wattage lamp set by a mattress on the floor. The blinds on the two windows were drawn tight.

"I'm being followed," she proclaimed defiantly, but without raising her voice, as she hunkered down at the head of the mattress bed. "And watched. The house is being watched. I've seen them."

"By the police?" I asked, still feeling mighty incredulous. Fennel simply shrugged, and I sat myself down, facing her from the end of the bed. She looked really stressed out; her eyes, darting between the windows and the door, flashed white again and again, as if she were signalling for help in a code I didn't understand. "Well, did they tell you not to leave town or anything like that?" My first impulse was to not believe her, to put her down as paranoid, but there had been a murder, after all, so who knew?

She shook her head no and then added, "How could they? We didn't have anything to do with it, we weren't there, we didn't see anything."

"They questioned you, though?"

"Fuckin' pigs," she rasped.

I heaved an internal sigh and plodded on. "Why didn't you leave town with the others?"

Fennel shrugged her shoulders again. "Wanted to finish school," she said. "Sally said I could stay here, and we're in a lot of the same classes, so we could go and come back together. Seemed safe enough at the time." She sounded dubious about her own judgment in that respect, and I wondered in passing how the unknown Sally was holding up under the strain of an omnipresent Fennel in her life.

"And Clove?" I prodded. "What happened to her?" Last I'd heard, from Jan, the Furies were on the point of disowning their littlest member for her accidental squealing to the police.

"Went back east, I guess. Where she came from." Clove was not an interesting subject, apparently. Talking about her didn't alter either the dull timbre of Fennel's voice or the voltage of her body's charged nerves.

"Okay, let's talk about Barb."

Now that got a reaction. "What's your role in all this?" Fennel demanded, suddenly fastening her restless brown eyes on mine. "Why should I talk to you about Barb or anything else?"

Faced with the need to explain my self-imposed mission yet again, I found myself overwhelmed by a feeling of deep repugnance. Death, grief, paranoia— what the hell was my role in all this? Why did I continue to dig into people's lives when all I found was...well, people's lives. Glimpses of pain, mostly, with no answers included, no tidy clues forming a neat little path toward revelation and understanding. The memory of Heidi's face twisted with pain was still very clear in my mind, and for a minute there, all I wanted to do was forget the whole thing.

I think I was actually on the point of getting back on my feet and walking out the door when another memory flashed in my mind: the eerie, impossible moment when Heidi's face, seen through the distortion of a windshield wet with rain, reminded me so forcefully of Barb behind the double wall of her flat, white face and the thick glass of the visiting room window. Yes, Barb has a point of view in this business, too, I reminded myself; and unlike me, she doesn't have any choice in the role she has to play.

"I'm trying to help Barb," I said at last. "She says she didn't kill Simpson— ex-husband or not. The police say she did, and I want to make sure her side of the story gets a chance to be heard. I guess if there's one thing you and I could agree on"—I looked at Fennel without a great deal of hope—"it's that a lesbian, and especially a lesbian separatist, might not inspire the police in this city to go the extra mile when they've already got a case they think will stick. So I'm trying to rustle up some alternative scenarios, some other answers to the case besides the ones the police have fixed on, because that might provide a reasonable doubt that she killed Ted Simpson."

Fennel's eyes had flicked back to the window. But, "Okay," she said reluctantly. "What do you want to know?"

I took her through my usual questions, and a few specifically Fury-oriented ones, with even fewer results than I'd expected. No, Barb had never mentioned Simpson to any of the Furies. No, they didn't know she'd spent her days at a friend's house instead of the factory where she'd said she worked. No, they hadn't seen or heard anything unusual or relevant on the night of Simpson's death. No, Fennel could add nothing to what I already knew from other sources—Jan and Barb herself—about what happened during the police intrusion at Athena House and the subsequent hours at police headquarters. The interview was a washout.

"Okay," I said, dejected but not quite ready to give up. "Now tell me about Barb."

Fennel snapped a quick, suspicious glare in my direction. "What?" she demanded.

"You knew her better than most people," I told her. "Do you think it's likely that she killed Simpson? Is she a violent person? What brought her to a group like the Furies? And why did she tell so many lies?"

For the second time since I got there, Fennel's eyes fastened on mine. "You want to know about Barb?" Her dull, stifled voice was almost mocking now. "Okay, I'll tell you about Barb." And she did. She told me about the uncle who molested Barb from early childhood, raping her when she was twelve. She told me about Barb's fumbling attempt to tell her mother and her mother's response that, "You'd feel so much better about yourself, Barbara, if you'd just lose some weight." She told me about the beginning of Barb's decade of obsession with food—eating until she was sick, then fasting for days at a time, or eating and making herself throw up—and always, always hiding her activities, her thoughts, herself, hating herself.

She told me all this in almost clinical detail and then said: "You were at the fat oppression workshop. Felt better afterwards, didn't you? Felt relieved you didn't have to hate yourself anymore for not being skinny. That's the way women like you always react, just ripping off the analysis to make yourselves feel better instead of admitting that you really ought to feel worse until you do something about the oppression of fat women. You never think about someone like Barb and what the radical analysis of fat oppression meant to her. So I'll tell you what it meant to her: it meant she could stop hating her body long enough to pay attention to something else. It meant she could free up her mind to remember what happened to her—the rape, the molestation, the way her mother abandoned her. You hear our analysis and walk away feeling liberated and happy. But Barb, who helped make that analysis, what kind of liberation does it give her? It liberates her into pain, that's what. Pain and anger. And then you have the gall to ask what brought her to a group like the Furies. You make me sick."

There was silence for a blessed minute while my brain reeled. Yes, it was easier to understand Barb after hearing what Fennel had to say. But on the other hand.... Not every abused girl-child becomes a Fury. I couldn't immediately carry that thought to any conclusion, so I shelved it for the moment, along with my hurt feelings. They could wait—and would wait—till later. Meanwhile, as a woman who'd been victimized and survived, Barb had plenty of reason for her fury against men. The question was, of course, whether she'd kept that fury within the bounds of analysis and spray-painting, or had lost control one night and let her anger wield the knife that killed Ted Simpson.

Fennel looked like a woman who needed to cry. Well, she wouldn't feel free to do so in my presence, I rationalized, so the best thing for me to do was leave. There didn't seem to be much more I could learn from her, anyway. Or maybe I just didn't want to learn what more she had to tell me.

My exit from the apartment was a mirror image of my entrance, including Fennel's peering out the kitchen window to check for spies. She didn't respond to my embarrassed "thanks" as she let me out the door at the bottom of the stairs.

Now what, Terry?, I asked myself as I reached the street. I felt upset, unsettled, and sad, and I didn't know whether I needed the solace of solitude or the comfort of company. As I walked through the damp evening air, I tried to figure out who I felt like being with just then. Ellie? Peg, maybe, or Jan? To my surprise, another name burbled up from my brain: Sarah, the woman I'd talked to at the Crescent on Wednesday night. Unfortunately, I didn't know her phone number. You could look it up, said a little voice in my head as I reached the top of the hill up to Fifteenth. Yeah, I countered, but do I really know her well enough to call her up and invite myself over out of the blue like this? So who says you have to invite yourself over? Just a friendly call.... Who knows, maybe she feels like company, too.

The debate continued as I walked south on Fifteenth and turned west on Pine Street. It felt good to be walking, and if I was headed more towards the Crescent than home, well, I could righteously claim to be heading toward a bus stop, too.

When I got to Broadway, I had to make a choice. Bus stop or not? I glanced left and there, on the far edge of a discount gas station one block down, was a telephone booth glowing like a sign from on high. I dug in my pocket for change.

My footsteps became audible halfway down the deserted block. This late in the evening, even on a Friday, the crowds would be further up the street, where the taverns and moviehouses are. *There is absolutely no cause for alarm.* I silently parroted the line from a Monty Python sketch for reassurance as I entered a shadowy patch of sidewalk that the streetlight failed to reach. That's when I heard the car behind me.

It sounded at first like the squeal of brakes, and I looked over my right shoulder to see why a car would need to stop that suddenly on an otherwise deserted street. As soon as I saw it, though, I realized I'd been wrong. It wasn't the squeal of brakes, it was the squeal of tires suddenly accelerating on damp pavement. The car was at the far end of the long block, headed south just like I was. Crazy driver, I said to myself, ready to dismiss the sound and the car from my mind. But then I saw the car veer out of the righthand lane and head across the center line. It was heading directly towards me.

There was a flashing instant of blankness, and then my body took over. That car was headed right at me, and accelerating all the time. If my mind had been in charge, I'd have turned around before I started to run; the car would have lost some speed if it'd had to turn that sharply. What I did instead was run straight ahead as fast as my legs would carry me.

I had at least half a block head start, and that's all I had. No door to dash through to safety, nothing massive to hide behind. Somewhere in my brain the thought appeared: nothing between me and the car except the bump of the curb. And then the curb disappeared. I'd reached the gas station, and the sidewalk melted down into the street, positively inviting the car to enter and run me down.

Nooooo! Was I screaming? I still don't know whether that desperate denial ever left my throat as I threw myself between two gas pumps and dove behind a green metal dumpster. It sat next to the gas station building between a low concrete divider strip and a wall of concrete blocks. Fortunately, I was going so fast when I hit the wall behind the dumpster that the impact knocked me off my feet, so the car's virtually instantaneous arrival caught me already on my way to the ground. If I'd been standing straight up, chances are my head would have been crushed between the dumpster and the wall. As it was, my body was batted back and forth a few times between the two. I don't remember that half-minute in any great detail, but I do remember the noise. It was incredible.

And then suddenly, incredibly, there was silence. Somewhere nearby, above my head, metal was creaking and groaning. I was just working up to some groaning of my own when I heard a shout: "Hey!" A man's voice. There was a shriek of metal, and the world rocked above me. Then the sound of running feet, light-sounding feet, running away. And then the man's voice again, "Hey! Hey, wait!" More running feet, coming closer this time.

"Jesus Christ! Did you see that!"

"Shit, man, that car just—! Must be some kinda lunatic to—! I mean, shit!"

The breathless voices came closer with the footsteps. Two men. They sounded young. "We gotta call the police, man," said one of them, "get a ambulance in here!"

I groaned. "Hey, I'm okay. How do I get out of here?"

There was a split second of silence, just long enough for me to panic at the thought that maybe I'd imagined those voices after all, and then I heard soft movement on my right and a face appeared in a square of darkness I hadn't yet identified as open air. The sense of relief was overwhelming. Maybe that's why I passed out.

Next thing I knew, I was lying flat on my back on the gas station pavement with a policeman crouched over me. A second policeman in the background said, "Ambulance is on the way."

"Just lay still," said the crouching policeman. "Just take it easy."

"You boys probably shouldn't've pulled her outta there. Always best to let the experts handle these things." I turned my head the other way to find who the second policeman was talking to. Two young men were standing just a few feet away. They shifted their feet uneasily and looked down at me, and then away to the sky-blue car that had merged with the dumpster.

"It's okay," I told them. My voice didn't come out loudly enough that time, so I tried it again. "It's okay. I appreciate your help." They ducked their heads in shy acknowledgment.

"Hard to believe it happened, even when you saw it with your own eyes," said one, and "Musta been a lunatic," said the other again, so now I knew which was which. It was speaker number one I'd seen so briefly from my prison behind the dumpster, his black hair fringing his face as he bent to peer in.

"I'm all right—" I started to tell the patrolman crouching by my side, but just then the ambulance arrived. The next fifteen minutes were a blur of frustration as I was retained in forcible isolation by the paramedics. The policemen were talking to the two young men, but I could hear only snatches of their conversation.

"Sure we saw it!" Then a bit I couldn't catch, followed by, "—headed right at her!" and, a minute later, "No way, man! Couldn't have been no accident, because—"

"Do you feel any discomfort here?" Fingers dug into my stomach.

"Ouch! No! I'm all right. How many times do I have to—"

But the medic was inexorable. Nothing could stay him in his search for grievous injury until one of the policemen showed up at the ambulance door. He watched the proceedings for a while and then, perhaps reassured by my continued bleating of "I'm all right, for heaven's sake!" cleared his throat and said, "Mind if I talk to the victim for a minute?"

The victim. Wow. I'd never thought of myself in quite that light before.

"According to documents found in the glove compartment," the policeman said, "the vehicle is registered to a Fennel Bowers." I felt the blood drain from my head. "Name mean anything to you, Ms. Barber?"

I never lied to him directly. Not out loud, any way. At first I could only shake my head, and then, when I'd recovered enough to speak, I said one hundred variations on "I don't know, I don't know, I don't know anything at all." Keeping that up, and fending off the persistent attentions of the paramedic, required all my limited stamina for the next half hour. Eventually I managed a minor miracle: to persuade the police I was too upset to make a statement until morning, while simultaneously persuading the medical man I was well enough to go home. A patrol car was summoned to carry me there, and I arrived with the policeman's words still ringing in my ear.

"We'll be in touch," he'd said.

20.

Voices outside my bedroom door woke me Saturday morning. I'd crawled into bed the night before in shock, numbly glad no one was around to see the police car drop me off and ask me what happened. For a while I'd lain awake with incoherent questions pulsing through my brain. *Fennel's* car? Why would Fennel...? She wouldn't have any reason to.... But nobody else even knew I was there. Nobody except...Peg? Connie? Impossible.

And yet, someone had tried to kill me. Or...scare me? They'd certainly succeeded if that was their aim.

The thought I had to bury deepest before my body would relax and let me sleep was the realization of what the attempt on my life might mean. Instead of diverting attention away from Barb and the lesbian community, all my feeble investigating had done was to bring the focus back home: back to lesbians and, specifically, back to the Furies. Because surely the attack on me was related to Simpson's murder. I wasn't the most popular woman in Seattle, but I was damned sure nobody hated me. Not, I assured myself, enough to—

"She says yes," hollered Jeanne outside my door.

"Okay. Ready in ten minutes," Fran hollered back from downstairs.

I rolled over to look at the alarm clock and groaned. My body felt stiff and bruised all over. The clock said it was eight-o-four.

Ten minutes later I heard Jeanne and Gretchen clatter down the stairs. Time to get up, I told myself. The armed struggle workshop was scheduled to begin at 9:30 over on Capitol Hill.

I hauled myself out of bed and examined as much of my body as I could without contortion. Wasn't so bad, really, I decided after a few cautious bends and stretches to work the kinks out, although there were a few places where bruises were starting to show. For some reason I still felt reluctant to talk about what happened—maybe just because I didn't want to think too much about it myself. So I timed myself to arrive in the kitchen with only enough leeway for toast, coffee, and minimal conversation.

"Where's Peg?" I asked the room at large.

"Probably stayed the night up at 4017," said Toni. "Getting pretty serious, I'd say." She waggled her eyebrows.

"Just as well," remarked Fran. "Six is a better fit than seven—and thank goodness you don't have bucket seats, Gretch."

Everything seemed so normal as the desultory conversation proceeded. Maybe, came the sneaking, hopeful thought, I won't have to think any more about last night at all.

We were headed out the door already when the phone rang. "Hello?" said Fran. And then, "Oh yeah. Sure." She held the receiver out to me and whispered, "It's Barb!"

My heart sank. Barb was the last thing I wanted to think about right then. Barb and the jail, Barb and the murder, Barb and last night.

"Hi," I said neutrally into the phone, and was startled to hear a fuzz of long distance in my ear.

"Can you talk?" Her voice was between a mutter and a whisper.

"Well, I was just on my way out the door," I temporized. "But I plan to come visit this afternoon, so—"

"No," she said.

"No?" I was dumbfounded.

"I'm not there," she said. "I got bailed out. That's what I called to tell you. I'm in Montana."

"Oh." My mind didn't seem to be working very well. "Oh, well, congratulations. That's great." Jeanne nudged me with her elbow and looked a question at me. "Barb, there's people here waiting for me," I said. "Why don't you give me your number and I'll call you back later. There are some things we need to—"

"No," she said, "I'll call you. I can't—" She stopped abruptly, and when she spoke again her voice was so soft and quick I could barely catch the words. "I'll call you." And she was gone.

"Wow!" razzed Fran as all left the house. "Talk about real life drama! Here we are on our way to a workshop about armed struggle and what do we get held up by? A phone call from a murderer. What class!"

"So what's the story?" Jeanne asked, and as we climbed into the car I told them Barb had been bailed out and was back in Montana. The minute we were under way, I rolled the window down and let the wind blow full in my face. If it couldn't blow the tears back into my eyes, at least it would give me something to blame them on. It's just the wind, I could say, and not have to admit how angry and confused I was feeling. Like a flashback, everything I'd felt for that instant in Fennel's borrowed room returned to overwhelm me again with repugnance for the mess I'd so blithely gotten myself into. Let her rich parents take care of her, then, I declaimed silently. Why should I put my life on the line for someone who jerks me around like that, calling up to tell me when to visit and then when not to visit, and then hanging up on me before I have a chance to—. Going off to safety while I'm still here taking all the risks, and then not even willing to give me her fucking phone number!

I breathed deeply through my mouth, as I'd been taught to do for carsickness as a child. With the gradual calming of my pulse came the unwilling memory of Barb herself. The sound of her. She was whispering. In her own parent's house, presumably, the place I called 'safety,' she was whispering to me over the phone and hanging up because she heard someone coming, there in her Montana refuge. I sighed and closed the window against the wind. No matter how angry she made me, I couldn't shake the connection I felt with Barb. The more I learned about her, the more I ached to return to Barb the power I used to see in the rigid, uncompromising strength of her big, furious body. She'd gone so far along a path that tempted me much more than the path chosen by the people I'd be hearing about at the armed struggle workshop, and I wanted so much to talk to her about it. Maybe it's too late for that, I told myself, now that she seems to have decided to go back...home. That didn't mean I had to give up the investigation, though. Not only did I still feel a commitment to Barb, I also had a stake in the outcome myself now. Maybe I could have pulled out yesterday; but not after last night's hit-and-run. If I was going to be made a target, I damned well wasn't going to be a stationary one; I'd be no man's—or woman's— sitting duck.

And after the whole thing was over, I'd try to figure out why it was that Barb could be so real to me when apparently I wasn't real to her at all.

The closest Gretchen could find a parking space was four blocks from the church, but we were part of a gathering crowd from the minute we got out of the car. Streamlets of people flowed together from all directions and filled the pews to capacity. Lots of lesbians, of course, but lots of other people, too. Men with beards and women with skirts, a scattering of babies, kids, and folks with white hair. Almost everybody, it seemed, was wearing blue.

I was sitting between Peg and Fran in the unofficial lesbian section of the audience, which was also the section that had come, at least in part, to cheer Jan on. She looked nervous, up there in front with the other speakers-to-be, but very involved, very much a part of what she was doing and who she was doing it with. So much so, in fact, that I wondered for a minute if she'd think of us at all. Would she remember to look for us and to care that we were here?

"Hey Peg," said Fran leaning out across me, "whistle for me, would ya?" Obligingly, Peg's shrill whistle split the air and everyone in the church turned to look in our direction. "Jan, hi!" yelled Fran waving like a flag. I saw Jan laugh and wave and felt myself more at home.

Only ten minutes past the appointed hour, the workshop got underway with a "brief" history of popular struggle. That took about an hour and a half, and neither of the speakers was Jan. It was fairly interesting, even if a lot of it, especially the parts about India and the Civil Rights Movement, had more to do with nonviolence than with armed struggle.

After a short break, which I spent mostly in the line to use one of the church's two female toilets, it was Jan's turn. She had some notes on index cards, and she stood behind a little lectern to give us the class analysis behind the politics of the George Jackson Brigade. I couldn't help wishing she wasn't so nervous, and then I felt bad, as if I was criticizing her by even noticing. It must be scary to stand up in front of a couple hundred people and lecture about class analysis, especially if, like Jan, you're not much of a talker.

Forty-five minutes later, Jan stepped back from the lectern and sat down, yielding the floor to a man presenting the history of the George Jackson Brigade. By the time he finished, I found myself summing up the program so far with the thought: This should have been more interesting. It all sounded stilted; jargony and unreal. And yet the people were real—not only the speakers but the GJB members themselves. They were real individuals just like me, more or less, except they'd committed themselves to living out their politics more radically than I had. So why these oddly alienating reports of their politics and their lives? Surely the purpose of the workshop was to make us feel the connections, not the distances, between the GJB and the rest of us.

After the woman who was emceeing the workshop explained the logistics for lunch and the schedule of events for the afternoon, the entire roomful of people rose as a body and started to talk, talk, talk. I couldn't even hear what Peg was saying to me, and I knew I'd feel claustrophobic when the crowd got to milling around, so I mimed back my intention to head for the outdoors. Her response was a friendly wave as she put her arm around the woman who'd been sitting on her other side and the two of them headed for a door leading deeper into the church. She wanted to be close to the front of the line for lunch, I decided as I weaseled my way towards fresh air.

I heard my name being called from two directions at once. "Terry" to the left of me, "Terry" to the right. It felt awkward to be so much in demand when all I wanted was to get the hell out of there. At last I made it through to the front steps of the church and turned around to see if my callers were still in sight. They were not only in sight, they were in pursuit, and they reached their quarry simultaneously.

"Terry, I've decided—" said Letitia, and

"Terry, you look—" Sarah said.

That led, naturally, to a moment of silence, followed by a round of introductions and an opportunity for Letitia and Sarah to exhibit extreme courtesy to one another. Eventually, Sarah persuaded Letitia to go first, so the two of us went into a huddle while Sarah strolled off a short way to wait her turn.

Letitia was glowing with nerves and excitement. "I've made up my mind. I'm going to infiltrate the Peaceful Way cult. I'm sure I can get them to recruit me, and then—"

I was appalled. "No, Letitia! What are you talking about? For heaven's sake, you don't have to—"

"It's all right," she told me with magnificent self-assurance. "It's not your responsibility, I'm doing it entirely on my own."

"But we don't even know for sure that there's any connection with Simpson's murder," I protested. "We ought to make sure before anybody—"

"If we wait, it might be too dangerous." Her assurance was starting to seem downright eerie. "The more you investigate, the more chance they'll have to figure out they're under suspicion and the more dangerous it will be. Now's the perfect time, don't you see?"

"No, I—"

"And besides, even if it doesn't have anything to do with the murder, it ought to be investigated, right?"

"Yes, but—"

"What you told me about Jennifer's behavior sounds like the effect of drugs to me, and why else would they be locked in? If I can persuade them to think they're recruiting me—and I'm pretty sure I can—then I'll have a chance to find out exactly how they operate and—"

"But Letitia," I wailed, "it's too dangerous!"

"Only if I weren't on my guard," she responded instantly. "But since I will be, I'll be able to see the cult from the inside as long as it's safe and then—"

The beep-beep of a car horn interrupted her as a blue Beetle pulled up to the curb. A tall young man with wavy dark hair got out of the driver's seat and stood leaning on the open cardoor.

"There's my ride," Letitia said, "I have to go now. Don't worry, Terry, I won't do anything stupid," and she took off at a lope toward the car.

"Letitia!" I called and started after her. "Wait!"

Sarah joined me on the sidewalk, and we both watched the little blue car drive away. "Not a lovers' quarrel, I hope," she said ironically.

The intelligence and challenge in her voice and her face were a bit too bracing for me at that moment. "Oh, Sarah," I wailed, "Why in the world did I ever get myself into this." I felt tears of frustration welling up in my eyes again, and when Sarah put a tentatively comforting hand on my shoulder I felt a twinge of pain from the bruised and battered muscle. Next thing I knew, we were sitting on the steps of the house next door, Sarah was holding my hand, and I was pouring out my tale of woe. "...so I haven't even told anybody yet about last night," I concluded, "and then Barb calls this morning, and now Letitia.... It's just too much for me, that's all. It's just too much for me to handle." I huddled against her shoulder with a sigh.

"Well," she said after a little pause, "I'm not sure I caught all of that, but it sounds to me like you need a break. Think you can bear to miss the rest of this business?" She nodded back towards the church.

"Yeah," I admitted. "It's making me feel kind of alienated for some reason."

"Let's go back to my place and see if we can get you put back together. A battering like that requires attention, even if nothing's broken."

We were almost to the bus stop before I remembered Ellie. "Oh damnation. I told Ellie I'd spend the rest of today with her after the workshop."

"Do you want to?" Sarah enquired reasonably.

"No," I muttered.

"So call her up and tell her you can't make it."

It sounded so easy the way she said it. So easy and so reasonable that I decided, entirely against my usual habits and practices, to give it a try.

"Ellie, this is Terr," I said into the pay-phone a minute later.

"Hi, Terry! Is the program over already?"

"No, I.... Listen, Ellie, I won't be able to come over today. Or tonight."

"Oh?" Guardedly neutral. "Why is that, Terry?"

"I, uh...."

A beseeching glance at Sarah brought a shrug of the shoulders and a whispered, "Just tell her something came up."

"...Something came up, Ellie," I said. "It's hard to explain over the phone, but.... I'm sorry. I'll call you soon, okay?"

There was an ominous silence from the other end of the line. "Bye, Ellie," I said, and ran to follow Sarah onto the bus. My bruised muscles were getting stiffer and achier every minute, but I felt like a liberated woman.

Sarah had a studio apartment in a crumbly old brick building perched on Capitol Hill's extreme south side. The hallway and stairs of the building smelled like a century of dust and dead people's cooking, but her apartment on the third floor smelled like books and oranges. Before I had a chance to take in much more than that, Sarah kicked off her shoes and was leading me into the bathroom.

She turned on the water in the old-fashioned tub, stirred in some green bath salts from a glass jar on a shelf, laid a clean blue towel on the rim of the sink, and said, "Go ahead and get in as soon as the water looks deep enough for a good soak. Keep it as hot as you can. I'll be back."

Wow, I said to myself when she'd left the room. Then I took off my clothes, folded them neatly on the varnished wood toilet seat, and stepped gingerly into the steaming hot water. It felt wonderful, once I'd adjusted to the temperature, to relax and let the water hold me. At Everywhere House, I always took showers because it was quicker and I was always in a hurry. Maybe I oughta slow down and bathe more often. I watched the steam rise toward the single blue and green flower painted on the wall above the tap end of the tub.

Eventually, Sarah stuck her head in the door to see how I was doing. "I'll give you a massage whenever you feel like you've had enough. The space heater's on, so you shouldn't feel cold, but I can lend you my robe if you think you'll need it."

"Thanks, I'll be out in a minute." Sarah's matter-of-fact attitude made my latent embarrassment seem silly. I debated whether to keep the towel with me when I left the bathroom but decided against it. With or without the towel, I'd be pretty visible out there, so I might as well just be bold. Thanks to feminism, I'd come to accept and appreciate my body, I really had. But that didn't mean I didn't get nervous every time I exposed it for the first time to someone new.

I padded soberly out of the bathroom and onto the soft plush of the main room's light-blue carpet. No wonder she took her shoes off as soon as she stepped through the door, I thought. A carpet like that wouldn't last a week at Everywhere House.

Sarah had changed into grey sweatpants and a tee-shirt and she was standing by one of those futons that you can switch back and forth from a couch to a bed. At the moment, it was a bed; on it was a yellow sheet folded in half lengthwise. "Go ahead and lie down on your stomach," Sarah said. "Is it warm enough in here for you?"

"Yes," I told her as I lay down. "Very pleasant."

"Good," she said. "Just relax now. It'll hurt a bit when I work on the sore muscles, but it'll help in the long run so bear with me if you can. If something really hurts, though, be sure to let me know."

Then she set to work, and it was wonderful. Oh, it hurt at times, especially in the shoulders, and there was one hip muscle that must have been hit harder than I'd realized the night before. But it felt heavenly nevertheless, and the lotions she worked with smelled clean and refreshing as daisies in sunlight.

I fell asleep somewhere around the time she was smoothing out my back with long, sweeping strokes of her palm. When I awoke I was lying on my back with a pale yellow sheet over me The late afternoon sunshine breaking through the clouds bounced off the white wall across the room from the foot of the bed. My stomach growled in response to a delicious smell coming from beyond that white wall, and I heard some kitcheny pot-and-pan sounds from that direction, too. After a luxurious stretch and yawn, I rolled myself upright for a look around.

"Hey!" I called out to Sarah a minute later. "It's an egg!"

"Welcome back to the world of the waking," she said, appearing in the opening between the main room and the little kitchen. "And yes, it's an egg all right. How are you feeling?"

"I feel great," I assured her. "That was a wonderful massage. Did you do the painting yourself?" The three other walls of the room were painted the off-white, brownish beige of a bird's egg, mottled here and there with pale indefinite areas of delicate blue.

"I helped," she said, "but mostly just following directions. My sister's the artistic one in the family."

Sarah disappeared back into the kitchen, and I decided it felt like time to get

161

my clothes back on. Heading for the kitchen afterwards I stopped to look at three framed photographs hanging on the white wall. They were the only decorations in the place, aside from the single flower in the bathroom, the three birds-egg walls, and a white carved rabbit on a bookcase full of books I hoped I'd get a chance to look at later. The sun had sunk lower in the sky, and I had to squint to make out any details in the small black-and-white photos. One seemed very old; it showed a man and woman, dressed in what I supposed was traditional Japanese clothing, the man staring stiffly into the camera, the woman gazing down at the little child standing on a stool in front of them. The child's wide eyes looked fascinated by whatever they saw. Beneath that picture was a more modern one, again of a man, a woman, and a child. These folks were dressed up, too, but dressed up like, at a guess, a 1930's Sears catalog. The man wore a dark suit with a tie and the kind of hats men wore in all the old movies; the woman wore a short-sleeved shirtwaist dress and a hat with a flower on one side. Between them was a little girl about three or four years old, wearing a dress with a wide, flat, lace-trimmed collar. The last picture was even more contemporary. All it showed was the smiling faces of three children, two girls and a boy; their shoulders blurred out and ended at the oval of the picture frame.

"Is one of those kids you?" I asked Sarah as I reached the boundary between the main room and the edge of the kitchen.

"The one on the left," she said.

"And the other girl's your artistic sister?"

"Yeah." She smiled. "And my brother Pete."

"Do they live in Seattle?"

"No. Marian came back to help me fix this place up, but—" She broke off and concentrated for a minute on the vegetables she was slicing into a pan on the stove. Then, "Come on," she told me. "I'll give you the tour."

Back in the main room, she pointed to the top photograph. "My father's parents and my father. In Japan, right before they emigrated to South America. Then they moved to Hawaii, and then here." She tapped the second picture. "My grandpa and grandma with my mom. In Spokane, about eight years before they were sent to Tule Lake."

Her voice was tight, and I could see why. The picture suddenly vibrated, even for me, with unexpected poignancy. "That was one of the camps during the war, right?" I asked her.

"Right." She hesitated and then said, half grudgingly, "Congratulations. A lot of whites wouldn't know about that."

"And this," I continued where she'd left off, "is you and your sister and brother, who don't live around here."

"None of them came back," she said. "My parents still haven't. Not even to visit. Maybe some day. Maybe not." She led the way back to the kitchen.

We were silent for awhile as she worked at the counter. Then I unconsciously spoke my thoughts out loud: "What an adventure, though." Sarah looked around at me at me, surprise in her eyes, and I hastened to explain. "Immigrating from Japan to South America, I mean, and then Hawaii. That must have been, what? In the Twenties?"

I saw her body relax, her shoulders and elbows lower, as her mind followed mine away from the camps and back to her father's family. "Nineteen-thirteen, actually. My father's mother was eighteen."

"And then your mother and father met here in Seattle?"

"In eastern Washington. That's where my mom's folks are from. I mean, if you go back far enough you hit Japan, but as far as they were concerned they were Washingtonians. Right up till the war, anyway."

She started gathering stuff to set the dinette table, and I reached out to take the silverware from her. Together we set two places, and then she brought the food: stir-fried peapods, cabbage, and carrots over rice. I hadn't eaten since toast for breakfast, so I was starved and she let me eat in silence for a while.

"Filled up?" she asked when I'd gotten to the filling-in-the-corners stage. "Now tell me again what happened to you last night. I couldn't make much sense of what you were saying at the church, but it sounded terrifying."

"Oh, it was," I assured her. "It definitely was."

After I described the attempted hit-and-run, I had to go back and fill in the bigger picture—the investigation into Simpson's murder—before we could talk constructively about the whys and wherefores.

"So I've been hoping the murderer will turn out to be someone connected with the Peaceful Way," I concluded as she picked up the shrieking kettle and transferred its boiling water to the teapot, "but how in the world does that connect with someone trying to run me over?"

"You told me Fennel said she was being watched," Sarah reminded me. "If that's true and not just paranoia, maybe there's a connection between her and the cult. Or maybe somebody from the cult is watching her. They could have seen you arrive and then followed you when you left. It wasn't necessarily her in the car."

"Yeah!" I accepted the idea with enthusiasm. "Maybe that's it!"

"Let's list all the possibilities." She pulled a tablet of paper and a pencil from the window ledge behind the table. "Fennel."

"I can't believe she do anything like this. Furious or not."

"But it's theoretically possible, right? It was her car, after all."

"But there's no earthly reason why she should want to kill me."

"How about if the Furies were involved in Simpson's murder somehow? Or if Fennel herself was?" Sarah poured the tea while we considered the possibility.

"I just can't see it," I said finally. "I mean, I guess I can imagine the Furies being involved in killing a man, but if they were, why would Fennel try to kill me now? Why not just sit back and let the wheels of justice turn, so to speak? At this point, nobody's really in any danger except Barb, and for Fennel to attack me would just turn the spotlight back on her and the Furies, which is the last thing they'd want if they're involved in any way."

"Makes sense," Sarah admitted. "Okay, so who else could it have been? Had to be somebody who knew you were there, who knew why you were there, and who had a reason to want to scare or incapacitate you. Let's start with who knew you were there. Besides Fennel."

"Only Peg," I told her, "and that's ridiculous. She was in the living room when I made the appointment with Fennel, and I've talked to her about Simpson's murder, but.... No. She's my friend."

"I suppose it's possible she talked to someone else," Sarah mused, "not meaning to do you any harm, of course. You better ask her." She made some notes on her pad of paper and then looked up to say, "How'd you know where to find Fennel, anyway? She was sort of in hiding, wasn't she?"

"Definitely. But you know how it is with lesbians: somebody always knows. Jan, in this case."

"Did you tell her you'd made contact?"

"No, I've hardly seen Jan all week, she's been so busy with this workshop. And besides, Jan is out of the question even if she knew." Some things I was sure of.

Sarah accepted the finality of judgment in my voice. "Well, if that's everybody else you can think of, and barring the possibility of somebody from the cult staking out the place, that leaves us with...what did you say her name was? Simpson's girlfriend?"

"Heidi Bascom? No way. That's almost as ridiculous as saying Peg did it. I mean, aside from the fact that she didn't know where I was going, and that she doesn't know Fennel exists, and that she has no reason to do anything but sit back and let the system convict Barb, she's just not the type." Sarah's eyebrows looked skeptical, so I went on. "The woman is a basket case since Simpson's death. It's pitiful. She's one of those women who doesn't exist except when she's got a man to base her identity on, and now that her man is gone she's falling apart all over the place. She even told me she's thinking of quitting school because she can't handle going on without Ted to lean on. I feel sorry for her, of course, but she's a real mess. Socialized into weakness and helplessness. Sort of the opposite of a Fury, come to think of it." It was downright discouraging to recognize that, after all I'd been through, Barb was still the likeliest candidate as Simpson's killer. "I've just got to find out more about the leaders of that goddamn Peaceful Way," I declared. And then: "Oh my word! Letitia!"

"Who?" asked Sarah. "Oh, you mean that woman at the workshop. Isn't she the straight woman you told me about who's been helping you?"

"Yes, but Sarah, she told me today that she's going to try to infiltrate the

Peaceful Way! What are we going to do? We've got to stop her!" I couldn't believe I'd actually managed to forget Letitia's mad declaration for six whole hours.

Sarah calmed me down by pointing out that infiltration is usually a fairly slow process and therefore I didn't need to rush right out and do anything about it that night. "If worst comes to worst," she reminded me, "you can call in reinforcements. I don't ordinarily approve of using a woman's heterosexuality against her, but if it's a matter of keeping her out of immediate danger...."

"Jim!" I exclaimed as I caught on to her meaning.

"Is that the guy who picked her up at the church?"

"Must be. I've never met him, but I know Letitia lives with a man named Jim who works in the Philosophy department at the U."

"Well, there you go. As a last resort, I'm sure you can rely on him to keep Letitia from putting herself in too risky a position."

Our conversation turned more general as we toted our dishes the five steps back to the kitchen. In fact, conversation turned so general that an hour or so later we were back on the futon, lying peacefully side by side listening to a tape of some piano music. Sarah said she found piano music especially relaxing.

At the end of the tape, we turned towards each other simultaneously, and simultaneously forgot what it was we'd been about to say. We both felt shy for about thirty seconds. Then we saw in each other's eyes how funny that was and were about to laugh when we realized we'd rather kiss instead. After that, as they say, one thing followed another. The first time is usually hard for me, getting past the part where I feel like my body is being looked at with new eyes. With Sarah, though, the eyes didn't come into it. It was our bodies that got to know each other, limb to limb, breast to breast, vulva to ecstatic vulva. When I finally fell asleep, whenever that was, I was very, very happy.

Next thing I knew it was Sunday morning, and sunlight was flickering off and on outside the windows over the futon as a herd of fluffy clouds raced by. I crept in to the bathroom and then returned to lie next to Sarah again and enjoy the warmth of her bed. She was loosely curled on her left side, facing me and, after enjoying the look of her for a while, I gently wriggled myself backwards into the curve of her.

"Mmmmph," she said, draping her right arm around me. Quite a few minutes later she added, "Hmmmmaaaaaw"—a yawn—and then, shyly, "good morning."

I pulled her hand up to my lips and kissed it. "Morning," I said.

"How are you feeling?"

"Wonderful. Well, a little bit stiff at first, but definitely better than yesterday."

"Good." She detached herself a few minutes later and went into the bathroom. When she came back, she knelt down by me on the futon. "Hungry?" she asked.

"I suppose so," I said, reaching up to touch her face and then pulling myself up for a kiss. The kiss turned into a hug, but then she sat back to tell me, "I need to run this morning. Want to come along?"

"Where to?" I inquired, game but puzzled.

She laughed. "Not that kind of run. It's not that I'm in a hurry to get someplace, I just need the exercise. What I usually do on Sundays is run over to the Cause for breakfast."

"Ahhhhh." The light dawned. "Sure, why not. I probably won't be able to keep up with you, though."

"No problem. If we get separated, we'll just meet up again at the Cause. First one there orders the coffee, okay?"

She had it ready for me at a table for two when I finally puffed my way in the door of the Cause Celebre Cafe, not far from the church where the workshop was held the day before. After breakfast we strolled over to nearby Volunteer Park and spent several hours walking and talking, taking refuge in the big greenhouse twice during rainy spells. Sometimes we were talking politics, and sometimes we were telling each other stories from childhood; sometimes we were doing both at the same time and holding hands to boot. The hours seemed to race by, and all too soon the light began to drain back out of the sky.

"Damn," she said as a third soft patter of rain began to find its way through the darkening leaves overhead. "Guess I better split. Sunday is laundry day for me, and I can't afford to call in sick tomorrow just because I don't have anything clean to wear."

I couldn't answer for a minute, choked up by my desire to invite myself home with her—or her with me—but I knew she was right: it was time to go. "Yeah," I said sadly. "I haven't studied this weekend at all, and week after next is finals already."

We walked slowly, still hand-in-hand, out to the street and down to the corner where I'd catch the bus. Sarah said she'd rather walk, since the closest stop for a bus going to her neighborhood was almost halfway home. "You've been a life-saver," I told her as we said goodbye, "in more ways than one."

She smiled. "I'll see you Friday," she said—we'd agreed to have dinner, thank goodness—and walked off down the street without looking back.

Back at Everywhere House, I was startled to discover that everyone assumed I'd spent the weekend with Ellie. Oh hell, I reminded myself, I've got to call her soon and explain. Meanwhile, it was pleasant to be able to hug the memory of Sarah to myself and avoid the ribbing that would be inevitable when my housemates found us out. It was Connie's turn to fix dinner that week, so we had something genuinely tasty for a change. And then, after helping half-heartedly with the dishes and listening even more half-heartedly to the continuing discussion about Jan's "congratulations and welcome back from the workshop" party, I dutifully trotted off upstairs to study.

My bed felt unpleasantly soft after the futon, and lonely, too, but Spanish grammar is a good soporific. I was asleep by eleven, and no dreams came to warn me of what the future held in store.

I was stuffing my school things into my backpack the next morning when the doorbell rang. Footsteps crossed the bare wooden floor of the front hall. A minute later, I heard a quick squeaking from the stairs, like a burglar in a hurry. It was Fran, and her frantic hissing brought me and every other second-floor dweller out to the landing posthaste.

"What do I do now?" she demanded at the top of her whisper. "Should I open the door? It's the police!"

21.

We instantly went into shock, all of us. Two weeks earlier, we'd fantasized this moment: the rap of the billy club on the door, the intrusion of the police into our lesbian household. We'd dreaded it, but we hadn't done anything about it. We hadn't planned, and now that the fantasy had become reality, it was too late.

"Terry." Peg rapped out my name. "You're dressed. Go and warn everybody downstairs. Tell them we're meeting in the kitchen. Everybody else, get dressed and get there."

Thank goddess for the Voice of Reason, I gasped to myself as I prepared to tip-toe down the stairs as fast as I could. But she hadn't quite finished yet, and I lingered a few more seconds to hear her say: "Fran, get back down there and tell them 'just a minute'—through the door. Then get some clothes on fast and once we're all together, you can let 'em in."

"Oh shit, oh shit, oh shit," Fran wailed softly as the two of us hurried down. I heard her quaver, "Just a minute, please," as I reached the door to Jan's room across the hall from the staircase and the basement door.

"Jan!" I rapped quietly once and opened the door. She was standing on one leg by her mattress on the floor, putting her foot into the second leg of her jeans, her face grim under a tangle of short blond hair. "The police are here," I hissed. "We're gathering in the kitchen."

Her nod told me she knew that, and all she said, already turning away to grab a shirt from the pile on the floor, was: "Close the door." Any other time, I might have taken that to mean 'come in and close the door,' but not that morning. There was something in that room—fear?, anger?, I didn't have time to figure it out—that pushed me away. Whatever was there, it made me shiver as I hurried precariously down the warped and splintery basement stairs.

Toni and Connie had the two little rooms down there, and typically, Connie was much faster off the mark than Toni. "Wait! Waaa-i-i-t!" Toni was still pleading as Connie and I scurried up the stairs. Just as we'd almost reached the doorway into the living room on our way around to the kitchen, Fran's nerves couldn't take it anymore and—sort of accidentally, according to her later claim—she opened the front door.

"Ah, Ms. Barber," said Lieutenant White as he stepped into the hall. "And Ms.— ?"

"Moonchild," said Connie with dignity truly amazing under the circumstances.

"Prescott," squeaked Fran.

"Ms. Moonchild," repeated Lieutenant White, "Ms. Prescott. And this"—he indicated the other man who'd followed him into the hall, "is Sergeant Keegan." Keegan was a white man, taller and younger than White and, although he too wore a business suit, he seemed to strain its credibility. I had the sense that he'd probably feel more at home in a uniform. Maybe my imagination was over-reacting, but I could swear that when Connie said her name the reaction underlying White's neutral expression was skepticism, whereas Keegan's was a sneer.

"Sorry to bother you so early," White continued. "We wanted to catch you before you left for the day. Is there somewhere we can talk?"

He was talking to me.

"You remember Sergeant Keegan," he prodded when I continued to stand there in silence. "It took a while, but eventually somebody made the connection."

"The...." My brain wouldn't seem to function, and the nightmare quality of the morning intensified by the second.

"Keegan was one of the officers who questioned you Friday night." The Lieutenant could tell I needed help.

"Oh!" Oh, indeed. Now I felt really stupid. But, oh, of course, that's why they were here. Not for the house, not for anybody but me.

Connie stirred at my side and I looked at her to see if she'd tell me what I should do. Before she had a chance, though, the stalemate was broken by the eruption of Peg from the kitchen. She stomped through the living room like a woman with right on her side, and her arrival in the hall was like a declaration of war. "Do you have a warrant?" she demanded.

"And you are?" enquired Lieutenant White politely.

"I am at home and you are not," was the retort. "If you don't have a warrant, you can leave right now."

The Lieutenant stifled a sigh. "We didn't come here with the intention of searching the house. At this time. We came to talk with Ms. Barber. Unless you have some legal standing that permits you to interfere with that purpose, I suggest you let us get on with it."

"I—" That was me, but Peg hadn't finished.

"What do you want to talk to her about?"

"We prefer to discuss it with Ms. Barber herself." The Lieutenant hadn't lost his temper yet, but his control was becoming steadily more obvious. "Since you refuse to identify yourself, I have no reason to believe it is any of your business." Peg tried to speak, but she'd met her match. "If you are a friend of Ms. Barber, however," he said with emphasis, "I should think you'd be all in favor of an investigation into what may turn out to be attempted murder."

Peg was nonplussed. "Attempted murder of who?" she asked, her voice less aggressive now.

"Attempted murder of Ms. Barber," was the answer.

It was sort of embarrassing. No wonder Peg suddenly felt at a loss for words, hearing from the police instead of from me about something this serious. She looked at me, obviously uncertain about where to go from there.

"I—" I said again, and stopped again. Everybody was looking at me. "Why don't we go in the living room and sit down," I offered lamely.

Lieutenant White sat in the big chair, Keegan on a straight chair next to the rubber plant; that left the couch for me and Peg. Fran and Connie sort of side-stepped their way around us all and into the kitchen, from behind the swinging door of which came low, urgent whispers.

"Now, Ms. Barber. Why don't you start by telling us exactly what happened Friday night?"

"I already told him all about it," I shrugged, hooking a thumb at Keegan. If the Lieutenant told me Keegan was one of the cops that night, I was willing to believe it, but I sure couldn't have picked him out of a line-up.

"Yes, I know," Lieutenant White said, "but I'd like to hear it for myself."

So I told him, finishing with, "and then they brought me home and that was it." I felt Peg's eyes on me the whole time, and the reassurance of her presence was mixed with a certain amount of guilt: sooner or later I'd have to deal with her feeling slighted by my failure to confide in her.

"Why were you on the Hill Friday night, Ms. Barber?" enquired Lieutenant White with bland curiosity.

"I was on my way to see a friend," I answered, and—although I knew I was babbling—"but she isn't part of this, she doesn't even know any of the people involved." There, I'd done it, I'd admitted that the attack on me and the murder of Ted Simpson were connected. Damn!

The Lieutenant's hooded eyes caught my slip, but he didn't refer to the murder right away. Instead, he stayed fixed on my Friday friend. Where did she live? Had she been the one to set the time and place of our meeting? Did I often visit her on Fridays? In the evening? Where was I coming from when I reached the location of the incident?

Finally I persuaded him that Sarah (whom I refused to name) was a dead-end as far as his investigation was concerned. Then he started in on Fennel: "The owner of the vehicle, a Fennel Bowers, claims it was stolen, but she is unable to document her whereabouts at the time of the incident. As you know, she was a friend of the defendant in the Simpson case." He looked at me speculatively, but I refused to let my nerves loosen my tongue, and the questions continued. How well did I know Ms. Bowers? How would I characterize the relationship between us? Did she have any cause to feel angry at me? When was the last time I'd seen her? Did I have any reason to believe—he glanced at Keegan, his brown face unreadable—that Ms. Bowers knew of my interest in the murder of Ted Simpson?

I hardly knew Fennel, I told him, had only seen her around. We didn't know each other well enough for there to be any bad feelings on either side.

Those were the easy questions, the easy answers. From then on, I was in trouble. Should I lie? To protect Fennel? Because she was a lesbian? But what if, despite what I'd rather believe, she was the one who tried to run me down? "I saw her a few months ago," I stammered, "at a workshop, but…. I don't know if she…. I don't know who was in that car—there's nothing more I can tell you!"

"Lieutenant." Peg's strong voice cut across my dithering like a rope to a drowning woman. "I don't think Terry wants to talk to you anymore." Good old Peg. No matter how shocked and confused she might have been a few minutes ago, it just wasn't in her to let a woman down.

"Ms. Barber," said Lieutenant White, focusing on me all the power of his voice and eyes, "it seems likely that someone tried to kill you last Friday. Now unless you can offer me some other line of investigation, I have to assume that the motivation for that assault is connected in some manner with your meddling"—he made the word sound dirty—"in the Simpson case. Are you with me so far?"

I nodded as defiantly as possible.

"Good. So can't you see that it is in your own best interest to cooperate fully in this investigation? Not only is that the best way to ensure your own safety, it's the only way to get what you wanted when you came to see me last week. A re-opening of the Simpson investigation."

"Do you mean," I burst out, "that you're going to let Barb go?"

Over by the rubber plant, Keegan made his first contribution to the discussion: a snort. But White never took his eyes off me. "I mean," he said, "that if the assault on you proves to be related to the Simpson case, the investigation of the assault may turn up something new about the murder. But no," he added, as if forced on by his own standards of honesty, "the grand jury's indictment of Ms. Randall would not be affected by this new investigation. There is sufficient evidence against that defendant to support the charges filed, but the attack on you may indicate that there are others involved who have not yet been apprehended."

What he said sounded so reasonable. But could I, should I, trust him? After all, what if his investigation led to Fennel's arrest as well? Handing another lesbian over to the cops—wouldn't that be worse than trying to work it out ourselves? I needed time to think, without Keegan and Lieutenant White staring at me.

"I have to think about it," I said, and Peg's approving nod made the whole couch vibrate. "I'll think about it and then let you know."

"Ms. Barber." White's voice was like a whip. It stung, but it also cut off whatever Keegan had been about to say. Their eyes met, and both men were silent for a few seconds. Did they plan this out ahead of time? I wondered; did the Lieutenant make him promise not to talk? It was Lieutenant White who broke the short silence, his voice under control again, almost genial. "Let's move on for a moment. Perhaps I could have a few words with Ms. Grice. While you're thinking."

Ms. Grice? What did he want with Jan? "Why do you—?" I started, but Peg cut me off.

"She's not here," she declared.

The two cops looked at each other again. "Maybe you aren't quite sure of that," said Keegan, his voice an unpleasant purr. "Maybe I oughta take a little look around."

Peg stiffened into militancy. "Unless you've got a warrant, you've not taking one step outside this room except to get out of this house."

"Ms. Barber." Hearing the Lieutenant say my name again and again was starting to burn on my nerves. "May I ask how well you know Ms. Grice?" I stared at him, mute. "Do you know, for example, about her criminal record? Are you aware that you share this house with a convicted felon? An ex-convict? A repeat offender? A person who spent much of her childhood and youth in correctional institutions? Don't you think you owe it to yourself, to your own safety, to cooperate with the police instead of doing your best to hinder our investigations in order to shield the very people who may resort to violence against you?"

I couldn't believe my ears. Had the cops run all of us through their computers? Did he mean that Jan might have tried to run me over? Did he mean I should take up sides with him against Jan? Well, if that's what "cooperation" meant, then I wasn't confused any longer. Not about that, anyway. I wouldn't say another word, and as soon as they left I'd go talk to Jan. What he was saying might not be true, and even if it was, it couldn't mean what he was trying to make it mean.

"It's time for you to leave now, gentlemen," Peg announced, rising to full height and weight. "Right now."

The Lieutenant argued all the way to the door and tried to get me to say exactly when I'd be coming down to "make a further statement," but she swept them on out the door. As soon as they were gone, we joined the others in the kitchen—trailed by Toni who'd been crouching on the basement stairs all that time.

"Where's Jan?" I asked, puzzled, after a quick glance around the room.

"She's gone," was everybody's answer.

"Gone? But—"

"Almost scared me to death," Gretchen said. She'd been spending the night with Jeanne and got caught up in our adventure. "We'd just that second walked in the room and all of a sudden the wall opens up in front of me. I thought for sure it was the cops busting through." She gestured at the wall next to the old dresser where we keep the pots and pans, and I finally caught on. Set into that wall, and camouflaged with a covering of posters, was a door leading from Jan's room into the kitchen. That door was never used, but it was there, and that's how Jan left the house unseen even with the front hall full of cops.

I felt crushed into tearful disappointment and then, as everyone crowded around me demanding to hear my story, my disappointment flashed into anger. How dare she sneak out and leave me alone with the police! Peg had been there, of course, and if I hadn't needed her so much I probably would have resented the way she kept "handling" the situation for me. But Jan was different. Jan was the wise one among us. She should be there when I needed her. How dare she run off and leave me with nothing to counter the picture the police tried to draw of her. Maybe what they said was true. Maybe she wasn't the wise, trustworthy person I'd thought she was. Maybe she had some reason I didn't know about to run from the police. Maybe her decision to live in Everywhere House wasn't what it seemed to be, maybe it was a blind to cover her real life, like Barb's days at Carolyn's house had allowed her to construct a false identity for the other Furies.

I couldn't take it anymore—the uncertainty, the anger, the disappointment. I've got to talk to Letitia, said a voice in my brain; if I can't understand another damn thing about this mess, I do understand that I have to stop her from going through with that infiltration of the Peaceful Way. I dashed upstairs for my pack, and when Peg and Fran and the others tried to stop me at the front door I just blurted out something about school and kept going.

At the door of the classroom just as the bell rang for the end of class, I stationed myself where I'd be sure to see Letitia when she came out. Except she didn't. When the flow of students ended, I stuck my head in the door, and Letitia was nowhere in sight.

"Professor Gladwin," I said, "where's Letitia? Wasn't she in class today?"

"Why, hello, Terry. I noticed that you weren't among us this morning."

"Yeah, I'm sorry, it was…. Something came up. Suddenly. But…Letitia?"

Professor Gladwin's face turned somber as she gathered her books and papers together. "Something came up suddenly for her, too," she said. "I'm sorry to have to tell you, but she's gone."

At that point, I lost it temporarily. "Gone? What do you mean, gone? I just talked to her on Saturday, dammit."

Professor Gladwin, naturally enough, was not pleased to be addressed so rudely. "That's as may be," she said stiffly, "but I talked to her last night. She called me at home." My heart went thunk as I followed her toward the door, weaving our way past students already arriving for the next class.

"I'm sorry," I said once we'd made it through the worst of the crowd and could walk down the stairway side by side in comparative calm and isolation. "It's just that I really need to talk to her, and you took me by surprise."

Fortunately, Professor Gladwin wasn't one to hold a grudge—or to pretend she was a different species than her students, the way some professors did. "That's okay," she told me. "It's none of my business, but I'd guess you're having one of those Mondays, right?"

"One of the worst," I agreed. "Could you tell me where she went? Maybe I could call her."

"I really don't know, Terry, I'm sorry. She said she had to go back home because of an illness in the family, and that's all she said. I don't even know where home is for her."

"Did she say when she'd be back?" The wind seeped through my jacket like cold water as I followed her up the sidewalk.

"She didn't know exactly. I told her we would be able to work things out, though; she's a good student."

"Work things out?" I felt numb all over.

"Yes, she'll do a short paper on our last novel to make up for missing the last week of class. If she can't get back in time for the final, she'll do a longer paper instead and mail it to me in time for the grade deadline. I wouldn't feel able to do that for just any student, but with Letitia I felt—"

"You mean she might be gone for more than a week?" I interrupted.

"Apparently so." My desperation must have come through clearly, because Professor Gladwin stopped and turned to look at me with concern. "Would you like to tell me what's the matter, Terry? Maybe there's something I could do to help."

"Thanks, Professor," I told her sincerely, "but all I need is to talk to Letitia. Don't worry, though, I'll figure out some way to reach her."

On that optimistic note, we parted—with me in search of Cherri, my acquaintance doing work-study in the Philosophy Department. I spotted her leaving the building—my one bit of luck that entire miserable day—and called out, "Hi, Cherri, how are things in Philosophy?"

"Oh, hi. Okay, I guess. I'm just on my way to class." She obviously meant that as good-bye, but I stuck to her like a burr on a dog.

"Hey, maybe you could help me out, Cherri," I suggested brightly, as if the idea had just that second occurred to me. "There's this grad student in Philosophy that I want to talk to, but I can't for the life of me remember his name. He's kind of tall and slim, dark wavy hair, kind of cute.... Name's Jim something-or-other."

"Jim McVey probably."

"McVey, McVey. Could be, I guess. Is there more than one Jim in the department?"

Cherri thought for a minute as we walked. "There's James Wellington, but he's a full professor and I've never heard anybody call him Jim. No grad student called Jim except McVey, as far as I know."

"That's great, Cherri," I said, "Jim McVey. Yes, it's starting to sound more familiar to me now. Thanks a lot."

I made myself late for my next class by stopping in the HUB to call the number Letitia had given me. Come on, Jim McVey, I muttered as I listened to the rings on the other end of the line. Answer the goddamn phone!

Between that first call and the end of my work shift at five o'clock, I must have dialed that number a hundred twenty times. No answer, no answer, no answer. I tried persuading myself that Letitia really did have a family emergency, that she really had flown home to…. Damn, if she'd ever told me where she was from, I'd forgotten. Surely Sarah was right; Letitia couldn't have infiltrated the Peaceful Way already. So she must really be out of town. Something else must have come up to interfere not only with school but with her other plans as well.

I was almost willing to believe myself by the end of the afternoon, but all the same I knew I couldn't rest until I had some proof that Letitia was somewhere safe and free, even if the price was sickness or death for some other member of her family.

My mental state had reached such a low by five-fifteen that I actually changed a dollar in the library's change machine to see if a different coin might produce a better result. But still no answer from Jim McVey. Might as well go home, I told myself, and started across Red Square under a static, unbroken ceiling of dull grey hanging oppressively low from horizon to horizon.

Everywhere House wasn't where I wanted to be under a sky like that, I realized as I reached the Ave, so I climbed on the bus instead and started up the Hill.

Weownit Press was in a run-down section of Capitol Hill, a conglomeration of long-neglected brick apartment buildings, car body shops, dingy groceries specializing in beer and junk food, and the occasional storefront business venture. As Jeanne liked to say, the real business of the shop was to make its name come true. It was a struggle, but the four women partners were determined to succeed—and without compromising their politics. I'd been to the shop a time or two, just to say hello, and as I walked through the door that night I was struck again by the layered look of the place. It was almost archaeological the way you could detect the basic, decades-old dirt showing through like bedrock despite the efforts of the Weownit women to create a decent working environment. Overlying the tenuously imposed layer of cleanliness was the surface litter of a working press: paper, mostly, ranging from huge sheets to tiny fragments, scattered as if by a capricious wind or carefully stacked in piles. The chemical smell was so strong I kept wanting to rub my nose.

The little jinglebell on the door tinkled cheerfully as I shut out the cloudy sky behind me, and within seconds Jeanne stuck her head around the archway to the back room. "Hi, Terry," she said, "come on in."

In the back room, the real work area of the shop, the lighting was much brighter. The only person visible was Jeanne, but I heard muffled conversation coming from the darkroom set into a back corner. "Have you heard from Jan?" I asked, my voice sounding pitiful in my own ears.

"No, but I left the house not long after you did. You could call if you want." She pointed out the phone with a nod of her head and then, looking at me as if checking a job for typos, "I've been a lot more worried about you than about Jan, Terry. Why'd you run off so fast this morning? And why the hell didn't you tell us about almost getting killed? Good grief, woman, how can we support each other if we don't know what's going on? I can see you're in some kind of trouble—right now you're droopy as a wet noodle—but it's not really cool to leave your roomies out of the picture when you're involved in something that brings cops to the house."

"Hey!" came a shout from the darkroom, "anybody out there?"

"Yeah, I'm still here," Jeanne called back, "and Terry's here, too."

"Hi, Terry," several voices hollered, and then a single voice, "Don't go away, okay? This'll just take a minute."

"We're having trouble with the camera again," Jeanne explained, "and we've got to get this one last shot made tonight or our whole production schedule is shot to hell this week."

"Ready out there?" from the darkroom.

"Ready!" from Jeanne.

The next minute or two was full of questions and answers called back and forth, and also with mysterious grinding noises behind the darkroom wall and finicky adjustments by Jeanne to some piece of equipment that stuck out from that wall into the main room of the shop. Eventually there was a cry of, "All set. Time to pray to the Goddess!" There was a loud buzzing noise.

"Whew!" said Gretchen as she came through the two layers of curtain in the darkroom doorway a minute later, wiping her forehead with the back of her hand. "What a bitch. If that doesn't work, we're fucked, that's all there is to it." Rita and Mary followed her out through the curtains, and then came Sarah, blinking in the bright light of the shop.

"Isn't anybody gonna process it?" asked Jeanne plaintively.

"Sure," Rita answered her, "but we want a chance to talk to Terry, too."

I gulped. Rita and I had never exchanged more than hello and so-long in our lives. Damn, I told myself, I guess every dyke in town is talking about me now. So much for keeping my investigative activities a secret. I looked beseechingly at Sarah, and she immediately came over and gave me a hug.

"You look really down tonight," she said as she pushed me gently to a seat on a stool by the lightbox. "Maybe it would do you good to talk about it"—even to all these women, her eyes added silently before she turned around to pull up another stool nearby.

A brief battle ensued over who would make the sacrifice of returning to the darkroom. Mary lost, exacted a promise that she would hear the whole story before leaving the shop that night, and vanished through the curtained doorway again. "Now," said Jeanne, "begin at the beginning, go on until you get to the end, and then stop."

Gretchen grinned at me from her perch on a pallet stacked with boxes of paper, and some annex of brain remained alert enough to remark on the miracle she'd wrought in converting Jeanne to Lewis Carroll. "It's all connected with the murder," I began, and they listened in silence till I reached the events of that morning. "So now you know as much as I do," I concluded. Everybody but Sarah was looking at me as if I'd just done something miraculous. A very uncomfortable way to be observed. And I hadn't even told them yet about Letitia's plan to infiltrate the Peaceful Way, because that didn't seem to fit the flow of my story.

"Christ, girl, you could've been killed!" Gretchen exclaimed softly.

Mary emerged from the darkroom at that point, but she didn't get a chance to demand an instant replay because Rita started in on me, trying to get me to explain why I'd decided to investigate the murder in the first place. My first few answers didn't satisfy her, and the threat of a generalized discussion about separatism and (or versus) The Lesbian Community hung heavy in the air. Desperately, I threw my concern for Letitia into the arena, as if trying to distract the lions with a nice juicy heretic.

Sarah picked up on it right away. "You still don't know, though, do you? It could be true that she's had something come up that's not related to you or the murder at all."

"Yes," I admitted, "but.... I have to know for sure. I can't just sit back and maybe let her get into serious trouble because of me."

"Well, in the first place, you can't take all the responsibility like that." Sarah was leaning toward me, her left forearm along the paste-up counter, her face serious. "If this woman has done something already about infiltrating that cult, that was her own idea. For you to claim all responsiblity would be to disempower her. Just because she's straight doesn't mean she isn't capable of being responsible for her own actions."

"That's a really right-on analysis of the situation, Sarah," Jeanne said, "but I gotta say I can see where Terry's coming from. I mean, not to make you feel worse or anything, Terry, but if it was me I'd be feeling guilty as hell."

"And you wonder why Terry doesn't tell her housemates everything," mused Gretchen as if to herself, and got a poke in the ribs from Jeanne in reply.

"Why don't you try calling again?" suggested Rita, so I did, dialing the now-familiar number for Jim McVey under unwavering attention from five pairs of eyes.

Still no answer, and I hung up the phone feeling ready to cry.

"In books," Gretchen offered, "the thing to do at this point would be to solve the murder." We looked at her. "Well, that would be one way to make sure the murderer wouldn't...get anybody else."

"Thanks a lot, Gretchen," I sniffed. "That makes me feel a whole lot better. Now how do you suggest I solve the murder exactly, huh?"

She hunched her shoulders and looked sheepishly around the room for inspiration. "Well.... What other leads have you got?"

"Only David Ellis. He was a friend of Simpson's. His only friend, maybe. But he left town right after the murder. Went back home to Bellingham."

"Oh?" That was Rita. "Left town, eh. Sounds suspicious, don't it?" She was asking the room at large, and the room at large agreed that, yes, it did sound suspicious, especially when they dug out of me the information that he'd given a phony excuse to the U. "So why don't you go talk to him? Maybe he knows something."

"But.... Bellingham?" I protested.

"Why not?" countered Sarah. "I tell you what. Why don't you leave that phone number with me. I can keep calling all day tomorrow, if necessary. And meanwhile, Gretchen and Jeanne can take you up to Bellingham to see this Ellis guy."

"We can?" asked Gretchen and Jeanne, looking at each other and then back to Sarah with surprise.

"Sure, why not? You've got a car, Gretchen, and the two of you have been complaining for months about not ever getting any time off, never getting to go anywhere. Mary and Rita can take care of the shop for a day, can't you?" she turned toward them to say.

"We—oh, sure!" they chorused, willing if not enthusiastic.

"And I'll be here after work, of course," Sarah continued. Gretchen and Jeanne still hadn't caught fire, so she added, "Bellingham's a nice little city, you'll like it. There's good taverns and cafés, and parks, and beaches, and the University...."

The pair looked at each other again and Gretchen shrugged. "Why not? If we can scrape together the money for gas, I'm game."

"Me, too!" Jeanne said with a bounce. "About time we got a break!"

Well, I said to myself, at least it'll keep me from sitting around all day going crazy with worry about Letitia.

Everybody but me got back to work then, and I watched until they were ready to go. Mary and Rita were giving Sarah a ride home, so I didn't have a chance to do more than say "Thanks" and hug and be hugged hard by her for a minute before Jeanne, Gretchen and I headed up the block and the three of them headed down. "Until tomorrow night!" she called when they were almost out of sight in the chilly darkness.

22.

Jeanne, Gretchen, and I were on the road by nine o'clock the next morning, me full of guilt about missing a day of classes and struggling mightily to exclude from my mind all thought of the much greater burden of guilt I'd have to deal with if Letitia came to grief along the Peaceful Way. As long as I kept moving I could fool myself into thinking I was doing something constructive. The knowledge that Sarah would be patiently dialing Letitia's phone number all day was a big help. Maybe by the time we got back to Seattle we'd know for sure that Letitia was all right. And maybe I would have learned something that could help get Barb out of trouble, too.

I rode along calmly enough, thinking vague thoughts and watching the sky as Gretchen turned us north onto the freeway at Forty-fifth. It was still cloudy, but the sky was prettier, more various than the day before. Instead of an unbroken ceiling of cloud, there were layers. High and to the north, a dark stretch of cloud looked like sleek grey marble with veins of black and lighter silvery grey. Lower down, coming from the south just like we were, flowed a school of smaller, whiter clouds, looking like puffs of cotton busily intent on reaching the marbled cloud and polishing it to an even shinier finish. A morning paper lay on the seat beside me, and I noted that Patty Hearst's trial had moved to the back pages for the moment. Jeanne and Gretchen talked quietly together up in front or sang along with the radio, but I felt content for the moment just to sit back and commune with the clouds.

As agreed, we stopped at a gas station about thirty minutes south of Bellingham and I called the number I'd copied off the phone bill in the Linguistics office. The phone rang five times and I was beginning to worry when the voice of an old woman said "Hello?" in my ear.

"Hello," I answered gratefully. "Mrs. Ellis?"

"Yes, this is Mrs. Ellis."

"My name is Terry Barber, Mrs. Ellis. I'm a student at the University of Washington in Seattle. Right now, I'm on my way to Bellingham, and I wondered if I could stop by and talk to your son for a few minutes. He's with you now, isn't he?"

"Why, yes. Or rather, no, not right at the moment. That is, he's gone out to do a little shopping for me. I expect him back in twenty minutes or so, and I'm sure he'd be pleased to have a talk with one of his former students. Might be just the thing to cheer him up, in fact," she added more softly, as if thinking out loud. "I believe he's feeling quite out of things up here, poor boy."

I felt bad about not clearing up that incorrect assumption, but I briskly swallowed my qualms and jotted down the directions for getting to the Ellis' home. Less than an hour later, Gretchen and Jeanne dropped me off in front of a small white house on a street full of small white houses. "We'll meet you in that park on the corner in two hours," Jeanne promised.

"And bring me back something to eat, okay?" I pulled a five-dollar bill out of my pocket. "If they don't feed me here, I'll be ravenous by the time we start back."

Off they drove, leaving me to walk up the short path between two neat patches of lawn and ring the doorbell. Subconsciously, I'd been expecting Mrs. Ellis to answer the door, and I had a picture of her in my mind: a fragile, slightly bent old woman with white fluffy hair, pink cheeks, and bright eyes. It was David Ellis himself, though, who jerked open the door and stared at me like a rabbit that's just seen a shadow on the grass, the instincts warring: run or freeze? I don't know which of us was more startled by the other.

"Professor Ellis?" I stammered, automatically awarding him tenure.

"I don't know you," he accused. I got the feeling he'd worked himself up to confront some threat and it would take him a while to forgive me for my harmlessness.

"No, but...like I told your mother, I'm a student at the UW, and I'd like to talk to you." He wavered. "About Ted Simpson," I explained.

Instantly, the fear was back in his eyes. "What about him?"

"Well..." I looked around the front stoop for inspiration. There wasn't any. "Could I come in for a few minutes? Maybe sit down? There are a few things I've been told about Professor Simpson that I'd like to check out with you."

I'd used that line with Heidi Bascom and was pleased to find it worked with David Ellis as well. First, he too made a visual check of the area. Then, "Okay. I guess so." It was a grudging invitation, but he did step aside and let me enter.

I followed him into the living room and sat myself down on the chintz-covered couch. David hovered uneasily for a few seconds and then sat—too abruptly— in a large oak rocking chair with tied-on cushions matching all the other slip-covers in the room. Thunk! went the high back of the chair against a bunch of pale roses in the wallpaper behind him.

As if that were her cue, a woman appeared suddenly in the doorway next to the rocking chair. Mrs. Ellis, undoubtedly, but not exactly as I'd imagined her. There was some brown mixed with the white of her hair, she wasn't stooped at all, as far as I could tell, and her hands, which she carefully held away from the full-length and business-like apron she wore, were covered with dirt.

"Hello, dear," she said to me. Apparently her voice was the frailest thing about her. "I didn't hear you come in." Well, voice and ears, maybe. "Dave, have you offered your guest something to eat?"

"No, mother," he said, sounding harassed. "It's not that sort of visit."

"Oh, but some coffee or tea at least, after driving all that way."

"All right," he conceded ungracefully. "I'll fix it, though, mother. It's time for your rest now. Do you want me to help you to your room?"

"Of course not, dear, don't be silly. I'll just wash this potting soil off my hands and then I'll go and act like an old lady for a while." She smiled sweetly at me and said, "Make yourself at home, dear," before she disappeared.

"I'll be right back," muttered her son as he followed her through the door. When he returned a minute later, he was carrying two cans of diet soda, one of which he set on the coffee table near my left knee. He then sat back down on the rocking chair—more carefully this time, snapped open the other soda and said, "How come you're mixed up in this business?"

I looked at him and wondered where to begin. Dave Ellis was an ordinary-looking guy, in his late twenties with a hairline already beginning to recede from a bleakly ordinary face. He did not look happy. Away from the campus context that made him an adult and me an almost-child, the five or six years' difference in our ages almost disappeared. In his mother's house especially, perhaps. The whole time we talked, his left hand strayed erratically between the arm of the rocker, his mouth, and his left eyebrow. Apparently, he was trying not to bite his fingernails, but his subconscious mind seemed to have substituted an even more annoying habit: pulling on his eyebrow hairs. I did my best not to watch that hand wandering up and down, but it wasn't easy.

"I've been trying to find out more about Ted Simpson so I can understand why he was murdered. And by whom."

That brought the usual reaction. "I thought they already arrested somebody. His ex, I heard."

"Yes, but…I have reason to doubt that they've got the right person. Or at least I have reason to doubt that they've got the whole story." I realized I could say that with a lot more confidence now that somebody'd tried to run me over. "So I'm trying to find out who else might have had a reason to want him out of the way."

"Why not leave it to the police?" He'd have sounded bored except for the current of unease still tense in his face and his voice.

"Like I said," I told him, "I've been doing some investigating of my own, and some interesting things have turned up. Things the police don't realize might be more significant than they look."

He licked his lips nervously. "So why come to me? Ted and I were friends. Hell, I looked up to the guy."

"That's great," I assured him. "Everybody says"—all the best detective stories say—"that the key to any murder is in the character of the victim. So far, I haven't found many people who knew Ted well enough to tell me much about him, about what he's like. And as his friend," I prompted, "of course you're anxious to see his killer brought to justice."

"Sure, sure." At least he was a bit calmer now, swigging his soda and playing at making water rings on his jeaned thigh with the condensation dripping off the can. "So what can I tell you? And what can you tell me? Like you said, I was his friend, so if there's something going on back there...."

"Tell me about Ted Simpson first. What was he like as a friend? You said you looked up to him. Why was that?"

He rocked slowly and silently back and forth about ten times each and then began to speak, his eyes on the filmy white curtains behind my head, his left hand floating down from a bout of eyebrow tugging to rest on the arm of the chair. "What can I tell you. Ted was a great guy. He had a lot of charm, you know? When you were with him, talking to him, him talking to you, you felt like you were really onto something. He made things—ideas—exciting. Made you feel like just keeping up with him, being able to follow his thinking, meant you were pretty special."

He returned to silent, rocking reminiscence long enough that I felt impelled to nudge him into speech again. "Is that what you and he did together mostly? Talk?"

"Yeah, sure." His eyes slipped down over my face briefly. "That's what academics do, y'know. Talk. But Ted.... He made it seem like more than that. Like you were out there on the frontlines of thought, the avant garde." Dave chuckled dryly and drained the last of his soda.

"When I talked to Heidi Bascom—"

Whump! It wasn't the wall this time, it was Dave's feet hitting the floor as he suddenly brought his body—and the rocker—forward so fast and hard they both almost fell over frontwards. "You talked to her? What did she tell you?" It was a demand as much as a question, and I remembered what Heidi had said when I mentioned Dave Ellis' name, her obvious attempt to steer me away from talking with Ted Simpson's closest male friend.

"She told me that she and Ted were working together on some articles, and I got the impression that the work was very important, as far as she was concerned. That it was exciting, the same way you're saying it was exciting to talk with Ted."

Dave wiped sweat off his upper lip with the back of his hand. "Go on," he said.

"Well, that's about it, really. Except that she said she might leave the UW now, because—how did she put it? Something about their work being intermingled and she couldn't bear to go on with it on her own."

There were dents in the middle of the empty soda can now, his grip was so tight. "What did she say about me," he asked as soon as I finished my sentence.

"Nothing much," I told him. "In fact, she said it wasn't important for me to talk to you, that she could tell me as much as you could."

His anxious eyes searched mine for an instant longer, and then he relaxed, tossing the empty can towards a wicker woodbasket next to the fireplace and leaning back into the rocker. "Yeah," he said, "well, Heidi's all right."

After that, he was almost genial, not that it helped me get anything out of him. I danced around the subject of the Peaceful Way for a while before finally offering it up in the guise of information, in response to Dave's prodding me to tell him what I knew about the official investigation. As a revelation, though, it fell tremendously flat.

"Oh, that. I already know about that. In fact, Ted was grooming me as his successor," Dave admitted with a smirk that changed quickly to a pouting gloom. "But nothing ever came of it, of course."

"When was this?"

"He'd brought it up a couple times before, but the definite offer was that same day. The day he was killed."

"You saw him that day?" This was getting exciting.

"Sure. We talked."

"When?"

"About four o'clock, I guess. Ran into him at Bogey's, a tavern we used to go to."

"How did he seem to you?"

Dave shrugged. "Normal." He thought for a few seconds and visibly changed his mind. "Or kind of excited, come to think of it."

"Can you remember what he said?"

Another shrug and some eyebrow pulling. "He offered to let me take over the Peaceful Way gambit, as a matter of fact. The cult thing."

"Take over what, exactly?"

"Don't you know?" His eyes narrowed with speculation and suspicion.

"Sure, I know." It was time to bluff. All the best detectives do it. "I've been to the house on Fourth Avenue. Even talked to some of the inmates there." I used the word advisedly and watched his face as I spoke, but all I got was the left hand being brought under control again and lowered to the arm of the chair. "I guess I could ask Lieutenant White to get the details for me, if you don't want to talk about it. Of course, I'd have to mention your name...."

Dave looked faintly green. "That's the guy in charge? Lieutenant White?"

"Yeah. I've talked to him a couple times. Seems pretty sharp. Has he been to see you?"

"No." Now it was his voice that was faint, whereas the green tinge in the skin around his eyes was more pronounced. "I'd rather not...bring myself to his attention, to tell the truth. For...professional reasons. You understand. Gotta think of the old resumé...." He forced a hollow chuckle.

"Fine. You tell me everything you know about Simpson and the Peaceful Way, and I'll do my best not to give Lieutenant White any reason to be interested in you."

He avoided my eyes but shrugged his acquiescence.

"Right. So tell me: did Ted have any role besides being a recruiter?"

"Naw. He just reeled 'em in, and those other guys gave him a cut of the take, that's all." Despite a bad case of nerves, his voice betrayed the pride of a would-be insider.

"And that's what you said you'd take over," I mused, only to be brought up short by Dave's hasty denial.

"No way, man. I mean, I said I'd think about it, but that was just to—just because I didn't want him to think I was chicken or something. I never intended to really do it, though."

"Why?" I asked him skeptically.

Dave grimaced and ran his other hand through his thin brown hair. "No guts, I guess." He avoided my eyes, but I immediately felt kinder towards him for his honesty. "And besides," he went on to say, "I had to ask myself why Ted wanted out. He said he just didn't need it any more, but.... Everybody knows Ted was hot for tenure—hell, he'd tell anybody who'd listen, had a real hang-up about it. I figured, if he's getting out because he thinks the association might screw up his chances, well, I'll be looking for tenure too one of these years."

"So that day in the tavern, he was pressuring you to take over his operation. Must have put you in a pretty tough spot," I said with pretended sympathy. "Stay clean enough for tenure and lose your friend, or keep your friend and run the risk of getting caught enticing students into a cult scam."

"You've got that all wrong. That's not how it was. He didn't pressure me. Just made a friendly offer, that's all."

"Was he scared?"

"Ted? Hell, no, he wasn't scared. He was happy, really up. All hepped up about something. Nothing to do with me, nothing to do with that cult shit, but something big. Something good and big."

"But what did he say?"

"He said.... 'One last big score tonight'—talking about the guys from that cult house. At least, that's what I thought he was talking about. 'One last big score, and then I won't need that penny-ante crap any more.' Said he had something much bigger lined up."

"Did he say when it was going to happen, whatever it was?"

"That night, I guess. He said something like, 'this time tomorrow I'll be on my way.'"

My head was spinning. This had to be it. Simpson had something on for that night, something he expected to be profitable but proved deadly instead. And Simpson couldn't have been been referring to Barb, because there was no way he could've known he'd run into her that night. Nobody had known ahead of time that the other Furies would leave her alone, or that she'd decide to spray-paint her slogans on the APL building. Nobody could possibly have known or guessed all of that ahead of time. Except maybe Barb, a conscientious inner voice reminded me.

Meanwhile, though, I had an important witness in front of me. I reeled my brain back into the room and asked sternly, "If everything was so friendly between you and Ted that day, how come you left town right away? Kind of suspicious behavior, some people might say."

Dave forced a laugh and picked a piece of fingernail off the tip of his tongue. "That's ridiculous. I came back here because my mother isn't well and she needed somebody to take care of her. And besides, everybody knows the ex-wife did it. You should've heard him talk about her." He sounded genuinely amused by the memory. "Ted had a nasty sense of humor"—apparently that was a compliment, coming from Dave—"and some of the stories he told about that bitch were...." He stopped and let his eyes drip down over my face and body as he added, "He used to say she was a—"

I knew what was coming next and jumped in to forestall it. "It's Ted I want to hear about, not his ex-wife. What about his politics?" I asked, reaching desperately for any possible source of conflict. "Was he into politics? Would you say he was a radical?"

Dave shrugged. "Depends on what you mean. Ted wasn't into electoral politics, and he hated academic politics. But.... He was advanced all right, radical even, in certain areas."

Dave was teasing me now, telling a joke he knew I wouldn't understand. Sacrificing my pride for the sake of the cause, I asked innocently, "Which certain areas?"

"In-tuh-LEK-chew-ull areas, you might say." He drew the word out in a broad burlesque of itself, leaving me no nearer understanding than before.

"Philosophy, you mean?" Miss Naivete of 1977.

Dave slapped me with a dismissive glance of amused condescension. "You could call it that, I guess. *Applied* philosophy." Snigger, snigger.

Oh, that, I told myself with a jolt. He means *sex*.

For better or worse, Dave clammed up at that point, and I was left to wonder whether there might be anything important behind his smirks, or whether he was just a case of arrested (or as Toni calls it, normal male) development. Maybe he and Ted used to go out cruising together; who could tell what a guy like Dave would consider "advanced" or "radical" sexual behavior. Maybe they got together once a week and talked dirty about their women students, or women faculty. Ugh. I decided not to think about it any more.

"Thanks for talking to me," I said as I stood up. And then, realizing there was still an hour to go before Jeanne and Gretchen would be back to pick me up, "Could I use your bathroom, please?"

He led me through the doorway next to his rocker, saying almost in a whisper, "I'd appreciate it if you'd be as quiet as you can. My mother really isn't as strong as she thinks she is, no matter what the doctor says."

He let me find my way back to the living room on my own, but was standing ready to dismiss me from the house as soon as I returned. In the few seconds I had between my going through the door and his closing it firmly behind me, I turned to tell him as graciously as I could manage, "Please give your mother my thanks for her hospitality." He didn't even grunt.

Outside, it was chilly and dampish on that street of small white houses. Gulls screeched somewhere nearby, and I thought I could smell ocean in the air. An all-too-brief walk brought me to the little park where Jeanne and Gretchen would be picking me up, and I spent the intervening time alternately perched on a hard, wet rock and striding briskly in circles trying to keep warm.

You've really got something now, I kept reminding myself, sure the key to the murder must be hidden in what Dave told me. The guy was clearly afraid of something; afraid enough to talk to me just to keep me from mentioning his name to the police. I could believe a certain level of paranoia about tenure, but surely Dave was too nervous for that explanation to be plausible on its own.

When Jeanne and Gretchen pulled up and honked the horn, I jogged gratefully across the narrow width of the park and climbed into the car. "Am I ever glad to see you!"

They were glad to see me, too. In fact, they were ready to be glad about anything and everybody—the result, I gathered, of some hilarious rock-climbing on the beach, followed by several beers in a tavern. "To warm us up," Jeanne explained; "it's cold out there on the water."

"And then we realized it was time to come pick you up already," Gretchen added righteously, "so we didn't even stop for food."

That meant a detour off the freeway at Mount Vernon to look for a place Jeanne had heard about somewhere, a place we never did manage to locate. Instead, we wound up at a neighborhood restaurant that looked like a greasy-spoon but boasted a license for beer. "How about letting me drive?" I suggested an hour or so later. "The two of you look like you need a nap." I hadn't wanted a beer with my grilled cheese sandwich, so I was able to pilot us back to Seattle with confidence. Nevertheless, our lunch stop delayed us enough that we became part of the pre-rush-hour traffic, and it was five o'clock by the time I found a parking space around the corner from Weownit.

"Here we are, folks!" I announced with relief as I turned the key in the ignition. "And here's your keys back, Gretch," I added, swiveling in my seat to hand them over.

The two of them were huddled cozily together in the middle of the back seat. Gretchen blinked her eyes sleepily, took the keys from my outstretched hand, and shook her head awake. "Jeanne, honey," she said stroking the back of the head that rested half against the seatback and half against her breast. "We're back. Time to go to work."

Jeanne snuggled in closer for a second before stretching out her body as far as it could go in the confines of the car's backseat. Her face, meanwhile, remained buried, then rose to nuzzle in to Gretchen's neck. "Do we have to?" she said, but the way she said it made it more an expression of feeling than a question.

"Hey, look! Sunshine!"

The street ahead of us lay in a swath of almost cantaloupe-colored light. After a day of low sky, the sun had found a crack where the clouds meet the mountains on the western horizon and filled the east/west streets of the city with a flood of thick, rich light. The three of us reached the corner just in time to get the last of it dazzling in our faces. Then it was gone, as the sun's disk slid behind the double summit of The Brothers.

"Terry!" I knew it was Sarah before my eyes were adjusted enough to fill in the details of the figure trotting up the hill. I hurried toward her, and we met right outside Weownit's door, both talking at once, my "Have you found out about Letitia?" butting up against her "Any luck in Bellingham?" The sudden energy of our encounter seemed to affect even Jeanne and Gretchen, and all four of us were wide awake as we entered the shop.

"Well!" Rita's voice broke through our babbling. "We sure are glad to see you!"

"Uh oh!" Yes, Gretchen's spirits definitely had revived. "I knew we never shoulda done it, Jeanne, we never shoulda taken a whole day off. Now, no matter who screwed up what, it'll be our fault from here on!" She threw herself down in the dilapidated kitchenette chair that graced Weownit's front room, braced her body dramatically, and declared herself ready to hear the worst.

Five minutes later, everybody was busy but me. "We've got to get this job going," Sarah explained. "That's why I worked through lunch, so I could take off a half hour early. As soon as I get my part of it set up, we'll be able to talk while I work." Meanwhile, she suggested, I could try calling Letitia's number again. There'd been no answer there all day.

I picked up the receiver—it seemed to weigh about five pounds—and dialed the number that remained etched in my brain. There won't be any answer, I consoled myself silently; Jim's probably gone back east with Letitia for this family emergency. Maybe it's even his family emergency. By the time the phone on the other end had rung four times, I was fully launched into a hopeful fantasy about Jim McVey's grandfather's impending death from painless old age. A good time for the family to meet Letitia, I decided on Jim's behalf, so naturally they both—

"Hello," said a lilting tenor voice in the receiver. I immediately hit myself on the ear with the damn thing.

"Uh, hello," I stammered. "Could I speak to Letitia, please?"

"Sorry, she isn't here. Want to leave a message?"

"Could you tell me when she'll be back?"

"I'm not sure. A few days at least. Anything I can do?"

This man had information I needed, and I had to get that information from him without alarming him unnecessarily. "My name is Terry Barber," I began. "I'm in a class with Letitia and—"

"Oh yeah. Women's novels, right? She goes over to your place to study."

"Right," I answered almost without hesitation. Letitia and I had only gotten together to study once, yet he made it sound like a regular occurrence. Had Letitia told him we were studying when really we were sitting in the park on Phinney Ridge and going downtown to see Lieutenant White? "The prof told me this morning," I went on, "that Letitia might miss the rest of the quarter, and I was worried that something might have happened....?"

"No, thanks for asking, but she's fine. She had a chance to do a special project for one of her other classes, that's all. Sociology. She's gone 'undercover,' so to speak, at a shelter for battered women. Can't tell you where it is, though, because I don't know myself. One of their rules is not to disclose the location to outsiders. Especially men."

His slightly forced good humor reminded me of Roger's reactions sometimes. Jim McVey's feelings were hurt, in other words. Well, maybe that would make him more willing to talk. I prodded on. "You mean she's doing volunteer work?" I asked.

"Not exactly. As I understand it, she'll be living in the shelter for a few days and letting the other women there assume she's one of them. A battered woman, in other words."

"And there's no way to get in touch with her? I mean, what if she had a problem... got sick, or... if nobody knows who she really is...."

"Oh, the staff know," he assured me. "They're all trained professionals, she tells me, and she got their permission to do this project. So she's perfectly safe." He sounded wistful. Lonely, maybe.

"Well...." I couldn't think of a thing to say.

"Shall I just tell her you called, or do you want to leave some more specific message?"

"Just...tell her I called, please. And ask her to give me a call sometime. I'd like to hear about what it's like being undercover."

"She has your number?"

I told him I thought so but I'd give it to him again, just to be sure. Twenty seconds later, we broke the connection and I laid my bewildered head on the pillow of my arms crossed on the counter.

"What did he say?" demanded Sarah at the lightbox behind me.

"He says she's safely stowed away at a shelter for battered women."

"What?" The full chorus of Weownit women was astonished. Well, it was a pretty unusual thing for a man to say about the woman he lives with.

"…So the problem is," concluded my explanation, "that apparently Letitia doesn't tell this guy everything—"

"Smart lady," interjected Rita.

"—which leaves me with no way to find out if she really is at a shelter doing a sociology project or at the Peaceful Way house, maybe getting exposed as a mole and hustled off to California in a casket!"

Sarah stepped over and gave my arm a reassuring squeeze. "We'll think of something," she said. I wanted to believe she was right.

Fifteen minutes later, Sarah had Rita on the phone to a friend of hers who knew all there was to know about women's shelters in Seattle. I pictured her as a powerful but beneficent spider poised in the middle of an almost invisible web.

"No," Rita said into the phone, "if she is at a shelter we don't wanna bother her. It's just, she told her boyfriend one story and a woman friend something else, and if what she told her boyfriend isn't true, she could be in trouble." A listening silence and then, "Thanks. Hasta pronto, che." After hanging up, "She's gonna call back and let us know," she told us. "And now, you gonna tell us about Bellingham, Terry?"

So I did, and got excited all over again by the conclusions I'd drawn from David Ellis' answers to my questions.

"You think he had two deals coming down that night?" Gretchen's skepticism took me aback a bit.

"Doesn't it sound that way to you? He was collecting another payoff from the Peaceful Way goons, but that was such small potatoes he was ready to pass the scam along to Ellis. And that means there was something else he expected to have happen that night—something bigger and more lucrative, something that would really make a difference in his life. Professor Compton even heard him say he might not be staying at the University, remember." I looked from woman to woman, watching for the spark of my excitement to blossom in somebody's eyes.

Sarah had swiveled away from the lightbox and answered my hopeful gaze with a waggle of her X-acto knife. "That's not the only possible conclusion, Terry. Let's look at all the parameters. First, does his location tell us anything?" I must have looked totally blank, because she hastened to explain, "I mean, what can we infer from the fact that he was killed near the APL? Does that area link him to the Peaceful Way? Or does it point in some other direction?"

Good question. "Could be either, I guess. It's only about four blocks from the APL to the Peaceful Way house, so they could've arranged to meet there. Or—hey! Barb told me she did think Simpson heard somebody coming from the APL parking lot. That makes it sound like he had arranged to meet someone there, doesn't it? Maybe he told this other person to meet him there because it was handy for him. Easy to get to after he got paid off at the Peaceful Way."

"Sounds okay to me," Mary offered as she picked up a sheet of paper from the press. "Hey, come over here, somebody, and baby-sit the goddamn paper-feed for a minute."

"It's plausible," admitted Sarah as Jeanne crossed the room to Mary's side. "But it's not the only possible explanation. After all, he could have arranged to meet the Peaceful Way men there."

"They'd be coming from the other direction, though," I objected stubbornly. "The Peaceful Way house is...northwest of the APL, and the parking lot is southeast of where Simpson was killed."

Sarah grinned at me. "Good point. Maybe you're right. I hope so, anyway, because it would be nice at this point if we could be sure that the murder and the Peaceful Way have nothing to do with one another."

No matter how hard I tried to think myself away from it, we kept coming back to that one terrifying fact: Letitia might very well be in the hands of the Peaceful Way. And someone at the Peaceful Way might be the murderer who drove Barb's knife into Ted Simpson's body.

23.

Rita's friend finally called back at about eight, and almost as soon as Rita picked up the phone I could tell the news wasn't good. When she turned from hanging up the phone and shrugged the answer with her shoulders and her eyes, I moaned unintentionally.

"Hey, now, whoa," Gretchen told me. "Don't be in such a hurry to think the worst. Just a minute ago you had us all convinced that the cult had nothing to do with the murder, remember? And if that's so, the only danger your friend's in is that maybe she'll be converted, right? Not that I want to see her turn into a guru-groupy, but let's face it, that's not a matter of life or death."

For a few seconds I trembled on the edge of accepting Gretchen's tempting consolation. But... "I feel so responsible. No matter what the danger level, she just shouldn't be there."

"I think Terry's right." Sarah spoke firmly but with judicious calm. "Of course, Gretchen's right, too," she added before I had time to panic. "We can't be sure there's any danger involved, but it's also true that we can't risk doing nothing. Terry may turn out to be right that Simpson arranged to meet someone else the night he died—someone not connected with the cult at all—and that someone else might be his murderer. But unless and until we know that for a fact, I think we have to assume Letitia might be in a dangerous position if the men at that cult house find out she's there to spy on them."

We thought about that for a minute, and then I repeated my earlier question, this time gratefully adopting Sarah's pronoun. "What should we do?"

"What *can* we do?" The way she asked it, Mary's question told us she was unsettled by the realization that she'd somehow become part of this particular "we."

"Call the police?" Jeanne suggested tentatively. When no one reacted immediately she added, "How about that guy who came to see you yesterday, Terry? He already knows about all this, right?"

I groaned. "He's the only cop who'd know enough about the case and about me to be any help, but he's also the only cop in the world who knows Terry Barber as an uncooperative, biased lesbian, a know-it-all who sticks her nose in where it doesn't belong."

"I can't think of anybody except the police who could intervene in a case like this," announced Sarah after brief deliberation. "Isn't there someone else you could ask to talk to him for you? Somebody he'd be more likely to pay attention to, but somebody who'd be willing to call and say he or she is convinced that you have legitimate reason to fear for your friend's safety and believes the situation does warrant police attention."

"Yeah," I agreed slowly. "I guess that does make sense. But who?"

"How about Professor Compton? She not only knows you, she's also a former colleague of the murdered man. That gives her some faint connection with the case, so her interest doesn't have to depend just on you. If she handles it right, she can put herself across to White as someone with independent knowledge of the situation, just in case he isn't willing to act on the basis of your information alone. You could call her at her office tomorrow morning."

I tried to bury the trepidation I felt at the thought of approaching Professor Compton with the request that she call a Seattle Police Department lieutenant and use the authority of her hard-won position on my behalf. Clearing my throat, I gave in to the inevitable: "I guess you're right. That's probably about the best I can do."

"I think Sarah's right," Gretchen said. "We really don't have any reason to think anything bad's going to happen to Letitia tonight, not to mention the fact that we don't know anything bad's going to happen to her at all. If we go busting in there ourselves, *we're* likely to be the ones in trouble. It's not that I'd refuse to help a woman in danger, Terry, but damned if I want to get busted for barging in unnecessarily on some hokey scene of peaceful meditation. So let's pack it in for the night, okay?"

I could see her point, and so could everybody else. A few minutes later, I was pulling the hood of my jacket over my head and wondering aloud, "Think Jan's come home yet?"

Sarah hesitated on her way out the door. "How about I come home with you tonight, Terry? I've got my work clothes right here"—waving her little gym bag in the air—"and I guess it won't get me fired if I wear the same outfit two days in a row."

This time, Sarah and I were the two bodies merged into one on the back seat of Gretchen's car. Fran came out of the kitchen to meet us when she heard us come in. "No," she said in answer to my question. "She hasn't come back, or called, either. What do you think—?"

I don't know how Jeanne and Gretchen answered her question, but my answer was to keep on heading up the stairs with Sarah at my side, saying only, "It's been a long day, Fran. I'll talk to you tomorrow."

After I'd shown Sarah around upstairs—my room and the bathroom, that is—she never gave me a chance to start moping and worrying again. "This is nice," she said, "you keep it warmer in here than a lot of these old houses I've been in. It's warm enough to give a massage, I think, as long as we keep the covers over our feet."

So that's what we did. At first. We took off our clothes, pulled back the covers, and I lay face down on the bed, with Sarah straddling my back and both pairs of feet under the covers. This time, though, the massage loosened me up much more quickly, and as soon as she felt my muscles relax under her hands, Sarah's movements modulated from the therapeutic to the erotic.

"Goddess!" I gasped as her hand slipped between my legs. Next thing I knew, we were face to face and touching each other in a way I'd never experienced before. All the tension and urgency of the day translated into urgent desire. Instead of the tremulous elation I was used to in love-making, I felt the blazing, resilient strength of my body as, grappling and wrestling, we fought—together—to reach a much deeper part of our sexual selves. The world went away. All there was was two bodies struggling and challenging each other, daring each other to hold on, to hold out, to force our way a minute further, to push against each other until we burst with a fierce, shocking orgasm that drove a poem clear through my brain and out the other side.

Only later, as we lay on our sides, face to face, still clasped together to prolong the now merely blissful sensitivity of our clits and vulvas, did the identity of the poem come clear to my conscious mind. "Sweet, oh sweet." I'd heard Sarah moan, and now I laughed softly as my breathing slowed.

" 'Sweet, sweet, sweet, O Pan!' " I murmured, " 'Piercing sweet by the river! / Blinding sweet, O great god Pan! / The sun on the hill forgot to die, / And the lilies revived, and the dragon-fly / Came back to dream on the river.' "

"Mmmmmm," said Sarah.

Elizabeth Barrett Browning, I thought but did not say. From a book of poems I had when I was a kid. Some of those poems I'll never forget, I guess. I'd tell her all about it some day. But not right then.

24.

The next morning I walked Sarah to the bus stop on my way to campus. "Promise you'll be careful?" she repeated for the third or fourth time, and then, "Promise you'll remember what you promised?"

"Of course," said I. As far as I was concerned, the hard part would be over once I'd persuaded Professor Compton to call Lieutenant White. I didn't expect the cops would welcome my participation on the raid itself. "You do think I'm right to bring Letitia's boyfriend in on it?" I asked as we reached the stop and it was time to say goodbye.

"Yes, I do." Sarah's thoughtful look was becoming familiar to me now, but my breath was caught up and stopped for a second as my memory linked her morning face with the fierce lover of the night before. "For one thing, it's only fair to let him know what's going on. And for another, his being male and an interested party might prove useful if the police aren't willing to act on the professor's word alone."

So, after we'd said a long farewell and I'd gratefully turned down Sarah's second offer to call in sick so she could go with me, I headed off for the office of Philosophy. Professor Compton usually stopped by the office at about ten-fifteen on Wednesday mornings, a woman there told me. Would I like to leave a message?

"Yes, please," I said, and I hauled my notebook and pen out of my pack. Professor Compton, I wrote. It's absolutely urgent that I talk to you ASAP. Please wait for me. I'll come to your office right after my 9:30 class. Thank you very much. Terry Barber.

My next stop was the Linguistics office, where I left a message in the box labeled Jim McVey: Urgent that you call or come to Professor Compton's office, 284 Savery, 10:30 a.m., today (Wed.), or ASAP after that. RE: Letitia.

My class ended at ten-twenty, and at ten twenty-five I crossed the threshold of Professor Compton's office like a sprinter breasting the tape at the finish line. "You're here! That's wonderful," I gasped as I burst through the door.

A quizzical eyebrow told me she wasn't so sure, herself. "What is it, Terry?"

So I told her. When the phone rang at about 10:40, she was already five minutes into a firm cross-examination. "Oh," I interjected as she picked up the receiver, "I asked Jim McVey to call—"

"Hello?" she said. "Yes, this is Professor Compton..... Yes..... No, but I think you should…. Yes, she's here. We'll wait for you…. Of course. I quite understand."

Her voice was dry when she spoke to me again. "Perhaps you should tell me about Mr. McVey, too, Terry. He's on his way to join us."

"He's a friend of Letitia's, and…. I know you don't approve of relationships between teachers and students, Professor, but it isn't quite like that, really. I mean, they were friends before they moved out here. At least, I'm pretty sure they were. And it's not like they met as teacher and student or anything."

"Never mind that now, Terry. It isn't the major issue at the moment, apparently. But when you say they are friends, you mean…?"

"They live together. And that's why I think he should be in on this. Because he thinks Letitia is off doing a research project for a sociology class, and it would be pretty weird for him if he finds out from the police later on that she's really been—"

"Professor Compton?" I hadn't heard him coming up behind me, but there he was in the door of the small office, looking over my head at the woman behind the desk.

"Come in, Mr. McVey," she responded, rising. "Please sit down. This is Ms. Terry Barber. I don't know if you two—"

"We talked on the phone," I reminded him as he perched his lanky frame on the edge of a chair next to mine.

"You're Letitia's friend," he said, sounding baffled. "Did you leave me this note? But what—?"

"Ms. Barber feels she has reason to fear for the safety of your mutual friend." Professor Compton seemed determined to keep the conversation under her control, which probably was a good thing under the circumstances. "Apparently Ms.—what is the young woman's last name?" she asked either or both of us.

"Vedermann," Jim told her impatiently.

"Yes." She eyed him speculatively, as if measuring his capacity to respond maturely to what she was about to tell him. "Apparently Ms. Vedermann is not engaged in research at a shelter for abused women, as, I understand, she had informed you, Mr. McVey." He nodded, open-mouthed with incomprehension. "Instead, Ms. Barber believes, she has undertaken an ill-advised investigation into a local cult of some kind, and—"

"But—" exploded Jim McVey, "wait a minute! How do you know any of this? Are you saying Letitia lied to me when she—"

"Mr. McVey." Professor Compton's voice pulled him up short. "Ms. Barber has persuaded me that there is in fact reason to believe that Ms. Vedermann may be in some danger." She paused briefly to let that word sink in. "Therefore, it seems to me more important to discuss what is to be done than to indulge in challenging the validity of Ms. Barber's information. After all," she concluded logically, "if Ms. Barber is wrong and we act on her information, we will look and feel foolish. On the other hand, if Ms. Barber's information is correct and we do not act, the results could be far more serious than any fleeting embarrassment."

He seemed stunned. "You mean to say…" he asked incredulously, "she's in danger? Physical danger?"

"I'm afraid so," I muttered. "She said she was going to try to infiltrate the Peaceful Way, and there are these men there who…sort of threatened me once just for knocking on the door, so I'm afraid if they find out what she's there for…." The dawning horror in his face made me feel about an inch and a half tall. And it's all my fault, my conscience said to tell him, but I didn't. I had no doubt he'd be telling me that himself before we were through.

"Well, what are we going to do?" he sputtered angrily. "We can't just sit here and—"

"I intend to call the police," Professor Compton told him sternly. "A Lieutenant White, to be precise. Ms. Barber tells me he already knows the fundamentals of the situation."

"But—do you know where she is?" McVey swiveled back and forth on the edge of the chair, looking first at the Professor, then at me, like a bull deciding which target to charge.

"Ms. Barber?" Professor Compton threw the ball back in my court.

"I think so. They have a house not far from here, and—"

"Where." It was a demand, no, it was an order: tell me where.

"On Fourth Avenue between Forty-Second and Forty-Fourth."

"What number." His voice was hoarse with tension.

"I'm not sure. It's the rundown-looking place on the east side of the street with lots of weeds in the yard, all the curtains pulled down, and the doorbell hanging loose by one wire." My description was meant for Professor Compton, so she'd know what to tell Lieutenant White, but it was Jim McVey who acted first.

He shot forward towards the desk. "Call the police!" he demanded fiercely, and the next second he was gone, running out the door and away down the hall.

"Mr. McVey!" she called after him. "Come back! You can't—" but it was clearly too late to tell him anything.

We looked at each other wildly for the space of a breath, and then she too went into action. "Go after him," she told me. "Try to stop him from getting to that house if you can, but under no circumstances approach the house yourself. If you are unable to stop him before he gets there, then find someplace out of sight and stay there. It will be helpful to the police if you can tell them what has happened. Now go. But, Terry—" she sharpened her voice to stop me on the threshold of the office "—do as I say: stay away from that house."

"I will," I promised her as I headed after Jim.

My lungs were ready to burst by the time I reached the edge of campus, but I pushed myself doggedly on. Not until I was almost to Roosevelt Way did I even catch a glimpse of my quarry. He'd been caught up by a spate of heavy traffic and had to wait for an opening before he could dart across. After that, I managed to stay within hollering range, mostly because he slowed down a fraction the closer he got to Fourth Avenue. Must be trying to figure out what to do once he gets there, I told myself as I panted and wheezed and forced my aching legs to function.

"Jim," I croaked finally as I saw him ready to turn up Fourth. "Wait up!"

He turned in my direction without pausing at first, but then jogged rapidly back to meet me. "Show me which house," he said, squeezing the words out around the fear I could hear in his throat.

"Okay," I wheezed. "I'll show you, but don't go in, okay? The police...wait for the police, they'll—"

"Faster!" he cried. "Faster!"

I did my best to obey his command, and as a result was unable to speak another word until I stopped, finally, at the corner of Forthy-Second.

"Come on!" he said.

Gasping for air, I gestured no with a wave of my hand and bent over, hands on thighs, to recover enough so I could breathe and speak at the same time. Jim almost got away from me again at that point, but I grabbed his jacket as soon as I saw him start to move. "Wait!" I said. "Wait... can't just rush up. Have to ... make a plan." That seemed to reach him. He stayed by my side, anyway, for the minute or two it took me to get my breath back.

When I was recovered enough to stand up and look around, the first thing I saw was his face. The red of wind and running formed brilliant, almost grotesque patches in his cheeks and forehead; all the rest of his face was drained and white with tension. He looked like a man in a panic, and with a sinking feeling in my stomach I knew I'd never be able to make him listen to reason. "Are you going to help me or not?" he challenged, his voice hard and his eyes even harder.

"We have to wait for the police," I insisted. "They know how to do these things, they've been trained, and—"

Without even a word of abuse to match the scorn I saw in his face, he turned away from me and ran lightly up the east side of the street. He knew the house as soon as he saw it, and within seconds was pounding on the front door, kicking the front door, battering the front door, all the while yelling, "Open up! Open up, you fuckers, open the fucking door!"

"Oh, goddess!" I wailed, and promptly forgot every promise I'd made that morning, to Sarah as well as Professor Compton. Like a meteor captured by a planet's gravity, I flew to Jim's side. "It's no use!" I cried, pulling frantically on his jacket. "It's solid wood! You'll never break it down!"

"Another door!" He whirled and grabbed my shoulders. "There's got to be another door!"

"Around back," I said, "but—"

He pushed me out of his way and was gone.

197

"Jim!" I hollered after him, picking myself up off the ground. "Wait for the police!" I yelled at the top of my lungs as I headed for the side of the house. "The police are on their way!" If anybody in the house was listening, might as well let them know that blowing the two of us away wouldn't necessarily solve all their problems.

I'd almost turned the corner of the house when I heard a sound that jerked me back around. *Blurp!* It was a police car siren making that strange noise they make when they want to attract your attention but don't want to turn the siren on all the way. Already? Could they really get here that fast?

Apparently they could. The plain black sedan pulling up at the curb had a bubble light on its dashboard. Next thing I knew, a familiar black-suited form was emerging from the front passenger seat. "Lieutenant White!" I shrieked. "Am I ever glad to see you!"

My joy wasn't mutual. Lieutenant White looked plumb disgusted—in the split second before the official mask descended. He was reaching down to open the rear car door when Jim came racing back around to the front of the house.

"Police?" he hollered, still on the run. "Are you the police? We've got to get in there, we've got to—"

Lieutenant White's raised palm stopped Jim with only a stride left between them. Silently, he directed our attention to the man who'd emerged from the back of the car. "Mr. Peaceful," he said, grimly polite, "Ms. Barber and Mr. ...?"

"McVey." The two of us stared at Mr. Peaceful, who smiled benignly back. He was of average height and build, smaller than both Lieutenant White and the other policeman who had joined us from the driver's seat of the car. Like Jennifer Stone and her little pal Gary, the guru was dressed in light blue, but instead of overalls he wore a soft, wide-sleeved soft tunic over blousy pants that narrowed to a cuff at the ankles. A wide belt of matching blue fabric carried a small pouch to one side. On his feet, clean white sneakers, on his head, a white turban that set off the bronze of his face: the healthy tan of a young white Californian.

"Welcome to the Peaceful Way," he greeted us. "Shall we enter?"

"They won't let us in!" Jim blurted.

"They will." He smiled. "The Way will open."

Jim and I clomped meekly up the path behind the smooth glide of light blue, Lieutenant White and the other cop bringing up the rear. It was freaky the way he looked so normal—in a regular business suit, he'd have been indistinguishable from any other young executive on his way up the corporate ladder—and yet.... Without raising his voice, without a single gesture, the man had the power to gentle us. To mesmerize.

At his mere approach, the door flew open.

"Jonathan," stuttered the man behind the door. As we entered, he was bowing humbly from the waist, and so was a second business-suited man beside him. "We weren't expecting you," he offered lamely.

"A pleasant surprise, then." Jonathan Peaceful's voice was light, verging on the humorous, yet the two Guardians cringed as if he'd cracked a whip.

Jim was vibrating beside me like a six-foot tuning fork. "Mr. McVey, was it?" inquired the guru. Jim nodded jerkily. "I believe I heard over the radio in Lieutenant Harrington's car that you are concerned about a friend of yours who has come to walk the Peaceful Way."

Jim jerked his head up and down again, and then he snapped. "Where is she?" he demanded of the two Guardians. "What have you done with her?"

Their eyes flickered briefly over his face before re-adhering to the Velcro charisma of their Leader.

"Why don't we all gather in the living room," he suggested. "Perhaps you would summon the Walkers for us?" Directed to the Guardians, his question had the force of an order.

Jim and I—he reluctant, I bemused—led the way into the small, dingy room to the right of the entrance hall. Two chairs and several big pillows, all of them looking second or third hand, were scattered at random on the dirty gray-green carpet. After a few seconds, I settled uneasily on one of the pillows, a twenty-inch square of mustard yellow. Lieutenant White sat stiffly on one of the two chairs, and the other cop stationed himself like a sentry in the doorway. Before Jim had a chance to pace more than once across the room, we heard footsteps on the stairs. Jim immediately sprang out into the hall. There was a short delay—"Thank God!" we heard him say; "oh, thank God!" When he came back, followed by Gary and the Guardians, he had Letitia tucked under his his right arm.

"I'm fine," she protested faintly. "Nothing happened. Really." Her face was pale at first, and she looked more embarrassed than anything else. Almost sheepish. When she noticed me sitting there, though, her eyes bounced off me so fast it brought the familiar dusky rose back into her cheeks. I wondered whether she was embarrassed for Jim to meet me, for me to meet Jim, or simply because she realized that Jim and I both must know about the little lies she'd been telling.

A movement in blue drew my eyes back to the Leader. His legs crossed neatly at the ankle, he sank gracefully into lotus position on a pillow. "Please, sit," spoke the gracious host. Of all the people in that room, he was the only one who looked completely at ease. The Guardians, shame-faced, sat awkwardly on two of the remaining pillows—one of them obviously the seat cushion from a defunct sofa, and the other a huge, formless beanbag made of some plastic material that grated unpleasantly against the beans trapped inside. After Lieutenant White cleared his throat loudly for the second time, Jim detached himself from Letitia long enough to lead her to a seat on the room's second chair. He himself stood behind her, a hand on each of her shoulders.

The Leader smiled serenely as he looked over his assembled flock. Then, under Gary's adoring gaze, he said, "Perhaps you would like to begin, Lieutenant

White."

"Earlier this morning, Lieutenant Harrington was invited by Mr. Peaceful"—Lieutenant White managed to repeat that absurd appellation without emphasis or irony—"to visit the facilities his organization maintains in Seattle in order to clear up certain allegations of improper and possibly illegal conduct on the part of local members of the organization." I noticed the eyes of one Guardian flashing anxiously back and forth from Lieutenant White to the Leader; the other stared rigidly at the carpet. "Lieutenant Harrington, in turn, invited me to accompany them, because of allegations concerning a possible connection between that organization and a case of mine. Those allegations were brought to my attention by Ms. Barber and Ms. Vedermann"—he identified us each with a nod as he said our names. "We had completed our inspection of one facility and were on our way to this address when the call was received from a Professor"—he searched his memory— "Compton regarding a possible infringement of the law with regard to Ms. Vedermann. Mr. McVey, I understand, is here because of his concern for Ms. Vedermann's safety. A concern aroused in him by certain statements made by Ms. Barber and repeated, at Ms. Barber's request, by Professor Compton to the police at ten fifty-five this morning." He paused and looked evenly around the room. "These two gentlemen"—nodding at each Guardian—"are members of Mr. Peaceful's organization. Ms. Vedermann, of course, has been mentioned already. And...?" He lifted an enquiring eyebrow in Gary's direction.

"That's Gary," I said, the sound of my voice surprising even me. Every eye was instantly upon me, except for Gary's. He simply sat there on a hideous orange pillow and gazed with loving awe at his Leader.

"A Walker on the Way," surmised the Leader, and the intersection of his smile with Gary's all but dripped honey on that ugly green rug.

"Right." Lieutenant White's voice was dry. "Now that we all know who we are, maybe you'd like to tell us why we are here." He was speaking to the man he called Mr. Peaceful, and I was instantly aware of two very different kinds of power meeting head-on across the circle of on-lookers.

"Very well," the Leader agreed. "One of Lieutenant Harrington's California colleagues visited me a few days ago. We've talked several times over the past year, he and I, and I am happy to say he has come to a place of understanding, if not respect, for the Peaceful Way." The soft voice hypnotized, and I had to pinch a fold of skin on my wrist between the nails of the thumb and index finger of my other hand to keep my attention sharp as he lilted on. "What he had to tell me was distressing enough to bring me here today. Thanks to a phone call from his colleague in California, Lieutenant Harrington very kindly met my plane"—an angelic smile for Lieutenant Harrington—"and introduced me to Lieutenant White at their mutual headquarters"—an equal beam for the alert Lieutenant White's hooded eyes. "After a most interesting conversation there, we journeyed together to a lovely house on Queen Anne Hill. A delightful name for a neighborhood, isn't it?" He looked now at the two Guardians sitting uncomfortably on the floor side by side. The one who'd let us in looked white and full of dread. The other one had his head hung down so low I couldn't see anything but his drooping shoulders and the top of his brown-haired head. Neither man looked up to catch the speaker's smile, and it was clear to all of us that, despite his apparent calm good humor, they were deeply afraid of their Leader.

"I was able to act as navigator for our visit to Queen Anne Hill," he continued winsomely, savoring his own small joke, "because of a long talk I had before leaving California with a new Walker on the Way, Jennifer Peaceful." The Guardians twitched at her name, and I guess I did, too, because the Leader shot a piercing glance in my direction before he explained, "She was able to give me very specific directions because she had traveled there herself several times, she told me, to clean all the lovely furniture, the new appliances, the very impressive television and stereo equipment...."

His voice trailed lightly into a silence made tense by the cowering of the two Guardians. For a long moment the Leader simply sat there, a calm half-smile on his face. His next words were directed to the policemen: "As I said earlier, I deeply regret the behavior of these two lost Walkers, but I can assure you with complete confidence that the only harm they have done is to themselves."

Lieutenant Harrington rumbled to life suddenly and spoke with the deep rasp of a long-time smoker. "The law takes a different view of these things, Mr.—. Extortion and embezzlement are criminal offenses."

"Oh, come, come, Lieutenant, we've been through that already."

One of the Guardians had jerked his head in Lieutenant Harrington's direction at the words extortion, embezzlement and now looked at the Leader with mingled hope and fear in his eyes. They're playing good-cop/bad-cop, I told myself in amazement, looking from the Leader to Lieutenant Harrington. So much for separation of church and state .

"The money was diverted from its rightful Way, I admit," the Leader continued almost playfully, "but surely it remains a matter for the Family of the Peaceful Way to resolve. I can assure you—indeed, I have assured you—that it will be resolved. It is not the practice of our Family for some few to live in luxury at the expense of others. Especially when those others are newly come to us, and when the luxury is enjoyed in the form of a hide-away for indolent Guardians, leading them to neglect their duties and corrupt their loyalty to the Way." One of the Guardians turned green, and the other buried his face in his hands.

"Meanwhile," the Leader said brightly, "why don't we clear up this other matter. Francis." He spoke the name softly, but we all felt the power behind the delicate enunciation of each syllable, and the green-faced Guardian looked toward his Leader as if his muscles were controlled by a force beyond his will. "Lieutenant White is concerned about your relationship with Theodore Simpson, Francis. Do you think you can set his mind to rest?"

The Guardian choked slightly and looked down at his hands. "He was a First Follower, Jonathan." It was strange to hear such a big man, looking so adult in his business suit, stammering his reply in the placating whine of a child. "He helped people find the Way."

"And you gave him money, I suppose." The Leader spoke with tranquil self-assurance.

"Yes, Jonathan."

"And you and Timothy shared the rest between you, using your share to leave the Way of Peace and live in the Way of the World."

"Yes, Jonathan."

"And that is why this Path entrusted to you had become unable to contribute materially to the Project of the Generation."

"Yes, Jonathan."

The Leader sighed with the forbearance of a loving parent whose patience has been tried but not exceeded. "You have done great harm to the Generation, Francis, Timothy. Great spiritual harm. We will need to discuss what Path you must Walk to regain the Way." The Guardians looked both depressed and alarmed by the prospect. "Meanwhile, what can you tell Lieutenant White about Theodore Simpson's most unfortunate demise." That last word sounded like a threat, even in the Leader's soft voice.

Francis, the Guardian who talked, looked directly at Lieutenant White; his voice sounded twenty years older than when he spoke to his Leader. "We don't know anything about the murder," he declared. "I met Ted that night at midnight to give him his money, and that's the last I saw of him."

"Anybody who can verify that?" Lieutenant White sounded skeptical.

"I guess—" he frowned in brief concentration. "Wait. There is somebody." He looked surprised and then a sneering smile flitted across his face. "The best possible somebody: a cop."

"Go on," said Lieutenant White.

Francis shrugged and told his story in a voice that said It's all over anyway. "We'd arranged to meet on Forty-first in the mouth of the alley between Eleventh and Twelfth Streets."

"Across from Condon Hall?" interjected the Lieutenant.

Francis repeated his shrug. "Some big building."

"Go on."

"I gave him his money—"

"How much?"

"Five hundred."

"Cash?"

"Sure. In a plain envelope. Regular white business envelope."

"Go on."

"So then Ted tells me he's not going to be bringing in any more kids for us." Francis glanced at his Leader, who remained serene. "Says he's got another guy lined up to fill his shoes, so no big deal. So I tell him okay and we start to split when, wham, this cop car pulls into the alley and next thing we know there's a spotlight on us."

"City police?"

"No, campus cops. I didn't even know they pulled night duty. I quick haul out a pack of cigarettes and tap one out for Simpson to take, to make it look...more natural like."

"And then?" Lieutenant White still sounded skeptical, but maybe that was part of his interrogation technique.

"Then nothing." Francis had been losing tension all the while he spoke and now was thoroughly sunk into morose apathy. "He took a cigarette, said thanks, and we went our separate ways. Ask those cops, they'll tell you."

"Which way did Simpson go?"

"I dunno. Away. Away from me."

"And you went...?"

"Whaddya think? Back here."

The Lieutenant measured the man with his eyes. "We'll be taking you down-town now to make a statement," he said. "Unless anyone has any objections?"

No one did.

"Shall I accompany you, Lieutenant?" The Leader addressed his good-natured question to Harrington.

"If you wouldn't mind. I'll go call in, ask for a back-up vehicle, Claude."

He peeled himself away from the wall and left the room.

Claude, I said to myself. I never would have guessed.

Lieutenant White squatted in front of the fixated Gary. "Want to tell me your name, son?" The answering silence felt ominous to all of us.

For the first time, the Leader's smile looked a wee bit forced. "Would you like to come with us, child?"

"Yes, please!"

"You won't need us, will you?" Jim helped Letitia up out of her chair—not that she didn't seem perfectly capable of rising under her own power—and pulled her close with an arm around her shoulders.

"I guess not. We'll be able to find you if we need you."

"We'll be around," Jim assured him and headed for the door just as it filled up suddenly with the stocky form of Lieutenant Harrington.

"Patrol car's here," he told Lieutenant White. "You and the driver want to take these two"—he beckoned the Guardians towards the door as he spoke—"and I'll take Peaceful and the kid?"

"Fine with me," said Lieutenant White. "Okay, everybody out." He shooed at us with his hands as if we were a flock of chickens. "I'll take the keys to the house, if you don't mind." The keys were duly handed over in the front hall as he added, "You'll get a receipt once we get downtown," and Lieutenant Harrington rattled a set of handcuffs in an idle but signifying way.

A minute later we were all outside and Lieutenant White locked the door behind us. "Okay, into the car," he told the Guardians, and they trudged fatalistically over to the blue-and-white at the curb. Gary and the Leader, moving much more gracefully, were already entering the back seat of Lieutenant Herrington's unmarked sedan.

"Hey!" I exclaimed as it suddenly occurred to me that everything was over. "Hey, Lieutenant White!" I scooted over towards the curb and managed to reach him just as he started to lower himself into the front passenger seat.

"Ms. Barber," he said with the patience of a man who sees light at the end of the tunnel but has learned the hard way not to put too much faith in what he sees.

"So…. What happens now? I mean, you're not going to just take their word for it, are you? You're going to—"

"Ms. Barber," he said again. "I want you to go home now, or back to school, or wherever it is you ought to be. And I want you to think, I want you to think very carefully, Ms. Barber, about the fact that this little plot of yours might not have had such a happy ending."

"It's—" not my plot, I started to say, but the Lieutenant's hand made a stop sign, and he went right on talking.

"A few hours ago, you had the good sense to be terrified by the thought of what you'd done. I want you to remember how you felt back then, Ms. Barber, because that is the way you ought to feel when you act in such an irresponsible manner."

No fair!, cried my inner defenses. "That's not entirely accurate, Lieutenant White," I protested. "Letitia is a responsible human being, too, you shouldn't talk about her as if she's not capable of making her own decisions or—"

The Lieutenant looked past me, and I turned to see Jim leading Letitia down the path from the house to the sidewalk. Just as they reached the end of the path, Letitia seemed about to look in our direction. Jim was the closer of the two, though, and still had his arm tightly in place around her shoulders. With no apparent effort—but with readily apparent intent—he shifted his body forward to block us from Letitia's view and steered her firmly away from us, up the sidewalk and away.

Oh, swell, I was saying to myself when I heard the car door slam.

"Leave it alone, Ms. Barber." Lieutenant White spoke through the open window as he gestured for the uniformed driver to start the car. "Stay out of police business. All the way out. I don't want to have to tell you again."

25.

I dragged through the rest of the day like a sleepwalker. Right after Botany class, I made three phone calls: to Professor Compton, Sarah, and Weownit. Cravenly, I didn't call the Professor direct, though; instead I asked the woman who answered the phone in the Philosophy office to "please let Professor Compton know as soon as possible that Terry says everything is all right." Sarah was filling in for the receptionist when I called, so our conversation was interrupted about a million times by other calls she had to answer. Not the easiest way to achieve coherence at the best of times, and that definitely was not among them.

"Where are you?" was her first question. "Are you okay?" came next but was much harder to answer.

"I mean, yes, of course, I'm fine," I said to correct my initial gloomy reply of "I don't know."

"And Letitia?"

"She's fine, too, I suppose. I mean, she is. She's fine."

"I'm going to have to put you on hold, Terry," followed by twenty seconds of Mozart. "Okay. Now tell me what happened."

By the time I'd worked my way disconnectedly from hold to hold to hold, and Mozart had given way to an incredibly boring recital of the week's upcoming events in classical music, Sarah had figured me out. "An anti-climax, huh?"

"In several different positions."

"Well, at least that's better than finding her chopped into little pieces."

"Pollyanna," I chided. "You're right, of course. And it is a big relief. Except—"

"Damn. Just a minute."—*invite you to visit their newly remodeled showroom located just minutes from downtown Seattle and*—"Okay. You were saying?"

"Except it looks like the Peaceful Way isn't going to provide a murder suspect after all. If what the Guardian told Lieutenant White checks out, then it looks like they weren't involved in the murder at all. Or at least not in any way I'm gonna be able to find out about."

"That's too bad." The sympathy in Sarah's voice was balm to my wounded spirit, but—"Oh hell. This is ridiculous. Can you call me tonight, Terry?"

I said I would, and released her to the demands of other callers. Before leaving the booth, I talked briefly with Mary at Weownit. There was a lot of noise in the background—I mean, a *lot* of noise—so we didn't try to talk much, just "everything all right?" and "yes, I'll tell you all about it later on."

When I got home that evening, Fran met me in the hall looking worried and mysterious. "Jan's here," she whispered before I even got the front door shut. "She says she's moving out!"

My emotions locked into suspended animation. Toni tiptoed into sight in the living room, and soon there were three of us standing in the entryway straining our ears towards the rustley, thumpy noises coming from Jan's room. "She's got a friend with her," Toni muttered. "Came to help her pack."

Why are we whispering? I wondered, and yet I too stepped as if on eggshell as I walked towards the door of Jan's room. "Jan?" I tapped on the almost closed door with my knuckles. "It's Terry. Can I come in?"

A pause. And then, curtly, "Yeah."

I walked in on a scene of chaos. Full, half-full, empty, and not yet three-dimensional boxes were everywhere; Jan and another woman continued to pack as I entered, working at top speed. "Where are you going, Jan?" I asked.

She looked up briefly from a jumble of books and papers she was packing. "Outta here," she said.

"But...why?"

"Seems like a good idea, that's all."

I felt tears rising, tears of anger maybe. "I thought we all made a commitment when we moved in here, Jan. I thought we were friends, too, but even if I was wrong about that, there's still the commitment you made to the house. You can't just walk out on us without any warning."

She gave no sign of hearing what I said, just kept on packing.

"I guess I was wrong, huh?" I told her as she hastily tied up a finished box with string. "I guess you never did care about this house. I guess you never did think of me as a friend."

There was a pop as she finished the knot and cut off the excess string with her pocketknife. Then she straightened up and looked at me fully for the first time. "I wish I could, Terry," she said. "I wish I could be friends with you. Been seeming for a while like it was working out pretty good. You've been good to me, don't think I ain't noticed." Her friend, a husky woman whose leather jacket creaked every time she moved, reached out to take the ball of string from Jan's hand, and distracted Jan back to work again. She came towards me to gather up some socks and underwear piled on the foot of the bed, and the light from the hallway fell directly on her face, revealing lines of weariness and worry.

"So why are you going?" I pleaded for an answer I could understand.

"Because it ain't safe for me here anymore." Her voice was too flat for me to infer any regret. It was a statement of fact. The earth is flat. The sky is blue. It is not safe here anymore.

"Hand me that box, will ya?"

Mechanically, I took the flattened carton leaning against the wall beside me and handed it to Jan's friend. "I don't understand." Another statement of fact.

"You got the police coming here now. True?" Jan's eyes flicked up to meet mine, and the question was almost a challenge.

"Well, yeah. Once. But—"

"They asked about me. True?"

"Yes. They did. But Jan, I didn't tell them anything, I swear I didn't."

"I know that, girl. I know you doing the best you can."

"But it's not good enough?" The tears were very close now, but I fought them back with determination.

After a few seconds' pause, Jan put the finished box of clothes aside and sat down on the bed. "I'm sorry, Terry," she said, looking at her hands. "I know it ain't your fault. The way it is, though…. You didn't need to tell them police anything, did you? They was telling you, I expect." She looked up then, looking more like the Jan of the week before.

"They said you had a record," I confirmed unwillingly. "But that doesn't matter to me, Jan. I mean, I've been wishing like hell that you hadn't…gone away like that, so I could talk to you. But it didn't make any difference to me, what they said. I knew I was definitely on your side, even if it meant putting myself on the other side from the police."

Jan almost smiled, and her hand went up, forefinger gliding along the side of her nose, to push aside the blonde hank of hair that fell over her eyes. "You're good people, Terry Barber, but it just ain't enough right now." She sighed, and I stifled an incoherent protest as she continued. "You're just too dangerous for me to know right now. The way things are. You're just too dangerous for me to even like. Gets me to thinking like I'm…the same as you, almost. Like I can lay back and be your friend and everything's rosy. But it's not, not for me. You and me, Terry, we're different kind of people. We live in different kind of worlds. Your world's a much safer place to be. That's why I came here in the first place, trying to pull some of that safeness over my own head. My own life. But it just don't work that way. Never did, maybe. But definitely not when the police come into it.

"I know you mean for the best, Terry. I know you won't never do nothing you think might hurt me. But it ain't enough. It just ain't enough, girl. Your world's too safe for you, and that makes you too dangerous for me. And the proof is those police you brung here. No—" she shook my abortive protest away with her head, "I know you didn't mean to bring 'em. That's what I mean. You do dangerous things, like getting yourself mixed up with this murder, because you don't even know they're dangerous. You've been safe for so long, you don't know what danger looks like, don't know how to act when it comes." She shook her head again, at herself this time. "Guess I was outta my mind not to stop you when I had the chance. Guess I almost got to thinking I was living in your world now so I'd be safe too, we'd all be safe in this nice little world. Everywhere House. Shee-it. Ain't no 'everywhere' about it, girl."

There was silence briefly, and then the other woman in the room brought us all back to the work in progress. "Guess I might as well start taking things out now, huh? Looks like we about got the most of it."

"Yeah." Jan stood up. "Those ones first, then these ones here. I'll be finished by then, and we can throw on the rest and get the hell outta here."

"Hope the police ain't been following your friend here," the leather-jacketed woman said to the wall as she hefted two boxes at once.

"Ain't much else we can do but hope. Hope and hurry."

I felt so shut out that I didn't have anything to say. Instead I tried to make myself useful, adding the few remaining loose objects to likely looking boxes and then carrying a few of them out to the curb where Jan's friend put them one by one into the back of a small pick-up truck.

Before long, all the boxes were out of the house, and Jan came out the front door with her jacket on. Fran and Toni peeped out after her but stayed inside.

"You have a place to go?" The question sounded stupid as soon as I said it.

"Yeah."

"You're not going to tell us where, are you?"

She answered that one by not answering at all.

"What about...if you get some mail or something? We won't know where to send it."

She walked around the rear of the truck to get in the other side as her friend slammed shut the tailgate and headed for the driver's seat.

"Jan!" I followed her out into the street. "Wait! Will we ever see you again? Will you at least call me sometime?"

Her hand was on the door handle. She opened the door, facing away from me. "I don't know, Terry. Maybe." She turned, finally, and looked back at me. "You take care, now. You hear?"

As soon as the truck pulled away, I shivered and went back in the house. "Did she tell you why she's going?" demanded Toni.

The three of us peered into Jan's room, silently examining the stripped single bed, the battered old dresser with none of its four drawers quite closed, and the scatter of papers, dust, and empty hangers on the floor as if there were a velvet rope across the doorway. As if the room had become a museum exhibit, as if it had passed from our everyday world into history in the last two hours.

Toni hinted that the real reason Jan left was guilt: Jan was hiding something—from us and from the police—and fled to avoid discovery. Not surprisingly, she and Fran couldn't understand my counter-arguments. They hadn't spent the last few days seeing their status with the police go from that of bland good-citizenship to that of a self-confessed pervert obstructing police investigation in possible alliance with murder suspects. No matter how things turned out, I knew I would never feel as unselfconsciously at home in the world as I had before Lieutenant White sat in the living room of Everywhere House and forced me to choose either Jan or The Law.

26.

I got to campus early the next morning, hoping I'd get a chance to talk to Letitia before class. Oh, well, I told myself when the bell rang and she still hadn't entered the room, afterwards, then. Because surely she'd be hurrying in any second now along with Professor Gladwin. A minute later, though, here came the professor, alone, shutting the door behind her and sealing me into the Letitia-less classroom for fifty long minutes.

I got to the HUB as quick as I could after class and jammed a quarter into the nearest pay phone. Four rings later, "Hello?" she said.

"Letitia, this is Terry. You weren't in class."

"Oh. No."

"Are you okay? Is anything wrong?"

"No. I just decided I might as well go along with the plan Professor Gladwin set up for me. Instead of coming back to class for the rest of the quarter. Less explaining to do."

"But you're still going to your other classes, aren't you?"

"Yes."

"When can we get together and talk things over?"

There was a long pause, and I heard the plaintive note in my voice echo in the silence.

"I'll be pretty busy...."

Such an obviously made-up excuse roused me to protest. "Come on, Letitia, too busy for a ten minute conversation? I want to talk to you about yesterday, if nothing else. About what you did and what you found out at the Peaceful Way."

"According to that policeman, the cult has nothing to do with the murder." Another weak excuse.

"Just give me ten minutes. On campus. Between classes." She was quiet long enough to provoke a second level of reaction. "What's the deal here, Letitia? Why are you trying to avoid me? Did something happen that I don't know about?"

Another pause, a short one, and then she gave in. "All right. I could come early for my one-thirty class this afternoon and meet you...in that second floor student lounge in the HUB."

Better than nothing, I decided, though it wasn't at all the place I'd have chosen. "One o'clock?" I asked.

"One-fifteen," she answered.

"Okay. See you then." I hung up feeling an odd mixture of unease and firmly repressed anger. Don't jump to any conclusions, Terry, I reminded myself. So I spent the next three hours carefully nipping each speculation in the bud.

The lounge where we were to meet was simply an open space at the top of the main stairs from the first to the second floor of the student union building. A variety of battered, overstuffed chairs and sofas were scattered around, some of them arranged to form little "conversation areas," others obviously disarranged from any order at all. Unlike the cafeteria, where the general noise level substituted for isolation in allowing a genuine measure of privacy, in the HUB lounge you could never be sure that other students apparently sleeping or studying all around you weren't interesting themselves intensely in your private conversation.

Letitia arrived only two minutes late, but that was two minutes too long for me. I sprang up to greet her, but the words I might have spoken got lost in my throat when I saw the expression on her face. She didn't look grim, exactly; but she clearly had her mind made up about something, and the way she avoided my eyes seemed to indicate she knew I wouldn't like what she had to say.

"Where do you want to sit?" I asked awkwardly. She had a thin binder and a couple of books clutched to her chest like a shield, and she kept them in position as she led me towards two chairs as big as sofa sections, at right angles to one another and about a foot apart. When she sat down, she put the books and binder down next to her, filling up the extra space on the broad seat as if to foil any attempt on my part to get too close.

"I have a class at one-thirty," she said.

I sat down and covered my face with my hands. This was hard. "Letitia," I said, sitting up and turning towards her but carefully keeping my distance. "Last week, you wanted to be friends. Now you act like I'm a vector for the Black Plague. What the hell happened? If it's something I did or said, okay, it's a free country, you don't have to be friends with me if you don't want to. But I wish you'd at least *tell* me."

She blushed, and I felt again the pull of her dusky rose and black. "It's not you, Terry," she said, looking down at her lap. "Or at least, it's not you personally; it's not something you did. It's just…. I guess I just found out I'm not as brave as I thought I might be."

"What does brave have to do with anything?"

"You know. I told you. In that little park on Phinney Ridge." Finally she looked at me.

"You mean what you said about not feeling free to be whatever you wanted to be?"

She nodded.

"But why does that mean we can't be friends? Do you feel like I've been putting pressure on you? Because I definitely never meant to."

She shook her head and then looked up at me again. "I know, Terry. It's me that's putting the pressure on. Me and—" she gestured vaguely in the air, a circling motion of one hand—"everything else. Not you."

"So…. We could still be friends. Couldn't we?"

She sat absolutely still and silent for half a minute, and then her hands began to make small pleats in her skirt as she answered me. "I wish we could, but it just doesn't work for me. I can't stop feeling like I should…be doing more. Being braver. If I'm your friend."

Suddenly she looked me steadily in the eye. "That's what I wanted, right from the start. I wanted to be friends with you because I thought I wanted to be more than I am. I wanted to be braver and more involved in things. But now…."

"What's changed? Me? You? Or…what?"

"Me, I guess." Her hands smoothed at the wrinkles she'd made a moment before. "I thought if I couldn't be brave one way, I'd be brave another way. That's why I decided to infiltrate the Peaceful Way. You were so brave when we went to see that policeman, I was ashamed of how timid I was. So I thought if I could do something useful, something that really…challenged me…I thought it would make me more…. I don't know. More like you, I guess. I wanted you to be able to look at me and think I was strong and brave and out there doing things. Like you do." She bit her lower lip and bent her head again.

"Letitia," I exclaimed, full of rueful frustration, "that's crazy!" And then, on second thought, "No, I don't mean that. I mean…. I'm not brave, dammit! If you knew me better, you'd know what a chicken I am. Really! I'm famous for it. My mom used to have to write notes for me all the time because I'd be afraid to go to school because I didn't understand my homework and was terrified that the teacher was going to call on me and I wouldn't have the answer!"

She looked up from the corner of the eye to see if I was laughing at her, and then she had to smile at how obviously earnest I was. "But you got over it," she said.

"No, I didn't. Honest. I'm still lousy at standing up for myself. I mean, look at who it was that called and made that appointment with Lieutenant White. You did. What you've been seeing lately isn't bravery, Letitia, it's just… conditioning. It's just the way I was brought up. My parents always encouraged me to stand up for what's right, and I always find it easier to speak up for somebody else than for myself. In fact, it comes so natural to me that there isn't any question of bravery about it."

There was a depressingly stubborn set to Letitia's lips, what I could see of them behind the curtain of hair, as I finished my explanation. Tentatively, I pressed for a response. "See what I mean?"

A minimal shrug of the shoulders seemed about to be all the answer I'd get, but then she said, sadly, "I guess it doesn't matter what you call it. Bravery or whatever. Maybe I was just trying to get back at my parents by doing—or being—something that would shock them. I don't know." She looked at me briefly, despondently, then back to her hands. "I just know that, after talking it all over with Jim last night, I think it's better I stop trying to be something I'm not."

Jim?!, demanded an indignant voice in my mind; what's he got to do with this? I didn't want to give in to the obvious answer.

"Okay," I said. "Let's both just be what and who we are. And one thing we are is friends. Right?"

Letitia's hands clasped in her lap. She hesitated, then looked at her watch. "I have to go," she said, and for a second I thought she meant to walk out without another word. She did pick up her books and stand, but then, as I rose, too, she turned to me and said what she'd come there to say. "I wish we could be friends, Terry, but it's just…too hard for me right now. It's like Jim said, this friendship is too…unsettling for me. It makes me want to do things I have no business doing. Your world is just too dangerous for me, Terry, that's what it comes down to. You don't see it that way, because you're used to it. You're used to living out there on the edge, being different, a social outcast. I guess that's what makes it easy for you to…do what I call being brave. I admire you. I really do."

I think there were tears in her eyes as she threw those last words into the air in the approximate direction of my feet and ran off towards the stairs. Maybe not. Maybe she was as relieved as she was sorry. I certainly felt more like crying than going to class, and more like pitching a fit of angry befuddlement than either of the above.

Good little social unit that I am, though, I trotted meekly off to class. And then spent the rest of the afternoon exorcizing my sadness in the form of righteous anger as I raced through the stacks reshelving books at a mile a minute. Just try to be friends with straight women and see where it gets you! Damn that Jim McVey! Why doesn't he mind his own business!

By the time I headed home, I was back to feeling mostly sad. Two friends gone in as many days. And I still was no closer to solving the mystery of Ted Simpson's murder. If it was a mystery. If it wasn't simply Barb who killed him, exactly as Lieutenant White believed. Letitia would have told me, even in the process of dumping me, if she'd found out anything relevant at the Peaceful Way; I trusted her that much, I told myself morosely as I trudged across the porch and into the house.

I was headed straight for the stairs and up to my room, but a voice calling from the living room turned me around. "Terry! Hey, you guys, Terry's home." It was Jeanne, apparently on her way through to the kitchen.

The door opened as we neared it, and Gretchen stuck her head and a beckoning hand out to hurry us along. "We brought food with us, Terry, so we could eat while we talk. Now that you're here, we can get started."

"What's up?"

"You'll know all about it in a minute," she said, and the next thing I knew, there was Sarah.

She grinned at me from the other side of the table, and Fran busily shifted her chair over to make room for me between the two of them. "Hi, Peg," I said as, chair in hand, I passed her on my way to Sarah's side of the table. "What is this, some kind of house meeting extraordinaire?"

"You got it. Okay, everybody find a place to settle, and let's get down to business."

I looked around the room, wondering whether this many women had ever sat down to eat together here before. In addition to the Everywhere House live-in population—which minus Jan made six—there were three other women sitting down with us: Sarah, Gretchen, and a cheerful-looking woman with big, round glasses that had to be pushed back up her small nose every thirty seconds. That's Georgia, I reminded myself, Peg's friend from up the street at 4017.

Peg took a deep breath. "I asked you all to come here today because I have an announcement to make."

"Want me to guess?" That was Fran.

"Shush," Connie told her. "Have some of this eggplant stuff and let Peg talk."

"I thank you." Mock pontifical. "I am pleased to announce, with no further ado, that as of next week I'll be moving out of Everywhere House and into 4017."

My weak "Nooooo!" was drowned out, fortunately, by the babble of comments and congratulations that followed Peg's little speech. Peg and Georgia beamed like newly-weds in the center of everyone's attention. That, and the fact that everyone was simultaneously busy eating, gave me a chance to pull myself together.

"Okay, ladies," Peg soon continued. "Now for the business part of the meeting. I know I can't just walk out of here like I'm checking out of a hotel. Unlike some people I might name." A cloud seemed to pass over us, casting a chill as she reminded us of Jan.

"We've got to find two new housemates pretty damn quick, in other words," Toni said, "or the five of us are gonna have to pony up seven slices of rent."

Gretchen cleared her throat and dissected a slice of zuccini with her fork as we all looked in her direction. "I've been thinking," she said. "That is, Jeanne and I have been talking, and—"

"Great idea," Fran bounced in enthusiastically. "You've been here a lot lately, almost as much as Peg's been at 4017. Might as well make it official."

There was a murmur of approbation, quickly stilled as Gretchen spoke again. "Yeah. Well. The thing is…. I'm not sure I want to live in a place where I'd be the only…non-white woman." Her intent gaze moved from her plate to a point on my left.

213

"Hey!" I said slowly as the light dawned.

"Sarah didn't hear a word about this until half an hour ago," Jeanne put in. "She hasn't had a chance to think yet."

"But you'd consider it?" I asked her eagerly.

Now it was Sarah's turn to pathologize the remains of her dinner. "I don't know," she said without looking up. "It hadn't occurred to me to move. Although...there would be advantages."

Nobody snickered, I am happy to report, although it was clear to me that somebody—Jeanne and Gretchen, I assumed—had filled the others in on my new relationship with Sarah.

"As long as Sarah's working nights at Weownit, she'd have a ride home with us," Jeanne explained. "That is, if Gretchen...."

"Maybe you should tell us what your usual process is." Sarah looked around the circle of faces. "Most of you don't know me. Don't you usually interview potential housemates?"

"There isn't anything formal." Toni answered for all of us, making Peg's outsider status seem real for the first time. Ordinarily it was The Voice of Reason who spoke for the household. "The process has varied every time since I've been here. But this time...hell, if Jeanne and Gretchen and Terry say you're all right, that's good enough for me."

"Me, too," Fran chorused, and Connie said, "Do you have questions you'd like to ask us, Sarah?"

"Well.... Jeanne told me about the financial agreements, and they sound fine; living here would be a lot cheaper for me. I think the most important thing now is for Gretchen and me to talk. By ourselves. Other than that, the only difficulty I can see is that Terry told me the system here is that the newest housemate always starts out in the basement. What I like most about where I am now is the light, the windows; I don't know that I want to give that up for a basement room."

"I'm willing to make an exception," Connie said calmly. "The room I've got now suits me fine. How about you, Toni?"

"Yeah, I guess so. I mean, I haven't been thinking about changing, because I had no idea anybody was leaving. I hadn't got my hopes up or anything, so sure, fine with me."

We looked, en masse, back to Sarah. Who did not look at me. Will she? I was asking myself; could she possibly...? And if so, how much would it be for convenience and economy, and how much—if any—because of me? I thought of her quiet, egg-shell walls and my heart sank. She won't, I told myself; how could she ever even consider moving into this zoo?

"What do you think, Terry?" she asked me, her eyes still on the squished squash remains. "Do you think it's a good idea for me to think about living here?"

"Well, sure!" That got a laugh from Peg, and then, of course, we all had to smile. Her laugh was like that. "I know there could be problems—unexpected expectations and stuff like that. But nothing we couldn't handle, don't you think? I know it wouldn't be easy for you to move from your own place to a shared household. But...well, yeah. I think it would be fabulous. And I think you and Gretchen would be wonderful for the house. Losing Jan and now Peg is...." I cast my mind and my eyes around the room looking for a way to say it. What I saw across the table was Gretchen. "You know Elizabeth Bishop, Gretch?" I asked her.

"Not personally," she grinned. "I like what I've read of her poetry, though."

"You know the one called 'One Art'?"

"Don't remember it right off the bat. Can you hum a few bars?"

"Probably not. I'm a better reader than rememberer. What it's about, though, is what she called the art of losing. The first few lines say:

The art of losing isn't hard to master;
so many things seem filled with the intent
to be lost that their loss is no disaster.

Then she goes on and talks about how you can practice the art of losing till you get to the point where even losing someone you love is no disaster. The way she does it, though, you know she's just trying to convince herself she can bear the unbearable. That's kind of how I've been feeling today: like a crash course in the art of losing. I don't expect it to be one of the decisive factors in your decision-making, but the way things are going, I sure wouldn't mind having another poetry reader in the house."

"I'll keep it in mind," she said with a smile.

After that, conversation became general for the five or six minutes before Jeanne and Gretchen announced it was time for them to get back to Weownit. Sarah was leaving with them, of course, but she had a chance to ask me, between the kitchen and the front door, "Did you find out anything new from Letitia?"

"Don't ask," I groaned. "She's one of the losses I was talking about just now."

"Really? What happened? An argument?"

"No, nothing as repairable as that, I'm afraid. She just decided she didn't want to be friends after all." I hung on to her hand as we reached the porch. "No matter what happens, we'll still see each other tomorrow night, won't we?"

"Definitely." The crowd had disappeared, and Jeanne and Gretchen waited tactfully in the car at the curb. We kissed, her lips warm and alive, her tongue brushing mine into erotic life, as a car coming up the hill lit the street and the contrast gave the shadowed porch a sense of fleeting privacy. "See you tomorrow," she said. "And call me, okay? If anything happens. Or if you want to."

"Okay," I said. "I'll be talking to you soon, then."

27.

I tried calling Ellie that evening, but she wasn't home. Very unusual for her on a week-day, I was musing to myself when the telephone rang right beside me. Barb Randall's voice almost took my breath away. "Terry?" she said uncertainly.

"Yes!" I lowered myself to the floor, already straining every sinew of my psychic powers to keep her on the line. This time, I was determined to get some information from her. "We need to talk, Barb."

"Yeah. It's been...." Her voice trailed off, but only for a moment. "We can talk now. I'm alone here. Finally."

"How's it going?"

Another pause. "The lawyer was here yesterday and today. They must be paying him a fortune. He wants me to plead temporary insanity."

"Not self defense?"

"No. Undue influence leading to mental instability, crime committed while the balance of my mind was disturbed."

"I thought you and Ted hadn't seen each other for ages. Could his 'undue influence' have lasted that long?"

"He's not talking about his influence. He means the Furies."

The penny dropped: Barb's lawyer meant to put lesbianism and radical feminism on trial. I was temporarily speechless with indignation. "But you can't—"

"I know. It stinks. That's why I called. I don't want to go through that shit, but if you can't help me I have no choice."

"You could refuse, couldn't you?"

Silence. "I don't know."

"Barb! You've got to!"

"I don't know if I could. I don't even know if I could want to, once it started. Once we were in court. But if I did.... Mr. Winterstone says whatever I did, he could use it against me. He says it would just make me look crazier and crazier the more I tried to object. Especially since my parents would be right there with the papers to have me committed."

I was deeply shocked. "You mean your parents would go along with this shit even if you refused to? And even though you're innocent?"

"Of course. And that means if you don't find the murderer, they'll find a way to lock me up, one way or another. Prison or mental hospital, guilty or crazy.

There are no other choices for me. Unless they come from you."

Lord help us all. "There's about one chance in a million that I'll be able come up with anything, though I have been trying. But if I'm going to help you, you've got to help me. Quite a lot has happened since I saw you last, but at the moment I'm all out of ideas. I talked to Carolyn Enderly. She's very concerned about you, by the way. She asked me to clear out that room you used in her house; seemed to think her husband would hit the roof if he found out she'd let you come there every day."

"She's right. Bill Enderly is a prick. He'd bust a blood vessel if he knew his precious offspring had been exposed to a real live lesbian in the house. Not to mention a murderer."

"I read your notebooks." Silence. "Why did you do that, Barb?"

"What?" It was a delaying tactic, not a question, but I answered it anyway.

"Why did you lie to your friends about having a job in a factory? Why did you spend all that time and effort creating a fictitious life for yourself?"

I let the silence run until Barb was forced to speak. "You don't understand," she said.

"So explain it to me."

Again, silence. Finally, she gave in. "I wanted them to accept me. I wanted to be one of them. I *was* one of them. I was good at it. I was good at being a Fury. But.... I saw how they treated anyone who was privileged. They said the only good theory comes out of the experience of oppression, and I was good at theory, they could see that. But if they knew I wasn't really oppressed, they wouldn't have listened to me. So I made up a life. We all did, in a way. All of us sort of ... interpreted our lives so they'd sound most...legitimate politically. It's just...I had to make up more than the others, because I had more to hide."

"From what I can see, you've got too many problems—even before this murder business—to need to come up with imaginary ones. Fennel told me about your family—"

"You talked to Fennel?"

"Yes. She didn't have a whole lot to tell me, but listen, Barb, is Fennel paranoid? When I went to see her, she acted like a spy or something. Said she was being watched."

"We were all paranoid, I guess. If you can call it paranoia when you really are in danger. Plenty of bigots hated everything we stood for; even a lot of faggots and lesbians would have been glad to see us dead. But I wouldn't expect Fennel to think she's being watched unless there's a reason. Maybe the cops?"

"Yeah, I thought of that, but then.... After I left the place where Fennel is staying, somebody tried to run me down. In Fennel's car."

There was a sharp intake of breath on the other end of the line. "You think Fennel...?"

"I don't know. I hope not. Why would she want to do such a thing? You don't have any reason to think she was involved in the murder, do you?"

"Hell, no. I never told the Furies I'd been married, much less anything about Ted. And besides, all the rest of them were on their way to the fucking restaurant when it happened."

"That's what I thought. Okay. Now it's your turn. Tell me something that might give me a new lead."

"What kind of things do you want to know?"

"So far, I've had two possibilities in mind. One was this cult that Ted recruited for, the Peaceful Way. Did you know about that?"

"No. He'd do just about anything for money, though, I know that."

"For a while it looked like maybe he got too pushy with the people in the cult who were paying him off, and they killed him to protect their business. But yesterday the cops raided the cult house, and apparently the two men there who looked like good possibilities are out of the running now."

"What's the other lead you had?"

"Vague hints, that's all. I went up to Bellingham to see David Ellis—"

"Who's he?"

"A friend of Ted's. After your time, I guess. He worked in the Linguistics Department at the U until just after the murder. Anyway...he talked to Ted that afternoon, and he says Ted was expecting something to happen that night, something lucrative, and something in addition to his payoff from the cult."

"What kind of thing?"

"That's the trouble. I just don't know, and Ellis said he didn't either. I'm hoping you'll be able to tell me something about Ted that'll give me some clue, give me some idea what kind of things he might be into. Something lucrative and illicit. Ellis said he seemed really excited about it. What did Ted get excited about?"

"Money."

"Okay, but how? What did he have or do that he could turn a profit on? And get some kicks, too, from the way Ellis was talking."

A longish pause. And then, "He had a gun," she said. "A pistol."

I tried to imagine the profit opportunities offered by the ownership of a hand gun. "He wouldn't go in for stick-ups, would he?"

"Never. Too dangerous. Too...menial." We both lapsed into thought, broken eventually by the clearing of Barb's throat. "He did...photography," she said.

"Uh huh." Now that she mentioned it, I remembered Professor Compton's comment about Ted popping off flashbulbs. "Was he serious about it?"

"He used to be. For a while he said he was going to go professional, go back to school, even. But then when he realized how expensive it was...."

"So that's no help," I concluded gloomily, and was surprised to hear a sort of stuttering We-e-elll from Barb that sounded like disagreement. "You think he could have been all excited about a chance to make money from photography?"

I asked skeptically.

"He...." She was having trouble getting the words out. "He made pornography."

I was struck speechless. Momentarily. "You mean he...?"

"Took pictures. Photos."

"Of...?"

"His new girlfriend, for one. That's how I know he was still into it. That picture he sent me—she was sucking him off."

"That's really sick. I guess that's what Ellis was hinting about. He said Ted was 'radical' in some way, some intellectual way, but he kept sort of snickering...."

"Sounds like a friend of Ted's all right."

"Was he doing it when you were still married to him?"

"Not right at the beginning, but after a while.... He said it was the next stage in human development. After radical politics and the expanding consciousness crap, LSD and whatever, the next step was to free ourselves of inhibitions about sex. He used to read things aloud, articles by men who said we were all shackled by old taboos, afraid of our own impulses, ashamed of our bodies."

"Doesn't sound so awful."

"No. But Ted...."

"What?"

"He used it, somehow, to get you to do things.... Whatever he wanted you to do. To him, or for him, for him to photograph.... Do you know if they found any?"

"If who found any what?"

"The cops. If they found any of Ted's dirty pictures. I thought.... He might still have some of me."

"Jesus."

"Yeah. I didn't tell Mr. Winterstone about it. Do you think I should?"

I marveled at the tone of Barbara's voice. She spoke to me, for the first time, as if I really existed, as if I was as real to her as she was to me. "I don't know, Barb. It would be horrible if the prosecutor suddenly whipped them out in court, and I suppose it would be even worse if your lawyer didn't expect it. On the other hand...it might be better to keep quiet and hope the cops didn't find anything. Or don't plan to use anything they did find. Because, what if this Mr. Winterstone decided to...."

"I know. Make it part of the defense." Her breath sounded loud in my ear for a minute. "I wish I was dead," she mumbled, and the jerky breathing turned into wracking sobs.

My god, she's all alone there!, I thought, even knowing that the alternative—her family—would be worse. "I'll see what I can find out, Barb," I said as the sobbing diminished. "The policeman in charge doesn't think very highly of me, but... I'll try to find out if they've got any pictures"—though Goddess only knows how I can pry anything out of Lieutenant White at this point, I admitted silently. "And I'll talk to Heidi again. The new girlfriend. After all, Ted's porn could be the key to everything. Maybe this new deal he was so excited about had something to do with the pictures. And maybe Ellis was involved in it. Maybe that's why he left town so quickly, and why he was willing to talk to me, fishing to find out if anybody'd stumbled onto it yet."

I was babbling, making it all up as I went along, desperate to give Barb something to hang her hopes on. Not to mention some hopes to hang thereon.

"Just a minute," she whispered hoarsely. I heard the clunk of the receiver being laid down, and then some extensive nose blowing. "Okay," she said. "I'm okay."

She wasn't okay, but we both knew what she meant. "Is there anything else you can think of?" I asked gently. "Anything you know about Ted that might help me find a clue?"

"I don't think so." She sounded weary. "You talked to Carolyn. He was a very charming man. I hated him, and I bet I wasn't the only one. He could be careless, sometimes."

"What do you mean?"

"I.... I don't know. With people, women mostly. Underestimating them." She was fading fast, and I couldn't bring myself to demand more of her.

"Okay, Barb," I said. "You've given me a good lead. Let's give it a few days, see where it goes. Would you call me back—let's see, this is Thursday, so—how about Monday?"

"I don't.... I'm not sure I...." Her voice stopped for long enough that I was about to conclude we'd been cut off, but then, "all right. I guess so." She sounded tired to death. "I'll try."

"I wish there were something I could do for you, Barb," I told her, wishing with all my heart. "I wish you had somebody there to—"

"Goodbye," she said, very very softly, and the tenuous links between us disconnected.

28.

On Friday mornings, I was like the guy in Roethke's poem: "*I wake to sleep and take my waking slow.*" My first thought that morning, once I'd realized it was Friday, was, Oh good, Sarah tonight. Then I drowsed some more, and when next I surfaced, there was a thin, early-morning sunray teasing at the edges of the window shade and Barb lay on my mind like the last vestige of an unremembered dream.

Every time I'd seen or talked to her, I mused, there'd been a wall between us. A wall of anger, the first time, when she came thundering down the Lesbian Resource Center stairs and almost knocked me over. A wall of who-knows-what the second time, at the fat oppression workshop. Even though we sat in the same room for hours that day, the barrier between us had seemed as real as the thick pane of glass in the visiting area of the jail. A wall of glass. A wall of space. A wall of...projection, as in the Nemerov poem that came to mind as I rode the bus down the hill from Carolyn's house.

I stretched my body awake and lay back for a few more minutes of quiet thinking. When Barb was a Fury, I asked myself, was the barrier between us a projection from her or a projection from me? Did I feel cut off from her because I was projecting my expectations onto her, or did I feel cut off because she was projecting onto me her own feeling of being different—or her expectation that I'd reject her because of that difference? And Jan, now. What about Jan?—not to mention Letitia. Where did all the distance between us come from? We'd been pretty close, I'd thought, and getting closer, but then suddenly we were worlds apart. I'd seen woodcuts of people in the middle ages who were possessed by demons that were represented by long balloons of words pouring out of their victims' mouth. Maybe we're all possessed by demons. Secular demons that pour out of our mouths as invisible, intangible forces that push us relentlessly apart from one another. Maybe we walk around projecting demons out of our eyes. Out onto the blank white walls of space....

At the last possible moment, something jerked me back into full consciousness, ready for the first item on the day's agenda: a phone call to Heidi Bascom. Studying was urgent, too, but Heidi had been talking about leaving town, and I didn't want to run the risk of missing my chance to ask her about Ted's photographic proclivities. But what tack should I take? When last I'd seen Heidi Bascom, she was a quivering mass of pain. How much could I expect her to have recovered in the intervening week? Did I want to bash my way into her confidence by starting out with: 'Hey, I understand Ted took a picture of you with his prick in your mouth. Mind if I come over so you can tell me all about it?'

On the other hand, Heidi was my only source for information about Ted's recent pornography. The more I thought about it, sitting there with my hand on the phone, the uneasier I felt. No way would it be easy to talk with Heidi about her dead lover's sex life, even assuming she'd been a willing participant. I was just about to allow myself to decide it was a decision better made after consultation (meaning, I could put it off till after my evening with Sarah) when another realization turned my thinking right around. If Ted sent Barb a picture of Heidi and Ted, that meant there had to be a third party involved. A delayed-action or remote-control shutter was a possibility, but what kept coming back to me were Dave Ellis' snickery hints about Ted's "applied philosophy." Maybe Dave was the third party in the photo sessions. That would explain why he'd reacted so strongly when he heard that I'd talked to Heidi.

The more I thought about a Ted-Heidi-David triangle, the better it sounded. Not only could I imagine Ellis getting talked into Ted's sexy photo business, I could imagine him freaking out at the thought of what he'd done and the evidence he'd left behind. I could even imagine Ellis flipping out to the extent that he'd argue with Ted over the pictures, pick up a knife so conveniently supplied by the fleeing Barb, and lash out against this man he'd looked up to—this man he'd idolized, who now merely laughed at his distress, perhaps taunting him, sneering at his failure of nerve. Yes, I could see Dave Ellis as a killer all right. Not a cold-blooded killer, but a man simply driven past his limit. He'd lashed out at Ted and, when he realized he'd had the bad luck to kill him with one blow, he'd panicked and run away. Next day, still fearing disclosure despite Barb's arrest, he'd used his mother's poor health as an excuse to leave the area and put the entire episode behind him.

No wonder he was scared when some stranger came to the door asking questions about Ted Simpson. If it had been anybody but an obviously benign and undangerous creature like Terry Barber, he might have been provoked into violence again. Instead, he'd seemed pretty confident, after the initial panic, that he could play the innocent for me and thus allay any possibility that I might suspect him and go to the cops. If the man was guilty of murder, of course he'd lie, of course he'd say he'd turned down the offer of Ted's part in the Peaceful Way scam, especially if he'd been with Ted that night to watch him take the payoff from Francis. Ellis might even have tossed me a red herring with that story about Ted's lucrative new venture, trying to lead me even further off the track. Well, from now on I'd let the police handle Dave Ellis. Once I'd persuaded them to question him.

That thought brought me back to Heidi Bascom again. She could tell the police about Ellis's involvement in Simpson's porn games. Surely they'd want to check into something like that. So all I had to do was persuade Heidi to talk to me and then to the police. I picked up the receiver and started to dial.

"Hello." I couldn't recognize the voice on the other end of the line.

"Heidi?" I ventured.

"Who is this?"

"Terry Barber. Is this Heidi?"

"Yes."

"You remember me? I—"

"Yes."

Her voice sounded a lot stronger than when I'd heard it last, but she still didn't sound…natural. Normal. But then, what do you know about how grief affects people? I reminded myself.

"Listen, Heidi, there's something I need to talk to you about. I wish it could wait until you've had more time to…. I wish it could wait, but it's urgent. So if we could—"

"What?" Her voice broke sharply into mine.

"I'd rather tell you in person. It's kind of…delicate, something that concerns you directly, you and Ted—and the phone always seems so—"

She cut me off with just her breathing that time, suddenly sounding fast and loud in my ear as if she'd been running. Oh hell, she's crying again. But no. When she spoke, her voice was dry. "Can you come over now?"

"I can be there in…twenty minutes."

"I'll be here," and she hung up.

When I left the house—setting out without my pack for once, because after all I'd only be gone an hour or so—the sky was mostly blue in the diffuse light of a northern March morning. Little puffs of flat-bottomed cloud, a creamy almost-yellow on top, then white shading down into gray at the base, made me feel like a fish swimming free under waterlilies in bloom.

By the time I got to the ugly building where Heidi lived, the sunny morning was giving in to the usual gray. On the way, I'd tried to imagine the mental state of a woman in love with a man whose hobby was taking pictures of their sexual acts. There was no doubt in my mind that Heidi loved Ted, so I had to assume that he'd managed to charm her into acceptance of his "radical" sexual philosophy. Or maybe he hadn't needed to. Maybe she'd enjoyed playing sex games and showing off before the camera. That was hard for me to imagine, so I stopped trying.

Heidi looked awful as she gestured me silently into the apartment, as skinny as I remembered her from the week before, but sort of puffy now, too. Definitely unhealthy. She looked like she hadn't done anything all week but sit inside the walls of that cinder-block hive and cry.

"Thanks, Heidi," I said as I sat down on a chair standing alone in the middle of the room. "I appreciate your letting me come over and talk."

Thin people get cold easier, I reminded myself; that's why she's wearing that coat in the house. Amazingly, the buttons hadn't come off yet, though she continued to twist them mechanically as she sat down on a straight-backed chair between me and the door. That put the thinly-curtained window almost behind her and, since no lights were on in the room, made it hard for me to read the expression on her face.

"What I want to talk about," I began after a deep breath, "is Ted's photography."

No reaction from Heidi, except her hand froze onto one button.

"Barb told me…" I spoke as carefully as I could, "about his interest in photography when they were married. And she told me he sent her a picture of you. And him. Together."

The silence was becoming eery. Every once in a while I'd catch a signal from the outside world—a door slammed shut, a truck passing on Eastlake—but inside the apartment, my voice was the only sound. Had Heidi's roommate left for work already?

"Heidi, I know Ted took…sexy pictures. And I know he took at least one of you, because he sent it to Barb. Now, believe me: I don't care about the pictures. What people do in the privacy of their own homes is their own business. All I want is for you to help me persuade the police to talk seriously to David Ellis."

"Dave Ellis!"

"Yes, I went up to Bellingham on Tuesday and—"

"You talked to Dave Ellis."

"Yes, that's what I'm trying to tell you. I wasn't sure when I talked to him, but then I talked to Barb last night, and now I am sure. Ellis is the one who killed Ted. He's the only one who makes any sense, and—"

"No." She leaned abruptly forward, hands on her thighs, coat falling open and hanging down on both sides of the chair just as her hair hung down on each side of her face. "You're wrong," she said. "It was his ex-wife who killed him. You've got to accept that. The police have arrested her and it's over."

"It's not." Her flat insistence made me stubborn, and that made me react more strongly than I'd meant to. "I know Barb didn't kill him, and that means someone else did."

"There's no evidence," she countered.

"We don't know that. If I'm right about Ellis, the motive was those photos. Ellis must have panicked when he realized that Ted had pictures showing him in compromising positions. That's what I want you to tell the police."

"What pictures?" Her voice had faded.

"The photographs. You know. They must be somewhere. Ted's apartment, probably, or wherever his things have been stored. The police will know."

"They didn't find any." Her back was rigidly vertical again.

"How do you know? Did they tell you that?"

"They would have told me if they'd found any."

I thought it over. "I don't think we can be sure of that. But if he kept them someplace else, the police might not have found them. I'm sure there is evidence somewhere. He sent Barb a photo, so he might have sent them to other people, or there might be evidence or witnesses from wherever he got the film processed. We can use the one he sent Barb, if we can't find the others," I lied desperately. "The important thing is to persuade the police to talk to Ellis. Once they know about the pornography, and once they start talking to Ellis, who's so ready to break it's almost pitiful, I'm sure they'll be able to—"

"No." She positively snapped it out.

I took another deep breath. "Now look, if it's the pictures you're worried about, I think you'd be a lot better off going to the police with me. If you cooperate with them, maybe they'll do what they can to keep your name out of it, at least as far as the pictures go. And you can bet that I'm going to the police with this story, whether you go with me or not. So for your own sake, why don't you—"

Heidi didn't interrupt me. I interrupted myself. When I realized she'd reached down into the pocket of her coat and taken out a gun. A gun that she was aiming straight at me.

Believe it or not, the first thought that flashed into my mind was the last lines of Ferlinghetti's poem, "The World Is a Beautiful Place..."

Yes
   But then right in the middle of it
                      comes the smiling
             mortician

That took maybe a quarter of a second, and then my brain lost all capacity for rational thought. Otherwise, how can I explain why I really, truly did not understand the significance of what I saw? Boy, she's really upset, I told myself. She's so worried about anybody seeing those pictures that she'd rather let Barb take the rap than take the risk of helping me get the police onto Dave Ellis' track.

So, "Heidi, take it easy," I said. "We can work this out. I'm sure the cops can find a way to prosecute Ellis without bringing you into it. Barb's already in it up to the eyeballs, and she can testify about the pornography as well as you can."

The only answer I got was a distant rumble of thunder, a sound unusual enough in Seattle to make me glance in automatic surprise towards the curtained window. A few seconds later, rain was hissing down and I realized how much darker it seemed—outside and in—than when I'd arrived.

Heidi stood up and backed the few steps it took to get her to the window, still keeping her eyes and the gun trained on me. With her left hand she drew the curtain back and looked outside. Grey rain pelted the window, despite the overhang of the next story's walkway, and the sound of rushhour traffic was louder in the downpour. It had gotten so dark outside that the yellow gleam of headlights was visible even on the second floor, flickering sporadically through the gloom like the eyes of distant fish swimming by.

"We'll wait until the traffic lets up," she said as she dropped the curtain and resumed her seat across from me.

Inevitably, her words flooded my mind with another of Ferlinghetti's poems. I shook my head like a dog with burrs on its ears, and bits and pieces of "I Am Waiting" were flung off and spattered around the room.

I am waiting for my case to come up
and I am waiting
for a rebirth of wonder....
and I am waiting
for linnets and planets to fall like rain
and I am waiting for lovers and weepers
to lie down together again
in a new rebirth of wonder....
I am waiting for the day
that maketh all things clear....
and I am waiting
for the green mornings to come again
youth's dumb green fields come back again....
and I am waiting
for the last long careless rapture....

Oh, Sarah!, my spirit wailed, and I think that's when I finally started to begin to understand. "I don't believe it," I said involuntarily.

Heidi had been watching me in an abstract sort of way. Hearing my declaration, she raised her eyebrows in polite inquiry.

"I don't believe you killed him," I expanded.

"Oh," she said, "...but I did."

"But—you loved him!"

"Yes."

We stared at each other, and then I saw her jaw begin to work, like the Tin Woodman after a squirt or two from the oilcan. She hasn't had anybody to talk to, I realized; she hasn't been able to talk since it happened. And I wondered if the floodgates were about to open.

It was a very strange scene, psychologically speaking. There she was, on the verge of opening her heart to a woman she held at gunpoint. And there I was, half my mind in total denial and the other half split into fractions of panic and desperation. I'd read quite a lot about women's self-defence, even tried out a few moves on my own, following the instructions in articles and pamphlets with names like "Women Fight Back!" and "Victims No More!" Nothing I'd read had prepared me for Heidi, though, and my feelings were still so confused I wasn't sure I'd be able to whack her even if I had the chance.

Meanwhile, I knew I definitely did want to stay alive as long as possible. Decades, preferably; certainly well past the end of the morning's rushhour. Stall, Terry, screamed one of my mental fractions; stall like hell, it's your only chance!

"I don't understand, Heidi," I said, hoping she couldn't see the tremors fluttering through my body. "But I'd like to."

"He was a fool." It burst out of her.

"But you—you just said, you just agreed that you loved him."

"I made a mistake," she said fiercely. "I believed him when he said we could be—we were intellectual companions as well as lovers. Oh, he was one smooth character, let me tell you."

"Yes, do. Tell me."

She needed no further encouragement. "He was a fake, an absolute fake. Intellectually. That's what fooled me. I thought he was brilliant!" The gun wavered for the first time as she unconsciously matched the scorn in her voice with a throw-away gesture of her dominant hand, and I suppressed a gasp of panic as I realized I might have to take advantage of a moment like that and try to overpower her. Her eyes glittered flat with anger and her left hand clenched viciously in her lap.

"So...when did you first realize you'd been deceived?"

"Not for a long, long time. Too long. I can't believe how stupid I've been, to be taken in by a shallow-minded fake like that. Intellectually fake!" She was into it now, leaning forward slightly, the gun slightly lower, resting on her knee. "His mistake was that he thought he could rip me off and get away with it."

"What was he—oh, you mean the pictures? He was trying to make you give him money for—"

"Not money. My work. *My* work, most of it work I'd done for my thesis, work he supposedly was 'helping' me with. What a laugh! Ted couldn't think his way out of a paper bag." A ghastly mask of humor twisted round with pain distorted her fleshless face, but the gun never wavered.

"You mean he was taking your work and putting his name on it?"

"Exactly. He had to get published to get tenure. But he was a nothing, an intellectual nothing. He was a pretty good teacher at the undergraduate level, but that's all he could ever be. His mind just wasn't good enough. He'd never get beyond the basics on his own, and that's why he needed to steal from me."

I thought back to what Carolyn Enderly had told me. Poor Ted, she'd called him, failing to last out the summer working in the mine, failing to gain the status and wealth he thought he'd achieve through marriage with Barb, failing, finally, to hold on to that marriage or to Barb. Heidi's picture of Ted made sense, though it was about the only thing that did.

"But what about the pictures, Heidi?" I blurted. "They have to come into it somewhere, or else you wouldn't...react so when I brought them up."

She looked away for an instant, but my reflexes just weren't up to it. By the time my mind reacted, she was back on track again. "That's part of how he kept me fooled," she said. "That's what he used sex for. To keep me believing he was more 'advanced' than I was. Even when I might have started to suspect what he was really like, that he needed me more than I needed him, and that this great intellectual companionship he talked about was really me helping him look better than he was...."

"Barb said something about that, too. She told me Ted had a theory about sex being the frontier of knowledge."

"He made it sound so intellectual." She laughed, with a sound that felt like when you're grating a carrot and your hand slips. "We were out on the edge, together. Where no man has gone before. Not just doing it, doing it as an 'expansion of the intellectual limit.' What crap."

"But you believed him. For a while."

She looked at me speculatively, as if searching for some sign that I might be able to understand. "You know what it's like when someone uses your insecurity against you? When he knows that you feel unsure of yourself—your sexual attractiveness, your performance, even—and he uses that to make you do whatever he wants you to? Because if you don't do it, if you even say you don't want to, that proves he's better than you are, braver than you are, more 'advanced' than you are."

I felt sickness rising in my throat. Any minute she might decide it was time, time for whatever she had in mind for me. I choked down the bile and tried to keep her talking—focused on the past, not the present and not, definitely not, the immediate future. "Was David Ellis part of Ted's sex games?" I asked her.

"Oh, yes. He got roped in, too. I'm not surprised to hear he was upset when you came around. But I bet he was relieved to hear that Ted was dead, especially when the days went by and nothing came out about the photographs." Another eerie smile stretched her thin lips as she thought about Dave Ellis. It went away as she said, "The picture your friend got, the one of me and Ted. Dave probably took it. Ted liked to make him watch."

For my own sake, I wanted to get her off the subject of sex. It made her fingers clench, and one of them was very close to a trigger. "Tell me how it happened, Heidi. Tell me why you killed him. Couldn't you just go to the Dean, or something? If he was stealing your work?"

"He threatened me," she responded, her voice making it sound reasonable that murder should follow threat. "I told him I wanted my own name on my work and he threatened me. He said he'd found a buyer for the pictures."

"Maybe that's what Ellis was talking about," I said, remembering the "big score" Ted had been counting on in the days before he died.

"What do you mean? What did he know about it?" The gun jerked up off her knee again.

"Nothing," I protested. "Ted told him the day he was killed that he was about to get a lot of money. Ellis thought it was some scam, something more lucrative than the Peaceful Way, but he didn't know what."

Heidi snorted through her tight-drawn nose. "Ted was a bigger fool than I thought, if he really believed he could make a killing in the porn biz. But then, he always did fancy himself a photographer."

"He was going to sell the pictures, though?" I ventured cautiously.

"That's what he said. I thought he was just doing it to punish me, but maybe he was stupid enough to think he could punish me and get rich at the same time. Or...," she thought about it. "I suppose he thought he could get enough for the pictures—he had drawers full, not just of me—to pay for him to set up as a pro. Darkroom equipment, some training to bring him up to speed." Her tone told me Ted's plans were of academic interest only.

A brief silence lasted until I saw Heidi's eyes glance towards the window. "Tell me exactly what happened then," I said. It was the first thing that came to mind, and it worked. She shrugged, her bony shoulders barely able to lift the heavy peacoat, and allowed herself to become absorbed in telling her story.

"I spent that Friday night at Ted's place, and I meant to tell him then. About wanting my name on my work—as one of the authors, not in some footnote at the bottom of the page. But I couldn't make myself say it. He was in one of his sad little boy moods, wanting his hand held and his tired brow soothed. Jesus, I can't believe I ever fell for that crap—and it's only, what? Eight days ago? Anyway.... I decided to tell him in the morning, and I did. I finally just laid it all out for him. I wanted my name up there at the top of the page when he submitted the articles we'd worked on together, or else I was going to the Dean.

"Right then the phone rang, and Ted dashed into the bedroom to take it. When he came back, he was grinning all over his face and it looked like he'd forgotten all about what I'd been saying. 'Who was it Ted?' I asked him, and he said, 'Oh, just a man, calling about a dog.' And then he laughed. Big joke.

"'I really mean what I said, Ted,' I told him. He stopped laughing then and sat down again, but a minute later there's this big smile on his face again, and he says, 'Oh, I don't think so, honey.' I was furious! The man was laughing at me! But I was curious, too. I asked him, 'What the hell do you mean?' And he started going on about how maybe he didn't need me any more, maybe he didn't even need the fucking tenure committee any more. He's thinking of moving into a career where his talents would be recognized. And finally he says, 'I tell you what, we'll get equal credit.' Like he's doing me a big favor. And I say, fine, that's all

I was asking for. But all the time I'm getting more and more nervous because of the way he's acting. You didn't know Ted, did you?"

She had me so mesmerized, what with the normal, run-on sound of her voice and the abnormal, steady-as-a-rock look of her gun, that I almost missed the question. "No," I piped up belatedly. "How was he acting, exactly?"

"He was...strutting. I mean, he literally got up from the breakfast table and marched around the room, bragging and showing off. Said he was going to give the U one last chance to grant him tenure, but if not, well, it would be their loss, not his, he'd be on his way to Easy Street. And I'm sitting there thinking, what the hell is he talking about. And why did he give in so easy on the article by-lines.

"Well, with Ted, the only way to get something out of him is to bluff him or flatter him. So I put on my big-eyed-little-miss face and beg him to tell me what it's all about. When he finally feels like he's got me on tenterhooks, he says, 'Stand over there by the window and I'll show you,' and then he disappears into the other room. When he comes back, he's got a big manila envelope in his hands. He holds it up and says, 'This, my dear, is the beginning of a whole new career for yours truly.' 'What is it?' I ask, but he makes me stand there and beg before he undoes the clasp and opens the flap—everything very slow, like a magician working a trick—and pulls out a blowup of a photograph. First he looks at it himself for a minute, grinning away, and then he looks at me and says, 'Would you like to see it?' I start over to him, but he says 'Stop!' and holds the picture up over his head, still with its back to me so I can't see what it is. 'What'll you do for me if I show you?' he says."

Heidi's voice had been flowing easily, but now it snagged on the bitterness of the memory. "Did he show it to you finally?" I asked, wanting somehow to help her over the worst of it—and not wanting, really, to share in that particular memory myself.

"Yes. It was one he took of me. And there were others. Of me and.... Well, it doesn't matter. He wouldn't let me get near them, wouldn't let me touch them. I was crying by that time, and next thing I knew the envelope was gone and there I was on the couch with Ted's arms around me, him going, 'There, there, now, maybe we weren't quite as grown-up as we thought. Maybe we're not quite ready to play grown-up games and take credit for grown-up work. Maybe we'd rather just leave things the way they are for a while.' And I couldn't stop crying. Does that ever happen to you?"

I nodded, unable to find any words.

"He didn't come right out and say it, but he sure as hell implied that he was offering to trade the pictures for the publication credit. I mean, that he'd keep the pictures private if I'd let him appear as sole author on the articles. So that's the way I played it. I let him think he was comforting me, and that I was agreeing to his bargain. I even let him kiss me, and pretended to kiss him back. But I knew all along I had to destroy those pictures and the negatives. Even if it meant destroying him along with them."

"I can see why you didn't want the pictures made public. But…wouldn't it do Ted just as much harm professionally, if people at the U found out what he was doing—the sex and the pictures and the Peaceful Way recruiting?"

"They wouldn't necessarily find out, even if the pictures were published. Not if he sold only the ones he didn't appear in. And he could always deny he'd taken them, couldn't he? Once they were out of his hands. But that's just quibbling. I didn't give a damn about him or what might happen to him if the pictures got out. As soon as I opened my eyes that morning and saw what a fool I'd been, as soon as I saw him for what he really was, I knew that what I had to worry about—and all I had to worry about—was my own career. Because I already am what Ted only hoped to be. I'm the one with a real career ahead of her—and I'm not just talking about tenure and rank and salary, I'm talking about the important things. I have a real contribution to make. The field of philosophy needs people like me. It would be madness to let a…a nothing like Ted Simpson destroy that promise. And I knew I couldn't trust him. I knew he'd try to sell those pictures sooner or later. Once Ted got an idea in his little mind, he'd hang onto it like a leech. A blood-sucking leech.

"And then—" She broke off into her scary little laugh again. "Do you know what? He actually asked to borrow my car. Can you believe the gall of the man? He's just said he plans to sell my life down the river, and then he turns around and asks to borrow my car. Luckily, I had pulled myself together enough to ask why."

"And he said…?"

"He said he had an appointment late that night with his 'contact'— that's the language he used when he talked about that cult place—and he wanted to be able to leave the car nearby. 'Your sticker lets you park any time in the W10 lot. I don't want to risk a parking ticket tonight, not tonight of all nights.' Ted always did have a misguided sense of the mysterious. He was having so much fun, thinking I hadn't a clue, thinking I'd believe that all he meant to do that night was pick up his pay-off from the cult. But I was sure, just from the way he looked so satisfied with himself, that he still meant to go through with whatever he'd set up on the phone that morning."

Heidi's eyes showed she was reliving that moment with great clarity. Deep inside me, a throbbing timpani said, You're going to die, you're going to die, you're going to die. "So what did you do?" I managed to ask her out of my misery.

"I decided to get the pictures and destroy them," she answered succinctly. "I told him he could borrow my car because I didn't want to make him suspicious—and because I figured it might give me an advantage, and I was right." She sounded triumphant. Heidi is brilliant, QED. "He drove me home and then took off again, in my car. As soon as he was gone, I got my other set of car keys and took the bus back to his apartment. My car was parked outside, so I waited around out of sight until he came out and drove off again. I knew he wouldn't be able to resist the chance to use somebody else's wheels for a day. He'd never given me a key to the apartment, but the manager lived in the basement and had seen me with Ted several times. So all I had to do was go to the little grocery on the corner and buy a few things. Then I knock on the manager's door and say could he let me into Ted's apartment because I want to surprise him by cooking a special dinner for him. The guy sees a bunch of celery sticking out of the bag, thinks, 'here's a girl who knows how to treat a guy,' and lets me in. Easy.

"But then I find out the sneaky bastard's taken the envelope with the picture away with him, and I just about died right there. What if he's doing it now? I thought. What if I'm wrong and he really did want the car just for getting his payoff from the cult, not for the meeting about the pictures? I tell you, I was in a state. Threw up, even. But then I pulled myself together again and decided I'd just have to do what I could. The fact that Ted was carrying the pictures around with him during the day might not be significant at all; he probably just wanted to hang on to the feeling of power they gave him. So I searched the apartment and took away all the photographs and negatives I could find that might implicate me, and then I went back out and waited for Ted to come home."

"That must have been hard," I ventured.

"Well, it wasn't easy." She sounded almost genial. Almost proud of herself.

"Did you have to wait long?"

"No, he came back about an hour later. When I searched the car, though, the envelope wasn't there."

She seemed to want my reactions now, so I dutifully fed her another line. "Did you panic again at that point? I know I would have."

"I was beyond panic by then. I decided to stick with my original idea, that the meeting was set for that night. That's what it sounded like when he first started going on about it, and sometimes first impressions are the best. Not that I had much choice."

"So...you came back home?"

"Yes. And waited."

She glanced towards the window again, where we could hear the rain gradually winding down. No!, screamed every cell of my body, No, please, not yet! "But Heidi," I said, trying to sound genuinely interested rather than desperately manipulative, "I still don't understand how you managed to work it out—to...do it, I mean. And not only not get caught, but set Barb up so perfectly."

"That was partly luck," she admitted. I was fascinated by the way she looked at me. I might have been a student come in for extra help, her gaze was so abstract despite its steadiness. She might have been thinking about something else altogether—what to have for dinner that night, maybe—and at the same time staying alert for the signs of how well I was catching on to the information she was feeding me, silently evaluating my rate of absorption. "There's a skill," she instructed me, "in making the best possible use of the luck that comes your way."

"I know Ted met his Peaceful Way contact that night. Were you there, too?"

"No. I watched him park my car in the W10 lot and set off on foot, but I didn't follow him. He'd told me where the cult house was, so I figured he was picking up the money there first. And meanwhile, I wanted another look in the car. If the envelope wasn't there, I figured I'd have to hide in the back seat and take it from him when he got back. I had this already"—she waved the gun back and forth a fraction of an inch, moving the trajectory of the bullet from my heart to my right lung and back again. "Took it when I went through his apartment that morning. So if worst came to worst...."

"But you didn't. Shoot him."

"No. That's where I got lucky. The first thing that happened, though, was, well, I froze." Defiant refusal to admit embarrassment, and I thought, Lady, I wish to hell you had. "I was just about to stand up from the damn bushes I'd been crouching in when all of a sudden a car came driving up the road behind the APL building. You can imagine how I felt when I saw it was a cop car. Campus cops, but still!"

"Wow," I said, because I obviously had to say something.

"That's why I froze. It was horrible. The cops just sat there. Looking. And smoking. They had their windows rolled down, and I could see them. Finally drove off after about fifteen minutes, but it seemed like forever.

"I stayed put for ten minutes after that, just to be safe. And then I went to my car. After that, everything was easy." A ripple of laughter like a flock of dislodged pebbles rolling down somebody's driveway. "My god it was easy. Ted had left the envelope lying on the front seat. All I had to do was unlock the door and pick it up. I checked the glove compartment and took a look in the back, too, but he didn't have any more negatives or photos with him. I had locked the car and was almost on my way home when I heard Ted's voice, and then his and a woman, and decided to check it out."

"You.... You weren't necessarily planning to kill him? At that point?"

"No. I would have killed him to get the pictures if I'd had to, but like I said, they were just lying there on the seat."

"So.... What made you decide to...."

"The luck of it. Like I told you. When I saw what a perfect set-up it was, I—" She stopped herself and frowned thoughtfully down at the gun. Then she looked up at me again and said, "That's not exactly true. With hindsight it's true, but then, at that precise moment when I killed him, I can't claim to have been entirely objective and...rational about it."

Her eyes demanded a response, and I felt my way out onto my words like a tightrope walker over the Grand Canyon. "I'm sure any well integrated person would have experienced a variety of…things in that situation. I mean, the human mind is not just—"

"Exactly!" I'd passed the test. "Just because a decision contains a certain emotional component does not ipso facto make that decision irrational."

"Not at all," I murmured in the space she left for me to fill.

"The merits of the decision must be judged according to outcome. By which standard, it's clear my decision was good. No matter what I…."

"I see that, Heidi," I assured her as she trailed off and I feared she'd reached the end. My end. "Barb told me she thought Ted heard someone coming from the parking lot. Was that you?"

"Yes. I was in the bushes there all along. Ted was standing on the sidewalk talking to this woman. Sneering at her, laughing at her, calling her a fat slob. That's when I figured the woman must be his ex-wife. He was always going on about her. Always telling me I better watch out or I'd get just as fat and ugly as his wife, always watching what I ate and saying, 'You've put on a few pounds, haven't you? Better watch it. There's nothing more disgusting than a woman who lets herself go. Fat. All jiggly and ugly. Better not eat that cracker, better not drink that juice, your pants are looking a little tight, better not, better not….' "

"But Heidi!" I almost reached out to her, despite the gun in her hand and the sneer on her face, because the anger and the sneer couldn't mask the pain in her voice. "Heidi, you're skinny! You're nothing but skin and bones!"

She shrugged convulsively and gripped the gun with both hands while she struggled to get her mouth back under control. My heart almost stopped as I watched the blood drain from her hands.

"I'm not sure I'd ever really hated him before. I should have, but… sometimes it takes a while. You know? That night, when I heard him laughing at her, I don't know…. It's like he was laughing at me, too. And I had to stop him. I had to make sure he would never laugh at me like that, and the only way to make sure was to stop him right then. To kill him right then and there. He got the knife away from her, and then he dropped it. She ran off, and he just dropped it right on the ground."

"What a jerk," I said tentatively as she looked for my reaction.

"Not just a jerk," she told me gleefully, "a fool. A complete and total fool. All I had to do was step out there, pick up the knife, and he walked right into it. All I had to do was hate him—hate him purely—for that one second, and he was over. He was lying on the ground at my feet. A white envelope was hanging out of his pocket, and there was blood on it. That didn't look right. It almost scared me. So I picked it up and took it with me.

"And then I got in my car and went home. Some of the blood from the envelope got on my gloves, so I had to burn them. Along with the envelope. But there was five hundred dollars inside, and I kept the money, of course. He owed me a hell of a lot more than that."

234

We sat and looked at each other. Heidi seemed calm. But as I watched, her eyes went hard again. Flattened out. She cocked her head toward the window. Nothing but a steady whisper of traffic noise, an occasional distant hiss of water striking the bottom of a car as it went through a puddle, and the intermittent rumble of trucks on the freeway. Suddenly she was on her feet, stepping quickly to the side and then behind me, her eyes and the eye of the gun barrel sticking to me like the most tenacious of burrs, making my skin prickle with the feel of them even when I couldn't see them any more.

"We can go now," she said.

"Where?" I croaked.

"My car. I still have two possibilities in mind. One is more...elegant, but... I think I'll go for safety, after all. You've been very helpful, you know."

"I have?" Her left hand was on my shoulder, and I was shivering all over.

"Yes. You've told me exactly what I needed to know."

"What? Tell me."

"You are curious, aren't you? Your mistake. But why not. You told me that the police still believe they arrested the right person. Because why else would you be working so hard to get them interested in Ellis? I know you've talked to them. You did, didn't you?" She shook my shoulder, jolting me into speech.

"Yes."

"I knew it. It was risky, bringing you to their attention that way. You didn't know that was me, did you? In that woman's car? I almost thought I'd made a mistake. It didn't stop your snooping. But it worked out well, in the end."

"No, I didn't know—" The sweat was pouring off me, soaking my shirt under my light jacket. How can I sweat when I'm so cold? "How did you know where I was?"

She laughed. "How did I know? I took you there! Don't you remember? Not right to the door, but close enough. I'd just been there myself. Did you know that?" I felt my body turning to ice. I'd never be able to move, never. All this time I'd been trying to keep her talking, and now she didn't seem able to stop. She wanted to tell me everything. I was the only one she could tell. Crazed with fear, I longed for oblivion, for an end to her presence behind me, the weight of her bony hand on my shoulder, the sound of her voice, alternately taunting and confiding, in the darkness of the room. "Did you know?" she insisted.

"No. No. I didn't know. I didn't know you knew her."

"I didn't know her, but I found out about her. You're not the only one who can find things out. Pat—you remember Pat, don't you? she let you in, before. She's interning at the *Times*, and the crime editor's one of those old guys who loves to have a sweet young thing hanging on his every word. He told her about that weird group Ted's ex-wife belonged to; he told her they all left town but one, and he even knew where to find her. In case Pat wanted to practice interviewing suspects. What a laugh!

"I'd just that minute come in from seeing her Friday when you got here, still out of my head with worry that the police wouldn't be satisfied with the scene I'd left for them at the APL Sunday morning, afraid there was something I'd overlooked, something that would lead them back to me. She was the only one I could think of to talk to. The only connection with her, Ted's ex-wife, and I had to find out what the police were saying, what they were doing. She didn't know, of course. She wasn't any help at all. But no sooner do I get home then you come along. Exactly the person I should have been looking for all along. You couldn't have done any better for me than if I'd programmed you myself."

A bus coughed its way to a stop out on Eastlake, and I felt her shift her weight behind me. "Better wait till that's gone," she said.

"Why?" My voice startled me.

"Why did I try to run you down? At the time I thought it was because you might be dangerous, and because I thought I could kill two birds with one stone. I'd taken that woman's keys just on spec, just because I'd seen them lying there in that bowl by the door and thought they might come in handy. I put them in the weeds by the door on my way out, so I could find them again if I wanted them. And maybe, just maybe, out of spite, too. A little bit. She was so frustrating. I couldn't get her to tell me anything! I liked the idea of her crawling around looking for those keys. After you got out of the car, I drove on a ways and parked, and then I walked back there. You could have been going someplace else but I was pretty sure. You had to be going there. I needed you to be going there. And you did.

"At first, when you came out I followed you because I was trying to think of how I could make you talk to me, tell me what she'd told you. She would tell you more than she'd tell me, wouldn't she? Because you're both queer. Aren't you? Aren't you?"

The second repetition came with a pinch on my neck, a sharp pain that bit through the glacial isolation of my fear with shocking heat, but I couldn't answer. I simply couldn't.

"I wish I had killed you then, I really do." She sounded irritated. "It might have worked all right. They'd have thought it was her, wouldn't they? Since it was her car. And that would have tied in with the ex-wife. Since they were friends. But...."

Something told me she was ready to go, and a new blast of panic sent my mind spinning around. Now, instead of an irrational desire to move, I felt an overwhelming need to stay fastened to that chair. She could stand there and talk for hours, for days, and I would listen, if only we didn't have to move.

"You haven't said what I told you," I blurted.

"You could figure it out, if you thought about it. But I guess you won't have time, will you? So I'll tell you. You told me that the police, even after you'd been so dramatically thrust upon their attention, didn't think there was any reason to investigate further. And you told me...." She seemed to be ticking off the points as she spoke; I could feel a soft, slow tapping on my collar. The gun, I realized. "...that Ellis, on his own, was not about to blab about the photographs. And that the police were not interested in the photographs. And therefore that you were the only dangerous factor, the one remaining source of possible danger for me. Because you were going to tell the police about the photographs whether I went with you or not. And what good did it do me to kill Ted if those pictures came out anyway?

"You told me I had to kill you, in fact. And that once I did it, I'd be safe. I thought of making it look like that woman did it. Fennel. Silly name. Silly woman. There would be a sort of pleasing symmetry in that. But.... What if she's not home this morning, eh? So, no. We'll stick to the simpler way. A nice, simple, neurotic suicide. Come on."

Suddenly she pulled on the shoulder of my jacket, and I felt the icy barrel of the gun jabbing into my neck, prodding me up and out of the chair. "Walk," she ordered. I took one step. Her hand still on my shoulder, the gun grazing the back of my neck. And then we heard the hollow clang of footsteps coming up the concrete and metal stairway outside.

The hand on my shoulder clamped down. They'll go to the next floor, I thought hopelessly. They'll walk right by. But the footsteps stopped. Outside Heidi's door.

Pain shot through my scalp as she grabbed a thick handful of my hair and twisted, wordlessly commanding me to silence. My heart and the blood racing in my ears almost drowned out the knocking on the door. The gun was jammed tight under the right side of my skull, a cold pain to balance the hot pain on the other side.

An endless pause, and then knocking again, and a voice. "Ms. Bascom?" Knock. Knock. "It's Lieutenant White. We'd like to talk to you for a few minutes."

I'm here! I'm here!, my soul called out to him, but all that left my mouth was a gasp of pain as Heidi twisted her grip viciously, pulling my head over at an impossible angle, and I felt bone—my bone—grating against the metal of the gun. It seemed inevitable that her finger would slip, that the muscular strain would at any second contract the tendons in a spasm that would send a bullet crashing through my brain. *Breathe, breathe.* A message from somewhere deep inside. Breathe. Stay still. Don't move. The slightest involuntary movement could set her off.

My hearing cleared, and I strained to decipher the murmur of voices outside the door. Instead I heard the footsteps again. Going away.

Her hand gradually relaxed its hold in my hair, not releasing me but easing up, allowing my neck to unkink, and the pressure of the gun also was reduced and became more bearable. Her body, which had been bowed forward, pressing up against mine, flexed back into vertical as her breathing slowed and its harsh rasp softened to the panting of a runner after a race. A measureless expanse of time passed. Her left hand dropped from my hair to my shoulder, and again she said to me, "Walk."

I took a step and she took a mirroring step behind me. I felt not only her hand on my shoulder and her gun on my neck but her face floating invisibly in the air behind me, just slightly above my head. Smash the heel of the hand up against the bottom of the nose. Hard. The bits and pieces of advice from the self-defense manuals were returning to my mind. Punch quickly at the voicebox with your fist. Jab at the eyes with your fingers.

We reached the door. "Open it," she said. I did, and the gun left my neck, sliding down to nudge me just above and to the left of my right elbow. Her left hand grasped my jacket just above my waist. "Walk slowly," she said, breathing the words softly into my ear with a voice sounding brittle, ready to shatter into splinters sharp enough to penetrate through to the bone. "To the right and down the stairs. We're going to get in my car. I'd rather not shoot you, but I will if I have to. It would be harder, but I feel sure I could manage. Grieving fiancée harassed by radical lesbian fanatic. Don't think I won't."

As we stepped out of her apartment and she pulled the door closed behind us, I believed her. I thought she would shoot, and I tensed my shocked body into readiness. She was going to shoot me, and I would have one chance to survive. If I could move first, maybe I could live. Maybe the bullet she fired into my body wouldn't kill me.

We turned together, like kids playing choo-choo, and we saw them together, too. Lieutenant White and another man were near the top of the stairs, coming towards us.

Instantly her hand was in my hair again. *I can't stand it.* The thought slid through my mind and disappeared into the static.

We froze, all four of us. With my peripheral vision strained to the utmost, I could see a blur of color to the right of my head that I knew must be Heidi's hand. She was holding the gun so they could see it. Lieutenant White's hand was on the metal bannister. He was about four steps from the top of the stairs. The top of the stairs was about fifteen feet from where I stood. Not moving, he spoke under his breath, and the man behind him disappeared.

"Stop!"

Her shout brought me back into focus, made the world around me real again. "Heidi," I said. "Listen."

She jerked me back against the wall by the door of her apartment, her own back to the wall and her hand twisting, twisting in my hair, pulling my head to the left as the gun barrel pressed into the flesh of my neck. Her left arm, bent by the grasp of her hand in my hair, held me pinned between her elbow and her body. I heard a scuffling sound from down below. The other policeman. Heidi moaned deep in her throat and slid us a half step to the left. I heard the stairway creak. Lieutenant White. And then a louder sound in the zone of silence we created around ourselves by our force of our attention: another stairway creaked, the one at the other end of the walkway. She moaned again and I felt stress vibrate through her body.

"Listen," I said again, muttering urgently with the little breath I could find. "You said you could manage and you can. If you don't shoot. You can do it. You can figure it out. Ted exploited you. Abused you. He threatened to ruin your life. I know a lawyer. She said Barb could plead manslaughter. Self-defense. So can you. It's the only way out now. You know you can do it. Use your brain. Think, Heidi. Think."

I felt her start to waver. Her grasp loosened and the distance between our bodies widened slightly. Now or never, Terry, I told myself, and shut my eyes against the pain I knew I was about to feel as I pulled myself sharply out and twisted with all the strength I had in the direction my scalp least wanted to go. My right elbow smashed into her belly, my left arm grappled wildly over my ducked head, frantic to deflect the gun before it fired.

What happened next was a kaleidoscope, a whirl of images in which real and unreal, present and past were mixed in a crazy Rorschach test as my mind temporarily went on overload and blinked out of control.

There were sirens almost immediately, as if my elbow had driven a hole in the silence and let the sounds come pouring through. And a man was standing on a balcony—no, on the walkway beside me—pointing. Reverend Abernathy, I thought. But he was pointing down. In the pictures he was pointing up, up towards where the shot came from that killed Dr. King. Was there a shot? I turned, half expecting to see a body stretched on the cement at my feet. But it was Heidi's body, and a man had pushed her up against the wall, her hands behind her back and her bony elbows sticking out on either side of his dark suit. Her head was turned to the side, mashed against the wall, and I felt I should do something. I should try to help her. Protect her. Her skinny arms. Victim or terrorist? Either way, the police would shoot her. That's what the lesbians in the SLA said about Patty Hearst, her skinny arms cradling a machine gun, and her head pressed against the gritty cinderblock wall. I felt the pain in my own head and when I touched my hair a piece of it came away in my hand. I'm going to scream, I thought wildly as police uniforms surrounded me.

29.

I didn't scream. I sat down. My legs gave out with minimal warning, and down I went.

The kaleidoscope gave way to a slide show—isolated cross-sections of events, like a series of photographic images. Somebody switched off the rain, and a stray beam of sunlight turned the bubble lights of a police car parked in the street below me into a marvel of brilliant blue and chrome. Then the sun was gone again and I was on my feet as the heart of a police sandwich heading down the stairs. When we reached the bottom, the avid faces of on-lookers flashed across the screen of my mind. The air felt wet and cold, molding itself around me with clammy persistence. Suddenly I was looking at Heidi. Her eyes met, assessed, and rejected mine from behind the rain-dimmed window of a police car on its way to away.

And then it was my turn. Behind the window this time, looking out through the left-over rain at people gathered loosely on the sidewalk. They don't know me, is all I remember thinking.

I was driven downtown, where the police car pulled into the official-use-only garage under the Public Safety Building. From there, I was led into an elevator and out again, directed to a chair, and temporarily abandoned. Occasional details were incredibly clear—the splinter on the edge of the doorframe across the narrow hall, a blue-headed tack sticking in a bulletin board, the squeak of many shoes on the linoleum floor.

"Take her in there and get a preliminary," said a voice that turned out to mean me. I dutifully rose as requested and followed somebody into a room down the hall. It could have been the room where Letitia and I talked to Lieutenant White except that it contained an old table instead of an old desk, and a younger, white policeman instead of the Lieutenant. Another man, this one in police uniform, sat scrunched up in a corner, a pad and pencil in his hands.

I don't remember what I said, really, but I know I answered questions. "Just tell me in your own words," he'd said at the beginning, but I didn't have any words of my own at that point, so he quickly resorted to asking question after short, pointed question, and I answered him like a robot programmed to mimic basic human speech. "What time did you reach the subject's apartment?" "About eight-thirty." "How long had you been there before she displayed the weapon?" "A long time. An hour?" "What transpired during the time between your arrival and her display of the weapon?" "We were talking." "Were you arguing? Fighting?" "No. Just talking." "Did you at any time threaten the subject with bodily harm?" "No."

It went on and on. After a while it felt sort of soothing. As if I were talking in my sleep, or hypnotized. The spell was broken eventually by the entrance of Lieutenant White. "Are you—?" he started to say to the man behind the table, but then he stopped. "Why is she crying?" he demanded. I looked around with vague curiosity to find the other woman in the room, but she wasn't there. The woman who was crying was me.

The Lieutenant stepped back into the hallway behind me. "Get a nurse in here," he told someone. "Now."

A few minutes later I was undergoing a different kind of interrogation. How do you feel? Are you cold? Hot? Dizzy? Do you want a doctor called?

"I'm all right. I'm all right," I said automatically. But then, as the blue-uniformed woman laid her hand on my forehead, I realized I wasn't quite as all right as all that. "Is there a bathroom here I could use?"

"Have her lie down for a while," the Lieutenant instructed as we passed him, "if you think she doesn't need medical attention."

Five minutes and a mild bout of diarrhea later, I was lying down on a cot in a little alcove off the women's restroom. The nurse spread a blanket over me and said, "If you need anything, just holler and someone will come."

I slept for several hours, as it turned out, awakened still heavy with sleep by the need to empty my bladder. Splashing water on my face helped revive me, and a policewoman who came in as I was drying my face reported my awakening to the outside world.

After that, it got pretty boring. Somebody took my statement again, and this time I was able to tell it "in my own words." Except that I found myself being very careful, trying to give only the bare facts. Heidi had meant to kill me twice, and she'd been perfectly willing to let Barb take the punishment for Ted's murder, and yet.... Something lingered in my mind from the whole experience— from everything that had happened since I started investigating the crime—that left me unwilling to relax into unwary confidence with the police, either.

I was set back out in the hall for a while after the taking of my statement, and the nurse passed by and discovered me there. "How are you feeling?" she enquired with professional concern.

"Hungry!"

"Roy," she called, and a young man in cop clothes came to join us. "Would you run downstairs and bring Ms. Barber something to eat?"

"Okay, sergeant." And then to me, "What do you want? Ham and cheese? Roast beef?"

"I'm a vegetarian."

The news seemed to stymie him completely, but he trotted off, returning eventually with an apple, a bag of potato chips, and a half-pint carton of orange juice. A veritable feast, under the circumstances.

I'd long since finished eating and was just debating the chances that no one would ever notice if I simply got up and walked out, when I heard someone calling my name. It was yet another uniformed officer, this one beckoning me down the hallway and into yet another small, anonymous room where Lieutenant White awaited me.

He looked sleeker than before. More relaxed. A shade more cordial. Satisfied. "Feeling better now?" he asked politely.

"Yes. There's something I want to know, though. Why were you there? At Heidi's?"

I could see him deciding to answer me. "Routine police procedure," he said, with just a hint of smugness beneath the bland surface of his voice. "Day before yesterday you passed on the rumor that Simpson had arranged to meet someone that evening, in addition to his contact with the cult. As a matter of routine, I checked the incident reports, both city and campus, for that night, and two items of possible significance were found. A patrolman reported seeing a car known to belong to an individual active in various...vice activities here in Seattle, and a campus officer automatically recorded the license number of a car observed parked in a University lot close to midnight.

"I didn't attach any particular significance to those facts to begin with," he continued, speaking to me over the tips of his fingers as he held his hands in prayer postion, lightly tapping the edge of his lower lip at every pause. "But I did arrange for some routine follow-up. And when the report came back from Bellingham, from the officer there who spoke with Mr. Ellis, and the Bureau of Motor Vehicles identified the parked car as Ms. Bascom's.... A further conversation with the lady seemed to be indicated. A matter of tying up loose ends before the case came up in court.

"After we knocked the first time and got no answer, we went and looked in the garage. Her car was there, so we decided to give it one more try. The rest, I believe you know."

We regarded each other in silence for a moment. Then his hands came down to the desk, business-like. "And now, Ms. Barber," he said, "we'd like you to read through this typed transcript of your statement and, if it is an accurate representation of this morning's events, we'd like you to sign it. Then you'll be free to go."

A bubble of rebellion tickled up through my mind: the temptation to say "I told you so" was almost overwhelming. The wish to get the hell out of there was even stronger, though, so I meekly sat and read through the pages of the statement.

When I came to the end, the Lieutenant gently pushed a ballpoint pen across the desk in my direction. "Sign at the bottom of the last page," he directed, " and initial each of the other pages, please."

I picked up the pen and stared at the black letters marching crisply across the white paper in front of me. Then I looked up at the man behind the desk. "It's not really accurate," I said.

The skin on his face seemed to tighten. "The facts given in that statement do not correspond with the events as they occurred?" There was a repressive edge to his voice that merely raised my hackles further.

"It's got the events right," I said, "but not the feeling of the events. Not the context. I mean, the man said I should tell it in my own words, but this doesn't sound anything like me at all. I'd never say I 'exited' a building and 'proceeded in a northerly direction.' And besides, this makes it sound like Heidi was a complete stranger to me."

The Lieutenant sighed away a bit more of his unusual good humor. "Ms. Barber," he said. "The statement we are asking you to sign is an official police document. It is not a psychological case study. It is not a novel. It is not even a report on the case as a whole. It is simply a statement of fact about what took place in that apartment this morning. Who did what to whom. That is all it is, and that is all it is meant to be. Now, unless you find something in that statement that is factually untrue, I suggest—I strongly suggest—that you sign it and let us both get on with other things. Will you do that, please?" After I'd done so, "I'll get a car to drive you home," he said as we both stood up.

My assigned driver turned out to be a woman. "How does it feel to have that gun on all the time?" I wanted to ask her but didn't. Instead, noticing a clock on the wall by the elevator, I said, "Would you drive me to Capitol Hill, please?"

And thus it was that I not only arrived at the shop in a police car, but entered with an armed escort. There was nobody in the outer room, as usual, but a full house awaited us in the rear, and the expressions on my friends' faces were priceless. I know because Jeanne and Gretchen told me about it later. At the time, I didn't really see anybody but Sarah—for the two seconds it took me to cross the room and fling myself into her arms.

She took me home soon after that—to Everywhere House—and gently guided me through several phases of recovery. At first all I wanted to do was huddle. By the time we got to the house, talking was what I needed. Sarah and several other household members listened open-mouth to my excited re-play of the morning's events. When Connie arrived I had grabbed Fran by the hair and was forcing her across the kitchen with a finger pointed at her skull. The others quickly filled Connie in on the general scope of things (while I sort of chittered in place), and she listened carefully for about three minutes before taking another look at me and asking, "Have you had anything to eat?"

"Yeah, sure. At the station," I babbled. "I had an apple. And...and some potato chips!"

"You're speeding, Terry," she told me kindly, and I slumped quivering into the chair next to Sarah, who promptly rose to help Connie get a meal underway.

A tense, vacant silence overtook me as I ate. Sarah had to take me by the hand and lead me into to the bedroom, I was so out of it.

Once in my room, my speaking equipment snapped on again as if a switch had been thrown. "Why was I so dead wrong?" I demanded, pacing up and down beside the bed where Sarah sat watching me calmly. "I told you, didn't I? I said no way could it be Heidi. I said she was such a weak little thing, all broken up, a typical feminine female. Remember? Even when she pulled out the damn gun I didn't believe she was the one. I mean, how stupid can you get!"

"You're not stupid," Sarah said as soon as I lapsed into shivering silence again. "I think we tend to forget what it's like for women who live with men. A lot of them have had to learn to be sneaky and tough. Didn't you tell me once that she reminded you of Barb?"

"You're right. So maybe Ted subconsciously picked the same kind of woman every time. Or picked women he could manipulate, anyway. But what about Lieutenant White, then? And Letitia? And Jan?"

"What do you mean?"

"I've always believed people were people, and that even if we get ourselves divided up by history—women from men, black from white, nation from nation—we still could always…overcome that, as individuals. If we had to. At least, I always thought that I could. With Lieutenant White, though—" I shivered again. "I guess what bothers me is that I feel like I can't trust him to react, to respond to me, like a person instead of a cop."

"He is a cop," Sarah said.

"Yes, but…. I don't know, it just freaks me out when anybody does that—puts their role before their selves. Like people who became Nazis. I look at Lieutenant White, and I think, 'Can I be sure he wouldn't torture me if he were a member of the SS and I was a member of the underground resistance?'"

Sarah looked rather taken aback by my analogy. "That's just an example," I explained. "What I mean is, if you can't count on people to see you as a human being instead of a category, then you can't count on them to be decent. Can you?"

"No," she said. "You can't. As many of us have learned the hard way."

"Oh lord. I guess this must sound really feeble-minded to you, Sarah." She smiled slightly and shook her head, but her eyes were deflected from mine by something else in her mind, and there was a bitter curl at the edges of her mouth. The manic phase was over, and I sat down next to her on the bed.

"Gretchen and I were talking along those lines," she said, and held out her hand for mine. "More or less. When we were talking about whether to move in here. We were talking about how it's not a conscious thing, people just tend to form cliques. We get into ways of talking and acting that we share with the people we spend time with, and those patterns turn into codes nobody else knows. And that's how we keep other people out, whether we want to or not. We don't have to put up a sign saying 'Outsiders not welcome,' because everything about the way we behave says it for us."

"Projections," I said. "Yeah. That's something I've been thinking about a lot lately." The warmth of her hands and the warmth of her body next to mine were making me feel sleepy and safe. "Walls. One way of acting inside, another way outside, and almost impossible to get across."

"It makes us feel safer," Sarah mused. "A lot of times we need to protect ourselves like that, but it can be overdone. If you go so far as to carry a gun for protection from outsiders, the way cops do.... And it's always more extreme when you have a social role and an identity reinforcing each other like that."

"What do you mean?" it was my turn to ask.

"I think a cop's occupation and social role are probably pretty well merged. More than for most of us. Cops see the world all the time as cops. I sure don't walk around thinking of myself as a secretary when I'm not at work. Not even when I am at work, sometimes."

I giggled. "But Barb does. Or did."

"She wasn't a secretary, was she?"

"No. She was a professional dyke. Her social role and her occupation merged." Another giggle. They were escaping out of me like hiccups now.

Sarah laughed softly. "I see what you mean. No wonder she was so hard line. She was the lesbian equivalent of a cop."

I started to laugh so hard I choked, and Sarah immediately stood up and dragged my hands up above my head, holding them there like dead weights. When I'd recovered enough to breathe again, the painful laughter had vanished from my body and my mind, leaving only weariness behind. "I'm okay now," I told her, seeing worry in her eyes.

"Ready for bed?"

"Ready whenever you are," I said.

Epilogue

I tried to call Ellie the next day, since it was Saturday, but got no answer. That night Jeanne and Gretchen insisted on a household night out, in celebration of my near escape, and there she was at the Slipper, dancing with a woman I'd never seen before. Trudi, Ellie's Scrabble-fiend neighbor was at the bar.

"Know who that is with Ellie?" I asked her.

She scanned the dance-floor, though I felt sure she already knew damn well. "That's Chris," she told me finally. "I guess they're...going together now. You didn't know?"

"No. But it's okay," I hastened to add before the situation had a chance to go baroque. "Ellie and I have been...growing apart for a while now."

There was relief on Trudi's face. "I'm glad to hear it, because I'm laying odds on Ellie moving to Tacoma before the end of next month."

"Tell her I said 'hi,' if you think of it." And I made my way back to my friends with a pitcher of beer in both hands.

My friendship with Letitia, on the other hand, did not stay stopped. On a campus of 34,000 students, the only ones you never see are the ones you're looking for. If you try to avoid someone, you see her daily. The first few times our paths crossed, we both averted our eyes. Next came a few vague acknowledgements mumbled in passing. "Hi." "Hi." We might have gone on that way forever—or at least until graduation—if the huff slowly building inside me hadn't bubbled up through a previously undiscovered crack just when Letitia and I chanced to meet in the middle of Red Square one sunny morning early in May. "Hi," she said, as usual, and was already almost gone. But I refused to complete the ritual.

"Hey!" I said loudly to her passing profile. "Hey, look at me for once!"

She couldn't help but obey, it was such a shock.

Once I'd got her attention, I opened my mouth and let it all pour out. I said that I was tired of watching a potential good friend pass by again and again for no good reason, that no matter how much I tried I just couldn't see why it was necessary for us to ignore one another for the rest of our lives, and that if she didn't think she was smart enough to know when Jim was totally out of line, and strong enough tell him so, well, she had another think coming, that was all. Under the stress of the moment, I didn't manage to say it quite that temperately. I simply raved, right there in the middle of Red Square.

I don't know which of us first noticed how much I was enjoying myself, which of us first caught the beginnings of a grin on the other's face. Before too long, we both simply threw back our heads and laughed—a fine example of how an element of theater can erupt into your life and triumph over habits of respectability, with beneficial results for all concerned.

That shared laughter didn't solve all our problems, needless to say, but it did get us past the biggest barrier. It got us talking. And we kept talking, too. We kept violating each other's assumptions, challenging each other's basic definitions, and prodding each other unwillingly past the limits of our previous opinions. According to me, Letitia had a bad habit of lying. According to Letitia, I was woefully narrow minded and stubbornly unwilling to consider alternate perspectives on reality. "My god, why do you have to be so fucking white all the time!" she said to me once. When I pointed out, in response, that we were both white, she smacked her forehead with her hand and said, "Oy, what a literalist she is!"

And I guess she was right. By now, what with Letitia's influence and the push and pull of life in general, maybe I could claim to be a recovering literalist. I spent my childhood following the White Queen's advice (to believe six impossible things before breakfast), but it took the second and third decades of my life to convince me effectively that things are seldom what they seem.

As for Barb Randall......

A few days after I spotted Ellie dancing at the Slipper, I got the number from directory assistance and called Barb's house in Montana. The woman who answered the phone sounded too formal to be a member of the family. "Miss Randall is not at home right now," she stated politely. "Would you care to leave a message?"

"Yes, please. Ask her to call Terry Barber. She has my number."

"I will see that she gets your message," said the voice on the other end of the line.

Despite her courteous assurance, however, I never heard from Barbara Randall again.